Burning Bright

Going Down In Flames, Volume 5

Chris Cannon

Published by CC Publishing, 2018.

Edited by Erin Molta
Cover design by Chris Canada
ISBN 9781964956084
First Edition June 2018
Second Edition July 2024

Chapter One

It had been three months since the Rebel dragons had attacked campus...three months since Rhianna had died... three months since Bryn had released Valmont from being her knight...three months since it felt like she'd had her heart ripped out of her chest...three months since anything had seemed normal or right or good in the world.

Summer had passed by in a flash. There had been far too many funeral pyres and not enough contact with her friends or her parents. Despite Bryn's intentions to hang out with Clint and Ivy, her grandparents had kept her hopping from one Blue event to another. And the singular constant at these events had been Jaxon. Not that she hated her former nemesis, but she didn't want to spend all her free time with him, either. Whenever they were together, her grandparents constantly mentioned their impending marriage of doom. She had finally mastered the art of not flinching when people brought up her marriage contract to Jaxon, although she sometimes experienced a tic in her left eye.

Then there was the problem of her parents, or rather, how the Directorate was dealing with her parents. All hybrids and disenfranchised dragons had been shuttled off to a town on the far side of the forest. Sanctuary seemed like an ironic name for the old mining town with rundown cabins. Of course they were building better housing, but that would take time. It was a place where mixed-Clan dragons didn't have to hide their true identity, so maybe the name wasn't a bad choice after all.

Once her parents had settled in, she'd hoped to spend time with them. That hadn't happened because until the Directorate decided that all the dangerous rebels had been rooted out, the citizens of Sanctuary weren't allowed to leave their new town. Which made the place more like a free-range prison. Bryn had been allowed to call her parents, but not visit them in person.

"Bryn, are you ready?" Her grandmother pushed her bedroom door open. "We leave for the Institute in fifteen minutes."

The Institute for Excellence was a school for shape-shifting dragons that masqueraded as an expensive boarding school.

"I'm all packed." Bryn pointed at the suitcases by the door. "But I'm not sure I want to go."

"It's your senior year," her grandmother said. "Not that you'll understand this at your age, but enjoy it, because the older you become the faster time flies. It feels like these past three months went by in the blink of an eye."

"They did," Bryn agreed.

"I know you're disappointed about not being able to visit your mother, but I think that might change in the next few weeks."

"Really?" It was about damn time.

"The Directorate has finished their background checks on almost all of the dragons living in Sanctuary. The students have been cleared to return to school."

That was great news. For the first time, she wouldn't be the only hybrid at school. Of course, she might still be the only Red-Blue hybrid because the middle class and the elite didn't mix very often. On a different note, her parents should have been cleared of suspicion from day one. They hadn't had anything to do with dragons since they'd run away to escape their arranged marriages. Bryn found it ironic that she was legally bound to marry the son of the man her mother had rejected all those years ago. Not that she faulted her mom, because Jaxon's father, Ferrin, was the most loathsome asshat on the planet. Still, fate seemed to have a twisted sense of humor.

"We should go," her grandmother said. "You don't want to keep Jaxon waiting."

Bryn managed not to roll her eyes. but couldn't help muttering, "I'm sure he's counting the minutes since he's last seen me."

...

Bryn was thrilled to find Clint and Ivy, her best friends, waiting for her outside the Blue dorm. After spending all summer with the golden-skinned, blond-haired Blue Clan, it was refreshing to see her friends from the Black Clan— dark-haired, ivory-skinned dragons with tattoos and wild hair. She hugged Ivy. "I missed you guys."

"We missed you, too. You were hardly ever there when we called," Ivy said. "What in the heck were you doing?"

"Socializing," Bryn said. "Which means networking, and smiling, and nodding while trying to keep up the facade that I fit in with the Blue Clan."

"Sounds dead boring," Clint said.

"There was usually food, so that was the one saving grace." Bryn opened the door of the Blue dorm. "Come in with me while I put my things away."

"Now that you're all upper class, shouldn't you have a maid do that for you?" Ivy teased.

"I volunteered to take care of this myself," Bryn said. Her grandparents had maids, and cooks, and staff who took care of normal everyday life activities. "I'd rather put my own things away so I know where they are." Plus sitting back and watching someone do something she herself was capable of made her uncomfortable.

Clint and Ivy followed her inside. Most of the students in the first-floor lounge glanced her way and nodded in acknowledgement, which was weird. Last year at this time few of them would have spoken to her except to insult her.

"That was different," Ivy said as they climbed the steps to the second floor.

Clint yawned. "Less talking and more coffee...and bacon. I feel the distinct need for bacon."

As if on cue, Bryn's stomach growled. "Breakfast sounds good." When they reached her room, Bryn unlocked it with her key. She stepped across the threshold and stared at the couch where she had spent so much time with her knight and former boyfriend Valmont. A spot in her chest ached as the bittersweet memories assaulted her. "I wonder if my grandmother would care if I bought a new couch."

"I could accidentally electrocute that one for you." Clint produced a ball of lightning in his hand.

"I might take you up on that." Bryn carried her suitcases into her room.

"Have you heard from Valmont?" Ivy asked as she followed Bryn.

"No and it's probably better that way." She pointed at the room across the hall from hers. "I still think of that as Rhianna's room."

"When you add Valmont and Rhianna together this dorm room has way too many emotional memories," Ivy said. "Why don't you ask if you can move to a new one?"

"I couldn't do that, because that would show weakness. At least that's what my grandfather would say."

"Blue Clan logic is weird," Clint said.

"You have no idea. The day after all the funerals, my grandmother scheduled me for this whirlwind of events where I had to spend time with Jaxon. When I asked why we were acting like we hadn't just lost people we cared about, she said that was the point. It was our job to show we were strong enough to go on and the Rebels hadn't won."

"That is some screwed up logic," Ivy said. "Black dragons binge-watch television, eat ice cream, and cry their way through several boxes of Kleenex."

"That's what I did after all the stupid parties...when I was alone in my room," Bryn said. "I'm betting that's what all the other Blues secretly do but they'd never admit it."

"I never thought I'd ask this question," Clint said. "But how is Jaxon coping?"

"For the first month after Rhianna's funeral, he barely spoke to anyone, which I understood. Then he went through a robot phase where he talked but showed zero emotion. As of a few days ago, he's sort of back to his normal self but with a hair-trigger temper which makes him loads of fun to be around."

"I wish life would go back to normal," Ivy said.

"I'm not sure what normal is anymore." Bryn's stomach growled.

"You need to be fed," Clint said. "and that is normal."

A knock sounded on Bryn's door.

Please don't let that be Jaxon. And that thought made her feel like a bad person. She opened the door and, of course, there stood Jaxon. "Hello, what's going on?"

"If you'd invite me inside, rather than leaving me standing in the hall, I could tell you," Jaxon said.

Chapter Two

Bryn tamped down on her instinct to snark back and waved Jaxon into the room. He spotted Clint and Ivy and frowned.

"Bryn," he said. "We need to talk."

Nope. "We were heading down to breakfast. Whatever it is, it can wait until after I've had coffee and bacon."

"No. It can't." When he spoke to her using his holier than thou my father is Speaker for the Directorate tone, she remembered why she had once shot a fireball at his head.

"Do you really want to come between me and my coffee?" Bryn asked.

"Fine. Then I'll accompany you to the dining hall and we'll eat breakfast together." Jaxon said this like he was issuing a challenge.

She could see where this was going. He'd insist on joining them if she didn't give him his way. At this point she'd rather hear him out than spend breakfast with him. "You have five minutes to speak your mind, and then you'll go away so I can eat in peace with my friends. Deal?"

"Deal." Jaxon glanced at Clint and Ivy.

"Do you mind?"

"Do we mind what?" Clint asked, like he didn't realize Jaxon wanted to speak with Bryn alone.

"Why don't you guys go to the dining hall and save me a seat?" Bryn said, just to move them along.

"Sure. We'll fly from your terrace." Ivy grabbed her boyfriend and pulled him down the hall.

Once they were gone, Bryn said, "What's on your mind?"

"I think you should change rooms."

That wasn't what she expected him to say. "I'd love to change rooms, but is that what my grandfather would want me to do?"

Jaxon's gaze traveled toward the door where Rhianna used to live when she was Bryn's roommate. "If it was just due to your knight, I'd agree, but I believe he'd understand why I'd wish for you to relocate."

When he put it that way—more about Rhianna and his feelings than about her not wanting to be reminded of Valmont, it made sense. "If you put in the request rather than me, I'd be more than happy to move."

"Thank you." His upper-class Blue demeanor slipped. "Being back here at school...there are so many memories... it's harder than I thought it would be."

And now she felt like a total jerk for giving him crap. With a normal person, Bryn's first instinct would be to hug him. She didn't think Jaxon would be okay with that maneuver, though, so she settled for touching him on the shoulder. "Let me know if there's anything I can do to help."

...

Bryn caught up with Clint and Ivy in the dining hall and explained Jaxon's request.

Ivy opened her mouth to speak and then stopped, blinking her eyes furiously. "I can't even talk about the attack without crying. God forbid if something had happened to Clint... I have no idea how Jaxon is holding himself together."

"It's our senior year," Clint said. "And not to sound petty, but I never imagined death and destruction would be a part of my high school experience."

Bryn stirred sugar into her cup of coffee while she thought about something. "My grandmother says our job is to remember the ones we lost while moving forward and trying to make the most of what and who we still have."

"Okay. Let's talk about what we have." Clint pulled out his class schedule with a flourish.

"That's not what I meant." Bryn laughed. "But go on."

"Give me yours so we can compare," Clint said.

She and Ivy both passed over their class lists and watched as Clint lined them up on the table.

"We have Mr. Stanton for Advanced Elemental Science first hour. Ivy and I have History second hour. Bryn you have Beginning Quintessential Medicine."

"I can't wait to start learning Quintessential medicine for real." Everything she'd done up to that point had been based on a small amount of training and a lot of instinct. The results hadn't always been optimal.

"Third hour we have Basic Movement," Clint said.

"Next is lunch and then all of us end the day with Proper Decorum."

"How many more forks can there possibly be?" Bryn asked.

"Maybe we'll learn something exciting this year," Ivy said. "Like how to fold napkins into origami swans."

Bryn sipped her coffee and tried to be subtle about checking out her fellow students because her grandmother had been on her all summer about staring at people. The tables seemed emptier than normal. Orientation wasn't until tomorrow, so some students might not arrive until then…still, it seemed like they were missing a third of the normal crowd.

"Why do you think we're missing so many students?" There had been casualties among the students, but not this many.

"Some students finished their college degrees so they won't be coming back," Ivy said. "Plus Orientation officially starts tomorrow, so maybe some students aren't coming until then."

"Not to sound ungrateful to my grandparents for all that they've done, but I couldn't wait to come back to school." Bryn leaned in close and spoke in a quiet voice. "I spent every waking minute with Blues, and I had to constantly be on my best behavior, which was exhausting. I mean, why does anyone care if you put your elbows on the table?" To make a point Bryn put both her elbows on the table.

"You're such a rebel," Ivy said.

"I've been going on about myself," Bryn said. "Tell me about your summer."

"It was pretty good," Clint said, "but it felt like there was a layer of sadness and disbelief floating in the air."

Ivy sighed. "I keep feeling like I can't relax or have fun because that would be disloyal to the dragons who are no longer with us."

Bryn had heard the phrase survivor's guilt but hadn't really understood it until now. "During the battle, if I had been faster..." She blinked her eyes rapidly to hold back tears. "If I'd managed to intercept the second dragon attacking Jaxon, then Rhianna would still be here."

"You can't think like that," Ivy said. "Rhianna did what she did out of love."

Clint put his arm around Ivy's shoulders. "I'd sacrifice myself to protect Ivy and she'd do the same for me. It was Rhianna's choice."

Bryn nodded because her throat felt too thick to speak. Several nights a week, since the attack on campus, her brain had replayed the battle. Over and over again she'd seen Rhianna fall from the sky. What Clint said was true. Rhianna had thrown herself between Jaxon and the second attacker because saving him meant more to her than her own life.

It was a sad realization that there was no one in the world who cared about her like that, and there probably never would be. She and Jaxon were legally bound together by a marriage contract, but she had no delusions about him ever truly caring for her—or she for him—as anything more than a friend.

"Let's talk about something happier," Ivy said. "We're supposed to be celebrating the beginning of our senior year."

"I'd love to do something fun," Bryn said. "What are our options?"

"We could go to Dragon's Bluff," Ivy said. "And shop for cool stuff for your new room."

Dragon's Bluff was a town populated by humans descended from knights. The town had a symbiotic relationship with dragons and the Institute. They protected the dragon's secret and in return their businesses prospered. But there was more to it than that. Every person in Dragon's Bluff carried a latent magic spell in their blood. If they stepped up to defend a dragon, to protect them from a perceived threat, they were transformed into a knight and became magically bonded to that dragon.

Valmont, a waiter in Dragon's Bluff, had performed an act of chivalry and become Bryn's knight. The magical dragon-knight bond she'd had with him had been wonderful, but then they'd fallen in love which had been awesome at first, until everything had gone to hell.

"I managed to avoid seeing Valmont all summer. I don't think I'm ready to see him yet," Bryn said. She may have broken their dragon-knight bond but that was only after he'd broken her heart.

"Are you over him?" Ivy asked.

"I don't know." Bryn played with her napkin while she thought about the question. Part of her life felt empty without him and she missed what they'd had together, but thinking of him no longer caused her physical pain. "I think I am."

"If you saw him with another girl, how would you feel?" Clint asked.

"If you'd asked me that three months ago I would have wanted to roast him, but now I think it would just make me a little sad. I guess that's an improvement."

Clint sat up straight and muttered, "Incoming."

Bryn turned and saw Zavien striding her way. He was no longer the spiky-haired rebel who'd impressed her so much when she'd first come to school. He wore his dark hair short, and his cheekbones were more pronounced than she remembered, as if he'd been ill and lost weight. Dark circles stood out under his eyes.

He approached their table, like he wasn't sure if he was welcome. "Bryn, can we talk?"

It's like someone had flipped her life into an alternate dimension. How many times had she wanted to speak to him and he'd blown her off? All of that seemed so long ago and childish now...and slightly embarrassing. He'd been her first crush, and the first guy who'd disappointed her, but all of that paled in comparison to the attack on campus.

"Have a seat," Bryn said.

"I thought maybe we could go for a walk." Zavien gestured toward the doors of the dining hall.

"That wouldn't be appropriate," Bryn said. Was it wrong that she enjoyed throwing that statement in his face? He'd said it to her often enough.

"That's a nice bit of irony," Zavien said.

"I think so," Bryn agreed.

He sat and stared at her for a moment. "I don't have the words to say how sorry I am about Nola. I want you to know that I had no idea she was involved with any of that madness."

Even though he'd turned out to be a huge disappointment as a friend and more than that, she knew he'd never meant to hurt her. "I know."

He continued talking. "She always acted like she had another agenda, but I had no idea she could be so—"

"Psychotic?" Ivy offered.

"That's one way to put it," Zavien acknowledged.

"I know you don't condone violence and that you worked for peaceful change through your petitions," Bryn said. "If you'd known anyone's life was at stake you would have turned Nola in."

"I would have." He sighed and reached up to rub the back of his neck. "I don't understand how she hid so much from me. When they questioned me after the attack they asked if I knew Nola was behind the attack on the theater building. I had no idea. She was so distraught over all the destruction. I never would have guessed she faked all that emotion."

"She majored in theater," Clint said. "Apparently, she was one hell of an actress."

"Maybe that was it," Zavien said. "Anyway, I just needed you to know." He tapped his fingers on the table.

"Did they find out how deeply she was involved with the Rebels?" Bryn asked.

"She was one of their inside spies on campus. No one has confirmed this, but I think she's the one who poisoned you."

Anger boiled up inside of Bryn. She wanted to unleash a torrent of fire and ice against Nola, but that would do little good. Nola was dead, and the plan to kill Bryn had failed, but thinking about the crazy dark-haired Barbie made fire crawl up the back of Bryn's throat. A wisp of smoke drifted from Bryn's nostrils as she exhaled. She took a moment to compose herself. "I wondered about that."

"I have something I wanted to give you...sort of as a peace offering."

"Okay."

He reached into his book bag and pulled out a black folder. "I made it awhile ago, but I still hope it makes you smile."

Now she was curious. She opened the folder. There was a pamphlet inside. On the front in elegant script it said:

BRYN'S PRIMER

Inside the pamphlet there were sketches of dragons from each Clan and a list of their traits and their breath weapon.

Red Dragons—Breathes fire. Strongest, with slightly scary tempers

Black Dragons—Breathes lightning. Most artistic, with a penchant for tattoos

Green Dragons—Breathes wind. Smartest, lacking in sense of humor

Orange Dragons—Breathes sonic waves. Plant whisperers who can kick your ass

Blue Dragons—Breathes ice. Elite lawmakers, chronic snottiness, second fastest fliers

Red/Blue Hybrid Dragon—Breathes fire & ice, kick-ass chick, fastest flyer

Bryn grinned. "I love it. When did you make this?"

"A few weeks after you came to school, which seems like a lifetime ago," he said. "After everything that has happened, I know I don't deserve this, but is there any way we can be friends again?" Vulnerability shone in his dark brown eyes.

There were so many answers she could give him and none of them were simple. "You were a good friend to me when I first came to school and didn't know anyone. I appreciate that because I would have been lost without you, and you literally saved my life after I was poisoned... but then you turned into an asshat. If it was up to me, I might agree to give our friendship another chance, but as an official member of the Blue Clan and Ephram Sinclair's granddaughter, I'm not sure I can."

Zavien gave the lop-sided grin she used to love. "I'll respect that answer for now, but if you ever change your mind, or you need someone to talk to, I'll be around." And with that, he stood and headed toward the dining hall door.

"Well, that was interesting," Ivy said.

"That's one word for it," Bryn leaned closer to her friends. "I wasn't wrong, was I...about not wanting to be friends with him?"

"No," Clint said. "He did some shady things to you and he was involved with someone who tried to kill you and destroy life as we know it."

"Ahh, when you put it that way, I don't feel so bad." She closed the folder so no one else could see it because not everyone would find it as amusing as she did.

Chapter Three

"We're about to have more company," Ivy said.

Seriously? Who was coming to brighten her day now?

Jaxon walked over to the table and held out a set of keys. "You're three doors down and across the hall from where you were before."

She took the keys from his hand. "Thanks." With a curt nod, Jaxon left.

"Want to help me move my stuff?" Bryn asked, like she was offering them a special treat.

"That has fun written all over it," Ivy said.

It didn't take long for Clint and Ivy to help Bryn move her clothes and the few personal items she had from one dorm room to another. The setup was the same—two bedrooms and a large front room divided into a living room with a couch and a study area with a library table and bookshelves featuring random pieces of art.

Clint plucked a small silver treasure chest from the shelf. "Mind if I open this?"

"It's too small to contain a dead body, so knock yourself out," Bryn said, referring to the root cellar door Clint had opened which had led to a tunnel where a family of hybrids had been murdered and left to rot.

He turned to glare at her. "Was that really necessary?"

"Sorry." Why had she said that? Maybe because being back on campus was bringing up all sorts of memories.

"Are you sure you don't want the comforter your grandmother bought you?" Ivy asked.

"No. Everything from that room reminds me of Valmont or Rhianna. I want to start fresh." And there was only one place to do that. "So unless you have other plans, I think I'm ready to suck it up and deal with going to Dragon's Bluff."

"Here's a test," Clint said. "Are you ready to eat at Fonzoli's?"

Was she ready to eat at Valmont's family's restaurant? Her gut said no. "Only if you have an uncontrollable craving for Italian food. Otherwise, I'd rather do without the side of possible drama and go with burgers and caramel corn from the Snack Shack instead."

"I'm not really in the mood for drama," Ivy said. "Burgers for lunch it is."

They headed out the window to Bryn's terrace and shifted into dragon form. She didn't even have to think her way through the transformation anymore, it was just second nature. She closed her eyes, felt something inside of her unfurl and then her center of gravity shifted. She opened her eyes and stretched her wings.

Ivy and Clint stood next to her with their black scales gleaming in the sunlight. The outline of their human faces flashed across their dragon faces for just a moment, which was how they recognized each other in dragon form.

Clint tilted his head and studied Bryn. "Did you mean to do that?"

"Do what?" Bryn asked.

"You have alternating red and blue scales," Ivy said. "It's cool, but that's not your normal look."

"Crap. Hold on." Her grandparents would have a fit if she presented herself as a Red-Blue hybrid rather than a Blue dragon. Closing her eyes, she imagined herself entirely blue.

"You could leave one red scale," Ivy said. "Like the stripe in your hair."

"That would be cool, but I'm not sure it's worth the family issues it would cause." When she had thought her parents were dead, she'd moved in with her grandparents. Her grandfather Ephram Sinclair was one of the most powerful individuals on the Directorate, the ruling council for the dragon clans. He helped balance out Jaxon's father's extremism, but he was supremely proud of his Blue Clan heritage and took Bryn's habit of coloring her hair as a personal insult. They'd settled on her going blond with a single red stripe. She missed her tri-colored red, black, and blond hair but some things weren't worth a fight...especially since she liked her new hair color.

Bryn launched herself into the air, soaring up and away from the Institute, leaving it and all the issues it contained far below. She was supposed to head for the back gate, but the lure of flying was too strong. She performed a diving roll and then banked right, enjoying the sensation of sunshine on her wings.

Clint and Ivy joined her in some aerial acrobatics. After ten minutes, Ivy flew alongside Bryn. "Are you ready to go shopping now?"

"Sure." She didn't want to come back down to earth, but it was unavoidable. Bryn had practiced her landings over the summer, something she seemed to have more trouble with than the average dragon. She discovered if she hovered above the ground for a moment and tucked her wings to drop into a sort of crouch, she did much better than when she tried to stick a landing.

"Hey," Clint said, "you didn't stumble."

"Thank you for noticing," Bryn said.

They shifted to human form and headed for the back gate. When she'd first come to the Institute, students had to sign in and out before exiting through a simple gate and flying to Dragon's Bluff. Now the exit had a reinforced steel fence, a turret with some sort of gun on top, and a small building where several guards were on duty at all times.

When they arrived at the gate, the guards glanced at them like they found their presence irritating.

"We want to go to Dragon's Bluff," Bryn said.

"You may go, but you're required to have an escort," the closest guard said.

"What does that mean?" Ivy asked.

"All students leaving campus will be escorted and driven by a guard. We'd like to keep flying off-campus to a minimum to ensure students' safety." He waved at another Red standing by several parked SUVs.

The Red dragon climbed into the vehicle, drove over to the gate, and rolled the driver's side window down. "Hello, I'm Manuel, and I'll be your driver today."

Guarded transportation to and from campus was new. Not that it was a bad idea, but it did bring up a question. "Once we're ready to return to the school what do we do?"

Manuel said, "I'll wait for you and then bring you back."

That seemed like a lot of manpower for students to leave campus. The Institute probably didn't want to stop students from visiting Dragon's Bluff because the town was still recovering from rebel attacks and keeping the businesses prosperous was a step in the right direction of returning to a normal life.

Bryn and her friends climbed into the SUV. "Does everyone get an escort to town," Clint asked. "Or is this because of Bryn's grandparents?"

Manuel smiled. "Bryn's grandmother and the Blue Women's League came up with the proposal, but it benefits all students. Plus, it gives us something to do rather than stand around waiting for trouble. It's a win-win situation."

Bryn was thankful that this hadn't been something afforded only to her, due to her status as Ephram and Marie Sinclair's granddaughter. So many aspects of her new life made her feel uncomfortable.

"Where to first?" Bryn asked to change the subject.

"I heard that Bath and Beauty expanded their store to include towels and sheets," Ivy said. "I bet they have comforters, too."

Clint groaned. "Not the smelly lotion store."

"I don't understand your objection to Bath and Beauty," Ivy said.

"It's a girl store. When I walk in there my testosterone level probably drops by ten points."

Manuel the driver chuckled.

"See, he agrees with me," Clint said.

Too bad Clint didn't have a guy to hang out with while she and Ivy went into the store. In times past, he would have waited for them while he talked to Valmont. It was weird to realize that there would never be a fourth person added to their group again because she'd never have another boyfriend. She'd have Jaxon, but he wouldn't hang out with them. And she was pretty sure Clint wouldn't want to pal around with him, either.

"Why do you have that look on your face?" Ivy asked.

"What look?" Bryn asked.

"You look sad. Are you sure you're okay with going to Dragon's Bluff?"

"It's not like I can avoid it forever." There wasn't any other place they could go while they were in school. She just needed to face the sad memories head-on. "And I do want to go shopping, so I'm just going to have to deal with it."

When they reached town, the driver parked in a covered lot that hadn't been there a month ago. The Directorate had done their best to make it blend into the rest of the town. The lot had a roof that matched the shops, which made it look like a strange house that had lost its walls. There were steel beams holding the roof in place and what looked like a small office off to one side where a Red sat at a desk.

"There are several lots like this throughout town," Manuel said. "If you are near a different lot and want to return to school you can ask someone there to take you. Just make sure you have them call me so I know you've gone back."

"Okay," Bryn said. "Thanks for the ride." She climbed out of the SUV, feeling like she should pay him or give him a tip.

They headed down the street. When Bryn had first seen Dragon's Bluff it had looked like a town out of a fairy tale, with its matching red brick buildings, bright yellow awnings, and yellow flowers in the planters that lined the sidewalks. Most of the awnings had been burned in the battle and whoever had been in charge of replacing them had chosen black instead. It shouldn't have made a difference since they all matched, but somehow it made the town feel more somber. Maybe that was the point...to remind people that there had been an attack and to keep their guard up.

When they reached Bath and Beauty, Clint opted to go across the street to a bookstore. "I'll be over there reading manly books while you shop for girly stuff."

Ivy chuckled and gave him a quick kiss. "Have fun."

Inside the store, there were more changes. The entire area had once been devoted to scented lotions and shampoos and any other body care product you could think of. Now half of the space offered sheets and towels and shower curtains.

A navy comforter with a gray stripe caught Bryn's eye. She wandered over to look at it. "I like this one."

Ivy pointed to another comforter which was hot pink with yellow flowers. "That's so bright it would keep me awake at night."

"But that one is cool." Bryn walked over to check out an aqua comforter with random width white stripes.

"And it's happier than the navy one," Ivy said. "Although the inconsistent stripes might make me crazy after awhile."

"It would probably make my grandmother crazy, too, but I kind of like that it's not symmetrical." The perfection of everything at her grandparents' estate sometimes gave her a headache. There was too much pressure for everything to be just right. Bryn grabbed the matching sheets and then investigated the bathroom accessories.

"Look at this." Ivy held out a smiling green frog with long eyelashes and some sort of lotion pump on its head.

"What is it?" Bryn asked.

"It's a soap dispenser. And even though it doesn't fit my kick-ass tattooed image, it makes me smile."

"Then you should get it." Bryn followed Ivy over to the other soap dispensers displayed with a sign that said: *Find one that makes you happy*. "Great marketing campaign," Bryn said. After all the fighting and bloodshed, finding little things that made you smile was a good idea.

She debated over several cute animals and then picked a plump blue bird. "This one works for me."

After paying for their items, they went outside to find Clint arguing with a Red Guard.

"What's going on?" Bryn asked.

"Loitering is not allowed," the guard said.

"He wasn't loitering," Bryn said. "He was waiting for us."

"No one is allowed to stand around in the street or on the sidewalk. When you come here you shop, or eat, and then leave."

"Okay." Bryn wanted to argue, but the guard looked like he was minutes from exploding. She could play the do you know who my grandparents are card, and if the guard had tried to arrest Clint she would have, but right now it was easier to make peace and then figure out what was going on later. "We're going to eat now."

The guard loomed over Clint. "Do not let me catch you disobeying the rules again."

Clint held up a piece of paper. "Maybe someone should hand these out to people as they come into town. It's hard to obey rules when you don't know they exist."

The guard opened his mouth to counter Clint's argument. Ivy grabbed Clint's arm and tugged him down the sidewalk. "Time to eat."

"What was that about?" Bryn asked as they walked at a brisk pace toward the Snack Shack.

"Let's wait until we're inside before we talk," Clint said, "because something about that didn't feel right."

Bryn inhaled the scent of caramel corn as they entered the restaurant. "That smells amazing."

After they were seated and had placed their order for burgers and fries, Clint said, "I was standing there, minding my own business, when the large, angry guard came over and started to lecture me about loitering. When I acted clueless, he pulled out this list. I swear he was ten seconds from arresting me. And this list is ridiculous.

Anyone in Dragon's Bluff who is not shopping shall be detained for loitering.
Anyone in Dragon's Bluff who is not dining shall be detained for loitering.
Loitering or congregating without purpose is not allowed.

"So the moral of the story is, don't stop to tie your shoe between shops or you could be arrested?" Bryn asked. "What's this about?"

Their waitress delivered their drinks and a bucket of caramel corn. "Be careful," she said. "They aren't kidding about arresting people. My boyfriend was waiting for my shift to end, and they took him in. I had to go identify him before they'd let him leave."

"Where did they take him?" Ivy asked.

"Those huts at the parking lots aren't just places for the guards to hang out. There are cells inside."

After the waitress left, Bryn said, "What's the purpose of this? Why pass laws to detain people who aren't doing anything?"

"No good reason comes to mind," Clint said.

Ivy frowned and examined the list again. "They escort us here in armed cars, and then harass us? That doesn't make sense."

Bryn leaned in and spoke in a quiet voice. "I'd bet money that the Women's League did not sponsor the anti- loitering campaign. That sounds more like Ferrin."

"You're probably right," Ivy said.

"I hate that we feel like we have to whisper these conversations when we're in public," Bryn said. "Like we don't have the right to discuss things in the open anymore."

"That's not on the list," Clint said.

"No, but common sense tells me that whoever is behind the list is looking to make an example of someone," Ivy said.

Chapter Four

Bryn's phone rang half an hour before curfew. Who could that be? She had a sneaking suspicion but hoped she was wrong.

Crossing her fingers for luck, she answered the phone. "Hello?"

"Hello, Bryn," her grandmother's voice coming through the phone was a relief. "I know it's late, but I wanted to stop by for a visit."

That was strange. "Is everything all right?"

"Yes. I'll be at your door in five minutes."

"I moved down the hall," Bryn said, in case her grandmother didn't know.

"I'm aware," her grandmother said. "How do you think I knew which room to call?"

"Right." She hung up, feeling sort of stupid. Whatever. Her grandmother knocked exactly five minutes later.

Bryn opened the door and was surprised to see Lillith by her grandmother's side. Jaxon's mom was due to give birth any day now.

Bryn stepped back to let them in and then gave her grandmother a hug. "It's nice to see you, but what's going on?"

"We've heard rumors that students aren't being made to feel welcome in Dragon's Bluff," her grandmother said.

"And we wanted to make sure that students weren't intimidated at Orientation tomorrow," Lillith said. "So we thought you and Jaxon could act as a hospitality committee to show everyone they are truly welcome at school."

Bryn had learned to keep her sighs of frustration on the inside. Outwardly, she smiled and nodded. "Sure. We can do that."

Lillith looked at the couch and then chose to sit in a chair at the table. "I'm afraid if I sit on the couch I won't be able to get up without assistance." She stroked her belly. "I keep telling Asher that he can make his appearance any time now."

"I thought you had another two weeks until your due date," Bryn said.

"I do," Lillith said. "But I swear there isn't any more room for him to grow."

Someone knocked on the door. "Are we expecting someone else?" Bryn asked.

"That will be Jaxon," her grandmother said.

Great. Bryn walked over and swung the door wide. Jaxon stood there looking as happy as she felt. "What fun new event are we attending now?" he asked in a tone that sounded like he was mentally rolling his eyes.

"We're hosting student orientation," Bryn said with obviously fake enthusiasm.

"How wonderful." Jaxon entered the room and nodded at her grandmother. "Mrs. Sinclair, Mother...how nice to see you both."

"Young man, I doubt your sincerity," her grandmother said.

"As you should." Jaxon walked over and sat on the couch. "It's been a trying day. Please explain what you'd like me to do so I can return to my room."

"Coming back to school must have stirred up so many memories," his mom said. "Are you all right?"

Jaxon glanced at his mother and then reached up to rub his forehead. "Which answer would you like...the truth or the socially acceptable response?"

"The truth," Lillith said.

Jaxon stared down at his hands. "Everything reminds me of Rhianna. I'd literally rather be anywhere other than here."

"I'm sorry," Lillith said. "But I'm not sure what I can do to help."

"The only thing that helps with this type of loss is time and distraction," Bryn's grandmother said. Her tone was more kind than Bryn would have expected.

"What do you want us to do tomorrow?" Bryn asked, hoping to move this along. Maybe she could talk to Jaxon after his mother and her grandmother left.

"You can greet incoming students with enthusiasm... fake enthusiasm is acceptable as long as it's believable," her grandmother said. "Once everyone is seated, one or both of you should give a short speech about the exciting prospects of the year ahead."

Bryn and Jaxon both snorted at the exact same time, which made Bryn laugh.

"I'll give this speech, you can give the next one," she said. "Although I have no idea what to say."

Her grandmother pulled an envelope from her pocket. "I took the liberty of writing down a few points you can discuss if you can't come up with anything appropriate."

"It's the appropriate part that might be the issue." Bryn took the envelope from her grandmother, removed the paper inside, and read the message aloud. "We'd like to welcome you back to the Institute for Excellence. A new school year is always exciting. Now that hybrids and throwbacks are out in the open, dragons can no longer be categorized by Clan color alone. Individuals must be judged on their deeds and their intentions and their loyalty to the Directorate." Well that was interesting. "What dorm will the hybrids stay in?" Bryn asked. Everyone was normally assigned by Clan.

"I think dragons should be allowed to live with the Clan they identify with," her grandmother said.

"So if a Black-Red hybrid identifies as Red then he'll live with the Red dragons?" Jaxon said. "What if the Reds aren't interested in taking him in?"

"That would be rude," Bryn said.

"They didn't want you," Jaxon stated.

"Asshat much?" Bryn asked.

He glared at her.

"Jaxon raises a valid, if somewhat rude, point," Lillith said.

"He does, which is why I've talked Bryn's grandfather into opening the Orange dragons' dorm up to hybrids or anyone else who doesn't feel that they would want to live in one of the traditional dorms. And before you even make a smart-ass comment," her grandmother said, "no, you may not move to the Orange dorm."

"I know you too well to even ask that question," Bryn said. "I might have thought it, but I wouldn't have asked."

"If you're clear on your role tomorrow, then Lillith and I can let you both return to your regularly scheduled evening." Her grandmother stood gracefully.

Lillith leveraged herself out of the chair. "Excuse my awkwardness."

Only a Blue who was nine months pregnant would be embarrassed at her lack of grace. Any other female would be happy they'd managed to get up and out of the chair.

Bryn hugged her grandmother and Lillith. Jaxon followed them to the door and kissed his mother on the cheek. Once the women were gone, Bryn expected Jaxon to bolt. She was surprised when he shut the door and paced back and forth in the living room.

Not sure what to say, Bryn waited.

Jaxon stopped walking and dragged his hand down his face. "I should go."

"You can stay, if you want," Bryn said and then mentally kicked herself. Why had she told him that? She didn't know what else to say. "I wish I could help somehow."

Jaxon nodded and then he headed for the door, letting himself out without another word.

...

The next morning, Bryn dragged Clint and Ivy along to Orientation. "Why are we here again?" Clint asked.

"Because misery loves company," Bryn said. "Plus I think you'll make the other tattooed dragons feel more comfortable, since Jaxon isn't exactly relatable and I'm the odd man out."

"You're not the odd man out anymore," Clint said. "Hybrids have been invited back to school."

Yes, but will they come? If Bryn had had a choice a year ago, she would have agreed to be homeschooled in a heartbeat.

Tension flowed through the room like a murky fog as soon as she entered the dining hall. The students had congregated by Clan, which wasn't surprising. Along with the Red, Blue, Orange, Black, and Green groups there was a group which appeared to be predominantly Black, but some of the girls had auburn or hazel hair instead of the standard black. There was another group of students who had the dark complexion of Green Dragons, but their eyes were blue rather than brown. The combination of dark skin and light eyes was striking. There were several students with coloring that hinted at intermixed heritage that must have gone on for generations. A pale blonde with green eyes resembled an ethereal elven princess.

The dragons from the traditional Clans seemed to be eyeing up the hybrid and throwback dragons with suspicion. The breakfast buffet sat mostly untouched.

"Is it me, or is this awkward?" Bryn said.

"You're always awkward," Jaxon said. "But this time it isn't just you."

Bryn considered huffing a small fireball at his head, but in this tense climate she might start a battle. "Keep it up, and I'll tell your mom that you want to be present at Asher's birth but aren't sure how to ask."

Jaxon grimaced, which made her laugh.

"Use your superior event-planning-knowledge to find me a microphone and we'll get started."

Jaxon stalked off.

"That was fun," Clint said. "What's next?"

"No one is eating. Why don't you and Ivy go through the buffet line and maybe some other students will follow your lead."

"I suppose I can eat bacon for the greater good," Clint said, like he was making some sort of sacrifice.

"Grab me a cup of coffee," Bryn called after them as they walked off.

Jaxon returned with a cordless microphone. "I can make the speech if you aren't up to it."

She held out her hand. "No. I've got this." She'd stayed up until midnight coming up with what she hoped would be the perfect speech.

Pushing the button to turn the microphone on, she said, "Good morning, everyone." People turned toward her. Some of them seemed curious. Some looked annoyed. "I know it's early and it's your first day here. The good news is there's coffee and bacon on the buffet. The bad news is none of us knows what this year will bring. Last year, I thought I was the only hybrid around, but now I know that wasn't true. Having other hybrids and throwbacks out in the open will make me feel more comfortable, but it may take the traditionalists a while to adjust."

"And I can't believe I'm about to say this, but the Directorate did investigate and approve every student before allowing him or her on campus. After the attack, I know they wouldn't take any chances with our safety, so please don't feel like you have to be suspicious of the student sitting next to you." She glanced over at Jaxon. "You may find some people annoying or overbearing, but none of them should wish you any serious harm."

A few students chuckled. Jaxon was not one of them. "This year is a fresh start for all of us. Now that no one has to hide who they really are, we can all get to know one another. The Directorate has opened the Orange dorm to any student who may not wish to live in one of the traditional dorms. If you're a hybrid or throwback who identifies with a certain Clan because that is how you were raised, then you can move into that Clan's dorm. Basically, you can present yourself as whoever you want to be." She reached up and touched the cherry-red stripe in her golden-blond hair. "Rather than hiding your heritage you can be proud of it. Or, if you're a more laid-back person who'd rather not attract attention, you can blend in. Basically, this school year is about options. If you have any questions you can ask to meet with Jaxon or myself since we represent the Student Directorate."

She turned to Jaxon. "Anything you'd like to add?"

He held his hand out for the microphone, which surprised her, but she passed it to him. He cleared his throat. "Many of us have lost loved ones or friends. I've been informed that Miss Enid, the librarian, will be hosting a support group in the library Thursday evenings. Everyone is welcome. Now, please feel free to visit the buffet."

Bryn decided that meant she was dismissed, too, so she went over to join Clint and Ivy at a table. Ivy pushed a cup of coffee toward her. "This is for you."

"Thank you." Bryn grabbed a packet of sugar and ripped it open. Half of the sugar crystals landed on the table. "I'm glad Jaxon wasn't here to see that." She dumped the remaining sugar into her coffee cup and stirred before sweeping up the stray sugar with her napkin.

"Nice speech," Ivy said.

"Thanks. My goal was to make sure that no one felt as uncomfortable as I did last year."

"Hard to believe that a year ago Jaxon had a hissy fit when he found out who you were, and now you're planning on getting married," Clint said.

"Agreed," Bryn said. "But I'd appreciate it if we could bring up that fun fact as few times as possible. I like living in denial. It helps me cope."

"Understandable," Ivy said. "So what's next on the agenda? Do we have to stay here, or can we go roam the campus?"

Her grandmother would say that since she was sort of hosting, it was her duty to stay until everyone left, but her grandmother wasn't here. "I'm going to grab some food. After we eat, I think we're free to leave."

Bryn scarfed down half a dozen pieces of bacon and a stack of pancakes without dripping anything on her blouse, which was an accomplishment. She finished off her coffee and smiled. "All done. Now what?"

"Let's go flying," Ivy said.

"Good idea." Bryn spotted Jaxon across the room, talking with some Blues. "My grandmother's voice in my head is telling me that it would be polite for me to let Jaxon know I'm leaving."

Clint frowned. "You should look into having that voice removed."

"I'd love to, but it seems to be part of my new Blue life." Bryn pushed to her feet. "I'll meet you guys outside in a few minutes."

Jaxon noticed her approach and frowned. She smiled just to annoy him.

"Did you need something?" he asked before she could get a word out.

"No. I just wanted to let you know that I'm leaving, so if anything comes up, you can handle it."

He nodded and went back to his conversation. It's not like she was thrilled with this situation, but if he didn't start being a little nicer, she was going to have to come up with ways to annoy him...like telling his mother that he wanted to go shopping for baby clothes for Asher.

Before she made it to the door, a girl with auburn hair and brown eyes stepped directly into her path. "Your mother asked me to give you this." She held out a folded piece of paper. "She said you should read it later when you're alone."

That probably wasn't going to happen. How could she be sure the letter was real? "Thank you. Who are you and how do you know my mother?"

The girl smiled. "I'm Veronica. I met your mom in Sanctuary when she and your dad helped fix up my family's cabin. She hoped to come meet you today, but the Directorate seems to be blocking the adults from leaving the town."

"My grandmother thinks that those restrictions will be lifted soon," Bryn said.

"Your grandmother?" the girl said in a snotty tone. "Wow. You really have gone native."

What the hell? "You don't get to judge me because you don't have a clue what I went through when I thought my parents were dead, or what my grandmother went through when she mourned my mother twice. I suggest you drop the attitude because I may look like a Blue, but I still have a Red's temper."

The girl smiled. "Your father will be happy to hear that."

Wait a minute. "Did you just set me up to see if I'd lose my temper?"

"Yes. Some of us were afraid that you'd lost your connection to who you were. I'm glad to see that's not true, even if you are going to marry a Westgate."

"I really wish people would stop mentioning that," Bryn said. "Well, thanks for delivering the letter. Tell my parents I hope to see them soon."

The girl nodded and went back to her table. That was weird. Bryn headed out the front door and down the steps of the dining hall. There was no way she could wait to read the letter from her mom, so she walked around the side of the building and stood under a shade tree.

Her heart beat fast as she unfolded the piece of paper.

Dear Bryn,

Your father and I can't wait to see you. If what we've heard is true we should be able to meet with you soon. I'm not sure where we can meet because my father still hasn't spoken to me, although my mother has responded to my letters. There's so much we need to discuss. I'm proud of the young woman you've become. I'm afraid you're trapped by choices your father and I made. Please don't agree to anything you don't truly want to do.

Too late on that front, but she wouldn't go back on her word. If Jaxon wanted to bail, she'd be okay with that. Not that he'd ever consider doing that since his loyalty was to his Clan. And after having her heart broken, she wasn't looking to jump into any sort of romantic relationship, so the frenemies thing she had going with Jaxon suited her just fine...for now.

She glanced back at the letter. If her grandmother or Jaxon came upon this information there would be hell to pay, so she focused on one of her elements, which was fire, and shot flames through her fingertips, burning the note to ash. Now to join her friends.

Clint and Ivy had already shifted into dragon form and were flying overhead. Their black scales gleamed in the sunlight. Bryn closed her eyes and focused her life force, allowing it to grow and expand as her body shifted to what felt like her true form. She stretched, enjoying the warm sensation of the sun on her wings and then launched herself into the air. Pushing down with powerful wing strokes, she gained height, catching up with her friends who were flying figure eights. Nothing compared to the sensation of flying. Bryn looped around in a lazy circle, not trying to fly fast, just basking in the sensation of freedom brought on by the air flowing over her body.

Ivy performed a diving roll, and Bryn followed suit. They played the dragon version of follow the leader. Other dragons joined them in the sky, but kept their distance interacting with their own friends. There was a single Blue dragon flying along the edge of campus; without seeing his face flash across his dragon features Bryn knew it was Jaxon. She couldn't imagine the pain he must be feeling right now.

Ivy came to tread air near Bryn. "Can you think of anything that might help him?"

"No. And I know Valmont broke my heart, but there's a chance he and I could become friends again one day. If he'd just vanished from the world...that sense of loss and lack of closure would make me crazy."

Chapter Five

The next morning the alarm went off in its usual annoying arrhythmia-inducing fashion. Now that she was back to living alone, she had to turn off the alarm in the empty bedroom, too, which was ridiculous. If there was no occupant, the alarm should be disconnected. What did they do for the empty rooms? There had to be a way to turn the blasted things off.

She met Clint and Ivy in the dining hall at their usual table. It took two cups of coffee before she felt capable of stringing words together in a sentence.

Ivy yawned. "I forgot how much I hated those stupid alarm clocks."

"Me, too." Bryn checked the time. They'd need to leave for class in fifteen minutes. "How come time flies when you're eating or being social and it drags when you're in class?"

"Good question." Clint slid lower in his chair. "Do you think Mr. Stanton would mind if I napped on my desk?"

"I'm going to go with yes." Bryn leaned closer to her friends and spoke in a quiet voice. "Do you think the Directorate still has spy cams everywhere?" They'd been installed when tensions had escalated with the rebels during the last school year.

"I'm sure there are," Ivy said. "But maybe they aren't watching them as closely."

"I looked forward to coming back to school like I was coming home." It was hard to put into words what she was feeling. "But now that I'm here everything feels off-kilter."

"Like you said in your speech, this is a new year for everyone," Clint pointed out. "It might take all of us awhile to adjust."

"Maybe," Bryn said, "but I swear, it feels like I'm waiting for the other shoe to drop."

"The biggest shoe of all has already dropped. Or several big shoes: the attack on campus and the approval of your marriage contract," Ivy said.

"True. Those were two big whammies...not to mention the whole mess with Valmont." How could she explain? "I have this feeling the bad stuff isn't over yet. Like we need to stay on watch."

...

When they entered Mr. Stanton's class, the seating chart on the board was comforting until she noticed that she was seated next to Jaxon. Seriously? What was up with that?

Mr. Stanton sat behind his desk, flipping through a booklet like he'd lost the page he was on. Students filtered in. Bryn smiled at Keegan when he waved from across the room. Both of his eyes were green, a Red Dragon trait, so he must have chosen to continue wearing a green contact lens to hide his throwback trait of one brown eye. Octavious and Vivian, the only two Orange students on campus last year were seated nearby with their heads together, whispering about something.

Once everyone had found his or her seat, Mr. Stanton stood. "Welcome back to school. I hope this year will be a little less exciting than last year. It is, however, your senior year which means you have some decisions to make. What do you want to focus your studies on now and in your college years? What do you want to major in? What classes can help you achieve your goals in life?"

"No pressure," Clint muttered loud enough for everyone to hear.

Several students chuckled, and Mr. Stanton nodded. "Clint is not wrong. It's a lot of pressure to decide what you want to do with the rest of your life when you're seventeen or eighteen. Some of you have family businesses you wish to become a part of. Others are striking out into new areas. Just know that the choices you make now will affect your future, but very few choices can ruin your future. So if you start down a path and decide it's not for you, it's okay to change course. No single decision will make or break you. This year is all about figuring out who you are and what you want."

That sounded good in theory, but Bryn felt like she had very little choice in the way her life was going.

"In the past, I've been assigned as counselor for the Green Clan. This year I've been asked to work with all of you, so we are going to spend some time discussing what your options are and what course of curriculum you will need to take to achieve your goals."

He grabbed a stack of booklets and handed some to the first student in every row, who dutifully passed them back. "In the past, we have all been defined by our Clans. Blues were the elite lawyers and lawmakers. Reds were the middle- class workers who kept our businesses running. Greens were the scientists, medics, and professors. Blacks were the artists and musicians. Oranges were the agriculturalists. No one strayed from the paths laid out for them. Today, what I'd like you to do is study all your options. Put a star next to anything that catches your eye, whether it's a major that someone in your Clan typically aspires to or not. Of course, the Directorate will have to approve what areas of study students will be allowed to pursue. Having more hybrids on campus could open doors for everyone, allowing dragons more choice in their professions."

Wow. That was something Zavien had talked about... something that Jaxon swore the Directorate would never allow. How would Ferrin and other rabid traditionalists handle this? They weren't exactly good with change.

Bryn read through the information about Quintessential Medicine, which was the act of healing others with your life force. She'd already healed several people and while it could be terrifying, it was also fulfilling. It made her feel like she served a purpose in this world, like she could contribute to the greater good.

Since there was no I want to be speaker for the Directorate section in the booklet, Bryn tried to see what Jaxon was looking at. Law? He wanted to be a lawyer? That made sense. He did love to quote Directorate law or maybe he hoped to change some of the outdated laws. How would his father feel about that?

Jaxon caught her looking at him. "What? Did you think I'd aspire to be a topiary artist like Ivy?"

"Only the coolest people can be plant whisperers," Clint said in a slightly defensive tone.

Jaxon didn't respond. He flipped through several more pages and frowned. "Did you notice what's not in here?"

Bryn checked the table of contents. She scanned down what seemed like a fairly inclusive list of professions. "What's missing?"

"Librarians," Jaxon said. "Historians, journalists... anyone who documents and archives history."

"That's weird." Curious, Bryn raised her hand, and Mr. Stanton came to her desk. "Why aren't historians and librarians listed?"

"I was wondering that myself," Mr. Stanton said. "We'll always need individuals to keep track of and report on important events and archive our history."

"Does that mean the Directorate wants to take over doing that?" Bryn asked.

"It was probably just an oversight by whoever designed the booklets," Mr. Stanton said.

Right. What were the odds that he was correct, and not that the Directorate wanted to control how information was reported and recorded?

When class ended, Bryn was excited to attend her Beginning Quintessential Medicine class. It was the first class that would lead toward her goal of becoming a Medic. Hopefully it wouldn't be boring.

Half a dozen other students, all of them from the Green clan, were already in the room. That wasn't unusual since Greens, who were recognized as the smartest Clan, had always been Medics and professors.

Medic Williams who had healed Bryn on more than one occasion, smiled at them from the front of the room. "I know you're all excited to start healing, but there will also be reading assignments and tests."

Great.

"I'm going to pass out a basic medical kit." Medic Williams walked to each of their desks and deposited a small green-zippered case. "Go ahead and open it."

Was this just going to be a typical first aid kit? Bryn unzipped the case. A pair of silver scissors, Band-Aids, and what looked like different types of healing salves and some pain killers were organized on one side. The other side contained several foil plastic packets of what appeared to be licorice, chocolate, and peppermint.

"Over time, you can replace the candy with whatever you want, but you should always carry extra calories with you. If you run out of energy when you're trying to heal a patient, you could both suffer injury or death."

Totally valid reason for carrying chocolate at all times. Score.

"As you know, Quintessence is the essence of all things. It's our life force. You can manipulate your life force to heal or to alter something about yourself." Medic Williams held out her hand and her fingernails changed from pink to red. "I'm sure some of you can already do this, but we're going to practice on ourselves today. You need to be able to focus your life force at will." She held her hand up again and her nails shifted through a rainbow of colors. "Let's get started."

Bryn gathered her life force in her chest and then focused on her nails. She changed them from red to a deep purple. Medic Williams walked around the room checking on their progress. She nodded at Bryn and checked the rest of the class.

"Okay, now that I know you can focus your Quintessence, we are going to go over some ground rules. Anyone who injures their friends, even with their permission to practice healing, will be kicked out of the program. The only person you will practice on is yourself and adult volunteers who I will bring to the classroom."

Who would ask their friends to do that? The irritated expression of some of her classmates showed that her opinion might not be the popular one. Greens were known for being clinical, but she couldn't picture Garrett purposefully injuring someone just to test his skill.

"You've healed real injuries, haven't you?" a girl next to Bryn asked.

"Yes." She wasn't about to go into gory details.

"You're lucky."

Bryn blinked. "No. I'm the opposite of lucky. Seeing people I care about wounded and bleeding hardly makes me lucky."

The girl's eyes widened. "Of course not. I meant you are one of the few who's been able to practice this skill. I wouldn't wish injury on anyone."

The girl's social skills could use some work, but Bryn would like to have a friend in class, so she let it slide. "Right. Sorry I got defensive. I'm Bryn."

"It's amusing that you think you need to introduce yourself. I'm Janelle." The girl smiled. "Can I show you a trick I've been working on?"

"Sure."

Janelle's dark hair lightened shade by shade all the way to white and then shifted to dark brown again.

"That is so cool," Bryn said.

"Thank you. I thought it was fun." She grinned like she'd done something she wasn't supposed to. "Greens don't usually do things just for fun, so no one else has appreciated it."

"I find fun is an important part of life," Bryn said. "I like to use Quintessence instead of makeup."

"You can do that?" Janelle asked. "Show me how."

"I usually need a mirror," Bryn said.

"Use one of the foil pouches in your kit," Janelle suggested.

"Good idea." Bryn held up one of the foil pouches and focused on her lips. She turned her natural pink color to a coral red. "Just focus on the color you want. I've used it for blush, too."

"Awesome." Janelle held up her own foil pouch and looked at her reflection, changing her lips to a brick red. "Greens don't normally bother with makeup, but I like it."

"That color looks great on you." With her dark complexion and chestnut-colored eyes, Janelle was beautiful without makeup. But the deep color on her lips made her look amazing.

"That's not what your skills are for," a girl next to Janelle said.

"If Medic Williams can do her nails, I can play with lip color," Janelle said.

"I've always wondered if I could change someone else's coloring," Bryn said. "Like if a certain someone annoys me, can I shift his hair color to electric yellow?"

"That would be fun to try," Janelle said. "I guess it depends on how annoying the other person is." She nodded toward the girl who'd commented on the lip color.

Bryn laughed. Janelle was pretty cool.

Chapter Six

After classes were finished for the day, Bryn returned to her room. Over the summer, at her grandparents' estate, she'd adjusted to living in a room by herself. Here back at school, she missed having someone to hang out with in the evenings. Valmont had always been there for her. The pain over his defection had turned into a dull ache, but she missed having someone around. She could call Clint and Ivy, but she'd see them for dinner. Maybe it was time to broaden her circle of friends. Could she talk to Zavien? Part of her wanted to, but she wasn't sure they could go back to being friends. And Jaxon would have an apocalyptic fit if she started hanging out with an ex-boyfriend who'd been betrothed to one of the key players of the Rebels.

Janelle had been fun, and it wouldn't hurt to have someone she could study with. Did making friends ever become less complicated? When you were a little kid the only thing that mattered was that you both liked the same cookies or cartoons. The older you became the harder it seemed to make connection with people.

It's not like she could call Janelle and ask her to hang out. They'd just met today, and she didn't want to look like a creeper. So...where did that leave her?

Maybe she'd go to the library and check out one of the Legends books which told stories of times when dragons were allowed to fall in love by instinct instead of being forced into arranged marriages. That thought gave her pleasure for about thirty seconds and then she realized that the books might not seem as entertaining to her as they once had now that she was involved in her own debacle of an arranged marriage. After witnessing the unstable hybrids who had attacked campus, the books didn't seem so romantic, either. Maybe Miss Enid could suggest something else.

Rather than walking down the stairs and dealing with the social niceties of nodding and smiling at the other Blue students in her dorm, which she didn't feel like doing, Bryn decided to fly down. She went through the window which led to her terrace. Standing outside, she took a deep breath of the fresh fall air. There was a hint of wood smoke in the wind, like someone had started a fire, or blasted someone with a fireball.

She shifted with ease to her dragon form and then dove off the terrace into the evening sky. Flying was the best. The cool evening air felt like a caress. Bryn aimed for the green space in front of the library and came in slow. She treaded air for a moment and then tucked her wings, dropping to the ground. Not a bad landing. She shifted and entered the library.

The librarian sat behind the front desk, working at her computer. When she looked up and saw Bryn, she frowned. What the heck? Miss Enid had always been someone she could count on as a confidant and she'd thought of her as a friend.

"I'm sorry, should I leave you alone?" Bryn asked.

"What?" Miss Enid blinked and then shook her head. "Sorry. I was off in my own little world."

Thank goodness the frown hadn't been directed at her. Bryn felt her shoulders relax. "How was your summer?" she asked.

"It was unsettling."

She knew why her summer had been odd, but she didn't know what Miss Enid had dealt with. "Feel free to tell me to mind my own business, but what happened?"

"Nothing specific," Miss Enid said. "It seems like there are several political forces at play, and I'm not sure what their goals are. I know your grandfather is trying to keep the peace, but Ferrin seems bent on crushing anyone he even thinks might be a problem. I had a new student, who happened to be a Green-Red hybrid, organizing an area on the second floor. When she didn't return in a timely manner I went to check on her and discovered that a guard had grabbed her for questioning. She'd been approved to attend school and had passed another set of approvals to work for me. The guard had no cause to suspect her. He'd just grabbed her because her auburn hair didn't match her dark complexion."

"That's ridiculous." And it reminded her of something. "Have you heard about the No Loitering rule in Dragon's Bluff?"

"No."

Bryn told her about the guards almost arresting Clint.

"That's absurd." Miss Enid drummed her nails on the wooden desk. "I don't understand why someone would go through the trouble of clearing students to return to school if they planned on targeting them afterward, anyway."

"I have another question." Bryn glanced around. "Why won't they let any of the adults leave Sanctuary?"

"Interesting. It's almost like they're purposely separating the children from their parents."

"Why would they do that?" And then Bryn had an odd thought. "What about the students who aren't old enough to attend the Institute? Where are they going to school?"

"Some of the hybrids were teachers, and they've set up a school for the younger students," Miss Enid said.

"Oh...well that's good. What are the adults doing all day?"

"I've heard that everyone is pitching in to build housing." That made sense. "Enough reality for the moment. Can you recommend some books that have nothing to do with dragons?"

"How do you feel about demon hunters?"

"I'm willing to give them a shot," Bryn said.

...

Bryn was one hundred pages into her book when someone knocked on her door. She'd just seen Clint and Ivy at dinner, so who did that leave? Wait, she knew the answer. She slid a bookmark between the pages and went to see what Jaxon wanted.

She opened the door and sure enough, the blight of her life stood there with a sour expression on his face...and he'd gripe if she tried to talk to him in the hallway. "Come on in."

He entered and went to lean against the library table. "We need to talk."

"Here I thought maybe you dropped by to play charades."

"I'm not going to dignify that poor attempt at humor with a response." He crossed his arms over his chest. "We should start eating our meals together in the dining hall."

"Hell no." She was not giving up her friends.

"I'm just as thrilled about it as you are, but people are talking about us not spending enough time together."

"What people? And since when does a Westgate care what other people think?"

He opened his mouth to speak and then paused. "Good point, but for the sake of appearances, we should eat together a few times a week."

This was not a conversation she wanted to have standing up. She walked over and flopped down on the couch, putting her feet up on the coffee table. "Fine. Let's negotiate. You don't want to eat at my table and I don't want to eat at yours, so we should share the awkwardness on some sort of schedule."

Jaxon came to sit in one of the winged-back chairs and pointed at her feet. "A table is not a footstool."

"This one is," Bryn said. "Back to the irritating topic at hand. I'll join you for dinner on Tuesdays and you'll join me for dinner on Thursdays."

"Fine. We should probably eat lunch together, too."

Nope. "Lunch is for scarfing down food before going to your next class. Let's stick with dinner. It's more date-like."

"I guess you're right. We'll start with dinner two nights a week and see if that takes care of the issue. We still need to discuss weekends."

She was going to regret asking this question. "What about the weekends?"

"Your grandmother and my mother spent all summer throwing us together. Did you think they'd stop just because school started?"

"Son of a bitch." Bryn slid lower on the couch.

"Agreed. Apparently, they are bringing events to campus rather than dragging us off to other peoples' estates. My mother claims it's about helping to unify the student body and making them feel welcome."

"Good to know other people will be sharing the fun." On a positive note, at least with students from all Clans and multiple versions of hybrids, she wouldn't stick out like she normally did at Blue events.

"So...this weekend we're having a Homecoming Gala where we're supposed to mingle and be seen."

"Can we do that in jeans, because the dress code isn't in force on the weekends?" Girls were required to wear skirts and blouses and archaic panty hose to class everyday and she relished her evening and weekend yoga pants and jeans time.

"I'm sure you know the answer to that question."

"You're just the bearer of all sorts of good news," she said.

"Just sharing the joy that is our inexplicably intertwined lives." He stared down at his hands. "I understand now why they test bloodlines. There are certain traits you definitely don't want brought to light. I'd like to see how they determine which bloodlines are compatible. You'd think there would be more than just a few good matches for every dragon."

"I don't understand why Mr. Stanton and Miss Enid were denied without a reason."

Jaxon's brow wrinkled in confusion before he seemed to understand. "They were denied, and they didn't accept the Directorate's alternative partners, which is why they never married."

"Exactly. They've been seeing each other all this time. And honestly, since they're past the age of having children, what would the harm be in allowing them to marry?"

"As far as I know, something of that nature has never been discussed," Jaxon said. "Dragons who chose not to marry have always stayed single, but if they are no longer at risk of producing dangerous offspring, they should be allowed to marry."

"I know it's not really the Student Directorate's place to advocate for teachers, but we could say that some students asked," Bryn said. "Because we're students and we wondered."

"Bothering my father with anything other than a life or death situation right now is not advisable. He's barely home and when he is, he isn't in a social mood."

Poor Lillith. "I could ask my grandmother if she thinks we should ask the Directorate about this. My grandfather seems like his normal self, but I have no idea what he's dealing with right now."

Jaxon stood. "Let me know what she says."

"Okay." Bryn followed him to the door and locked it after he left. While she wasn't looking forward to eating several meals a week with him, it was nice to have someone to talk to about these Directorate issues. Did he feel the same way?

Chapter Seven

The next morning at breakfast, Bryn shared the joyous news about Jaxon joining them for dinner one day a week.

"So you have to eat dinner with him tonight?" Ivy said.

Bryn nodded.

"Everyone knows your marriage contract was approved, so why do you have to be seen digesting food together?" Clint asked.

"I don't know...something about presenting a united front or showing everyone that our family alliance is strong or some weird Blue Clan crap like that." Bryn sipped her coffee. "Did I mention that there's going to be a Homecoming Gala this weekend? Posters will probably go up later today and it's my job to mingle and be seen with Jaxon."

"It's almost funny," Clint said.

"Almost," Bryn said, "but not quite. The good news is there will be food. The bad news is, it's dress code compliant."

"But it's the weekend," Clint whined.

"I had the exact same reaction," Bryn said.

"How's your Medic class going?" Ivy asked.

"Interesting. I met a Green named Janelle. She's pretty cool. How's history class, part two?"

"They haven't found a replacement teacher yet, so we're reading historical articles," Clint said. "Mine was about a secret society of Silver dragons who possessed all the breath weapons. They took dragons as prisoners and siphoned their Quintessence."

"That's downright evil," Bryn said.

"True," Clint said. "It reads like a horror story. Hard to believe it was real."

"Why would someone need to do that in the first place?" Bryn asked. "If you're tired, you rest or eat...you don't go all Quintessence Vampire on someone."

"Some people just don't play well with others," Ivy said. "They want all the toys for themselves and they don't care who they hurt."

Bryn had a mental image of Ferrin hoarding toys and refusing to let anyone else play with him. "Sounds like someone I know."

"Does his name rhyme with Darren?" Clint asked like he was trying to solve a puzzle.

"How'd you guess?" Bryn asked.

"I'm brilliant like that," Clint said.

As the weekend approached, Bryn waited for word that her parents would be allowed to visit, or that she'd be allowed to visit them in Sanctuary. She received no such message.

At dinner Thursday night she griped to Clint, Ivy, and Jaxon, who sat at their table looking like he'd rather be eating behind a dumpster.

"I don't understand," Bryn said. "I thought the powers that be would have all that crap straightened out by now."

"The Directorate has been convening day and night for months," Jaxon said. "And they probably prioritize everyone's safety above your concerns."

Bryn glared at him. "I'm aware of that," she added a silent asshat to her statement. "But a reliable source told me my parents would be allowed to visit soon. And I won't apologize for wanting to hug my mom and dad, who I thought were dead...so back off."

Jaxon's eyes narrowed. He leaned toward her so that their faces were inches apart. "But unlike Rhianna, they aren't dead, so you will be able to see them again." Frost shot from his lips as he spoke. "Stop complaining when you have no idea of the scope of issues the Directorate is dealing with."

Flames crawled up the back of Bryn's throat. She knew he was hurting but he'd crossed a line. She pushed the flames down but could still taste the smoke. "I know you're still grieving, and I miss Rhianna, too, but that doesn't give you the right to be a condescending asshat. We're supposed to be a team, which means we support each other, not tear each other down."

Instead of responding, he just stared at her for a moment and then he went back to eating his dinner. Was he admitting she was right? She couldn't read the blank expression on his face.

Clint and Ivy made small talk while they finished their dinner. Bryn finished her food before Jaxon. Now what? Did she have to wait for him? Maybe if she asked him, he'd feel better because he'd have an answer for something, which might soothe his ego.

"When we eat together are we required to exit the dining hall together?"

"Yes." Jaxon glanced at her plate. "My appetite is gone. We can leave now if you want."

Now he just seemed sad which made her feel guilty. Reaching over she laid her hand on his forearm. "I'm sorry." His skin was surprisingly warm to the touch.

He seemed genuinely confused. "For what?"

"For the whirlwind of crap that our lives have become."

"That's a fairly accurate description." He gave a tight smile. "From now on, I'll try to remember that we're on the same side."

She exited the dining hall with Jaxon. They didn't speak as they walked back to the Blue dorm, but the silence wasn't awkward. He walked her to her dorm room and said goodnight. Clint and Ivy knocked on her terrace window fifteen minutes later.

She let them in and they went to sit in the living room.

"That was uncomfortable," Clint said.

"At the end it was kind of sweet," Ivy said. "Which was strange, in its own way."

"I know." Bryn rubbed her eyes. "Half the time I want to smack him, and the other half I want to comfort him but I'm not sure what to do."

"Yeah...he doesn't seem like the hugging type," Ivy said.

"On to a less awkward and far more interesting topic," Clint said. "I found more articles about Silver dragons. Supposedly, they were part of a cult and they took Quintessence from specific dragons in order to gain their breath weapons."

Bryn sat forward. "Try saying that again in a way that makes sense."

"The dragons sucked Quintessence from each Clan with the help of some ancient spells that gave them the ability to reproduce each Clan's breath weapon. Think about it," Clint said. "A dragon who can breathe fire, ice, wind, lightning, and sonic waves would be badass."

"And slightly crazy," Bryn said, "due to the whole vampire-type thing."

"True. But it's still intriguing," Ivy said. "And the article hinted at the idea that possessing all the breath weapons would make them invincible...like no breath weapon could hurt them."

"Wow," Bryn said. "If that were true they could do whatever they wanted."

"I think that was their plan. They wanted to be superior to all Clans, even the Blues, so the Silvers would then be the rightful rulers."

"Wow. I can't believe the Institute, much less the Directorate, lets students even read these articles."

"It's not like any Silvers are around today," Ivy said. "The last cult member died more than a hundred years ago in a Directorate-sanctioned public execution."

Bryn cringed. "That sounds medieval."

"They weren't nice dragons," Clint said.

"I get that. Do these articles say which Clan these crazy dragons were from? And please don't say they were hybrids. We've gotten enough of a bad rap lately."

"No mention of the term hybrids, but it did say they were the result of some sort of rare combination of genes, so that could mean hybrid."

"Great." That's all she needed.

"When you think about it, the driving force behind any cult is the need for power or control, so I'm guessing any clan could be susceptible. The Silvers claimed it was their duty to evolve into superior beings, like super dragons, so there would be peace among our kind."

"But didn't they kill the dragons they sucked Quintessence from?" Bryn asked.

"There is that minor detail," Clint said. "Although some of them kept dragons around and fed off them routinely, like vampires feed off fang groupies."

"Fang groupies?" Bryn asked. "Seriously? Is that a thing?"

Ivy laughed. "Depends on what paranormal television shows you watch. In some of them there are vampire groupies who allow vamps to feed off them for the sheer joy of being around the undead."

"Can you say abusive relationship?" Bryn asked.

"I didn't say it was a mentally healthy lifestyle choice," Clint said. "And small public service announcement— vampires aren't real. Though the comparison works. The Silver dragons had groupies who hung around and lived on their lavish estates in exchange for allowing the Silvers to feed."

"Are you sure this isn't some twisted up vampire story you're reading?" Bryn asked. It sounded way too bizarre to be true.

"Who knows?" Clint said. "But there are a lot of historical articles about it, and it's far more interesting than reading those Directorate Law journals."

"It's kind of a guilty pleasure," Ivy said. "We should go to the library and see what Miss Enid knows about them. I bet she could point us in the direction of some great articles for our research papers."

"A bonus of being in Quintessential Medicine is that we haven't been assigned a research paper."

"Yet," Clint said. "Research papers seem to be a right of passage for senior year."

"I hope that's not true."

...

When they told Miss Enid what they were interested in, she balked. "That might not be a wise topic choice."

"Why not?" Clint asked.

Miss Enid glanced at Bryn. "I'm sure I don't have to tell you not to share this, but there have been recent reports of Silvers that you don't know about. Around a dozen years ago it was rumored that someone had tried to bring the cult back to life. Students started coming down with a strange illness that left them exhausted for days at a time. It took the Medics a while to realize that someone was siphoning Quintessence from them."

"Umm...how could you not notice that?" Bryn asked. "Because I can feel it when I use too much of my Quintessence when I'm trying to heal someone. It literally feels like your life force is bleeding out."

"That sounds lovely," Ivy said.

"The cult members were very adept at engaging unsuspecting victims in conversation. They'd brush their hand across the chosen dragon's forearm a few times. Eventually, they'd lull the victim into sleep. Then they'd siphon what they wanted, perform some sort of spell on the victim to change their memories of where they'd been, and walk away to prey on someone else."

"That is all sorts of wrong," Bryn said.

"It is, which is why anyone found guilty of this crime had their wings amputated."

Bryn's stomach rolled. "That thought literally makes me want to vomit."

"Right there with you." Ivy clutched at her midsection.

"The Directorate had to take a harsh stand against the felons who did this because apparently, Silvers can be oddly charismatic. They were adept at luring people to their cause. If the punishment wasn't extreme, more dragons might fall prey to the cult's radical ideas."

"What was their big sell?" Clint asked. "Come join us and suck the life from your classmates?"

"The Silvers thought of themselves as the next step in evolution for dragons...a superior race."

"The Hitler of dragons," Bryn said. "I guess humans don't have the market cornered on racist egomaniacal hate- spewing dictators."

"Unfortunately," Miss Enid said, "they do not."

Maybe that was another reason the Directorate screened bloodlines with such care. She couldn't ask Miss Enid about that because her marriage contract had been denied due to something they'd found when they combined her blood with Mr. Stanton's. And the Directorate, being the all-powerful council that they were, didn't give an explanation why. But there was something else Bryn could ask.

"Could I talk to you in private for a moment?" Bryn asked Miss Enid.

"Of course." She scribbled something on a Post-it note and passed it to Clint. "This is where you'll find more information on the Silvers. Make certain that anyone you speak to knows that you believe the group was a bunch of radical terrorists. If it sounds like you admire them in any way, someone will probably drag you away for questioning."

"Understood," Ivy said. She and Clint headed toward the back stairs.

"What did you want to speak with me about?" Miss Enid asked.

There was no way to bring this up without it being awkward. "I know that couples have been denied marriage due to the possible issues in their bloodlines, but I was wondering if one of those couples who never married...if they were past the age of having children, would they be allowed to marry if they still wanted to?"

Miss Enid opened her mouth and then closed it. "I...I have no idea. No one has ever even mentioned...I'm not sure...have you spoken to anyone else about this?"

"No. It's just a question that popped into my head. Jaxon and I spoke of it, but he would never mention it to anyone else."

Was Miss Enid angry or confused? It was hard to tell. "I'm sorry if this was rude. It's just with all the talk of marriage and hybrids and—"

Miss Enid placed a hand on her shoulder. "It's okay. No one who grew up in our culture would ever ask such a question. They wouldn't even think it."

Since Miss Enid wasn't angry, Bryn asked the next logical question. "Is getting married something you'd be interested in?"

"I can't even answer that right now, but you've given me something to mull over."

Chapter Eight

Bryn joined Clint and Ivy on the third floor where they sat at a library table, flipping through what looked like newspaper articles bound together in giant black leather books.

"Find anything interesting?" Bryn asked.

"Disturbing as hell," Clint said, "but interesting."

"Apparently the Hitler of this group, who was named Eric, had been extremely charming. He convinced students and adults to be donors for the dragons who were trying to evolve. He promised those who gave Quintessence would then be allowed to evolve once they recruited more donors."

"A Quintessence-sucking pyramid scheme?" Bryn said. "Are you kidding me?"

"Nope," Ivy said. "This Eric guy promised power and wealth and a crazy amount of dragons joined him."

"I still don't get it. How does anyone agree to let someone suck their life force for money and power?" Bryn asked.

"Medics use their life force. They willingly give it away to heal other dragons," Clint said.

"That's completely different," Bryn said. "As a Medic you heal, and do good, and then go chow down on a dozen chocolate bars or cookies. You don't do it for personal gain...unless you count gratitude and some respect."

"True," Ivy said. "Medics do what they do to help others. Silvers only wanted to help themselves."

"But both trade in Quintessence," Clint said. "I'm just saying."

"You're just being annoying," Bryn shot back.

Clint puffed his chest out with pride. "It's my special skill set."

Bryn rolled her eyes. "Perhaps you should aspire to something else."

"But it's so much fun to piss people off," Clint said with a good-natured grin. "Seriously though, I know that Medics and these Cult whack jobs are miles apart, but if Eric was trying to convince someone that it wasn't a big deal, he could use an argument like that and some people might fall for it."

"And people believe strange things all the time," Bryn said. "Like decaf coffee deserves to exist when it's just useless brown water."

"Speaking of useless things," Ivy said. "What are we doing for the Homecoming Gala this weekend?"

Bryn laughed. "I thought you liked excuses to dress up."

"Dances and Galas are not the same. And while my enthusiasm for dances has decreased slightly since every dance we've had at this school has ended in some crap-tastic life-altering disaster, they are still better than Galas."

"Remind me what a Gala is," Clint said.

"Like Ivy said, we dress up and we stand around in awkward groups, pretending that we're having a marvelous time while we have uncomfortable conversations with people we normally wouldn't talk to. And as an added bonus, I'll be attending with Jaxon and, since you're my friends, you'll be hanging out with us, sharing the joy of Blue small talk."

"Maybe we should rethink this whole friendship thing," Clint teased.

...

Saturday afternoon, Bryn and Ivy hung out in her room trying on different outfits.

"I can't believe your grandmother had one of the boutiques ship these dresses to your room." Ivy stood in front of the mirror, modeling a black silk dress that fit her like a glove on top and flared out at the bottom. "And I can't believe she included some for me. This dress is amazing." She twirled, and the dress spun out into a full circle.

"I used to think Blues hoarded their money, but my grandmother is generous. So is Lillith." Bryn checked her reflection. It was strange, but when she'd dated Valmont she'd picked out dresses she hoped he would think made her look good. She never tried to look special for Jaxon...because he'd always be prettier than her...which sort of sucked. Now she just tried to find dresses that looked appropriate for the occasion and gave her a boost of confidence. The navy spaghetti-strap dress she currently had on wasn't doing the trick.

"I am not feeling this dress," Bryn said.

Ivy pointed at a pale-green dress. "Try that one. I think it will look great with your skin tone."

"Most dresses don't scream this should be worn with pale freckled skin." Bryn tried the dress on. It had a wide boat neck and was made of some ethereal floating fabric that skimmed over her curves without looking clingy. She turned in front of the mirror. Since the dress wasn't full it didn't flare out like Ivy's had, but it still made her feel good. "I think we have a winner."

"Time for hair and makeup," Ivy said. "And since this is an early evening Gala rather than a late evening dance, I will skip the theatrical makeup."

"Good, because I don't want to listen to Jaxon gripe about my level of taste."

"Is it just me, or has he backslid into being more of an asshat than he used to be?" Ivy asked.

"It's not just you." Bryn sat on the edge of the bed while Ivy grabbed her makeup kit. "And I keep telling myself he's suffered a terrible loss and I need to cut him some slack, but there are times when I want to roast him."

"Totally understandable," Ivy said. "I love Clint and there are days I want to zap him. You're forced to spend time with Jaxon and you two aren't even really in a relationship...at least not the traditional sort."

"You make it sound like we're involved in some strange affair." Bryn closed her eyes as Ivy applied sea-foam green eye shadow.

"How would you describe your situation with Jaxon?" Ivy asked.

"It's like we're teammates who tolerate each other. Occasionally, it seems like we're friends." Bryn felt a lump rise in her throat. "There are days where I can't believe I'm going to have to marry him. I keep hoping something will change, but I'm pretty sure it won't, and if I think about it too much I have to breathe into a paper bag so I don't hyperventilate in desperation."

"At least he seems to respect you. That's a good start. Maybe something good will come of it in the end."

Bryn opened her eyes. "I've always counted on your honesty in all things. Please don't start lying to me now."

Ivy sighed. "I'm trying to be optimistic."

"Thanks. Let's talk about something else."

"Okay." Ivy dug into her makeup kit. "Do you want regular dark green eyeliner or dark green eyeliner with glitter?"

"What the heck," Bryn said. "Glitter me up."

Half an hour later, Clint knocked on Bryn's door. When he saw Ivy his face lit up just like it always did. "You look amazing." He grabbed Ivy's hand and pulled her in for a kiss.

Bryn looked away to give them a moment. Another knock sounded on the door. Jaxon would be on the other side looking handsome and annoyed. He might tell her that her dress was pretty, but his compliment would be fake... just part of the Blue dragon code of conduct and would have nothing to do with her or how she actually looked in the dress.

Taking two quick strides across the room, she opened the door. Jaxon wore a tuxedo that emphasized his broad shoulders and trim waist and made him look like he should model high-end clothing for a living. If only he didn't look perpetually pissed off.

"Hello, Jaxon." She stepped back so he could enter the room. "Are you ready for an evening of fake fun and boring small talk?"

"We should go," he said without looking at her or acknowledging that she'd spoken.

"I was trying to be funny," she said.

"Trying and failing," he shot back. "And I refuse to fake politeness until we're at the event. So let's get this over with."

"You might want to dial back the attitude," Bryn said.

"I'm not giving you attitude. I'm being realistic. We played this game all summer and I'm tired of pretending that life is wonderful. I will smile and nod when we're in public, but I see no need to fake my feelings in private." Jaxon stalked out the door.

Bryn fantasized about blasting him. She turned to Clint and Ivy. "It's like he doesn't realize that I could kill him, incinerate his body, and scatter the ashes where no one would ever find him."

"And we'd totally be your alibi," Ivy said.

"Good to know." They exited Bryn's room and she hurried to catch up with Jaxon while Clint and Ivy stayed a few paces behind.

"Just so you know," she said. "I plan to smile, and nod, and bail as soon as possible."

"Finally, something we can agree on."

The Homecoming Gala was set up in a conference room located in the theater building. Like most school sponsored events, the students were splintered into groups by Clan. Unlike all the previous gatherings, there were now hybrids sprinkled among the groups. All except the Blues, of course. And she had been the one to change that, much to their annoyance.

She followed Jaxon over to a group of Blues which included Quentin and his girlfriend. She smiled and nodded politely while they talked about the weather and the upcoming holidays, and absolutely nothing of any consequence. Small talk was so boring. What was the point? No one cared that much about the weather. It took effort to focus rather than slip off into a daydream.

They worked their way around the room and engaged several other couples in the same meaningless conversations. Bryn participated as little as possible, which seemed to suit everyone just fine. When the most recent conversation reached a lull, Bryn spotted Garrett standing with a group of Greens. "I'm going to say hi to a friend. Would you like to come with me?"

"No thank you. We can meet up later," Jaxon said.

"Works for me." Bryn headed across the room to Garrett. His left arm still hung in a sling, but his eyes no longer looked haunted. Working on the prosthetic wing and regaining the ability to fly had given him a renewed interest in life.

"Hello, Bryn." Garrett smiled like he was happy to see her. That was nice. And they would actually have something interesting to talk about.

"How's your work on the wing going?" she asked.

"It's great," he said. "Actually, I'd love to show you how far it's come since you helped me test it. If you'll meet me out at the stadium after dinner tomorrow evening I can give you a demonstration." He glanced across the room at Jaxon. "It would be best if you came without your other half."

"Gladly. Do you care if Clint and Ivy tag along?"

"No," Garrett said. "They're friends."

And Jaxon wasn't. It was pretty simple when she thought about it. Over time, would Jaxon become friends with her friends? Who knew? It might make her life easier. Then again, she didn't want to hang out with his Blue friends, either. Maybe it was better if they kept their social lives separate.

"I've been working on other prosthetics," Garret said. "For dragons who have issues with their legs."

Most dragons who suffered wing injuries had corresponding injuries to their legs. A small percentage, like Garret, had injuries that corresponded to their upper extremities.

"That's great," Bryn said. She'd been told that her father had suffered damage to his legs, not that she'd been allowed to see him for herself, which was a whole other irritating topic of conversation. Still, it was good to know that Garret might be able to help him fly again.

"How is your Medics class going?" Garret asked.

"So far so good," Bryn said. "I've been talking to Janelle. She seems nice."

"She mentioned that you'd talked," Garret said. "Honestly, I think she's a little intimidated by you."

Bryn laughed. "You have no idea how ridiculous that sounds to me. I feel like my life is this crazy roller-coaster ride where the lap bar doesn't work and I'm trying to hold on for dear life."

Garret nodded. "I understand that because I've known you since you first came here, but to other dragons you're an outsider that came in, kicked ass, and somehow ingratiated yourself to the two most powerful Blue families."

"I guess it's all a matter of perspective," Bryn said. "My grandparents have been great, but the whole situation with Jaxon makes my head spin on a daily basis."

"Do you trust him?" Garret asked.

"Yes." She didn't even have to think about it. "He may be cranky and snobby sometimes...make that most of the time, but if I need his help he'll be there for me. He'd probably complain loudly the entire time, but he'd be there."

Garret grinned. "That sounds like an accurate description." He glanced past her and said, "If you'll excuse me, I see someone I need to speak with. I'll see you tomorrow evening at the stadium."

Now what? Bryn plastered a fake smile on her face and checked out her options for conversation. There wasn't anyone she was dying to talk to. Jaxon was conversing with yet another group of Blues. Clint and Ivy sat at a table drinking coffee and eating cookies. That seemed like a much better way to spend her time, so she headed over to join them, stopping at the buffet along the way to pick up half a dozen chocolate chip oatmeal cookies and some coffee.

As she sat down, Clint said, "How long do we have to stay here?"

Ivy poked him on the shoulder. "We've only been here half an hour."

"And that's about twenty minutes too long," Clint said.

"I feel your pain." Bryn stirred sugar into her coffee. "I think the Gala is supposed to last two hours. I say we sneak out in thirty minutes."

"Sounds good to me," Clint said. "Do you have to check with your other half?"

Bryn rolled her eyes. "Probably." She glanced over where Jaxon had been talking to Quentin and a few other Blues. Now he was talking to a Blue female she didn't know. They appeared to be deep in conversation, with their heads close together.

"Who's that with Jaxon?" Ivy asked.

"I don't know." And something about how the girl smiled at Jaxon bothered her. That was ridiculous. He was probably making standard Blue small talk.

"Did you and Jaxon set any ground rules for your not quite real relationship?" Clint asked. "Because that looks a little too friendly."

Okay. It wasn't just her. "We haven't really defined our situation." It's not like she expected what was going on between them to be real, but she certainly didn't expect him to see other people, either. Some students dated discreetly while they were in school even after their marriage contracts were approved. Jaxon had that sort of arrangement with Rhianna before she was injured. Afterward, he'd spent all his time taking care of her and they'd fallen in love.

Did she really need to talk with Jaxon about not seeing other people? It's not like they were seeing each other, but still. She leaned in and spoke quietly to her friends. "How in the hell am I supposed to even bring this up to him? Before, I had Valmont and he had Rhianna. Now neither of us has anyone, but the way that girl is touching his shoulder is really pissing me off."

"He's not interested," Clint said. "You can tell by the way he's backed away from her when she's tried to come closer. Maybe you should go rescue him."

That sounded absurd. Jaxon didn't need rescuing, but maybe she needed to make a point to the other Blue females who might think he was open to some sort of discreet relationship.

Bryn wiped her hands on a napkin. "Okay. I guess I'll go let him know that we can leave whenever he's ready." She headed across the room, trying to figure out why this annoyed her so much. It wasn't that she wanted him. It was more that if she couldn't have anyone then neither could he. And that sounded petty but it was the honest truth. They could be miserable together, because she sure as hell wasn't going to be miserable alone.

When she reached him the other girl barely acknowledged Bryn's presence. "Enjoying the Gala?" Bryn asked him.

He raised an eyebrow. "Almost as much as I enjoyed the half dozen we attended this summer."

"I was hoping we could leave," Bryn said. "What are your thoughts?"

He checked his watch. "If your grandmother or my mother were here I'd say no, but since we're on our own, I think we can leave in ten minutes."

"Works for me." Bryn smiled at the girl. "What were you two talking about before I interrupted?"

The girl gave a tight-lipped smile. "Nothing important. Excuse me." And then she walked away.

"I don't think she liked me," Bryn said.

"She isn't open-minded to the new students on campus," Jaxon said. "And she was fishing for information about the Directorate's approval process."

Ten minutes later they joined Clint and Ivy and walked back across campus.

"From a Blue Clan point of view," Ivy said. "What was the purpose of that event?"

Jaxon didn't respond, so Bryn prompted him. "Excuse me, Son of the Speaker, I believe that question was directed at you."

"Social gatherings are supposed to improve unity," Jaxon said, "and shore up alliances."

"And here I thought I was just eating cookies and drinking coffee," Clint said.

Bryn and Jaxon headed to the Blue dorm while Ivy and Clint went to the Black dorm. When they reached her dorm room, Bryn felt the need to say something but didn't know what to say, "Would you come in so we can talk for a minute?"

"Nothing would please me more," he said, laying on the sarcasm.

"First off, bite me," she said. "And second, this will only take a minute."

"Fine."

Once they were in her living room, Bryn paced back and forth while Jaxon stood staring at her. "This is going to sound strange, but you and I have never discussed certain issues about our situation." Her face heated. She should just spit it out. "It looked like that girl was flirting with you, and I wouldn't want other people to think you were open to discreet relationships."

Jaxon backed up a step like he wanted to put some distance between them while simultaneously looking at her like she was insane. "The entire purpose of all these ridiculous events is for us to present a united front. I can't imagine anyone being stupid enough to consider that either of us would be open to something like that."

"As long as we're on the same page," Bryn said.

"Of course we are," he said.

"Good, because like you said, we're putting a lot of effort into this non-relationship in order to make it appear real."

Chapter Nine

Sunday after dinner, Clint, Ivy, and Bryn walked across campus, admiring the newly planted landscaping. A couple of adult Orange dragons were walking among the trees, touching them, sending Quintessence into the trunks and making the trees grow. Limbs shot out, reaching for the sky, and leaves popped out as tiny buds blossomed and then tripled in size.

"That is so cool." Ivy stopped walking.

"It is," Bryn agreed. Orange dragons had a connection to the earth. Their power of sonic waves could open fissures that would swallow a person whole or create agricultural feats like the forest Jaxon's parents had commissioned inside Westgate Estate...as in they had a forest in their house... which was weird but amazing.

"I don't know that I could ever be that skilled," Ivy said. "I can make plants grow into twisted topiaries, but I can't make them mature like that."

"How do you know?" Bryn asked.

"I tried over the summer. I transformed all of our houseplants. I can twist the vines into hearts or corkscrews but I can't make them grow."

One of the Orange dragons stopped working and came toward them. She was an older bronze-skinned woman who wore her dark hair in two long braids. "You want to learn how to make plants grow?"

Ivy nodded. "I like doing topiaries, but it doesn't feel like enough."

"Given our population's decline there aren't enough of us to continue our work. So maybe it's time we teach those willing to learn. Come." The woman led Ivy back to the trees. "Let me show you what it feels like. Place your hand on the bark."

Ivy placed her palm on the tree trunk and the woman placed her hand on top of Ivy's. "I will direct Quintessence through your hand so you can understand what we do."

Wide-eyed, Ivy nodded.

The woman closed her eyes and Ivy sucked in a breath.

A huge smile lit her face.

After a few moments the woman pulled her hand away from Ivy's. "Now you try."

Ivy took a deep breath and then laughed. "It's silly, but I'm nervous." Closing her eyes, Ivy furrowed her brow like she was concentrating. Nothing happened. "Maybe I need to keep my eyes open. I'm used to looking at the things I'm working on." Ivy moved her hand to a low branch and stared at it intently. The branch shook and shot out several new leaves. "I did it," Ivy exclaimed.

"Yes. You did." The woman beamed. "Do you want to stay and help us?"

Ivy looked at Bryn questioningly. "Stay. Have fun," Bryn said.

"I think I'll hang around too just in case she tires herself out," Clint said. "This summer she went overboard with the rose bushes at my house and I had to feed her half a pizza before she was back to herself."

"No problem. You two enjoy yourselves."

Garrett was flying around in the stadium when Bryn arrived. The last time she'd seen him he was basically hang gliding. This new wing moved up and down. The motion was a bit jerky, but it allowed for more realistic flight.

When he spotted her, Garrett came in for a landing. He stutter-stepped, but his landing was no more awkward than hers. "What do you think?"

"It's amazing," Bryn said. "You've made so much progress."

"I worked on it during all my waking hours this summer," Garrett said. "It's not perfect, but I can take off and land by myself."

"Show me," Bryn said.

Garrett crouched down and shot up into the sky, flapping his prosthetic wing in time with his one functional wing. He didn't get a lot of vertical lift, but he was able to get off the ground under his own power, unlike the last time she'd seen him, when she'd had to lift him up into the air and drop him so he could glide. Once he was aloft, he flapped both wings and climbed higher.

He circled a few times and then landed again. The wing retracted until it looked like he was wearing a large black leather backpack.

"That's so cool," Bryn said. "You could wear it all the time, if you wanted."

"That's the idea," Garrett said. "I have something else to show you. Follow me."

What else could he have to show her? She trusted him but wasn't sure why he was leading her to the back side of the bleachers. What she saw took her breath away.

"Dad?" Her father stood there, leaning on a cane with some sort of black plastic brace on his right leg. He looked oddly weak, but the smile that lit up his face was exactly the one she remembered. Running to him she threw her arms around him. "I've missed you so much."

He hugged her one-armed and lifted her off her feet. "Bryn," his voice broke as he said her name.

Tears streamed down Bryn's face as her dad set her back down. She kept her eyes on his face, not wanting to look at his leg. "I'm so happy to see you."

He kissed her on the forehead. "I was getting ready to storm the campus if they didn't let us out to visit you."

Bryn laughed. Wait a minute. "Us?" Was her mom here, too?

"Hey, baby." Her mom stepped out of the shadows.

"Get over here," Bryn said, holding one arm out so they could have a family hug.

Her mom laughed and joined them. "Garrett managed to get us day passes out of Sanctuary. He's a good friend."

"Yes, he is." Bryn stepped back and looked for Garrett who stood off to the side, smiling. "Thank you."

"You're welcome. And you don't have to stay hidden back here. You can go to your room or hang out on the bleachers. Mr. Stanton knows they're here."

She had no idea how long her parents would be allowed to stay, and she didn't think her father would want to make the trek across campus to her room. "I'm good with staying here."

"There's an office for the referees over this way," her mom said. "We can sit in there and have some privacy."

"Sounds good." Bryn followed her parents to the small office. Her dad actually moved at close to a normal pace, which made his injury a little less unsettling. Once they were seated in the small office, her mom said, "How's your senior year shaping up?"

"Seriously?" Bryn laughed. "I'm okay. I've been worried sick about you guys. I don't know why they wouldn't let you come visit or allow me to visit you."

Her dad frowned. "Ferrin kept interrogating all of us, making us drink those stupid potions where you spill your guts and then feel lightheaded afterward. I understand that they're trying to root out anyone who might want to attack the campus or start a war, but he seems to be going overboard."

"He does love to exert his power," Bryn said. "Which is why I can't believe I'm stuck in this crap-tastic marriage contract with Jaxon. I was sure he'd find a way to outmaneuver mom's parents."

"Please tell us that Jaxon is not the complete jackass his father is," her mom said.

"He's not. He's crabby and snotty, but he's also noble and loyal and he can be kind when he doesn't have his Blue panties in a bunch."

"Do you like him?" her dad asked.

"I don't hate him like I used to. Which may not sound like a lot but I'm trying to look on the bright side. I hope one day we'll become friends, but that's probably the best I can expect."

Her mom and dad exchanged a look and then her dad said, "We could leave. Go back to living the way we did before, alone in the human world."

"Tempting offer, but I don't think that would work."

"We made it work before," her mom said.

"That's because you two were running away to be together. You gave up everything for love. I understand that, but I don't have love, and I probably never will. But I do have flying, and friends, and dreams of becoming a Medic."

"Is that enough?" her mom asked.

Part of her brain screamed no. "It kind of has to be, since I don't have a better option."

"I can't believe I'm about to say this, but what happened with Zavien?" her dad asked. "He's the lesser of two evils and he liked you."

This was going to be awkward. "We dated before I realized he was already promised to someone else...who happened to be one of the leaders of the Rebels."

"Then I'm guessing she's dead," her mom said. "The Directorate wouldn't let her live after the damage she caused."

"You're right. She's gone," Bryn said. "And they interrogated him the same way they did you guys...probably worse. He didn't have a clue what she was up to. It blindsided him just like the rest of us."

"So Zavien could be an option again," her dad said.

"Not after what happened between us." Bryn sighed. "He really let me down. Finding someone else is a nice fantasy. While I don't have the warm fuzzies for Jaxon, I do respect him."

"Does he feel the same way about you?" her mom asked. "There have to be other Blues that lost their intended mates. Maybe he could be with someone else."

"Maybe, but I'd appreciate it if we could change the subject because I prefer to live in denial."

"Okay," her dad said. "We just want what's best for you."

"Tell me about Sanctuary," Bryn said.

"It's coming together," her dad said. "The remaining hybrids and throwbacks are going out of their way to fly under the radar. Everyone is being painfully polite and respectful to the Directorate and the guards they've stationed there to keep tabs on us."

"I'm amazed at the supplies and building materials that have been donated. It's not like we're living in luxury, but they added on to the original Miner's Hall, turning it into a community center with cots and an industrial-sized kitchen. Everyone is allowed to stay there until enough houses are built. There were dozens of old cabins that we helped fix up and they've started new construction which is designed to resemble the existing cabins."

"So it will be a Stepford town, like Dragon's Bluff, where all the buildings match?" Bryn asked.

"Pretty much," her mom said. "So anyone who doesn't want to live in a semi-rustic-looking log cabin is out of luck. Honestly, I'm just grateful that we have heat, indoor plumbing, and food. We camped in the woods for weeks before they opened the Sanctuary, and I'd hate to live that way for the rest of my life."

"I still don't fully trust the Directorate's motives," her dad said. "They're almost being too civil."

"I think they're trying to bring everyone back into the fold. The Rebel attack took them completely by surprise. If they make the hybrids and throwbacks feel welcome and semi-respected, then there's no reason to start another war."

"We raised a smart girl," her mom said. "I'm sure that's why they are doing it."

"I was stunned to find out that there were other hybrids," her dad said. "Here I thought we were the lone rebels."

"You were the only rebels out in the open," Bryn said. "It's nice to know that I'm not the only hybrid, but it's terrifying to see how many other hybrids were sort of insane."

Her mom nodded. "I never really understood the bloodline tests the Directorate based their decisions on, but now I understand why they'd be cautious."

"You have to wonder about nature versus nurture," her dad said. "How many of those hybrids would have been normal if they hadn't been raised to hate the Directorate?" His question reminded Bryn of the first time she'd met Jaxon. "Funny, but Jaxon was raised to hate me. After we were forced to spend time together and ended up helping each other, he saw that I wasn't the evil person his father claimed I was."

"I can only imagine what Ferrin said about me," her mom said.

"You don't want to know. I suggest avoiding him at all costs," Bryn said. "But I think you'd like his wife Lillith. She's really nice."

"Poor woman," her mom said.

"She's checked out emotionally, like it seems all Blue wives do with their husbands, but she seems happy most of the time." And that gave Bryn hope for her future.

"I forgot how crazy this world was," her dad said.

"It's plenty nuts," Bryn said. "But the flying and magic kind of balance things out."

"Speaking of balance." Her dad pointed at the brace he wore. "Your friend Garret is a genius. This brace has made a huge difference in my ability to move around."

"Good. Garret is probably the first dragon to work on prosthetics since injured dragons used to be shunned." Bryn thought of something ironic and grinned. "Did Garret tell you who funded his research and development of these products?"

"No," her dad said.

"Your father-in-law," Bryn said. "I asked him to help Garret, so he funded the whole thing."

Her mom stared open-mouthed. "I have no idea how you worked your way into their hearts, but I'm so glad you did. I think you've had a positive influence on them."

"They've been good to me," Bryn said. "I care about them. I know they still care about you, and I'm hoping they'll let you back in to their lives."

"I wouldn't bet on that," her mom said. "I committed an unforgivable crime in their eyes. I'd love to make amends somehow, but for now, I'm grateful that they've taken care of you."

"Your mom and I are prepared to live in Sanctuary so we can be near you. We have no illusions that we'll be welcomed back into Dragon society. I hope your mom can visit her parents, but I have no plan to ever step foot into Sinclair Estate."

That wasn't what she wanted to hear. Not that her grandparents would welcome him with open arms, but she hoped they could all be together one day. "Maybe for special occasions like Christmas you could visit," Bryn said. "Because honestly, Christmas without you guys last year, when I thought you were gone..." Bryn teared up. "Worst holiday ever. I really want us all to be together this year."

"We may be able to meet on neutral ground," her mom said. "But I don't expect to be invited into my parents' home. Truthfully, it might be better that way."

"You are ruining the family reunion I've spent many hours planning in my head," Bryn said. "And I'm only sort of joking."

Her mom grabbed Bryn's hand and squeezed. "Having you back in our lives is a miracle. I knew that once you attended the Institute and had a taste of living like a dragon...flying whenever you wanted...using magic...you'd never be satisfied with the human world again. So being able to visit you, and eventually having you visit us, is enough for me. Don't push my parents to make amends. I don't want to upset the balance of your new life for something that will probably never happen."

"Well, that sucks," Bryn said.

"Things could have been so much worse," her mom said. "We could have been tried for treason or tossed in a prison without a trial. The moral of today's story is be happy with what we have."

"I can do that," Bryn said. "For now." There was one other uncomfortable topic they needed to address. "Dad, when I came here I tried to find your relatives, but—"

"The car crash," her dad said. "I heard about that a few weeks ago."

"I'm so sorry." Bryn was grateful she wasn't the one breaking the news to him that his parents had been killed in a car crash, but it still sucked.

He nodded and looked away. After a moment, he cleared his throat and said, "I wasn't expecting a happy family reunion, but finding out they were gone was hard. Having you back is the most important thing."

Chapter Ten

Saying goodbye to her parents was a tearful affair, but it helped that she now knew she could see them again. Once she was back in her room, she felt emotionally exhausted but wired. She was sitting on her couch reading the book Miss Enid had given her when her phone rang.

Clint's voice came through the phone loud and clear and slightly panicked. "I think Ivy over exerted herself growing the trees. She's fallen asleep on my couch and I can't wake her up."

"Oh my God. Did you send for a Medic?"

"Yes. They're on their way, but waiting by myself is making me crazy."

"If it wasn't past curfew I'd be there in a heartbeat," Bryn said.

"I know. Can you just stay on the phone with me?"

"Sure." She'd never heard Clint so flustered.

"Distract me," Clint said. "Tell me about Garret's new wing."

Bryn rambled about how cool the new wing was. Clint made sounds like he was listening, and then she heard a knock in the background.

"Leave the phone off the hook so I can hear," Bryn said. Clint didn't answer, but she heard the phone land on a hard surface, probably the table, and that was followed by the sound of people talking. A few words drifted through the phone but most of it was unclear. Bryn waited not so patiently for Clint to come back on the line. Maybe she could just dash over to Ivy's room, but her grandparents would have a fit if she was caught out after curfew. She paced back and forth, waiting to hear something. Finally, someone came on the line.

"Bryn, this is Medic Williams. Ivy is fine. In her untrained enthusiasm she spent too much of her Quintessence growing those trees. I want to track down the Orange who let an inexperienced student do something like this, but Ivy can't remember the woman's name. Did you catch it?"

"No. I don't think she introduced herself while I was there."

"This is disturbing. Since all this information will go into an official file, don't be surprised if you're called in for questioning." And then Bryn was listening to the dial tone. That was weird. It's not like the Orange would have done this to Ivy on purpose. They'd probably track the woman down and warn her about working with untrained students. Poor Ivy. She'd seemed so excited about working on the trees. They probably wouldn't let her do it again.

Ten minutes later, Bryn's phone rang again. She answered, expecting it to be Ivy.

"It's Clint again. Ivy is sleeping."

"She's all right?"

"Yes, but something is bothering me. And it might be my overactive imagination, and the fact that I've been reading about Silvers—"

"No way." Bryn sucked in a breath as she guessed where he was going with this. "I mean that lady did have her hand on Ivy's to help her grow the tree, but the tree actually grew, so she had to be funneling Quintessence out, not sucking it in. Right?"

"After you left, the woman kept her hand on Ivy's forearm, supposedly to guide her. I sat there thinking 'what a nice Orange dragon.' Most of them are standoffish and kind of quiet, but this lady was really nice...almost too nice."

"Now my brain is spinning, too," Bryn said. "Do you think I should call my grandfather and mention this?"

"You could, but I'd hate to get a nice Orange in trouble, if we're just being paranoid."

What should she do? Bryn frowned. "Should we wait and ask Ivy what she wants us to do?"

"It might be better if you did it while she's sleeping. If she were awake she'd try to talk you out of it. She's kind of embarrassed about the whole thing."

Bryn sat on the couch and tried to consider this from all angles. "Medic Williams will file a report that someone on the Directorate will read, so my grandfather will hear about it sooner or later. I think I'll call him because if I don't and this ends up being an issue and he finds out that I knew and didn't say anything, he'll be mad."

"Your life is so complicated," Clint said. "I trust you. Do what you think is best. I'm going to lay down with Ivy. We'll see you at breakfast tomorrow."

"See you." Should she call her grandparents? She paced back and forth in the living room. Was she being paranoid? Probably, but "better safe than sorry" was a saying for a reason. Bryn dialed her grandparents' estate and spoke to Rindy the magical phone operator, who always sounded so happy to take everyone's calls. The woman must be on some type of medication. No one could be that happy to answer the phone.

"Just a moment, Bryn, and I'll put you through to your grandfather."

"Thank you."

"It's my pleasure," Rindy said, like she actually meant it.

"Hello, Bryn. What's wrong?"

She hated to think that she only called when something was wrong. She'd have to remember to call when good things were happening, too. Bryn told him about Ivy and about how Clint happened to read an article about the Quintessence sucking cult of Silver dragons. "And we could totally be blowing this out of proportion, but I figured I should at least mention it to you on the off chance it could be true."

Her grandfather was silent for so long that she thought maybe he'd put the phone down and walked away. "Should I not have bothered you?"

"No. I'm glad you called. As far as I know, the Institute didn't schedule any Oranges to help mature the trees. That doesn't mean a few well meaning dragons wouldn't show up and help of their own volition. Keep an eye out for this woman who worked with Ivy. I'll scan the videos from the remaining security cameras to see if we can discern her identity."

"Are there still cameras all over campus?" Bryn asked. It made her a little paranoid to think someone was always watching.

"Some were destroyed during the attack on campus and not all of them were replaced. Oranges are so rare these days that if a pair of adults were roaming the campus someone would have taken notice. Good night, Bryn."

"Good night."

Bryn took her book to bed and read until she couldn't keep her eyes open any longer.

...

The next morning at breakfast, Ivy looked like her normal self as she ate her way through a plate of French toast.

"All better?" Bryn asked.

"Yes." Ivy's face colored. "Clint told me about your far fetched idea. I'd hate to think that nice old lady was a villain. She seemed to care so much about the trees. She talked about them like they had souls."

Bryn sipped her coffee while she thought about what they knew. "She did seem nice. Hopefully, we're just being paranoid. Although that doesn't usually seem to be the case, if I'm involved."

"You are sort of a harbinger of doom," Clint said.

"I am not." Bryn laughed. "And I object to that characterization. I feel more like a Chaos Magnet."

"I guess that's a more accurate description, but it doesn't have the same ring to it," Clint said.

In Advanced Elemental Science Mr. Stanton lectured them about the multiple uses for their breath weapons and how they might be applied in different areas. "Now break into groups and discuss ways you think you might use your elements in a field of study. Be as creative as you want. Sometimes thinking outside the box spurs a new vocation." Bryn moved her desk toward Clint and Ivy's. Jaxon didn't move any closer. He just tapped his pencil on his notebook.

"Are you going to join us?" Bryn asked.

"I see no need. The only use I have for my breath weapon as a member of the Directorate is blasting an enemy."

"Okay." Maybe Jaxon wasn't capable of thinking outside the box. His loss. Not that she felt like arguing with him. She scooted closer to her friends. "Let's see. What can I do with my fire? I doubt there are many jobs where they'd want me to incinerate things."

"As Artists we can use our lightning to create sculptures or other pieces of art," Ivy replied. "As a Medic, they'll probably discourage you from frying your patients."

"Yeah...that would be counterintuitive, unless you were cauterizing a wound," Clint said. "I know. You could open a barbecue restaurant featuring flame broiled burgers with spit snow, snow cones for dessert."

Bryn laughed. When they'd been trapped under the library in a dusty old room, Bryn had exhaled a snowball into her hand because she was so thirsty. Neither of her friends had been interested in sampling her "spit snow" as Clint had called it.

"I'm not sure how happy people would be to eat flavored spit snow," Bryn said.

"Well, you wouldn't advertise it like that," Clint said.

Jaxon gave them a disgusted look.

"Lighten up," Bryn said. "We're having fun. You should try it some time."

"You're disrespecting our breath weapon," Jaxon said.

Bryn rolled her eyes. "No. I'm not. It's ice. I could build an igloo if I wanted to, or create an ice sculpture. It's not disrespectful. It's a fact."

"It's plebeian," Jaxon said.

"Did you swallow a thesaurus this morning?" Bryn asked. "Because no one talks like that and FYI, if they do, other people find them obnoxious."

"Only if those other people are uneducated peasants," Jaxon shot back.

"I've had just as much schooling as you," Bryn said. "And since you're being supremely obnoxious this morning, I'll point out that the last time I checked, my grandfather has more money in his bank account than your father does in his."

Jaxon went very still and then it was like he changed into another, far angrier, person. His eyes went flat and hard. The corners of his mouth turned down. He leaned in and spoke in a razor-sharp voice. "Your grandparents' wealth and the substantial bribe they offered my father, which they disguised as a business proposal, are the only reason we're stuck in this absurd marriage contract, because on your own, you have no worth."

Bryn sucked in a breath. It felt like he'd smacked her... and he'd done it on purpose. He'd meant to wound her, and she hadn't thought he was that person anymore. She knew he was hurting but there was only so much shit she was willing to put up with. "Let me make one thing perfectly clear. If you ever say anything that rude again, I will blast your snotty ass across the room."

"Class dismissed," Mr. Stanton called out in a voice that seemed louder than normal. And that's when Bryn noticed all conversation around them had died down and everyone was watching them like they might come to blows at any moment.

"We'll continue this conversation later," Jaxon said. "In private."

"No. We won't," Bryn said. "I'm done playing the polite game, so stay the hell away from me." She stood and stalked out into the hall. She could taste smoke in the back of her throat as she battled the fire in her gut. What in the hell was Jaxon's problem? Why was he reverting to his evil asshat ways?

Clint and Ivy caught up to her. "That was interesting," Ivy said.

"I want to fry him," Bryn said. "Literally. I want to blast him until he's a charcoal briquette."

"Totally understandable," Clint said.

"Yeah...but I don't understand how your conversation went from teasing to a death match in sixty seconds flat," Ivy said.

"Me, either." And the truth, which she was trying to ignore, was that her feelings were hurt. She'd thought they were friends...allies. And over the summer they'd bantered back and forth. They'd even shared private jokes. Where had that Jaxon gone and who was this elitist douchebag left in his place?

The conversation she'd had with her parents replayed in her head. Maybe there was someone else she could be paired with. Not that her grandparents would ever agree to that. Especially after all the trouble her grandfather had gone through putting together a business deal to entice Ferrin into accepting the marriage contract. God. That was a depressing thought. It's not that there was anything wrong with her. She just wasn't pure Blue, which is what Ferrin wanted.

Chapter Eleven

After dinner that evening, Bryn sat on her couch, wondering what type of repercussions she was going to have to deal with for going off on Jaxon in front of her classmates. She should have just laughed his holier-than-thou behavior off, but he'd blindsided her. She hadn't seen his mean side since she'd saved his sorry ass at her grandparents' house. Maybe she should remind him that he wouldn't be alive if it weren't for her.

That conversation wouldn't go well. She'd try to be the better person and just let it drop for now. Per Blue dragon custom, she and Jaxon should fake a civil relationship in public, though that would be difficult for a few days. And she sure as hell wasn't going to extend the olive branch. He was the one who'd gone nuclear. Maybe she'd make a game out of it. Wait and see how long it would take him to mention their fight. Then again, since he truly didn't care about her, he might not even be feeling bad about their confrontation. So...where did that leave her? And why was she constantly asking herself that question when it came to males and why did she always react to their baggage? Since she had no answers, she went back to reading her book. The guy in the story was being a jerk because he was possessed by a demon. That she could understand. Funny how fiction made more sense than real life.

A knock on her door made her cringe. "Who is it?" she called out.

"Let me in," Jaxon said.

"Wrong approach," Bryn shot back through the door. "Try again."

"We need to talk," he said.

"Why?"

"We're not doing this through the door," Jaxon said.

She had to bite her tongue to keep from pointing out that they were, in fact, doing this through the door. "If I open the door, you have to be civil," Bryn said.

"Fine."

She wasn't sure she believed him, but she opened the door anyway and stepped aside to let him enter. He scowled at her and headed for the couch where he flopped down in a most un-Jaxon like manner. He loosened his tie, ran his hands back through his golden blond hair, and then stared up at the ceiling.

She'd seen Jaxon covered in blood after a battle. Somehow a disheveled Jaxon was more disturbing. She sat in a wing-backed chair and waited for him to start the conversation.

"Do you know what day it is?" he asked.

Was this a trick question? "It's Monday."

He kept his gaze on the ceiling and spoke in a quiet voice. "It's Rhianna's birthday."

Son of a... Bryn threw her arms out wide. "Damn it. Now I can't even be mad at you."

"I'm sorry about what I said earlier. I'm just so angry abou—" His voice broke and he stopped talking.

Double damn it. If he cried she was going to lose it.

He cleared his throat and resumed talking. "It didn't help that the gift I commissioned for her months ago arrived today." He sat up and reached into his jacket pocket, removing a blue velvet case...it was long and flat...the kind that would hold a bracelet. "I don't know what to do with it." He looked up at Bryn like he hoped she might have an answer.

Damn. Damn. Damn. "Do you want me to hold onto it until you figure it out?"

He turned the blue velvet case over in his hands before leaning forward and setting it on the coffee table. "Perhaps that would be best...for now." He pushed to his feet and stared at her for a moment. "You're a good friend, Bryn. I'll try to be a better friend to you." He walked to the door and let himself out.

Bryn tried to bat away the fog of sadness Jaxon seemed to leave in his wake. "This totally sucks." She grabbed the phone, dialed Ivy's number, and unloaded her newfound knowledge.

"Oh my God," Ivy said. "That's so sad. And now you can't even be angry at him."

"I know and that pisses me off." Bryn picked up the blue velvet box. "This whole situation sucks." She looked at the silver hinges that ran along the side. "Would it be wrong if I opened the box to see what he bought her?"

"You want to open his dead girlfriend's gift?" Ivy said.

"When you put it that way..." Bryn set the box down.

"I guess you should open it. If you don't and it ever went missing you wouldn't be able to help look for it."

"Way to rationalize," Bryn said. She popped the lid open. A platinum diamond and sapphire bracelet lay on the blue silk. The stones in the middle of the bracelet were looped back around themselves into an infinity sign. On the lid of the box, in an elegant silver script, it said "Together Forever."

Bryn closed her eyes and swallowed over the lump in her throat. "I shouldn't have looked." She snapped the lid closed and told Ivy about the bracelet.

Ivy sniffled. "Wow. That's tragic."

"I gotta go." Bryn hung up the phone and took the emotional bomb of a gift into her bedroom. Where should she put it? She could call her grandmother tomorrow and ask to meet her for dinner and then give her the bracelet to take back to Sinclair Estate, but her grandmother wouldn't be pleased to discover the unbelievably romantic gift that Jaxon had intended for someone else. She opened her armoire and put the blue velvet box on the top shelf underneath her sweaters.

...

Beginning Quintessential Medicine was becoming Bryn's favorite class for several reasons. First and foremost was her love for the healing arts. The second, and slightly guilt inducing reason, was because it was the only class she didn't share with Jaxon. He'd been civil to her for the last couple of days, but he seemed distant and sad and sometimes she just needed a break.

"Who do you think our guinea pig will be today?" Janelle asked.

"I don't know." Bryn squirmed in her seat. "I know we need to practice on people and these dragons who volunteer to work with us are over eighteen, but I don't know why anyone would agree to being poked and prodded by amateur Medic students."

"I think they get extra credit," Janelle said.

"All right, class," Medic Williams said. "Today I'm setting you up with volunteers who have minor scrapes and cuts. I'll be monitoring your progress. Please respect the volunteer's privacy."

Bryn kept her eyes on the stream of older students and adults who entered the classroom. When Zavien walked in and headed straight for her, she was at a loss for words.

"Hello, Bryn." He sat between her and Janelle, looking more like his old self, minus the spiked hair.

"Zavien? What are you doing here?"

"I'm volunteering for the greater good," he said. "And for the extra credit." Amusement flashed in his dark brown eyes. "It was either this, or nude modeling for the art class."

Bryn's face heated. "That seriously can't be an option."

Zavien grinned. "Ask Clint and Ivy."

"So how do you two know each other?" Janelle asked.

"Sorry," Zavien turned on the charm, smiling at Janelle. "Didn't mean to ignore you." He held out his hand. "I'm Zavien. Bryn and I met when she first came to school."

That was one way to put it.

"I'm Janelle." She shook his hand.

"All right, class, now that you've introduced yourselves, please take turns healing your volunteer."

A nervous feeling settled in Bryn's stomach. While she'd fantasized about injuring Zavien when he'd ducked out on her during their pseudo-relationship, she had no desire to injure him now.

"So...why are you here?" He didn't appear to be hurt.

He unbuttoned his shirt cuffs and rolled up his sleeves exposing his forearms, which were covered in scrapes.

"What did you do?" Bryn asked.

"I was working on a wooden sculpture last night, but the oak fought back. I kept scraping my forearms."

"Why didn't you go to a Medic right after this happened?" Bryn asked.

"I did. She mentioned that I could volunteer today and receive extra credit." He flexed his forearm. "It's not like it hurts. It's more annoying than anything and if there's any way to graduate early and get out of here, I'm willing to give it a shot."

"Too many memories?" Bryn asked.

Zavien nodded and stared straight into her eyes. "Too many memories and too many bad decisions."

Bryn blinked. Was he talking about their failed relationship? No. He was probably thinking about Nola.

She broke eye contact and placed her fingertips on his forearm. "Let me know if this is uncomfortable." She focused her life force in her chest and then imagined the Quintessence flowing from her fingertips like beams of healing light.

Janelle worked on his right arm while Bryn worked on his left. Time seemed to slow down, and she traced her fingertips over the scratches and scrapes while she imagined the skin mending itself...returning to its unblemished state. The fact that she was touching Zavien made the whole thing disconcerting, and he was smiling at her like they shared some sort of secret. They didn't. At one time she had fallen for him, but it had been a first crush, not first love. Although it hadn't felt that way at the time.

What she'd felt after Valmont had broken things off with her...that had been far more devastating, but maybe that had to do with the dragon-knight bond they'd shared. At least she'd never have to worry about having her heart broken again. She'd never have the chance because she'd never have the opportunity to fall in love...which was depressing and reassuring at the same time.

It took ten minutes to heal Zavien's injuries. "There you go."

He held out his arm and turned it over, looking at it from all angles. "Thanks."

"You're welcome. Maybe you should invest in a pair of protective gloves."

"Not a bad idea. Or I could go back to painting. My paints never fought back."

"Sounds like a good plan." The way Zavien was looking at her and talking to her reminded her of how things had been when they'd first met...when they'd been friends, which was kind of nice.

Janelle was still working when Medic Williams came over to check on Bryn's progress.

"Nice job, Bryn." She checked the arm Janelle worked on. "Try focusing on one scrape at a time rather than healing the whole arm."

"Okay." Janelle frowned and concentrated. Soon the scrapes and cuts began to disappear.

"Much better," Medic Williams said.

Once Janelle was finished, Zavien stood and rolled his shoulders. "That was oddly relaxing."

Later, in Basic Movement, Bryn told Clint and Ivy about her experience healing Zavien. "At first it was awkward, and then it felt sort of okay. Is that wrong?" Bryn asked.

"No. He has kind of paid his dues," Clint said.

And then she remembered something. "Do people really volunteer to pose nude for art classes?"

"Yes," Clint said. "And most of the time it's someone our parents' age, which is disturbing."

"It's not sexy," Ivy said, "if that's what you're wondering. It's more...hellaciously awkward."

Bryn cringed. "I can't imagine. Have you ever known any of the people who have volunteered?"

"Not so far," Clint said. "And that's a good thing."

"What are we going to do today?" Bryn asked, gesturing at the joust station, the weight lifting area, and the treadmills.

"That depends," Ivy said. "Do you want to punch something or whack something with a giant cotton swab?"

The joust featured two platforms raised high in the air where students faced off with jousting sticks which resembled giant foam-tipped cotton swabs. You could push people around with them but not really hurt anyone. It felt like being hit with a couch cushion. Although being knocked off the pedestal into the pit of foam blocks below was still unnerving...especially since she'd once landed on a javelin buried in the pit.

She shook off the remembered sensation of the metal tip driving through her thigh. Jaxon had been the one to help her that day. Funny how that was one of her positive memories of him. "There are days when I feel like my life is a game where people keep changing roles. Jaxon used to be evil, now he's mostly my ally, with a dose of asshat and sadness thrown in. Zavien used to be my friend, my sort of boyfriend, the guy I most wanted to blast into a cinder, and now he's an acquaintance I could become friends with again."

"At least we've stayed your friends the whole time," Ivy said.

"Yes. You have," Bryn said. "Thank you for that."

"You're welcome. Now let's go see who we can knock off one of the platforms," Clint said.

...

At lunch Bryn was surprised when Zavien approached their table. He wasn't carrying a tray, so he probably hadn't been through the buffet line yet. "Can I ask you a question about what you did to my arms?"

"Sure."

He sat down, rolled up his sleeves, and held out his arms. "It may just be a difference in skill level, but the arm you fixed feels normal." He held out the arm Janelle worked on. "My right arm feels weak, and does the skin look strange, or is it just me?"

Bryn traced her fingers over the arm Janelle worked on. "It's not just you. You almost look dehydrated. Let me try something." She focused Quintessence through her fingertips into his forearm. His skin returned to a normal color and his muscles flexed and filled out. Once she stopped they compared the two arms. "There you go. You now have a matched set."

"Thanks." He rolled his shirt sleeves back down. "What do you think she did wrong?"

"I don't know. She's new at this. It's like she used your own Quintessence to heal your injuries rather than using hers."

"Maybe you should tutor her before she works on someone else." He grinned and headed for the buffet line.

Clint cleared his throat. "You're about to have company." Jaxon came to their table and he was carrying a lunch tray. Without asking he sat and said, "I hadn't planned on eating with you but since you were just seen touching your ex-boyfriend in a strange manner, I thought I'd come say hello."

"You mean Bryn hasn't told you about her forearm fetish?" Clint asked.

Jaxon snorted in response.

Bryn laughed. "It's not like I was groping him. He was one of the guinea pigs in my Quintessential Meds class today. My partner didn't do such a great job on his arm so he asked me to look at it." She explained about Janelle.

"Maybe she should change her field of study," Jaxon said.

"Or maybe she's a Quintessence-sucking vampire," Clint said. "A dragon-pire."

Jaxon paused mid chew and looked at Clint like he'd just said something insane...which he sort of had. After chewing and swallowing Jaxon said, "What are you talking about?"

Clint explained about the Silver dragons and the theory that the Cult might be making a comeback.

Jaxon reached up and rubbed the bridge of his nose. "We just fought off a Rebel uprising. For the first time in the history of the Institute, hybrids and throwbacks have been welcomed onto the campus. I am not mentally prepared to deal with an evil Quintessence sucking cult, so I sincerely hope you're wrong."

"But you're not dismissing the idea completely," Clint said.

"If this involved anyone but Bryn..." Jaxon didn't bother finishing his sentence.

"We've decided she's a chaos magnet," Ivy said.

Jaxon nodded. "Sounds about right."

"What can I say?" Bryn shrugged. "I lead an interesting life."

Chapter Twelve

That night after dinner, Bryn went to speak with Medic Williams in the infirmary.

The Medic looked up from the file she was reading. "Bryn, are you injured?"

"No. I wanted to talk to you about something and I didn't want to do it in front of the class."

"Okay." She closed the file and placed it on a stack to her right. "Have a seat."

Bryn sat in the hard-plastic chair in front of Medic William's desk. Hopefully she wasn't about to make a mistake. Maybe she should hedge her bets a little bit. "This is going to sound weird, and it's probably all in my head." And then she launched into the story about Zavien's forearms and Clint's dragon-pire theory.

"That is odd." She tapped her nails on the desktop. "Janelle is inexperienced, but that was also a low-level injury. Before we decide a dangerous cult is back on campus, I'll have a talk with her."

"I'm beginning to understand how those conspiracy theorists feel," Bryn said. "I feel like I'm overreacting all the time but if I don't say something I'm afraid it could lead to disaster."

"If it makes you feel any better, I think we all feel that way after the attack on campus. Dragons I'd known my whole life had been Rebels, and I never had a clue that they were anything but what they said they were. Feel free to bring your suspicions to me. I'm always willing to listen."

"Thank you. Hopefully, I won't have to take you up on that offer."

Later that night, Bryn tossed and turned. Her mind wouldn't stop spinning speculations about possible spies. Was Janelle part of a cult? Did Silver dragon-pires even exist? Why couldn't she stop focusing on all this weird crap and fall asleep? At least tomorrow was Friday. Not that she had any special plans, but two days spent either hanging out with Clint and Ivy or hiding in her room reading books, eating pizza, and avoiding the world in general, sounded fabulous.

...

In Quintessential Medicine the next day, before class started, Janelle was too quiet. Bryn got a funny feeling in her stomach. Had Janelle heard that Zavien had come to Bryn or that she'd spoken to Medic Williams? It's not like Bryn had ratted her out. If Clint hadn't put the idea of Quintessence sucking dragon-pires into her head, she wouldn't have gone to Medic Williams. Should she bring it up?

"Class, we are low on volunteers for healing at the moment, so we are going to read over some interesting case studies."

Bryn doubted the interesting part. She leaned toward Janelle. "I was hoping this class would be mostly hands on."

Janelle nodded. "Me, too."

Medic Williams passed out bound copies of case files. "The names and other personal information have been redacted. Focus on how the Medics diagnosed the patients rather than the actual treatment. Not every injury is clear cut. You need to be part detective to be a good Medic."

Bryn read the first few lines. A female dragon had been admitted to the clinic with a strange rash. Not exactly a page turner.

Janelle scooted her desk closer to Bryn's. "Can I ask you a question?"

"Sure." Please don't let this be awkward.

"Why did Zavien have you look at his arms yesterday?"

And it's awkward. How could she say this without putting Janelle's efforts down? "One of his arms felt a little weaker," Bryn said, not specifying which one.

"Crap," Janelle said. "I screwed up. Didn't I?"

"No." Bryn stalled for time. "I think you stopped just short of putting on the finishing touches. The skin was healed, but he needed a little bit more of a boost, if that makes sense."

"Medic Williams's watching made me nervous," Janelle said. "I guess I stopped when the cuts were healed and didn't think to finish up."

"No big deal," Bryn said. "We are here to learn."

"As a Green, there's pressure to always do the best job possible. Sometimes I get distracted. I'm not the perfectionist most of my fellow Greens are."

"That's not a bad thing," Bryn said.

Someone shushed Bryn. She rolled her eyes. "Speaking of perfectionists," she whispered, which made Janelle smile. Bryn went back to reading her case study. Thank goodness Janelle hadn't been offended.

In Basic Movement, Bryn ran on a treadmill next to Ivy while Clint used a stair climber.

"What are we doing tonight?" Ivy asked.

"What are our options?" Bryn asked.

Ivy reduced the speed on her treadmill to a slow jog. "We can go to dinner in Dragon's Bluff or eat pizza in your room and play cards."

"Are you still carrying around a deck of cards at all times?" Bryn asked Clint.

"Yes. I think of them as my good luck charm," he said. "Plus I rock at building card houses."

When they'd been trapped under the library, the hallways had seemed like a never-ending maze. Clint had left a card at every turning point in numerical order so they would know where they'd already been. Ever since then he'd carried a deck, just in case.

"I used to build those with my dad," Bryn said. And then another memory hit her. "I wonder if Valmont's dad went through with his plan to create those pizza-shaped decks of cards he told Valmont about."

"If you're talking about him, does that mean you're ready to go to Fonzoli's?" Ivy asked.

Was she ready to go visit Valmont's family restaurant?

Dragon's Bluff wasn't very big. She'd bump into him eventually. Maybe it was better if she did it on her own terms. "I might be willing to give it a shot."

"Cool," Clint said. "I've been craving Fonzoli's pizza, but I didn't want to mention it."

"And if it's too weird we can order carryout and come back to campus," Ivy said.

Bryn nodded. Hopefully, she wouldn't need to take that route.

They took one of the sanctioned SUVs into Dragon's Bluff that evening and had the driver drop them off down the street from Fonzoli's. Bryn inhaled the garlic and Italian-seasonings scent drifting through the air. "That smells amazing."

"It does," Ivy said.

Even though her mouth was watering, she wasn't quite sure about this. She wouldn't just be facing Valmont. His entire family had disapproved of their relationship... especially his grandmother. "If it's super awkward we can leave, right?"

"Yes," Ivy said. "If it's too much you can say you're running to All That Sparkles to pick something up, and I'll have them change our order to go."

"Okay." She could do this. Clint walked into the restaurant in front of them. Bryn trailed behind Ivy. The hostess smiled at them like they were just another set of customers. Bryn scanned the room for Valmont but didn't see him...thank goodness.

The hostess seated them up front near the window. "Megan will be with you in just a moment."

Holy crap. Bryn hadn't even thought about Megan, the cute young waitress who'd had a crush on Valmont...the human girl who could give him the simple, uncomplicated life he wanted...the life he deserved. Maybe coming here was a mistake.

Megan approached with a smile on her face. The smile slipped a bit when she saw Bryn. "Welcome back to Fonzoli's. Are you ready to order, or would you like me to bring your drinks while you look over the menu?"

"Clint and I want to split a large sausage pizza," Ivy said.

"I'll have two pepperoni calzones," Bryn said, like the situation wasn't all sorts of awkward.

Megan stared at Bryn for a moment. "Something you want to say?" Bryn asked.

Megan frowned. "Honestly, I'm stuck between wanting to yell at you and wanting to thank you."

And that's when she understood. The spicy scent which had made her hungry moments before now made her slightly nauseous. "You got your wish. You're with Valmont now."

Megan nodded.

Bryn's pulse spiked. "Is he here?"

"Yes, but he's not waiting tables anymore. He's cooking." Megan glanced around. "I hope...you're not here to try and take him back, are you?"

Bryn shook her head no. "I'm just here for the food." And to rip the bandage off an emotional wound.

Megan gave a nervous laugh. "Good. Should I tell him you're here?"

He'd probably hear it from one of the other waitstaff, even if Megan didn't say anything. "Tell him I said hello. He doesn't need to come out and see me...I know he's busy."

"Okay." Megan bit her lip. "Maybe the next time you come in it won't be so awkward. I'll be right back with your drinks."

Megan walked away. Bryn noticed the hostess and another waiter watching her. She gave a tight smile and turned back to Clint and Ivy. "Well, that was fun."

"At least it's over," Ivy said.

"Or not," Clint pointed to someone headed their way.

Valmont's grandmother, the evil woman who had told her she never should have been involved with Valmont in the first place, came to their table and sat next to Bryn. What was she going to do—ban Bryn from the restaurant?

"I never liked you," his grandmother said.

"Yes, you made that perfectly clear," said Bryn.

The woman narrowed her eyes. "But I wanted to thank you for doing the right thing. Valmont is better off with Megan. She makes him happy." And with that she stood and walked back toward the kitchen.

Bryn wanted to slump down in her seat. This was emotionally exhausting, but since she was part Blue she sat straight in her chair and acted like none of this bothered her. "I may never eat Italian again," she told Clint and Ivy.

"At least the drama is over," Ivy said.

"Unless Valmont comes out to say hello," Clint said.

Bryn froze. "He's not. Is he?"

"No." Clint said. "But I'll keep my eyes open for any more chaos that might be headed your way."

After Megan brought their food, Bryn was able to relax. She was on her last bite of calzone when Jaxon walked in the door and headed straight for her.

"What's wrong?" Bryn asked.

"My mother asked me to find you and bring you to Westgate Estate," he said, sounding less than enthusiastic.

"Why?"

"Asher made his appearance early this morning," Jaxon said. "And she knew you'd want to meet him."

Happiness bubbled up inside of Bryn. "That's so exciting."

"If you say so. Let's go."

"I have to pay." Bryn glanced around for Megan.

"We'll take care of the bill," Clint said. "Next time you can buy."

"Okay. Thank you." Bryn followed Jaxon out the front door.

A low-slung black sports car that looked like it was made from liquid metal sat parked right in front of the entrance to the restaurant. Jaxon pushed his key fob and the car's lights blinked. He opened the door for Bryn and she climbed in.

As she buckled her seat belt, he climbed in behind the steering wheel and took off.

"Is this your Christmas present...the Bugatti something?"

"Bugatti Veyron," he said. "And yes, it is."

"It's amazing," Bryn said. And she meant it. The car looked like a work of art.

"Thank you." He shifted gears and headed down the main road before taking a sharp right into the forest. He picked up speed, flying down the winding roads.

"Aren't you afraid something might run out in front of you?" Bryn asked.

"No." He pressed the accelerator and the engine growled.

"Not too chatty today, are you?" she asked.

He didn't bother answering. Bryn watched the forest whiz by as Jaxon drove down roads which barely seemed wide enough for the car. "Are these real roads?" Bryn asked.

"Of course."

Ten minutes later Jaxon pulled up to Westgate Estate. The wrought iron gates sported giant Ws, which Bryn found ridiculous. From past experience, she knew it only became worse in the house. The foyer floor was inlaid with a gold W, which was probably made of real gold. Even the silverware was monogrammed. Her grandmother had once informed Bryn that she would receive a set of monogrammed silver as a wedding present. That was one present Bryn might accidentally shove in a drawer and forget about.

Rather than pulling to the front of the mansion, Jaxon drove around the side to an enormous garage, which looked like it could hold a dozen cars. Several SUVs sat at the far end of the structure. Jaxon parked in one of the open spots and turned off the ignition. Bryn reached for the door handle to let herself out.

"Wait," Jaxon said.

Was this one of those stupid moments where she was supposed to let someone else, like a member of the Westgate staff, open the door for her? She didn't see anyone outside the car. She glanced at Jaxon for a clue. He stared at his key fob like he was searching for something.

"Jaxon?"

He sighed. "I don't know how I'm supposed to act."

And she was lost. "What are you talking about?"

"As a Westgate and a Blue, I've been raised to behave in the appropriate manner for all circumstances, but no one prepared me for this. How am I supposed to act around Asher?"

Okay, how should she handle this? "Don't get mad because I'm not making fun of you, I'm trying to help."

He nodded like he understood.

"Normal, and by that, I mean non-Blue individuals, are usually happy about having another family member. How do you feel about having a baby brother?"

"I'm not sure. I'm happy for my mother, but I'm worried about my relationship with my father."

Where was a psychology book when she needed one? "I'm an only child so I don't have any actual experience with this, but I've seen how proud your father is of you. That won't change just because he has another son."

"I suppose not...so I'll pretend I'm happy and go from there?"

A strange thought occurred to Bryn. "Do you spend most of your time pretending?"

"Doesn't everyone?" he asked like he actually meant it.

"No," Bryn answered.

"If there's one thing I learned from my relationship with Rhianna, it's that real feelings will only cause you pain. Pretending is a much better choice. We should go." He reached for his door handle and exited the vehicle.

Bryn was caught between wanting to hug him or yell at him. Maybe both. What did he plan to do? Keep a layer of ice between himself and the rest of the world...between him and her? Forever? Not that she expected him to fall in love with her...that was ridiculous...but she at least needed the warmth of friendship, of a good strong ally that she could depend on...hell, she'd settle for someone she could have a dinner conversation with.

Maybe they needed to discuss some ground rules for their current and future relationship. His personality had already been molded by Ferrin and polite dragon society. Maybe she could help Asher become a more normal, happier, healthier person...sort of balance out the strange proper Blue teachings with normal feelings. She opened her car door and caught up with Jaxon.

Chapter Thirteen

Lillith sat in the nursery, cradling Asher in her arms. When Bryn and Jaxon entered the room, she beamed at them. "Come meet your brother."

Jaxon approached his mother with a polite smile frozen on his face. "How are you feeling?"

"Tired but happy," she said.

He studied the baby like he wasn't sure what to do.

"Out of the way." Bryn scooted past him and reached to touch Asher's cheek. His skin glowed golden like his mother's and he had a sprinkling of curly blond hair. His chest rose and fell with every breath as he slept. "He's adorable."

"I know." Lillith grinned. "I may be biased, but I think he's the most beautiful baby I've ever seen."

"Every mother thinks that," Bryn's grandmother said as she walked into the room, "And every mother is right."

"It's a little crowded in here." Jaxon backed up toward the door.

"Your father is in the den if you want to join him," Lillith said.

"If you want me to stay—" He left the sentence hanging.

"Thank you for coming and bringing Bryn. You're free to go do manly things now," his mother teased.

Jaxon walked over and kissed his mother on the forehead before exiting the room.

"May I?" Bryn's grandmother reached for Asher.

"Of course." Lillith passed the baby off.

Her grandmother held the baby and did that walking bounce maneuver that seemed to be innate to all species. "I can't believe he's sleeping so well."

"He ate an hour ago," Lillith said. "So I'm expecting him to start fussing any minute."

"Westgates fuss?" Bryn acted surprised. "I didn't think that would be part of their genetic code."

Lillith laughed. "Not so much fussing as making their voice heard in the world."

As if on cue, Asher opened his mouth and wailed. Bryn's grandmother handed the baby back to Lillith.

"Bryn and I will take a walk in the arbor-areum. You can send someone for us when you're ready for company."

"Thank you."

They shut the nursery doors on their way out. Bryn followed her grandmother down the hall. "I'm hoping you remember how to find the arbor-areum because I have no clue."

"I've learned my way around Westgate Estate over the last few months," her grandmother said. "Even with its idiosyncrasies, it's a remarkable home."

"It sure is...something," Bryn said.

Her grandmother laughed. "The arbor-areum is amazing."

"True." They entered the glassed-in forest with its slate paths and mature trees, and headed for a park bench.

"So I hear that you and Jaxon have not been coexisting peacefully."

What was her grandmother talking about? Oh...their argument in Elemental Science. "We straightened it out. He was upset about something else." She couldn't tell her grandmother about it being Rhianna's birthday, so she improvised. "He came to me later and admitted he'd overreacted because something else was bothering him, so there's no lasting damage."

Her grandmother sat and stared at Bryn like she had two heads.

"What?" Had she broken some archaic Blue code of conduct?

"He came to you," her grandmother said. "He admitted fault?"

Bryn nodded.

"I have no words. Your grandfather has never admitted fault for anything in his entire existence."

Bryn shrugged. "Maybe it's because Jaxon and I started out as rivals who have come to respect one another."

"Whatever the reason," her grandmother said. "I hope it's a trend that continues in the new generation of Blues."

"Me, too." Maybe she could change the attitude of the Blue males for the better.

Lillith ended up sending word, via a maid carrying a sealed note, that she was going to take a nap with Asher and asked that they come back another time. She also asked that they not pass that information onto anyone else because she didn't want to seem rude.

"We'll come back another time," her grandmother told the maid. "And we can see ourselves out."

"Should I track down Jaxon and tell him we're leaving?" Bryn asked.

"I have a better idea. Let's tell him we're going to Suzette's for pie and that he's welcome to join us," her grandmother said. "Then we can do whatever we want and not worry about him or Ephram trying to locate us."

Bryn laughed. "Sounds good to me."

...

For a Friday evening there weren't as many people as Bryn thought there would be wandering around Dragon's Bluff. "Curfew isn't for another hour and a half," Bryn said. "Makes me wonder where everyone is."

Only a few families walked along like normal. Students moved quickly in small groups from one destination to another. "Is it me," Bryn said, "or does everyone seem to be rushing because they're afraid to be caught loitering?"

"I'm sure Ferrin or some male is behind that rule. They don't understand that part of enjoying Dragon's Bluff is leisurely wandering from one store to the next. It's supposed to be relaxed and enjoyable, not a race. Let's see if we can get to the bottom of this."

"You lead, and I'll follow," Bryn said.

Would anyone approach her grandmother in a rude manner? She doubted it, but it would be interesting to see how this played out.

"We'll start with that lovely little park that the Women's League paid for which no one is enjoying."

Most of the trees and foliage in Dragon's Bluff had been burned to ash during the attack several months ago. Over the summer the bare areas had been transformed into green spaces or small parks.

"It's beautiful," Bryn said. There was a multilevel circular copper fountain surrounded by plants and flowers. A fantastical swing set sat off to one side. Instead of normal swings, at the end of the chains there were horses that looked like they belonged on a carousel. Some were small enough for toddlers, but a few were large enough that Bryn thought she might fit on one. Next to the swing set was an array of wooden balance beams connected to one another, suspended a foot off the ground.

Benches were scattered around, so parents could keep an eye on their children or enjoy the fountain.

"You want to ride one of the horses, don't you?" her grandmother asked with a knowing smile.

"I do," Bryn said. "Would that be all right?"

"That's why we made some large enough for high school students. They're hard to resist. Go on. I'll loiter right here and wait to see what happens."

"I almost feel sorry for whatever guard is clueless enough to approach you." Bryn headed over to the horses and picked a white one with black spots. Would it hold her weight? Her grandmother and the other women would have spared no expense making sure this place was safe. Still... she sat and tested the feel of it before pushing off with her feet.

Her grandmother laughed as Bryn held onto the handles protruding from the horse's head and leaned forward and backward, making the horse swing higher.

A few students who'd been walking stopped and watched Bryn. They ran across to the park. One girl climbed onto a horse while the other walked on the balance beams. The boys stood and watched, talking among themselves.

A guard approached from across the street and walked up to the young men. Bryn slowed her swing so she could hear better.

"No loitering allowed," the guard declared. "Move along."

Before the young men could get a word out, Bryn's grandmother approached. "I'm sorry. Is there a problem?"

The guard turned to her and paused like he'd lost some of the wind from his sails. "There is no loitering allowed."

"But they aren't loitering," her grandmother stated. "They're enjoying the park."

The guard took a deep breath. "I have my orders. Students are not allowed to loiter. They are supposed to shop and eat and leave." He handed one of the papers to her grandmother like that would explain everything.

Her grandmother looked at the paper and flipped it over like there might be more information on the back side. "This is counterproductive to our efforts to restore Dragon's Bluff and ridiculous to apply when it comes to a park. Who gave you these orders?"

The guard shifted his weight back and forth on his feet. "My superior."

"Do you have a phone? Can you call him for me? I'd like to speak to him."

"I'm sure he's busy," the guard said. "Perhaps you should all just move along."

Oh no, he didn't. Bryn fought the urge to laugh. Time to sit back and enjoy the show.

"Let me rephrase my request. Call your superior and tell him his presence is required here, now."

"Uhm...he may not be available," the guard said.

Her grandmother crossed her arms over her chest and smiled at the guard. "I'll wait."

The guard walked away, pulling his phone from his pocket. After placing the call, he stayed where he was rather than returning to her grandmother.

Bryn pushed the swing higher and waited to see what would happen next.

A harried looking guard entered the park and sighed when he saw Marie Sinclair waiting for him. "Mrs. Sinclair, is there a problem?"

"Yes. There is. My granddaughter and other students are here to enjoy the town and the park. Your friend over there seems to find that objectionable. Can you explain why?"

"We are under orders to keep people from congregating."

"Yes, I've seen the pamphlet." She held it up. "Who gave you this directive?"

"A member of the Directorate," the guard said.

"Which one?" she asked.

"I'm not at liberty to say."

"Were you specifically ordered not to reveal who gave this ridiculous order?" her grandmother asked. "Or do you fear retribution?"

He glanced around. "It's almost curfew. I respectfully suggest you enjoy the park and then seek answers elsewhere so that my men and I won't receive the fallout."

"I understand your position. Answer me one question and I won't trouble you any more. When I search for more information, should I bother contacting Ferrin Westgate? He's a busy man and I wouldn't want to disturb him needlessly."

"He might be able to point you in the right direction." The guard stepped away from her. "Good night, Mrs. Sinclair."

Both guards retreated. Bryn hopped off her horse and went over to her grandmother. "Ferrin would have been my number one guess since he seems to suck the joy from most situations."

Her grandmother gave her a warning look. "However accurate your sentiment might be, we are in public."

Bryn rolled her eyes. "Fine. Where to now?"

"I'd like to sit here for awhile longer, if you don't mind." Her grandmother said. "It is a beautiful night."

"And you want to stick it to that guard," Bryn said.

"Possibly." Her grandmother grinned.

"Bryn, is that you?"

A male voice came from behind her. A voice that made her stomach clench.

She turned and saw Valmont walking toward her. Crap, was she ready for this? Pasting on the least-fake smile she could manage, she said, "Hello, Valmont."

"Mrs. Sinclair." Valmont nodded at Bryn's grandmother. "May I borrow Bryn for a moment?"

His words brought back painful reminders of cuddling on the porch swing behind the restaurant. She squashed the memories, shoving them down deep as she took a breath and prepared for a god-awfully awkward encounter.

"Of course. I'll just check on the fountain." Her grandmother headed toward the copper structure.

"Let's have a seat." Bryn gestured at the bench.

They sat, but he didn't make eye contact. "I wanted to thank you."

Bryn laughed. "For what?"

"For doing the right thing." Valmont raised his head and met her gaze. "I'll never regret being your knight, but the rest of it...us...never should have happened."

Wow. Whatever she'd expected him to say, that wasn't it. Her eyes burned. She blinked rapidly and cleared her throat. "And now you're with Megan and she makes you happy."

He nodded. "She does. What about you? Are you happy?"

A happily ever after probably wasn't in the cards for her. There was no true love on her horizon. Just Jaxon. Temperamental and sometimes kind, but certainly never loving. Not that she could explain any of that to Valmont and quite frankly, it was none of his damn business. "I have my parents back, Asher is adorable, and I'm enjoying my Medic class."

"And Jaxon?" he asked like he expected some declaration of love. Was he just looking to ease his own conscience?

"Jaxon and I are a good match."

"One day, I hope you'll be more," Valmont said. "You deserve to be happy."

"Good night, Valmont." Bryn stood and went to join her grandmother.

Chapter Fourteen

Saturday morning Bryn lounged on her couch in yoga pants and a tank top, drinking coffee and reading her book. So far, the boyfriend possessed by the demon was acting pretty much like Jaxon when he was in a pissy mood. Could the person who wrote this book have spent time around Blue males? It was an amusing thought.

Bryn's phone rang. She picked it up and said, "Hello, Bryn is reading and lounging right now. She's not doing anything that requires putting on real clothes."

"That's not how you're supposed to answer the phone," Jaxon said.

"Maybe I'm starting a new trend. Why are you interrupting my reading time?"

"We've been summoned to dinner at your grandparents' house this evening."

"Really?" That was weird. "My grandmother didn't mention it last night."

"Call her and see if you can figure out what's going on."

"Okay Mr. Crabby Pants. It's just dinner. Why are you upset?"

"Honestly, I've had enough family bonding time and I wanted to spend the day reading."

Huh. She hadn't known Jaxon liked to read. "I don't suppose we can claim that we have too much homework and then hide out, separately, in our own rooms, reading?"

"No." Jaxon said. "But the next time my mother insinuates that you and I need to spend more time together I'm going to tell her we have plans. And the plans will be that we're sitting in the same room, reading but not talking."

"Now that's a date I could enjoy," Bryn said. "In the meantime, I'll figure out what's going on with dinner."

She hung up and dialed Sinclair Estate. Once her grandmother was on the line, she said, "Jaxon said we're invited to dinner tonight."

"Yes, you are." Her grandmother's tone gave nothing away.

"Any particular reason?" Bryn asked. "Not that I don't want to come but you didn't mention anything yesterday."

"Your grandfather wants to have a discussion about your future."

"That doesn't tell me much."

"There's not much to tell," her grandmother said.

"You sound amused," Bryn accused.

"I don't know what you mean." There was a touch of sarcasm to her grandmother's tone.

"You're up to something. Should I be worried?"

"You have nothing to worry about. I'll see you at six on the dot. Don't be late."

That was weird. Bryn called Jaxon and explained the strange conversation.

"Oh no," Jaxon said.

"What?" If he was worried it had to be bad.

"Since your parents aren't included in our community, your grandfather is going to want to discuss our future plans."

"Our plans for what?"

"Children," Jaxon said.

"What about children?"

"It's tradition," Jaxon said. "Normally your father would pull me aside and talk to me about...family planning."

That didn't make sense. "You mean when we plan to have kids?"

"No."

And that's when she got it. "Are you kidding me? He's going to talk to you about where baby dragons come from?"

"Unless I fake a violent illness after dinner, I'm fairly sure that's what he plans to do."

"That's horrifying," Bryn said. "Can't you tell him that your dad already filled you in on that stuff? I mean he did... didn't he?"

"Of course he did," Jaxon sounded exasperated. "When I was ten."

Bryn was caught between wanting to laugh and wanting to go hide under her bed. "Why? Why is this a tradition? It's mortifying."

"Maybe every generation wants to share the horrible awkwardness of the situation with their own children."

"Is there any way we can get out of this?" Bryn asked.

"None that I'm aware of." Jaxon sighed like he'd given up hope.

"I'd be happy to fake a kidnapping...maybe go trap myself under the library." She was only partially joking.

"I'll be by your room at five thirty," he said and then he was gone.

Bryn stared at the phone for a moment before hanging up. What would her role be in this strange evening? If her grandfather was going to traumatize Jaxon, did that mean her grandmother was going to talk to her about sex?

Chapter Fifteen

They drove in silence to Sinclair Estate. Not that conversation was much of an option in Jaxon's sports car. Planes probably had quieter engines. Then again, he might be doing some unnecessary gear shifting to keep conversation to a minimum.

She was surprised when he pulled up to the hairpin drive in front of her grandparents' house and handed his keys over to one of the staff for valet parking.

"Are we ready for this?" Bryn asked as they walked into the main hall.

"No," Jaxon said. "But we don't have a choice. And as you've said before, that seems to be the theme of your life... so thanks for sharing that with me." His tone was sort of teasing.

"You're so welcome," she shot back.

Bryn's grandmother met them at the top of the stairs. "How nice to see you both. We're going to eat in the atrium since it's such a lovely evening."

That was new. Bryn would have bet they'd eat in the dining room. "Not that I'm complaining, but why the atrium?"

Her grandmother's grin looked a little wicked. "Just in case your grandfather wants to speak to Jaxon about something in his office."

Suspicion confirmed.

"Is there any amount of money I can bribe you with to keep him from giving me this talk?" Jaxon asked.

"No." Her grandmother smiled. "Now come along."

Jaxon glanced back at the stairs. "What if I accidentally fell and broke my arm?"

"Well, then Bryn could heal you and we'd reschedule this event." Her grandmother headed toward the next flight of stairs.

"I'm sorry," Bryn said as they followed along. "At least it's only a one-time thing."

The atrium was amazing. The entire back wall was glass, which turned the area into a greenhouse, bringing the outdoors indoors. Plants and flowers lined the hall and were used to create pathways to the white wrought iron tables in the center of the room. It smelled like flowers and soil and something savory, which must be dinner.

Her grandfather met them by the table where he hugged Bryn and shook Jaxon's hand. "Nice to see you." He smiled like he was highly amused by this entire situation.

"You're going to torment him, aren't you?" Bryn said.

"I have no idea what you're referring to," her grandfather said. "If you'll have a seat we can start dinner."

"It smells wonderful," Bryn said.

"It should taste even better," a woman dressed in a maid's uniform said, as she pushed a cart into the room with four domed silver plates. Bryn had learned the drill. Sit and wait until everyone had a plate. Once her grandfather had removed his cover, she removed hers. It was some sort of beef.

"Prime rib," her grandfather informed her. "One of my favorites."

They ate, and her grandmother made small talk, asking them about school and how their classes were going. Jaxon gave perfunctory answers and pushed his food around on his plate. Bryn enjoyed her food and tried to keep the conversation flowing.

"I have a question for you," Bryn said. "If a couple never married because their contract was denied, and they're past the age of having kids, is there any reason they couldn't marry now?"

Her grandfather frowned. "No one has ever asked that question."

"Can you look into it?" Bryn asked.

Her grandfather nodded. After dessert of peach sorbet, he stood. "Jaxon, why don't you join me in my study?"

Without a word, Jaxon stood and followed after her grandfather. Once they were out of range of hearing, Bryn said, "Is this the part where you ambush me with embarrassing conversation?"

"No"—her grandmother grinned—"I assume you know about the birds and the bees."

"I do," Bryn said.

"And I hope you're going to wait until you're married before you and Jaxon become intimate."

Bryn cringed. "You said this wouldn't be embarrassing, and there are no worries on that front." Because she and Jaxon would never be a real couple.

"I've said my piece," her grandmother responded with a grin. "I'm afraid Jaxon is going to get a much more thorough talking to about respectful behavior and responsibility to the Clan."

"This is a horrible tradition," Bryn said.

"Wait until you have your own children," she said. "Then you'll understand."

Half an hour later, Jaxon returned with a resigned look on his face. "I believe we're done," he told Bryn. "If you're ready to leave?"

"Sure." Bryn hugged her grandmother and then her grandfather.

"Did you traumatize him?" she whispered to her grandfather.

He grinned. "Just looking out for your best interests."

"You enjoyed this way too much," she said.

"I did," he agreed. In a louder voice, he said, "Go enjoy the rest of your Saturday evening."

Jaxon snorted and muttered something under his breath as he walked off. Bryn pressed her lips together to keep from laughing.

She caught up with Jaxon on the stairs. "I'm sorry," she said.

He didn't respond, which was strange. From her perspective this was sort of funny, but maybe he couldn't see that or wasn't ready to see that yet. Whatever. She'd wait until they were in the car to talk to him.

On the drive back to school the engine didn't growl nearly as much, and he didn't seem to enjoy driving. Something was wrong. But what?

When Jaxon pulled into a spot in the school parking lot, he made no move to turn the engine off.

"Do you want to talk about something?" she asked.

He didn't respond.

Well, crap. "Did my grandfather offend you in some way?"

"No. It's just that this shouldn't be happening." He turned the car off. "No offense, but we both know this will never be a real marriage."

His statement tugged at her insides. "I know it will never be like what you would have had with Rhianna or what I thought I could've had with Valmont, but we can be friends. We can make this work as a partnership. Isn't that what most Blue marriages are about anyway?"

"Yes," he conceded. "It's just that I thought I'd have something more...and now I won't." He reached up and rubbed the bridge of his nose. "We should go in. It's almost curfew."

They walked back to the dorm in silence. He didn't say good night, he just kept on walking to his own room. What a lovely evening this had turned out to be. She let herself in, changed into comfy clothes, and lost herself in a book.

...

Sunday morning she met up with Clint and Ivy for a late breakfast and told them about the strange Blue Clan tradition Jaxon had endured.

"That is...evil," Clint said. His eyes grew wide. "Your dad isn't planning on ambushing me like that," he said to Ivy. "Is he?"

"Absolutely not," she said. "Why would they do that?"

"It's like some sort of weird Blue hazing ritual," Clint said.

"That's exactly what it is. My grandfather looked like he had a wonderful time."

"On to a happier and far more normal topic," Ivy said. "Henna, the Orange female dragon who helped me grow the trees, is not an evil Silver dragon-pire."

"How did you figure that out?" Bryn asked.

"Someone must have tracked her down and told her how exhausted I was after growing the trees because she came in to speak to Medic Williams and apologize for not thinking about how the effects might be different for a Black dragon's system. Apparently, Orange dragon's sonic waves are like a never-ending source of plant growing energy, which is different than me using my own Quintessence. She can grow plants for hours and never require a nap. I did it for forty minutes and was down for the count, which is sort of embarrassing."

"I guess it makes sense, though," Bryn said. "Since their sonic waves are so powerful they must naturally have more energy to spend."

"And if I'd never read those articles about Silvers and their strange dragon-pire cult, I never would have suspected Henna of being anything other than what she was," Clint said. "A turbo-powered plant whisperer."

"It makes me kind of sad that I'll never be able to grow plants like her," Ivy said.

"You can still be the topiary queen," Bryn said. "And that's pretty cool."

"I think I'll go back to painting," Ivy said. "It's strange, but knowing I'll never be the real deal makes me not even want to try."

Kind of like her marriage to Jaxon. Wait...where did that odd thought come from?

...

Nothing strange or mortifying happened on Monday or Tuesday. Wednesday was odd because Jaxon knocked on her door after dinner, interrupting her reading. He held his own book and had a takeout box with two cups and a couple of giant cookies, which looked like they were chocolate chip.

"What's this?" Bryn asked as she let him in.

"A reading date," Jaxon said. "To appease the people who are making snide remarks about our non-relationship."

"People are talking about us? Since when?"

He set the box on the coffee table and sat in one of her wing-backed chairs. "Doesn't matter. One night a week we can meet to read and that should shut people up."

"Okay." She plopped back down on the couch with her book and then eyed the cups he'd brought. She couldn't smell anything so he hadn't brought coffee.

"It's milk," he said without looking up from his book.

"You brought milk and cookies?" It's like they were on a kindergarten date.

"If you're going to have cookies you might as well have milk," he said.

She grabbed a cup and took the lid off, broke off a piece of cookie, and dunked it before taking a bite. It was brown sugar, vanilla, and chocolate bliss. This type of dating totally worked for her.

She read and finished off her cookie before eyeing up the cookie still sitting in the box. Jaxon was deep into whatever he was reading. He hadn't touched his cookie, so maybe he wouldn't miss it.

She started to lean forward and he said, "Don't even think about it."

"You're not eating it," she objected.

"I plan on eating it," he said. "And you already had one."

"One," she said. "It's like you don't even know me." He shook his head and continued reading.

Ten minutes later he closed his book and picked up his cookie. She gave him puppy dog eyes.

"Fine." He broke a third of the cookie off and gave it to her.

"Thank you."

After finishing his cookie, he shoved his cup back into the carryout box. "Are you done with your milk?" he asked.

"Yes."

He shoved her cup back into the container and stood. "I'm at a good stopping point in my book, so I'll see you tomorrow."

"Are we still eating dinner together tomorrow, because we could read together several nights a week instead." Would he go for her plan?

"We still need to be seen together in public. What if I eat dinner at your table one night a week? Then I won't have to explain your lack of manners to my friends."

"You just couldn't play nice the entire time, could you?"

"I am a Westgate," he said with a fake air of snottiness.

"I'm well aware of that disturbing fact."

He smiled at her, and it was a real smile. That was nice.

"Good night, Bryn." He walked to the door and let himself out. Weird how she'd never thought he'd act so normal. He was usually so formal and Blue. Maybe this whole friendship thing could work.

Chapter Sixteen

Bryn had strange dreams about her book suddenly morphing to the size of a car. She lost her place and turning the pages was like flipping a giant blanket. The pages were heavy and awkward, and the letters were so big the text was hard to read. She ended up flipping the pages and then climbing a ladder to peer down at them but couldn't find the right perspective. She woke up and checked to see that the book on her nightstand was still the normal size. What a bizarre stress dream. Was her brain trying to tell her that she needed to think about how she was viewing her life?

Who knew?

At breakfast, Clint and Ivy weren't speaking to each other. And that wasn't normal. Neither of them looked angry. They looked sort of sad or tired.

"What's going on with you two?"

Ivy yawned. "I don't know. We're both wiped out today. And it's not like we did anything strenuous yesterday. It's weird."

Clint reached up and rubbed his eyes. "I feel like I'm in a fog."

That wasn't good. "When did this start?"

"We both woke up tired this morning," Ivy said, "but it's not like we stayed up any later than usual last night."

"Did you do anything different yesterday?"

"No," Ivy said. "I mean we went for a walk and bumped into Henna and her son, but I didn't try to grow anything."

"What did you do?" Bryn didn't like where this was going.

"They showed us a fall flower garden full of mums they're working on," Clint said. "Ivy wanted to try and make a plant grow, but I talked her out of it."

"Now I'm glad he did."

How could they not be putting two and two together? "It has to be Henna," Bryn said. "She was there both times something happened to you."

"No," Ivy said. "She's too nice, and didn't you say Medic Williams checked her out?"

"Can you give me another rational explanation?" Bryn asked.

Clint and Ivy didn't respond.

"Maybe as a chaos magnet I'm jumping the gun, but wouldn't it be better to speak to Medic Williams just in case?"

"What would we tell her?" Ivy asked. "I'm pretty sure she already thinks I'm an idiot."

"Now you're being paranoid. If you're embarrassed to speak to a Medic, why don't you talk to Coach Anderson in Basic Movement?"

"That might work," Clint said. "Because I'm not up to jousting or doing anything else that takes effort today."

In Quintessential Medicine Janelle seemed unusually quiet. "What's wrong?" Bryn asked.

"I went to bed at a normal time last night, but I feel like I need a barrel of coffee or a nap."

"That's weird." She told Janelle about Clint and Ivy.

"That is strange," Janelle said.

"Class," Medic Williams said, "today we have more volunteers asking to be healed. Some of these may be trickier. Don't hesitate to ask for help."

This should be interesting. The classroom door opened and a college-aged guy with auburn hair and the build of a Red came in with an ace bandage wrapped around his right leg from his knee to his ankle. He limped over to Bryn and Janelle's station.

"Hello," he said. "I'm George."

They exchanged introductions. "What did you do?" Bryn asked.

"I took a spill on my motorcycle yesterday. The medics healed the bones and muscles, but I've got a pretty good case of road rash. They said if I let you guys heal the surface scrapes I'd get extra credit. They already fixed the part that hurt so it didn't seem like a big deal."

"Okay. Janelle, do you want to start?" She didn't want to seem bossy.

"No. You have more experience, you should go first."

"Sure. George, can you unwrap your leg so we can see what we're working with?" Bryn asked.

He removed the bandage and Bryn worked at not cringing. It looked like someone had taken a cheese grater to his leg. "You're seriously claiming that doesn't hurt?"

"They gave me a pain reliever. Otherwise, I'd probably be uncomfortable."

That was an understatement. "Okay. I'll start by channeling Quintessence into your leg. If anything feels strange, let me know."

He nodded. Bryn focused on channeling her Quintessence out of her fingertips like healing lasers. The mottled, scabbed up skin turned a healthy color and changed back to a normal, flat surface. She worked on his knee and halfway down his shin before he laughed.

"What?" Bryn asked.

"I had freckles. Can you add those back?"

Bryn blinked and then looked at his other leg. Sure enough, the leg she worked on had pale unblemished, unfreckled skin where the other one had random freckles. "This is a problem I never thought of. Let me get some expert advice." She raised her hand and Medic Williams came over to join them.

Bryn explained the issue and the woman laughed. "This is one of those things you don't think of until it comes up." She touched George's shoulder. "I can restore your freckles after Bryn and Janelle do their work. It's a little too complex for them to handle at this point."

"Who knew freckles were complicated?" Janelle asked.

"Why don't you take over," said Bryn.

Janelle worked steadily, healing a little slower than Bryn had but her work looked good. Thank goodness. Bryn didn't want to have to point out errors because then she'd be the most annoying classmate ever.

By Basic Movement, Bryn hoped that Clint and Ivy would feel better, but they were still foggy. She approached Coach Anderson with them, but they had to wait to talk to her because another student was already complaining to her about not feeling right.

"You're the third student today who's told me they're not feeling well," Coach Anderson said. "I need to get to the bottom of this." She took out her whistle and blew it. Activity all over the gym came to a halt. "Anyone who feels abnormally tired today, come over here. I need a head count."

Bryn backed up as Ivy and Clint joined the group of at least a dozen students surrounding Coach Anderson.

Jaxon came over and stood next to Bryn. "What's going on?"

She explained what Clint and Ivy had told her.

"Maybe Henna is a dragon-pire," he said.

"I know dragons don't typically become ill like humans do," Bryn said. "But is there a dragon flu that sometimes goes around—like in the human world?"

"Not that I'm aware," Jaxon said. "This reeks of foul play."

...

Word went out late Thursday evening that Friday classes would be canceled. All students were asked to stay in their dorms while the Medics investigated the strange energy draining malaise that seemed to be going around campus.

Bryn wandered down to the Blue dorm restaurant in the lobby for breakfast Friday morning wearing yoga pants and a sweatshirt because if she wasn't leaving the dorm she didn't see any reason to follow the dress code. Unfortunately, the rest of the Blue students didn't think like her. Every person she passed, who looked at her like she was a homeless bum, was wearing their dress code-mandated skirts, blouses, and yes, even the archaic panty hose. Not the males, of course. They were in their shirts, dress pants, and ties. Whatever. She was just coming downstairs for carryout. Then she'd hide in her room for the rest of the day and not have to suffer Blue judgment for daring to wear comfortable clothing.

The waiter grinned at her as he handed her two large cups of coffee and a dozen bagels with different flavors of cream cheese.

"What?" she asked.

"You're so normal. Sometimes I forget what that's like working here."

"I'll take that as a compliment."

On the trip back up the stairs she ran into Jaxon. Okay. She didn't literally run into him, but she did cause him to stop and give her the once-over on the stairs.

"What?" she said. "It's not like I'm running around in my pajamas."

"You mean those aren't your pajamas?" he said. "Because I've seen you sleep in something like that before." Okay. Technically she did sleep in these same sort of clothes, but she hadn't slept in this outfit.

"I took a shower and put on clean, comfortable clothes. So sue me." She continued her climb up the stairs to her room.

Being judged by snotty Blues all the time was freaking annoying. If they were still on lockdown tomorrow she'd go down to the restaurant with bedhead just to spite them.

After eating her fill of bagels, she called to check in on Clint and Ivy. Clint answered Ivy's phone, which didn't surprise Bryn. Despite having separate dorm rooms, the two practically lived together.

"How are you guys doing today?" Bryn asked.

"Today we both feel mostly back to normal," Clint said. "Medic Williams gave us a clean bill of health this morning. Last night, she didn't know why we seemed weak."

"Did she mention a cold going around or does she suspect dragon-pires?"

"She didn't think the dragon-pire comment was amusing. She seemed stressed. I think they really are afraid some whacko Silver cult member is going around siphoning Quintessence from students."

"I still don't understand how anyone could energy-suck someone without that person noticing," Bryn said.

"Maybe they're like mosquitoes. They take a small amount of Quintessence and no one notices until it adds up over awhile. Either that or they lull unsuspecting victims into sleep mode, take what they want, and then wake the victims back up."

"This whole thing is creepy," Bryn said. "Were there any common factors between the students who showed symptoms?"

"The only thing they knew last night was that none of the ill students were Blue. I'm not sure what that means."

The information sent Bryn's brain spinning. "I can guess," she said, "Blues aren't touchy-feely...like they don't do casual hugs or pats on the back like the rest of us do."

"So having a stick crammed up your ass could keep you from being the victim of a dragon-pire?" Clint said.

Bryn laughed. "That's one way to put it."

After hanging up with Clint, Bryn did some homework and then read her book for a while. The guy in the story had managed to evict the demon from his body, but his personality changed as a result of what he'd gone through.

Understandable. She'd been through her fair share of weird crap and it had changed her view of the world. Nothing was as black and white as it had seemed before. She no longer thought the Directorate was evil, though she did think that they were a little too sure of their own importance and would benefit from sharing rule with a wider variety of dragons. Even Ferrin, as despicable as he could be, didn't seem like an evil monster. An arrogant asshat...yes. She'd seen him holding Asher and even though the dominant look on his face had been pride, there was some love mixed in there, too...at least she'd like to think there was.

A knock on her door pulled her out of her thoughts. "Who is it?" she asked.

"Who is the only Blue likely to stop by your room?" Jaxon asked through the door.

"Good point." Bryn opened the door. Jaxon still wore the same shirt he'd had on earlier, but he'd lost the tie and changed from dress pants to jeans. "I see even you opted for comfier clothes."

"I did," he said. "If you would put on something resembling appropriate attire to wear in public we could go to the restaurant downstairs for lunch."

"It's only eleven."

"I'm bored and since when are you not hungry?" he asked.

"Another good point." She opened the door wider so he could come in. "Give me a minute." She headed into her room and changed into a pair of dark jeans and a black cashmere sweater. He couldn't argue that cashmere wasn't socially acceptable.

When she came out, he nodded. "Much better. I'm surprised your grandmother hasn't burned all your yoga pants."

"There is nothing wrong with yoga pants."

"If the person wearing them is actually doing yoga, then there is nothing wrong with them. They aren't meant to be a wardrobe staple for people who are too lazy to put on real clothes."

"You're a guy," Bryn said, "so you don't understand."

"You can enlighten me after we're seated for lunch." He opened the door. "Let's go."

As they walked down the stairs, Bryn nodded at the Blues they came across. They all nodded back. It was so bizarre that being pledged to marry Jaxon had taken her off the social pariah list...at least when it came to greeting people in passing.

They had to wait a few minutes for a table because half the students seemed to have descended on the restaurant at the same time.

Once they were seated, Jaxon said, "Why does me being male keep me from understanding yoga pants?"

"Real pants aren't comfortable," Bryn said.

"They're pants," Jaxon said. "How can they not be comfortable?"

"Girls go in at the waist and out at the hips and the pants don't always follow the same line, which means the seam for the waistband can end up digging into your hip the entire day and that leaves an uncomfortable red mark which is why most women change into yoga pants as soon as they come home."

"You wear skirts to class," Jaxon said. "So your argument is invalid."

"Have you ever tried wearing panty hose?" She was pretty sure she knew the answer to that question, but it was fun to see the expression of horror on his face.

"Of course not."

"Well, they are ten times worse than pants—with elastic waistbands that never seem to hit in the right place."

"So basically, you're telling me that the clothes you wear in public every day are uncomfortable and you wait to go back to your room and change into yoga pants because they are comfortable."

"Yes."

"Maybe you should buy better clothes," he said.

She rolled her eyes and picked up the menu. After they ordered, Jaxon started a new topic of conversation. "Have you heard anything about how the investigation is going?"

"No. Clint and Ivy asked about Silver Cult dragon-pires, and the Medics didn't think it was funny."

"I mentioned your theory to my father and he said that kind of unfounded wild speculation would only cause panic."

"That's me," Bryn said. "A wild speculator."

Jaxon snorted. "I believe it's worth looking into because I can't think of another explanation."

"Here's an interesting fact. Clint said that no Blues had been reported ill."

"So you think a Blue might be behind this?"

"No. I mean, I hadn't thought that until you suggested it. I was going more with the idea that you guys aren't touchy feely. Someone has to touch you to siphon energy. Blues don't do casual touches like the other Clans."

"See, being an elitist is better for your health," he said.

Bryn laughed.

Chapter Seventeen

After lunch Bryn felt antsy. "I don't want to go back to my room. I wish we could go for a walk."

"We could walk the stairs," Jaxon suggested.

That didn't sound like a fabulous fun time, but it's not like she had a better idea. "Okay."

They walked up the three flights of stairs and were about to turn back around when Bryn noticed a side door that said Exit. She pointed at it. "Where does that lead?"

"To some sort of attic or roof access would be my guess," he said.

"Cool." She headed for the door.

Jaxon caught her arm before she could open the door. "You can't go out there."

"Why? Do you think Quintessence sucking dragon-pires are holding a secret meeting on our roof?"

"No," he said. "But we're supposed to stay in the dorm."

"It's not like I'm leaving the dorm. I'm just going to walk around on the top of it." She could tell he was considering the idea. "Come on. You know you want to check it out."

He frowned. "Only so I can keep an eye on you."

She pushed the door open and climbed the flight of stairs, which led to a short hallway and what appeared to be storage areas.

"I guess no one lives up here," Bryn said.

"I guess not." Jaxon pointed to a door at the end of the hall. It bore a sign that said Roof Access. Emergency Exit. There was a fire alarm to the right of the door. "If we open that it will probably set off an alarm."

Bryn walked closer to the door. "It doesn't say there is an alarm."

"Do you want to test that theory?"

"Yes." Before he could argue, she grabbed the handle and turned it. The door opened without a sound. Grinning, she turned back to Jaxon. "You were saying?"

He glared at her.

She laughed and walked through the door and into a stairwell, which led up to yet another landing. Before Jaxon could rain on her parade, she darted up the steps and pushed the door open and then...nothing. No one was on the roof. She inhaled the fresh air and enjoyed the sensation of sunlight on her face. Maybe they could just hang out up here for a while.

She heard Jaxon running up the stairs behind her. He stood by her side and looked around. "This is underwhelming," he said.

"Yes, but it's a nice day," Bryn said.

"We're not staying up here," Jaxon said.

"How'd you know that was my next suggestion?" Bryn had just thought of it herself.

"One of the side effects of us spending time together is that I've learned how you think."

"That's just one of the side effects? What's another one?" Bryn asked.

"I've developed the uncanny ability to find food, because I've been around you when you're hungry and it's not pretty."

She laughed. "You speak the truth." What had she learned about him? "You like everything to be planned out and to follow a schedule."

"And yet life never seems to work that way," he said. "Come on. We should go back downstairs before someone notices our absence and sends out a search party."

"Fine." She followed him back inside. As she shut the rooftop access door, she said, "Do you think this should have been connected to some sort of alarm?"

"Probably. I'll send word to my father. He can do what he wants with the information."

They headed back downstairs to the second floor; when they'd almost reached her dorm room door, Jaxon's friend Quentin approached from the opposite direction.

"I need to speak to Quentin," Jaxon said. "So I'll see you later."

"Excuse me?" Was he blowing her off?

He stopped walking and turned to look back at her. "We ate lunch and took a walk. I think that's enough bonding time for one day."

"Fine by me. This was your idea in the first place." She continued to her room. Once she was inside, she leaned back against the door. Huh? Why did it feel like she'd been blown off? And why did it bother her? It's not like she wanted to spend time with Jaxon.

She was, however, annoyed. Why? She headed for the couch, flopped down, and grabbed a throw pillow, playing with the fringed edge. Mentally, she ran over the day's events in her head. Maybe she was annoyed because she'd had fun with him. They'd talked and joked around. She'd had one of those even though my life has been hijacked and I'm being forced to marry my former frenemy it's okay because we're in this together kind of camaraderie moments. And then he'd declared his obligation done and headed off to be with his actual friend.

Then again, maybe she was irked because she didn't want to be alone right now, but none of her friends lived in the same dorm. That had to be it. She was irritated that he had friends while they were on lockdown, and she didn't.

Bryn's phone rang at eight thirty that night. Hopefully, it would be good news. She set her book down and picked up the receiver. "Hello?"

"Hello, Bryn." It was her grandmother. "How are you?"

"Feeling a little stir-crazy, but other than that, I'm good."

"You'll be happy to know that the restrictions should be lifted tomorrow morning."

"Did the investigators figure something out?" Bryn asked.

"You must keep this to yourself, but they've investigated every lead. They're going to let students roam about campus again, with heightened security in the hopes of capturing someone in the act."

"They're using students as bait?" Bryn asked. That didn't sound right.

"No. They are using several college students who volunteered as bait. Since one of them is your former friend, Zavien, I wanted to warn you not to speak with him because he'll be wearing a recording device."

"So if I said something snarky about Jaxon, his father would hear it," Bryn said.

"You can interpret my message that way if you like. I just didn't want you interfering in the investigation since you have a way of ending up in the middle of things."

"I'm hoping that trend is over," Bryn said. "Can I tell Clint and Ivy to watch what they say?"

"You can tell them security has been heightened so they should be careful with what they say, but don't mention the college students."

"I understand." While she had her grandmother on the line, she might as well bring up something that had been on her mind. "Do you think we could have lunch with mom at some point in the near future?"

"Well...Ephram is not ready to speak to your mother yet, but I think we could manage a civil lunch on neutral ground...maybe someplace in Dragon's Bluff, like Suzette's."

"I'd love that," Bryn said.

"How are things going with Jaxon?"

There wasn't anyone else she could talk to about Jaxon. "Something he did annoyed me." She told her grandmother about him sort of blowing her off after lunch, but she omitted the part about them heading up to the roof.

"So he asked you to lunch, went for a walk with you, and then went about his day like you were unimportant to him," her grandmother said.

That summed it up in a not so positive nutshell. "Sort of. Maybe I'm just being overly sensitive."

"Jaxon may be more evolved than men of past generations, but his actions today prove he isn't too far removed from them. You can expect his dismissive behavior to continue and you can let it annoy you or you can learn not to be bothered by it. I suggest the latter. Your life may be intertwined with his, but it is still your own. Develop your friendships and your hobbies because you will need both later in life."

That was not the answer she'd been hoping for. "I don't understand why he runs hot and cold. He acts like he's my friend and then once he's met his goal, he bails. It's weird. That's not how you're supposed to treat your friends."

"I'm not sure Westgates have friends," her grandmother said. "Ferrin has allies and enemies. That's about it."

"But Jaxon has friends he hangs out with," Bryn said.

He'd just taken off with Quentin.

"I hope he does, but I'm not sure you should count on being one of them."

"This conversation is starting to suck," Bryn complained.

"I'll always tell you the truth, even if it's not something you want to hear," her grandmother said.

...

Bryn strolled around campus after breakfast Saturday morning with Clint and Ivy. "Both of you guys are feeling better now?"

Clint nodded. Ivy said, "We're back to normal. I have no idea what that was about. At least it went away quickly."

"And hopefully, it won't come back," Clint said.

Bryn stretched, enjoying the warmth of the sunshine and the early morning breeze. "It feels so good to be outside."

"Agreed," Clint said. "It's not like I'm claustrophobic but the walls of my dorm room felt like they were closing in on me."

"I know what you mean," Bryn said. "And I only had Jaxon for company which was kind of depressing. Which reminds me, I want your opinion on something." She told them about Jaxon's dismissive behavior. "Am I just being a drama queen?"

"Not necessarily," Ivy said. "He does change moods on a regular basis."

"Here's my question," Clint said. "Why do you expect him to act any different than he always has?"

"Because of the way he acts like we're a team when we're in public," Bryn said. "I don't understand how it can totally be an act. Instead of acting like he's my friend, why not just be my friend? It's not that hard."

"As long as you're fed and caffeinated on a regular basis, you're pretty easy to get along with," Clint said.

"I know. So why does he flip back and forth like this?"

"Ask him," Ivy said. "You can guess all you want, but he's the only one who has the answer."

"True, but what are the odds his answer won't make me want to blast him to a cinder?"

"Given his history, zero to none," Clint said. "He is who he is. An elitist asshat with occasional moments of niceness."

Bryn sat on a bench under one of the new trees in the recently restored green areas. "Every time I think I have a handle on my life, someone switches up the cast or changes the rules."

"Look at it this way," Ivy said. "The cast for your future is pretty well set. Maybe not with the people you expected or necessarily wanted, but at least they shouldn't be changing."

"True." Maybe she just needed to sit down with Jaxon and hash this out. If he said he wasn't interested in a real friendship then she could move on...or flash fry him, depending on his level of rudeness.

"So have you heard anything about dragon-pires?" Clint asked.

"No, but I do know the powers that be are upping security again just in case someone evil really is running around campus."

"Great," Clint said. "So we have to assume that someone is watching us all the time?"

"Watching or listening," Bryn said. "And that used to annoy me, but now I kind of understand."

"It was only a matter of time," Clint stage whispered to Ivy. "Bryn has turned into the establishment."

"That is a scary thought," Bryn said. And it might not be far from the truth, which was truly frightening.

That night, Bryn called Jaxon's room. He answered on the third ring.

"Do you have time to stop by for a few minutes?" she asked. "I want to talk to you about something."

"How long will it take? I'm meeting friends in fifteen minutes."

That probably wasn't enough time. "Never mind. Call me when you have half an hour to spare."

"What's this about?" he asked.

"It's nothing life endangering," she said. "Call me tomorrow some time."

"Okay." And he hung up.

Maybe calling him had been a mistake. Asking him if he could be her real friend sounded sort of desperate and ridiculous. His actions would prove more than his words. She should just forget about having any touchy feely moments with him and move on with her life.

Chapter Eighteen

Bryn stared into her armoire, trying to find a balance between the person she was now and the person she was before she'd come to the Institute for Excellence. Her grandmother loved shopping and had succeeded in replacing most of Bryn's casual clothes with nicer high-end clothing. Not that Bryn minded. Her grandmother had been very generous, but sometimes the clothes made her feel like an imposter.

She grabbed her favorite jeans. Should she wear them? Would her mom wear jeans to a lunch this important? Then again, who knew what her mother had to wear. It's not like she could have brought much with her when she'd been running for her life.

Should she call her mom and ask if she needed to borrow something? Why hadn't she thought of this sooner? Nothing to be done about it now. She checked the alarm clock on her dresser. Her grandmother would arrive to pick her up in twenty minutes. Time to stop worrying about things beyond her control. She picked a simple navy dress and boots. That should appease her grandmother and not look too uppity to her mom.

How would her mom be traveling to Suzette's? That was another question Bryn hadn't thought to ask. The students who traveled from Sanctuary came by SUV, so hopefully transportation would be provided. Why was she focusing on these things? Probably because she was worried about how her mom and grandmother would deal with being in the same room after all this time.

Half an hour later, Bryn was hugging her mom in the nice back room of the restaurant while her grandmother acknowledged Sara with a nod.

"Mother," Sara said. "It's nice to see you."

Marie Sinclair gave a tight smile. "Nice to see you, too, Sara."

The waitress delivered a round of ice water and left them to read the menu. From behind the piece of laminated plastic, Bryn said, "I don't suppose there's a way to skip over the awkward part and just be happy that we're taking a step in the right direction?"

Her mom and her grandmother both snorted in the exact same manner. Bryn laughed. "That must be genetic."

"Perhaps," her grandmother said.

Sara set her menu down. "I want to thank you for all you've done for Bryn. I know it couldn't have been easy when you first met."

"We had a bumpy start," Marie Sinclair said, "but eventually we found our footing."

"I've corrupted her a bit," Bryn whispered in a conspiratorial tone. "She says things like 'That sucks' now."

Sara laughed. "I can't imagine those words coming out of your mouth."

"We've all changed," Marie said. "And no matter how at odds you and I may be, I commend you on raising such a strong-willed, loyal daughter."

"She is pretty great," Sara said.

Their food arrived. As they ate and made small talk, Bryn ignored the other patrons of the restaurant who seemed to be watching and waiting to see what would happen.

"Should I just stand up and announce that there isn't going to be a battle so everyone can go back to minding their own business?" Bryn asked.

"No," her mother and grandmother said in tandem. Again they sounded exactly the same, which made Bryn laugh. "I never noticed the similarities in your mannerisms and some of the things you say," Bryn said.

"How are things out at Sanctuary?" Marie asked.

"We're comfortable," Sara said. "And everyone there seems to be genuinely happy that they no longer have to hide who they are."

Marie opened her mouth like she planned to say something and then she paused. "There are so many things I want to say. Questions I want to ask about the path you chose, but this is not the place."

Uh-oh. It was only natural that her grandmother would be hurt by what her mom had done...running away in the middle of the night...rejecting everything she'd ever been taught about loyalty to the Clan.

"I'm sorry for the pain I caused you," Sara said. "But if I hadn't done what I did, Bryn wouldn't exist."

"Think of me as a sarcastic consolation prize," Bryn said in an attempt to lighten the mood.

Her grandmother didn't smile or respond in any manner.

Damn. Damn. Damn.

What could she say to appease her grandmother? "Maybe fate is trying to heal this rift by having Jaxon and I marry. The Sinclairs and the Westgates are coming together in a different way than originally intended, but it's still happening. Does that help?" Bryn asked, hoping she hadn't laid it on too thick.

"A bit," her grandmother said. "I suggest we stick to less inflammatory topics for the remainder of this meal."

Now what? Bryn racked her brain for an interesting topic. "Jaxon likes to read," she said. "So we're having reading dates. He brings cookies and milk and we each enjoy our books without talking to one another."

"A Westgate brings you cookies and milk?" Her mom laughed.

"I'm glad to see you're finding a way to make the situation work," her grandmother said.

Was that a slap at her mom?

Her mom didn't seem to notice, so Bryn decided to ignore it, too.

The rest of lunch was tense, but civil.

After they finished dessert, her grandmother said, "Bryn, why don't you come back to the house with me? I want to talk to you about the Christmas Ball."

And that was a pretty clear signal that her mom and dad wouldn't be invited, which is what her mom had expected and probably preferred. "Sure."

They exited the restaurant together. All three of them headed over to the corner lot where SUVs waited to drive passengers where they needed to go.

"It was nice seeing you, Mother," Sara said.

"It was. Over time I think it will become easier," Marie reached over and touched her daughter on the cheek. Then she dropped her hand and backed up a step. "But I'll never truly be able to forgive you."

Wham! Bryn sucked in a breath. It felt like someone had punched her in the gut. From the look on her mom's face, she felt the same way.

"I understand," Sara said in a tight voice. "I regret that my actions hurt you, but I don't, for one second, regret the path I chose." She put her hand on Bryn's shoulder. "Hopefully, we'll come to an understanding that will benefit Bryn."

"I believe we will. Bryn, I'll wait by the car while you say goodbye to your mother." Marie walked over to the black SUV where her regular driver sat waiting for them.

Feeling shell-shocked, Bryn just looked at her mom. "I don't know what to say."

Her mom pulled her into a hug. "There's nothing to say. I knew how this would end before we sat down to lunch, but she still caught me off guard. For now, this is the best happily ever after you can expect."

Bryn released her mom and backed up a step. "We'll plan a pre-Christmas or a post-Christmas celebration at your cabin."

"That will work," her mom said.

Bryn schooled her features into a non judgmental smile as she joined her grandmother in their car. Her best defense against becoming overly emotional would be to focus on something else. Something her grandmother would be excited about. "So what do you have planned for the Christmas Ball?"

"This year I thought we'd have silver and gold trees rather than the traditional green."

"Sounds pretty." Would the trees be made of real silver and gold? "What color ornaments would you use?"

"I'm of two minds. My first thought was to decorate with blue, but then I thought about decorating the gold trees with silver and vice versa."

"If you go with gold and silver, maybe the stars on top could be blue or have blue in them?"

"That might work. We'll draw up some samples and see which is more eye-catching."

Once they were back at the Sinclair Estate, in the atrium, Bryn watched as her grandmother sketched trees decorated with different color combinations. They had avoided any mention of the lunch or her mother and that's how Bryn wanted to keep it.

"Can we put a tree near Ferrin's table with a bunch of S's on it?" Bryn asked.

Her grandmother laughed. "I'm not sure he'd find that amusing, but that does remind me of something. Lillith has asked several times if you and Jaxon planned to move in with them while your estate was being built."

"Wait." Bryn held her hand out to signal her grandmother should stop speaking. "I hadn't planned on thinking about this until I was legally old enough to drink." Because the idea of living under the same roof as Ferrin was enough to drive anyone to drink.

"There's something Lillith doesn't know," her grandmother said. "It's something even Ephram doesn't know."

Now she was curious. "What?"

"I designed an estate for your mother. I meant to give it to her as a wedding gift."

"So you drew up plans for their home?" Bryn asked.

"I did," her grandmother said. "But there's more to it than that. The estate is partially built. We stopped construction when...when I realized the house would no longer be needed. Right now it's a shell with a few interior rooms. The plumbing and electricity haven't been hooked up. There's no flooring or paint on the walls, but the structure is there. Would you like to see it?"

"Yes." For several reasons. Not having to live in a house with Ferrin would be the best present ever. Plus knowing that her grandmother had put so much effort and care into something that had sat idle all these years made Bryn's heart hurt.

"Let's go." Her grandmother led her down to the hairpin drive where a car waited for them. She instructed the driver where to go. Five minutes of twists and turns through the forest and Bryn had no idea how far they'd traveled in a straight line when they came upon a house that looked like it belonged someplace sunny. The stone was the color of sand. There were columns along a massive front porch that led to a front door. The structure was at least three stories high and had wings that jutted out diagonally.

"It's beautiful," Bryn said. "And you designed it?"

"I did."

"Can we go inside?"

Rather than answer, her grandmother exited the vehicle.

Bryn followed her to the front door, which her grandmother opened with a key. Since there were no curtains on the windows enough natural light filtered in so that Bryn could see the amazing spiral design of the foyer floor. Unlike Sinclair Estate, everything in this house was made of light stone, mixed with off-white and light gray. Veins of silver ran through the floor and the walls.

"It's amazing. It's so light and happy."

"I'd hoped it would help your mother acclimate to her new situation."

Bryn looked at her grandmother. "You knew how disagreeable Ferrin was and you were trying to help by designing the most pleasant house possible."

Her grandmother nodded.

The depth of what her grandmother did hit home. "I can't imagine how hurt you were...and I'm so sorry. I hope I can make up for some of what she did."

"You have, and I think you will," her grandmother said. "It means a great deal to me that you understand and appreciate this house. I hope Jaxon agrees to move here."

Bryn laughed. "This is where I'm going to live, so he better plan on joining me."

"I considered giving this to you as your Christmas present this year as a surprise but Ephram would be furious if I didn't tell him about it beforehand, and Ferrin might be insulted if he was caught unaware."

"The part about insulting Ferrin sounds good," Bryn said. Should she mention something about how her mom had made the right decision? Even though she felt her mom was in the right, because she wouldn't exist if things hadn't worked out this way, she didn't want to offend her grandmother.

"Something you wanted to say?" her grandmother asked.

Crap. She needed to think of something else fast. "It's just weird to be thinking about marriage and moving into a house. I'm in my last year of high school and I have at least four years of college in front of me to become a Medic." A strange thought occurred. "No one has ever mentioned when I'm supposed to get married. I'm guessing after college."

Her grandmother nodded. "Most dragons marry after they finish their degrees, though some marry before."

"We'll be going with the after plan," Bryn said.

"That will give us plenty of time to finish your new home," her grandmother said.

Bryn glanced around. "It's lovely."

"I'm so glad you like it." Her grandmother blinked and looked away. "Your mother... she never noticed or recognized the things I tried to do to make her life easier."

Damn. Damn. Damn. She needed to say something. "I'm sorry for the pain she caused you, but I wouldn't be here if she hadn't abandoned ship. And I do see all the nice things you've done to help me acclimate to my new life and to the idea of marrying Jaxon and I really do appreciate it."

"Thank you," her grandmother said. "Now why don't we go home and look through some decorating magazines and I'll take you back to the Institute after dinner."

"I'd like that."

Chapter Nineteen

Bryn had just made it back to her room and changed into her yoga pants and a sweatshirt when someone knocked on her door.

"Who is it?" Bryn asked, even though there weren't that many people who'd be dropping by on a Sunday evening.

"It's me." Jaxon's voice came through the door.

Bryn opened the door and said, "Maybe we should develop a secret knock so I'll know it's you."

Jaxon walked in and headed for the library table. "When is it not me?" he asked as he pulled out a chair. "Clint and Ivy arrive by the terrace window. Who else knocks on your door?"

"Other people visit me," Bryn protested because he made it sound like she had no friends.

"Of course they do," he said like he didn't believe her. "What did you want to talk to me about?"

Crap. Did she really want to talk about the whole friendship situation? It might be best just to let this situation play out. If she didn't say anything what other reason could she give for asking him to come over and talk?

"Okay. This is going to sound strange," she said. "And you can't mention it to anyone...especially your parents."

Jaxon narrowed his eyes. "How scary is this confession going to be?"

"It's not a confession." Bryn laughed. "It's just something that I am supposed to be keeping secret but since it directly affects you, I wanted to let you know."

"Fine. I'll keep whatever it is to myself."

"Good." She sat across from him. "My grandmother, who has excellent taste and is an amazing interior designer, may have started building us an estate."

"Excuse me?" He leaned forward.

Not the response she'd hoped for. "If you remember correctly, your mother expected us to move in with her while our estate was being built. My grandmother loves to design things, and I have no desire to live at Westgate Estate. The good news is, nothing is definite yet as far as the interior goes, so you can still have input. Although I will veto any large W's that you might plan on sprinkling about the house."

Gobsmacked is the only word that fit the expression on Jaxon's face. "I'll just wait until you can form coherent sentences," she said.

"I've put zero thought into where we'll live or what type of house we'll have," he said. "That's years away."

"Four years," Bryn said. "At least that's what my grandmother said."

"Right. After we graduate from college...that's when we'd marry and move in together...into a house your grandmother decided to build for us. Doesn't that strike you as odd?"

"Nothing about my life falls into the normal range," Bryn said. "Telling you about this seems strange but keeping it from you seemed less than honest."

He nodded. "I appreciate that you shared the information rather than keeping it from me, but I'm not prepared to deal with that level of reality. Your grandmother does have impeccable taste. The only W's I'll require are on the front gates. That is non-negotiable."

"I can live with that." The monogrammed silverware she would bury in a storage closet somewhere, never to be seen again.

He eyed her suspiciously. "Do you have any other disturbing news you'd like to share, or are we done?"

"We're done."

"I'm going to pretend we never had this conversation." He stood and exited her room.

She locked the door behind him. Should she have mentioned the friend issue? Maybe, but it could have been so awkward. This way he wouldn't be mad at Christmas if her grandmother did give her the house as a present. The idea made her laugh. A house, actually a ginormous estate with more rooms than any sane person would ever need, might be given to her as a gift. Her life was bizarre.

...

The dining hall was noisier than normal for breakfast on a Monday. Bryn frowned as she stirred sugar into her coffee. "Why is everyone so chatty this morning?"

"Once again," Clint said, "you are out of the loop."

"Of course I am." She sipped her coffee, assuming either he or Ivy would fill her in.

"Rumors about evil Silver dragon-pires have gone mainstream," Ivy said. "And everyone is freaking out."

"Understandable, but how did people hear about them?" Bryn asked.

Ivy and Clint exchanged a glance. "Well...a college student was found last night after curfew. He was disoriented and feverish, so the guards took him to the Medics rather than throwing him into one of those lovely cells under the library."

"Thank goodness," Bryn said. "With the way things have been going around here, I'm surprised they didn't arrest him for loitering."

"Apparently, he'd volunteered to help track down any suspicious characters on campus," Ivy said. "And he ran into more trouble than he could handle."

A feeling of unease brushed across the back of Bryn's neck like a chill breeze. "Was it Zavien?"

"How'd you guess?" Clint asked.

She didn't want to mention that she'd known of his involvement and not shared, so she improvised. "After his involvement with Nola, it sounds like something he'd do to show whose side he's on."

"I'm sure you're right," Ivy said. "But there's more to the story. Supposedly, he was wearing a wire, but when they found him the recording equipment was gone."

"So whoever fed on him figured it out and took the recordings," Bryn said.

"That's the general theory," Clint said. "I'm surprised they didn't order us all to stay in our dorms today."

"The dragon-pire could be anyone or several anyones so there's no telling where you'd be safe. I guess the moral of the story is don't go anywhere alone," Ivy said. "And speaking of going places, how did lunch with your mother and grandmother go?"

Bryn slumped in her seat. "About as good as it could." She told them about her grandmother's announcement that she'd never forgive her daughter for what she'd done. "I feel like I'm caught in the middle of this surreal argument no one can win."

"What your parents did was incredibly brave," Ivy said. "Abandoning their entire way of life for love."

"Although karma does seem to be kicking you in the ass by tangling your life up with Jaxon's," Clint added.

"Did you talk things out with him yesterday?" Ivy asked.

"No. After lunch with my mother and grandmother it didn't seem like such a big deal." Plus she didn't want to seem desperate. "I figure my relationship with Jaxon will change and evolve over time. Asking him to define it will just make the whole thing more awkward."

"And it seems plenty awkward already," Clint said.

"Thanks for pointing that out."

In Advanced Elemental Science, Mr. Stanton hadn't bothered with a seating chart, which was unusual. Bryn sat next to Clint and Ivy. Jaxon sat a few seats away.

"Class, I need your full attention. I'm sure you heard that the guards found a disoriented student and escorted him to the Medics for treatment. It has been determined that someone drugged him and then siphoned off his Quintessence. While I have heard the term dragon-pire thrown around campus, there is no such thing. In the past there were cult members who attempted to feed off all the clans in order to obtain their breath weapons. Doing this supposedly made them more powerful overall and had the side effect of turning their eyes and hair silver which is why they were called Silvers. Given their level of mastery over Quintessence, they would then alter their hair and eye color to blend in with the general population."

"Dragon-pire seems more accurate," Clint said.

"It's also more inflammatory. And it implies some undead villain from a movie who converts people into children of the night. I don't know who coined the phrase, but whoever it was"—Mr. Stanton eyeballed Clint like he knew the truth—"should stop using the term."

"Not to be disrespectful," Jaxon said, "but what we call them doesn't really matter. What matters is finding them and stopping them."

"Agreed, and a lot of people are working toward that end. For now, keep in mind that the sole reason someone is doing this could be to cause friction between the Clans and the Hybrids. Don't jump to any conclusions about who is behind this. And... It would be best if students didn't travel anywhere alone."

After their last class, Clint and Ivy went to Bryn's dorm room to hang out and do homework, which meant that Bryn and Ivy did homework while Clint built card houses.

"Is it cheating if I push the first level of cards down into the carpet a bit?" Clint asked as he slid the card back and forth, embedding it in the carpet fiber.

"That's how my dad always started," Bryn said. She finished writing a five-paragraph essay and then set her pen down.

"Mr. Stanton was none too happy about the whole dragon-pire name," Clint said. "And he seems to know I started it."

"You do have that special skill set," Bryn said. "Annoying people far and wide."

"It's a gift," Clint said.

"In theory, any dragon could siphon Quintessence from another dragon," Ivy said. "I can't decide which would be better. The Silver cult reviving, or crazy dragons who want us to think the cult has revived to make us distrust hybrids."

"If it's just someone wanting to disturb the fragile peace," Bryn said, "there are a lot of easier ways to do that."

"Do you think someone could be doing it to create a distraction?" Ivy asked.

"Maybe," Bryn said. "But why? What activity are they trying to keep hidden?"

"Who knows," Clint said. "But they managed to shut down the campus for an entire day. If they were searching for something like more of those evil tyrant crowns or a secret doorway leading to a hidden treasure, they would have been able to explore the campus at will."

"That's an interesting idea," Bryn said.

A knock sounded on her door. Since both her friends were present, she said, "Jaxon, is that you?"

"Yes," he said.

She stood and opened the door. He was wearing a smirk which usually accompanied some mandate from his mother and her grandmother. She waved him into the room. "What joyous news are you here to share?"

"Apparently, we're having a pre-holiday celebration at your grandparents' house."

"We? Who's we?" Because she was okay with hanging around Jaxon and Lillith, but there was only so much time she could spend in Ferrin's company.

"My family, including Asher, and your family, minus your father."

It took her a moment to process what he'd said. "So my mother is supposed to mingle with your father?"

"I thought you'd be more upset that your dad wasn't included," Jaxon said.

Bryn laughed. "Inviting my father to spend time around your father would result in bloodshed, so that part doesn't surprise me. And I knew my mom wouldn't be invited to the Christmas ball, but I didn't expect this. Whose idea was it?"

"It may have been my mother's. I think she's feeling overly maternal and wants to make sure that your mother has a chance to spend part of the holidays with you."

"That's sweet," Ivy said.

"And a bit twisted," Clint added.

Jaxon shoved his hands in his front pockets. "I have no answers. I'm just delivering the news."

There was something he wasn't telling her. "There's more, isn't there?"

"We're supposed to exchange gifts," Jaxon said.

"All of us?"

"No. You and I are supposed to show how we're the perfect couple by exchanging the perfect gifts."

"Says who?" Bryn asked.

"Does it matter? Each couple is supposed to exchange gifts."

"Which means my mom will be left out of the loop, which is kind of bullshit."

"That may be the point," Jaxon said.

"So you're inviting Bryn's mom to a party so that she can be with Bryn during the holidays, but also so you can point out that she doesn't fit with the group," Clint said. "Or am I misreading the situation?"

"You're reading it correctly," Jaxon said.

"This sucks," Bryn said. "If your mom was the one trying to make nice, who insisted on the gift exchange?"

"Take your pick...my father or either of your grandparents," Jaxon said. "Honestly, I think you should suggest that your mom refuse the invitation. No good can come of this. You and my mother are the only ones who will be trying to make nice. Everyone else will be attempting to put your mother in her place."

"Including you?" Bryn asked. Because they needed to straighten that shit out right away.

"You've made no secret about your feelings for my father," Jaxon said. "While I won't be openly rude to your mother, I have no desire to spend time with her."

Well, crap. When he put it that way...

"You thought you had the moral high ground, didn't you?" Jaxon raised an eyebrow.

"No comment." Bryn cleared her throat. "Now that my parents are back in the picture, I will do my best to be grudgingly respectful toward your father, if you'll do the same for my parents."

"That's not really equal," Clint said. "Because you like his mom."

Bryn laughed. "Clint is right."

"That doesn't change anything," Jaxon said. "We'll agree to be civil and moderately respectful. If I were you, I'd call your grandmother and try to cancel the gift exchange idea. Tell her we'd rather exchange gifts on our own or something like that."

"Do we have to buy something for each other?" Bryn asked.

"It's Christmas," Jaxon said, like that explained everything.

"Can we just agree to give gifts to charities in each other's names?" Bryn asked because that would make her life so much easier.

"What does the Blue half of your genes say to that question?" Jaxon asked. "What are the gifts truly for?"

Bryn groaned. "That's right. I forgot. I'll be buying you a gift to show everyone how much money I have and you actually liking the present is irrelevant."

"Wrong," Jaxon said. "You're supposed to buy a gift the person will like that will also inspire jealousy in others because they can't afford it."

"Wow," Ivy said. "That's all sorts of screwed up."

"It's a game," Jaxon said. "And Bryn needs to learn how to play it."

Bryn stomped her feet like a toddler. "I don't want to."

"That was funny," Jaxon said, pointing at her obviously fake performance. "But you still have to do it."

"Ugh," Bryn said. "Any other happy news you'd like to share?"

"No. That's all the joy and light I have to shed on your life this evening," he said. "I'll let myself out."

Bryn watched as he left. Then she turned to her friends. "What in the hell am I supposed to buy a Westgate for Christmas?"

"A diamond studded jock strap?" Clint suggested.

"Ewww," Bryn said. "Thank you for putting that bizarre image into my brain."

Ivy laughed.

Chapter Twenty

Tuesday morning, Bryn whacked her alarm clock with her Proper Decorum book. It did little damage but at least the blasted alarm turned off. Now what? Maybe she'd ask her grandmother for a small coffeemaker for her room. Something she could keep on her nightstand so she could roll over and suck down some caffeine first thing in the morning before getting out of bed.

She stumbled to the other bedroom to turn off its alarm. Why hadn't someone invented an alarm clock that brewed coffee? Maybe she'd mention that to Garret. He or one of the other Green dragons could come up with a line of alarm clocks that made coffee and cooked breakfast...something simple like toast. That would make it way easier to wake up every day.

Bryn yawned and made her way to the shower. It felt like she was moving in slow motion this morning. Once she was clean and presentable per the school dress code, she grabbed her books and checked the time. She was running about fifteen minutes late, so she dashed down the stairs. She'd just hit the lobby when she realized she'd left her essay for Mr. Stanton on the coffee table.

Crap. She ran back upstairs to get it. Now she was running even later. No big deal. She could suck down breakfast faster than most people on a normal day.

She headed out the front door of the dorm and down the sidewalk at a brisk pace. The air had a nip in it that said snow might not be far off. She couldn't wait for the first snow. There were a few straggling students like her, walking down the sidewalk in a daze. She had to step off the pavement to avoid a student who was carrying a giant painting.

"Sorry," he said. "Curse of the art student."

Bryn smiled. No harm done.

"Excuse me," a voice came from a few feet away. Someone was standing under one of the new groves of trees that Ivy had helped to grow. The branches hanging down obscured the person's face. "Can you help me?" The person's voice was a bit hoarse, like they didn't feel well.

Bryn's safety alert went off. Should she walk over and see what the person wanted? There were a few students out and about, so it's not like she was climbing into a windowless van because some stranger offered her candy. Still, she didn't want to get too close. She walked over within a few feet of the person. "What's wrong?"

"I don't know. I'm dizzy."

A college-aged Green male Bryn didn't know came down the sidewalk toward her. "Hey, can you come over here?" she said. "Someone needs help."

The Green stopped walking and studied Bryn. "Why aren't you helping him?"

"I was going to, but I thought it might be better if more than one person offered assistance." Why does this guy not understand there's safety in numbers?

"He might need help walking."

"Okay." The Green accompanied Bryn over to the person standing under the tree. It was another Green male, but his dark complexion looked a little pale.

"What's wrong?" Bryn asked, feeling better about the situation now that she had backup.

"Nothing that a snack won't fix," the guy said. And then he lunged for Bryn.

What the hell? She stumbled backward into the arms of the other Green.

"Don't worry," he said. "I've got you." And then he smacked a white rag over her nose and mouth.

Bryn inhaled to blast the attacker with flames. The strong scent of chemicals filled her nose and made her lightheaded. She tried to shift, but her body felt fuzzy and distant. This could not be happening. She growled and sparks shot from her hands, but she couldn't concentrate to shoot a fireball. If she could get the damn cloth away from her face. Every breath made her lose a little more control. She tried holding her breath and shoving at the rag.

That didn't work, so she turned her head, opened her mouth, and bit down as hard as she could on her captor's arm through the rag. He yelped, but she hadn't even broken the skin. Stupid rag. Stupid drugs. Stupid dragon-pires. And the world went dark.

"Bryn?" Another chemical smell hit her. She tried to jerk her head away but moving was difficult.

"She's awake," a voice said.

Where was she? She opened her eyes but the world was blurry. Panicked, she pushed at the hands pressing against her head and shoulders.

"Don't fight us, Bryn. This is Medic Williams. We're treating you."

Thank God. The fight or flight instinct drained away as the sensation of warmth flowed over her body. Being treated with Quintessence felt like being wrapped in a warm cocoon. She was safe now. After a few moments she became more aware of the people around her.

"What happened?" she asked, her voice came out like a harsh whisper.

"Someone fed on you." Wait a minute. She recognized that voice. She turned her head to see if she was right. "Zavien?"

"You're dehydrated. Drink." Zavien held a glass toward her with a straw. She sipped the water as he held the straw in place. "You're disoriented, your head hurts, and your vision is blurry. It sucks, but give the Medics an hour and you'll be back to yourself."

Bryn released the straw. "Dragon-pires?" she asked.

"I don't find that name amusing," Medic Williams snapped.

"It's pretty accurate," Zavien said.

"What can you tell us about the attacker?" Medic William asked.

There was something she needed to remember. Who had attacked her? "Green," Bryn said. "They were Green."

"The people who did this to you? You saw them?" Zavien asked.

"Yes. Males...college aged and Green." Wait a minute. "What about the dragon-pires who attacked you?"

"I never saw who fed on me, but it was nighttime. What were you doing out by the stadium so early in the morning?"

Bryn blinked, and the room came into better focus.

Zavien sat by her bedside looking concerned. She had an odd sense of deja vu. He'd been there when she'd been poisoned the first time.

"Bryn, can you answer the question?" another familiar voice asked.

"Jaxon?" When had he come in?

Jaxon came closer and stood on the side opposite Zavien. "Were you going to meet Garret?"

"No. I was on my way to breakfast." Bryn shook her head, hoping to clear her thoughts, trying to bring the memories into focus. "I was near that new stand of trees and someone asked for help. I didn't want to go over by myself. There was a guy coming toward me. I asked him to come with me, just in case."

"You thought you were being safe," Jaxon said, "but you were being set up."

And that really pissed her off. She growled, and the taste of smoke filled her mouth. "I tried to blast them, but the towel was soaked with something...some chemical. I could barely fight, but I bit him."

Zavien laughed. "You bit the guy?"

"It was through the towel so I doubt I inflicted much damage."

"I don't suppose anyone came in to have their arm treated for a bite wound?" Jaxon asked.

"No," Medic Williams said. "But we'll keep watch for anything suspicious."

Bryn's stomach rumbled. "Can I eat?" It felt like she hadn't eaten in days.

"I brought you some chocolate bars," Jaxon said. "I can go grab some real food if that would be better."

"Any calories are good right now," Medic Williams said. "Bryn, try to sit up."

Bryn's muscles responded in slow motion. Sitting up shouldn't be so hard. Anxiety trickled through her brain. "What's going on?"

"Don't panic," Zavien said. "Your strength will come back to you."

He reached for her, but Jaxon said, "I've got this." Jaxon placed his arm behind her back and lifted her into a seated position. His expression was unreadable. That couldn't be good.

"You're wearing your nothing is wrong face," Bryn said. "How bad do I look?"

"Not as bad as the time you opened the door with the bomb attached to it," he said. "So that's a plus."

She closed her eyes. "I feel stupid and really angry right now."

"Eat," Jaxon said.

She heard him unwrapping a candy bar. The scent of chocolate made her mouth water. "Fine." She opened her eyes and took the chocolate he held out to her. And then a thought occurred to her. "Has anyone called my grandmother yet?"

"No. We wanted to treat you first," Medic Williams said. "Your grandfather knows what happened. We'll call your grandmother once you're able to move under your own power. I don't want her to be more alarmed than necessary."

That was probably a good idea. Bryn tried to wrap her head around the situation. "Who found me?"

"When you didn't show up for breakfast, Clint and Ivy came to me and asked if I knew where you were. We went back to your room, and when you didn't answer your door, we sent for a master key. Once we knew you weren't inside, we went to Elemental Science, thinking maybe you'd gone to speak to Mr. Stanton. When we told him about the situation he organized a search party. One of the guards found you unconscious near the stadium and brought you here."

None of this made any sense. "Why would someone do this?" Bryn asked. "I mean, besides the obvious psychotic need to feed on another dragon's Quintessence, why target a student in the morning? They had to know that friends or a teacher would notice that a student was missing."

"Which leads me to believe that they targeted you on purpose," Jaxon said. "Because of your connections."

"Unlike the dragon-pires who attacked me," Zavien said, "who more than likely needed to feed, this might have been more of a political attack."

Jaxon nodded. "That would be my guess."

"The guy whose face I didn't see sounded sick," Bryn said. "But you're right. It's weird that they risked feeding in broad daylight while other students were roaming around." One part didn't add up. "I was running late this morning. Normally, I would've been to breakfast by the time they ambushed me. There's no way they could count on me being the one who'd stop to help."

"Maybe it was all coincidence," Jaxon said. "But I doubt it."

"You do tend to be in the wrong place at the wrong time," Zavien said.

"It's my special skill." Bryn grinned at Zavien. "Not that I don't appreciate the concern, but what are you doing here?"

"Mr. Stanton contacted me to help look for you. I know how freaked out I was when I woke up, so I wanted to reassure you that you'd make a full recovery."

"I appreciate that."

"No problem." He stood. "Now that I know you're okay, I'll pass word on to Clint and Ivy. I'll leave you and Jaxon to deal with your grandparents."

"Thanks," Bryn said.

Zavien exited the room, and she turned to Jaxon. "Is there any way I wasn't specifically targeted?"

"It's possible, since you were running late, but even if you weren't they could have lured you away by asking you for help or for information," Jaxon said. "Which makes me think they wanted to target someone with strong ties to the Directorate to show them the campus isn't as secure as they think it is."

"Just what I wanted to be," Bryn said. "The poster child for you're not as safe as you think you are."

"Try picking up the glass and taking a drink," Medic Williams said.

Bryn managed to reach for the glass and even picked it up, but getting the straw from her glass to her mouth was beyond her coordination at the moment. "A little help," she said.

Jaxon adjusted the angle of the glass and the straw so that Bryn could manage a drink. "Thank you."

He nodded but didn't say anything. Rather than wearing his everything will be fine face, he seemed to be concerned. "Should she be recovering faster than she is?" Jaxon asked.

"I don't have a lot of case histories to go by," Medic Williams said. "I think she's responding appropriately. In half an hour she should be back to normal."

"Why don't you go call my grandmother," Bryn said. "She'll want to hear that I'm ready for visitors."

Jaxon left the room to use a phone in the front office. Bryn knew she only had a few minutes and there was something she needed to ask. "The

Greens who did this dumped me while I was unconscious. What would have happened to me if I hadn't been found until later tonight?"

"I can't answer that question," the Medic said.

"Let me rephrase it then. Do you think they meant to kill me?"

Chapter Twenty-One

"It's possible," Medic Williams said. "But I can't be sure. You could have passed out because they drugged you or because they drained you to unconsciousness."

"I wish there was a way to know if it was an attack on my life or merely an evil way for them to thumb their noses at the Directorate."

"I understand your frustration," Medic Williams said, "but I have no answers."

Jaxon came back into the room and took one look at Bryn's face. "What's wrong?"

Since she didn't have an affirmative answer, she recounted her question to the Medic.

"That is a disturbing thought," Jaxon said. "You probably shouldn't repeat it to your grandmother."

Fifteen minutes later, Bryn's grandmother stalked into the room looking like she wanted to rain hell down on someone but couldn't find anyone to take her wrath out on.

Thankfully, Bryn was sitting up under her own power and she felt almost completely back to herself.

"I'm okay," Bryn said.

"I am not." Her grandmother stalked over and glared at Jaxon. "You are not to let her out of your sight until these individuals are caught and incarcerated. Do you understand?"

"Yes, ma'am." Jaxon backed up a step. "I'll wait outside so you two can talk."

That was a smooth escape on his part. Bryn opened her arms. "Hug me before you yell at me."

Her grandmother hugged her tight and then sat in the chair Zavien had recently vacated. "I am angry at the world right now, but I have no intention of yelling at you."

"Thank you," Bryn said. "I swear I was minding my business walking to breakfast. I wasn't investigating crazy Silver cult dragon-pires or doing anything remotely adventurous."

"Tell me everything that led up to this event." Her grandmother pulled a small tape recorder from her pocket. "Leave nothing out. I'm passing this information on to your grandfather since he couldn't come himself, and I am fairly certain you don't want to deal with Ferrin."

"Thank you for that." Bryn launched into her tale of a good deed gone wrong which left her grandmother looking angrier than before.

"Is that everything?" her grandmother asked.

Bryn nodded, and her grandmother switched off the tape recorder. "I meant what I said to Jaxon. I don't care if this was a fluke or if you were targeted, since your marriage contract was approved you two are responsible for each other's safety. And since you seem to be the one more at risk for running into trouble, he needs to keep an eye on you."

"I'm sure he will," Bryn said.

Once she was able to walk under her own power, and her grandmother was satisfied that Jaxon would take his caretaker role seriously, her grandmother left.

"Sorry about that," Bryn said to Jaxon.

"She's not wrong," he said. "I guess it's time for me to stop focusing on the past and start focusing on my future."

Medic Williams released Bryn with the appropriate paperwork and a note excusing both her and Jaxon from classes for the rest of the day.

Jaxon escorted her back to the Blue dorm, stopping for some carryout food he'd ordered for her. When they reached her room, he followed her inside. She felt stressed and grimy from the drama of her day. All she wanted was a shower, food, and a nap.

"You don't have to stay here," she said.

"I do," he said. "Until I know you're one hundred percent."

She could argue with him, but that would keep her from a nice, hot shower. "Okay. Make yourself comfortable. I'm going to take a shower and try to wash away some of this stress."

He sat at her library table and opened his book bag. "You should eat first."

If she said she didn't feel like eating, he'd probably call out the National Guard, so she quickly scarfed down the sandwich he'd bought for her and then went into her room. She took a quick shower and changed into yoga pants and a big comfortable shirt. When she went back into the living room, Jaxon was still working on his homework. She walked over and stood where he could see her.

"I'm going to take a nap." She didn't need him sitting out here while she slept. "I'll call you when I wake up."

He set his pen down. "I guess that would be all right." In quick efficient motions, he packed up his bookbag. He stood and looked at her like he wasn't sure about the situation. "Perhaps we could stop these near death experiences you seem to keep encountering."

She laughed at his attempted humor. "Fine by me."

"Good." He opened the door and then paused. "Do me a favor. Wear your elemental sword bracelet at all times." He pointed at his shirt cuffs where he wore the cuff links that channeled his power into two frozen swords. "I plan to wear mine."

"That's a good idea." Even if she'd had her bracelet on when the Greens ambushed her she wasn't sure she would have been able to activate the sword, but it did make sense to keep a weapon handy in case anyone tried again.

He let himself out, and she locked the door behind him. Bryn went into her room and retrieved the sapphire and platinum cuff bracelet, which focused her elements. She put it on and squeezed the bracelet to release the safety. When she pantomimed holding a sword, a blade of fire and ice shot from the bracelet. Maybe she'd keep it on twenty-four hours a day, even if it did look ridiculous with her yoga pants ensemble. She turned the safety back on by pressing the top. Armed with her badass sword, she fell asleep within minutes of Jaxon leaving. Strange dreams of Green dragons stalking her plagued her mind. She never thought Greens would be behind something so ruthless. They were logical... like Spock from the old Star Trek shows her dad used to watch. They might be curious and perform experiments, but they didn't seem like the type to use people for their own ends.

She drifted into a strange dream where Jaxon followed her every move, like literally...he turned into some sort of shadow that mimicked everything she did, and she couldn't shake him. Whenever she thought she was alone, he would jump out at her. She woke up and checked her room. For a moment she expected to find shadow Jaxon standing there. That was ridiculous. Was her subconscious commenting on their impending marriage? Maybe.

She got out of bed and went to call Clint and Ivy. She needed to interact with real people to shake the strange dream. They showed up on her terrace fifteen minutes later.

Ivy climbed in the window and gave Bryn a hug. "You've got to stop doing things like this," she said. "You scared the crap out of us."

"I'd love to lead a calmer life, but the universe seems to have other ideas." She walked into the living room and they followed her.

"How did Jaxon deal with everything?" Clint asked. "Because he was doing that I'm a Blue and I have no emotions thing earlier."

Crap. Jaxon. She was supposed to call him. "He was okay. I need to call him really quick or he's probably going to be ticked off."

He might be ticked off that she called Clint and Ivy before him. "Would you guys mind participating in a little white lie by saying that you called me? I don't want him to think I forgot about him."

"No problem," Clint said. "It's for the greater good."

Bryn called and told Jaxon that she had company so he didn't need to worry about her.

"Don't leave the dorm by yourself again," Jaxon said. "Have your friends come here to meet you or call me and I'll walk you wherever you need to go."

"I want to whine and say that I don't need a babysitter, but I won't because there are evil dragon-pires out there."

"Glad to see you understand the situation," he said and then hung up.

Bryn sat in one of the wing-backed chairs and pulled her knees up to her chest. "So...did you hear any interesting rumors about the dragon-pires?"

Ivy laughed. "Everyone is talking about them. No one can believe they shanghaied you in broad daylight."

"That was pretty ballsy," Clint said. "Zavien told us how they lured you in. If I come across someone who needs help I hate that my first instinct will be to make sure they aren't trying to trick me and suck out my Quintessence."

"I know," Bryn said. "From now on, unless someone is in danger of bleeding out, I'm going to call for a guard."

...

Jaxon walked Bryn to breakfast the next morning, parting company with her when they reached the dining hall. They ate breakfast separately and she walked to Elemental Science with Clint and Ivy. She had most of her classes with her friends, except for Quintessential Medicine.

"I can walk to one class by myself," Bryn objected as Jaxon escorted her to the appropriate room.

"You could, but you don't have to," Jaxon said as they turned the corner into her hallway and approached her classroom. "And arguing this is pointless because it's my job to make sure you're safe."

That was so weird. "What a difference a year makes," she said.

Jaxon snorted. "If you'd told me a year ago that we'd be in this situation, I would have thought you were insane."

"Life is stranger than fiction." Bryn entered her classroom. It was weird how seriously Jaxon was taking his duties. In a way it was a good thing because now that he was focusing on her, he seemed determined rather than sad.

She sat next to Janelle, who looked like she was about to launch into a series of questions but wasn't sure what to say.

"Go ahead," Bryn said. "Fire away."

"I didn't want to be rude," Janelle said. "But now that you mentioned it, what in the hell happened?"

Bryn gave a succinct version of her misadventure. Everyone in the class seemed to stop talking so they could listen in.

"Any questions?" Bryn asked when she'd finished her story.

"Were the Greens students or adults?" Janelle asked.

"The one whose face I saw appeared to be a college student, but I don't know about the other one."

"Did they have you look at photos of students?" Janelle asked. "To see if you could identify anyone."

"No, but that's not a bad idea."

Medic Williams cleared her throat. "I think the Directorate assumed that anyone who let you see his face must have altered his appearance, but it wouldn't hurt to look at some pictures. Now, we're all glad that Bryn is safe. And the sad truth is everyone needs to keep their guard up. Let's turn to chapter ten in our books and read about treating puncture wounds."

After class, Medic Williams waited with Bryn for Jaxon to show up.

"How many days do you think I'll have to do this?" Bryn asked.

"I think this is your new normal until we find out who is behind these attacks," Medic Williams said.

"That's not the answer I wanted to hear." Something else was bothering her. "I hate feeling like something bad is out there waiting to pounce on unsuspecting students. And I hate that I fell for their act."

"Your pride is wounded?" Medic Williams asked.

"Yes," Bryn said. "I've fought in bloody battles but some guy with a rag soaked in chemicals did me in. It's embarrassing."

"It's not like you engaged in some risky behavior. You were trying to help someone."

"I know. And as someone who wants to be a Medic, now I'm going to hesitate when anyone asks for help. That feels wrong, too."

"We'll figure out who is behind this and then you won't have to second-guess your instincts," Medic Williams said.

Chapter Twenty-Two

Bryn came to accept Jaxon as her ever present escort. He didn't seem to mind, which was strange, and he even joked around with her. Maybe they were reaching a comfortable stage of their not quite real relationship.

At dinner Thursday night, Bryn was grateful to be alone with Clint and Ivy, which made her feel guilty. "I feel like a terrible person because all I want is to walk somewhere by myself."

"Being around Jaxon almost twenty-four hours a day has to be an interesting experience," Clint said. "Who knows, maybe you'll find some common ground."

"Maybe. And he's been great about everything, but I'm pretty sure he's over there telling his friends that he's tired of being my shadow."

Ivy peered past Bryn. "He's not at his table."

"What?" Bryn turned around. Quentin sat there with some other Blues, but Jaxon wasn't one of them. Maybe he was in the food line. She checked the buffet. Nope. "Okay, where did he go?"

"He could be in the restroom," Clint said. "Give it a few minutes before you panic."

It seemed like anyone within her gravitational pull eventually ended up in trouble. "I'm hoping my chaos magnet hasn't rubbed off on him."

When he didn't show up in five minutes, Bryn stood and approached Quentin. "Excuse me. Sorry to interrupt, but I noticed Jaxon wasn't here."

Quentin pointed at a plate of food, which looked untouched. "He said he'd be back in a minute, but it's been awhile."

"Not to raise any red flags, but I'm not a fan of people going anywhere alone."

"Understandable," Quentin said. "Why don't we go check on him."

Jaxon had known Quentin forever, so Bryn had no reason to mistrust him, but she also didn't know him very well. "Let's grab Clint just in case we're outnumbered."

Quentin didn't comment. He just followed Bryn back to her table. "Clint, come for a walk with us."

Ivy stood. "You're not leaving me here by myself." "The more the merrier," Bryn said.

"Let's check the restroom first," Quentin said.

When they reached the restroom, Clint and Quentin went in and came back out thirty seconds later. "We need to alert the guards. There's blood on the floor."

Damn. Damn. Damn. "Clint, you and Ivy go find a guard. Quentin and I will keep looking."

"If he wasn't injured, he would've come back to our table," Quentin said.

"Unless someone cut him off." She looked around, getting her bearings. There was a long hallway to her left. "There are private dining rooms down that hall." There was a short hallway to her right. "I think that leads to the kitchens."

"Let's go this way." Quentin headed to the private dining rooms.

Splitting up would save time, but it wouldn't be smart, so Bryn followed him, activating her elemental sword. Quentin glanced back and his eyebrows went up, but he didn't comment. They approached the first dining room but didn't see anyone inside.

Voices came from farther down the hall. The words were indistinct. Quentin ran ahead and threw open the door and then laughed. "It looks like we were worried about nothing."

Bryn pushed past him and saw that Jaxon had a Green male pinned to the wall with one of his elemental swords, while another Green lay bleeding at his feet, trying to stand back up.

"I wouldn't mind a little help." Jaxon's lip was swollen and bleeding and he appeared winded.

Bryn walked over and got a better look at the student on the floor. He was the one who'd pretended to offer help and then drugged her. She turned off her sword and nudged the guy with her foot. "Hello, there. Remember me?" Anger over what he'd done stoked the fire inside of her. She focused on cold and then blasted the young man with ice, building layer after layer until he was covered with ice from the shoulders down. "Not going anywhere now, are you?"

The sound of several people running came from the hallway. Quentin waved out the doorway. "We're in here."

Two guards entered and assessed the situation. One approached Jaxon. "Are you all right?"

Jaxon nodded. "I can see myself to the medical clinic."

"One of us will escort you there, for the sake of protocol. If you'll release him, I'll restrain him."

Jaxon released his elemental swords and the man who'd been pinned against the wall sagged with relief. The guard grabbed his shoulder, spun him around, and not so gently pushed him against the wall before putting on a pair of handcuffs.

The other guard pointed at the Green on the floor. "Who did this?"

Bryn held up her hand. "He's one of the Greens who ambushed me, and sometimes payback is a bitch."

The guard nodded. "I'll have to defrost him."

"That's a shame." Bryn approached Jaxon. "Where are you hurt?"

"Just my face and my pride," he said.

"Can you give a rundown of what occurred?" the first guard asked as he pulled a small recording device from his pocket and pressed a button.

"There's not much to tell. These idiots tried to jump me when I was leaving the restroom."

"That didn't go how they expected it," Quentin said.

"No. I'd just washed my hands and reached for a paper towel when the one on the floor tried to grab me and sedate me with a drug-soaked rag. I elbowed him. The other one caught me by surprise with a sucker punch. I activated my elemental swords. After that it was me chasing them down so they couldn't escape."

"Your story is way better than mine," Bryn said.

"I am a Westgate," Jaxon said in a fake snotty tone.

Bryn laughed.

"So everyone is good?" Ivy said from where she and Clint were peeking in the doorway.

"Yes," said Jaxon.

After one of the guards hauled their prisoners away, the other guard said, "I could call for a Medic to come here."

"No. My father would want me to follow protocol."

Bryn and Jaxon went to the Medical Center with their escort, while Clint and Ivy went to finish dinner with orders to bring two boxes of carryout food back to Bryn's room.

When they reached the Medical Center, Bryn was less than pleased to find Ferrin waiting for them but held her tongue. Jaxon explained what had happened in a very modest fashion, which surprised her.

"Once again, you have made me proud," his father said. "I'll let you know when we have some answers about who these two criminals are and why they went after you."

Jaxon beamed with pride as his father exited the building.

"If you'll let me heal you, you can go have your dinner," the Medic said.

The Medic scanned Jaxon, placing her hand on his head. As Bryn watched, the swelling of his lip receded, and the cut healed to a fine pink line. The woman continued the scan. She probably wanted to be thorough since he was the Speaker's son. She frowned. "Did you forget to mention that one of those men hit you in the ribs?"

"Maybe," Jaxon said. "I'm sure it's just bruised. It wasn't a big deal."

"One is cracked," she said. "Take your shirt off."

Jaxon frowned as he loosened his tie and removed his shirt. An ugly purple bruise decorated the left side of his rib cage.

"What the heck?" Bryn asked.

Jaxon frowned. "They came at me out of nowhere. When the first punch didn't take me out, the other guy tried to tackle me and rammed me into the sink. I was too busy activating my elemental swords to brace for impact."

"So the sink cracked your rib?" Bryn said, trying not to smile. She really shouldn't find any of this funny, but she did. Maybe because it made her feel better that his ambush hadn't gone as perfectly as he'd said.

"Yes, and that information will not leave this room," Jaxon said.

"No, it won't. This falls under patient-client privilege." The Medic placed her hand on his rib cage and the bruise faded.

Jaxon gave Bryn a questioning look as he put his shirt back on.

"No one will hear it from me," she said.

He started to knot his tie and then let it hang loose instead. "I think I can be excused for not following the dress code just this once."

Bryn smiled. "Next thing you know, you'll be wearing yoga pants."

He laughed, his eyes sparkled, his hair was kind of tussled, and with his tie undone he looked so much more normal...still devastatingly handsome and undeniably hot... but normal. Bryn froze. Wait. Did I just think Jaxon was hot?

Where did that thought come from?

"What's wrong?" Jaxon asked.

"Nothing." Nope. Nothing was wrong. She did not think Jaxon was hot. She did not. "Clint and Ivy will be waiting for us outside my room with food. Let's go eat."

"Sounds good." They walked to the Blue dorm. Guards were positioned outside of every building and along the sidewalk. Despite the heightened security, it seemed like any other night. A normal night. Not a night where she suddenly found herself attracted to a certain asshat... because that was so very very wrong.

When they entered the Blue dorm, it looked like the entire Blue student body was in the main lounge waiting for them. Jaxon acted like nothing was out of the ordinary, so Bryn followed suit.

Clint and Ivy sat on the floor outside Bryn's room playing Go Fish.

"There you are," Ivy said. "I was beginning to worry."

"We're fine," Bryn said. She opened the door and they all sat at the library table where Clint placed four carryout boxes.

"Before you try to finish off all this food, Ivy and I call dibs on this container of nachos." He pulled a container over toward himself. "You guys can split the rest."

Bryn popped open the other containers to reveal nachos, hamburgers, and an entire container of French fries. "Since you were injured, you can pick first."

Jaxon ripped the lid off one of the containers, placed two burgers in it and two handfuls of fries. "You can have the rest."

"Challenge accepted."

Clint and Ivy left after they finished their food, but Jaxon hung back like he wanted to talk with her.

She finished off the last of the fries while she waited for him to start.

"Do you think those Greens targeted you and then me because of our Directorate connections or was that a coincidence?" he asked.

"Your father should be finding out the answers to those questions right now." The two Greens would be dosed with a drug that would make them talk, which was much more civilized than she'd thought dragons would be.

"I think they must have come after us for some reason," Jaxon said. "There's no way they just happened on both of us."

"When it was just me I was willing to believe it was the luck of the draw, but I think you're right," Bryn said. "We were probably targeted for some reason."

He leaned back in his chair and stared off into space like he was thinking. "Which means they weren't after Quintessence."

"Um...I seem to remember them sucking out a lot of my life force," Bryn said.

"Maybe they just did that to cover something else up," Jaxon said.

"Like what?"

He ran his hand back through his hair. "That's where my theory falls apart. I don't know what they could be after. It's not like you or I have access to some secret information."

"I could call my grandfather and ask what they've found," Bryn offered, because she really wanted to know what the heck was going on.

"No. My father said he'd call when he had answers. I'll share whatever he tells me. I guess I should say thank you for coming to look for me."

"You're welcome, though you seemed to have the situation taken care of by the time we got there."

"Mostly," he said. "But it's nice to know someone notices when I'm not where I'm supposed to be."

And now this felt awkward and a little too serious. "I guess it really is our job to look out for each other now, isn't it?"

He grinned. "I'd like to point out that I'm normally a lot less trouble than you are, so you're getting the better end of this deal."

She rolled her eyes. "Yes, I'm one lucky girl."

He acknowledged her joke with a grin and then pushed to his feet. "Do try to remember that." He walked to the door and let himself out.

She locked the door behind him. Weird how she felt closer to him now. Shared drama probably had that effect on a relationship. Whatever kind of relationship she had with Jaxon, it seemed to be shifting...which was natural given their strange circumstances. Nothing to worry about. Nothing at all.

Rather than think too hard about the absurd state of her life, she grabbed her book and relaxed on the couch. The now non-possessed hero of the book was declaring his undying love for the main character when Bryn's phone rang. She reluctantly set her book down, hoping whatever she was about to hear would make her feel safer.

"Bryn," Jaxon's voice came through the line. "The Greens they questioned claimed they chose us because we were alone. Apparently, it's their job to collect Quintessence from unsuspecting students so that they have enough to share with the higher-ups in their dragon-pire ring. They called themselves feeders. They haven't been doing so well with that, and their bosses take what they want from them, so they were ambushing people to try and stock up. They fed off several other students in this same manner but were successful in making the students forget so the incidents went unreported. They were desperate when they attacked you, and tonight when they came after me, because they'd just given so much energy to their higher-ups."

"So, normally they don't ambush people and drug them?"

"No. They just touch them in passing. Contact for a few minutes allows them to siphon off a dose of energy and the victims don't remember a thing. That's how they usually operate."

"So they were behind the students who were so tired, like Clint and Ivy?"

"Yes, but my father said their answers in that area led them to believe there were other feeders on campus."

"Well, that's just fantastic," Bryn said.

"I think the good news is they weren't targeting us in particular."

"I guess that makes me feel better."

"I'd feel better if they'd learned who the ringleaders of this group were, but the higher level dragon-pires never let anyone see their faces," Jaxon said. "They wear masks, robes, and gloves to conceal their Clan colors."

"Speaking of Clans, were they able to determine if the dragon-pires they arrested were hybrids?"

"Yes. And you can't share this information with anyone. Not even Clint and Ivy."

"They wouldn't tell anyone."

"I'm not telling you unless you promise not to share."

Damn it. She hated keeping information from her friends. Still she wanted to know. "Fine. I won't tell anyone."

"They were Green-Blue hybrids."

"Wow." That was the only response she could come up with for a moment. "I'd never expect that pairing."

"I'm not sure how it would happen."

"If I were to hazard a guess, I'd say that the Greens were females who were denied marriage and the Blues were males who kept them as mistresses. The secret offspring of that union would have the brains of a Green and the ambition of a Blue."

"And an angry, ambitious, genius who is unstable might resort to extreme measures to achieve their goals," Jaxon said.

"I can't tell you how much I hate the fact that some hybrid combinations are unstable."

"Because it proves that the Directorate had a reason for creating the marriage laws," Jaxon said.

"Exactly. I don't get it," Bryn said. "I'm not unstable."

Jaxon laughed.

She almost threatened to blast him with a fireball but that would prove his point. "I'm not homicidally unstable," she corrected. "And you'd have to think that any dragon raised in a loving supportive environment wouldn't want to hurt other dragons."

"For centuries, dragons hoarded treasure and kept control of land. It's in our nature to seek out treasure and power. Some combinations of those genes lead to bad results."

"I guess."

After hanging up the phone, Bryn lay on the couch for a while, rolling this new information around in her brain. She had no answers to the Silver cult dragon-pire mystery or to her odd and most certainly one-time feeling of attraction to Jaxon. It must have been the stress or the fact that she'd been concerned for his well-being. When she saw him tomorrow she was sure everything would be back to normal.

Chapter Twenty-Three

News spread about the Greens that had been arrested and students seemed to grow leery of their classmates. Garrett approached Bryn during Basic Movement.

"This is ridiculous," he said. "Everyone is looking at us like we might go darkside and try to suck out their Quintessence at any moment."

"I'm sorry." She wished the Directorate would share that the dragon-pires were Blue-Green hybrids but understood why they'd want to keep that information quiet during their investigation. "Your entire Clan shouldn't be judged by the actions of a few random whack jobs."

"I feel like we need to put together some sort of PR campaign, like, 'Remember we're still the dragons most likely to heal you or help you with your homework so stop looking at us like we might slit your throat at any moment.'"

"We could put that on a poster," Bryn said. "Although, we might want to tone down that last part." He didn't seem to appreciate her attempt at humor. "I'm sorry. Is there anything I can do to help?"

"I'm not sure," he said. "As a Green, the illogical nature of this situation is highly annoying." And with that he stalked off.

Clint and Ivy had been standing in line behind her, so they'd heard the entire exchange.

"It is kind of ridiculous that people would be suspicious of the whole Clan now," Clint said.

"Do you think all the dragon-pires are Green?" Ivy asked.

"Who knows?" Bryn moved forward in the line.

"I'm just playing Devil's advocate here. In one way it makes sense," Clint leaned closer and whispered. "Greens are acknowledged as being the most intelligent dragons. What if a group of them were tired of being ruled by inferior minded Blues?"

Bryn snorted with laughter. "Sorry, I just had an image of Ferrin reacting to your description."

"That would not be pretty," Ivy said. "I hate that those dragon-pire lackeys were able to feed off us and then make us forget."

"That's really been bugging me," Clint said. "I have absolutely no memory of anything happening. No missing time. We weren't late for classes. How did they manage it?"

"I have no idea," Bryn said.

The line for jousting moved forward, and Bryn was next to go up the ladder to do battle with the giant foam-tipped cotton swab. She climbed the rungs with ease. When she reached the top, she discovered she was facing-off with a Blue female.

"Your marriage will be a joke," the girl said before swinging at Bryn's shoulders.

"Excuse me?" Bryn blocked the blow and swung at the girl's hips.

The girl dodged the blow. "You heard me. Jaxon deserves better than you." The girl swung at Bryn's head.

Bryn ducked. "I don't know who you are, and I don't care." She swung at the girl's legs. "And your opinion means nothing to me."

"Really? It seems to be upsetting you." The girl swiped at Bryn's shoulders.

Bryn smacked the girl's stick down, knocked her off-balance, and then whacked her as hard as she could, toppling her off the podium and into the pit of foam blocks below.

Who in the hell did that girl think she was? Bryn focused on cold. Tell-tale wisps of smoke drifting from her nostrils would tell everyone how pissed off she was. No one had been so openly rude to her in months. What was that girl's problem? She climbed down the ladder ready to give the girl a piece of her mind, but when she reached the floor her new not so friendly acquaintance was nowhere to be seen.

"Did you see where she went?" Bryn asked Ivy while Clint climbed up to take his turn.

"Who?" Ivy asked.

"The girl I just faced off with?"

"No."

Bryn gave her a summary of the lovely conversation. "She's probably jealous because Jaxon is higher up the social ladder than whoever she's contracted to marry," Ivy said. "Don't let it bother you."

Right. In theory it was easy to say that the girl's opinion meant nothing, but Bryn hadn't missed the random verbal insults from Blues and she wasn't happy to have them back. "I thought I wouldn't need to be thick-skinned anymore. Guess I was wrong."

"There's been a lot going on lately," Ivy said. "She probably just caught you off guard."

"You're right."

"Bryn," Jaxon's voice came from behind her.

She turned around to see him coming toward her with an amused smile on his face.

"That's your I know something you don't look," Bryn said. "What's up?"

"You won't find this amusing," he warned, "but we've been summoned to dinner at Westgate Estate this evening."

"What?" That had bad idea written all over it. "Why? And why do you think this is funny?"

"I'm not sure why we're having dinner, but I find it amusing because I've had to endure several meals at your grandparents' house and that last one was especially horrific."

"True." Which left her little room for griping. "I don't suppose you know who is going to be there?"

"My parents and your grandparents, as far as I know. But you might want to call your mother to find out if she's coming."

"What? I thought that was supposed to be a Christmas thing."

"I spoke to my mother about us wanting to exchange gifts at the Christmas Ball instead, and she agreed that would be better."

"That's a relief."

After their last class, Jaxon walked Bryn back to her room. She had two hours to mentally and physically prepare for what could possibly be the world's most uncomfortable dinner. First step, call her mom.

"Hello, sweetie. What's up?"

"This will sound weird, but were you invited to have dinner at the Westgate's tonight?"

Her mom laughed. "Are you joking?"

"No. I have it on good authority that Lillith has been trying to make sure that you're included in some sort of dinner out of misplaced maternal instinct."

"She wants to put your father and I in the same room with Ferrin?" Her mom snorted.

"Uhm...no. Here's the crappy part. If it happens, Dad isn't invited."

"If that's how the invitation is extended, I'll refuse it," her mom said. "When I told you that I'm just happy to be part of your life and I had no illusions about being accepted back into dragon society, I meant it."

"While I don't love that answer," Bryn said, "I'm beginning to see your point. I'd like to see both you and Dad. Can I come visit you tomorrow?"

"We'd love that. Why don't you come out for lunch?"

"Should I stop and pick up some carryout?"

"No. I'll cook," her mom said.

There was only one problem and she wasn't sure how to explain it to her mom. "There have been some safety issues on campus, so I'm not supposed to go anywhere alone. I bet I could get Clint and Ivy to ride to Sanctuary with me, and then they could go to Dragon's Bluff for lunch."

"What type of safety issues," her mom asked. "Did something happen to you?"

"I'm fine, and that's all you need to know right now. I'll explain everything else tomorrow."

"Yes," her mom said. "You will."

"Before you become upset, just be thankful that you won't be spending time with Ferrin tonight."

Her mom snorted. "I'm grateful for that fact every day of my life. See you tomorrow."

Bryn called Clint and Ivy to see if they were okay with her plan. Once they were on board, she went to stare into her armoire. No matter what she wore, she wouldn't be mentally prepared to deal with Ferrin. She reached out and touched her favorite pair of jeans. How funny would it be to show up for dinner in jeans and a sweatshirt? Her grandmother probably wouldn't find it amusing. Speaking of her grandmother, maybe she should touch base with her.

"You're having dinner at Westgate Estate tonight?" Her grandmother sounded surprised. That wasn't good.

"So I'm guessing you're not?" Bryn said.

"Not that I'm aware of," her grandmother said. "Maybe Lillith wanted to keep it just the immediate family."

"That is not a good idea," Bryn said. "There won't be anything to distract Ferrin from his hobby of disliking me."

"If he's hosting the dinner, he shouldn't be openly rude to his guests," her grandmother said.

"I don't find that comforting. "

Bryn changed outfits three times before settling on a black skirt with an aqua cashmere sweater set. It wasn't super fancy, but it was upper class, and that's what she was aiming for.

When Jaxon came to collect her at six o'clock he was wearing a black suit with a navy tie. "Are you ready?" he asked.

"Why does that feel like a trick question?"

"Probably because it is. No matter how you think my father is going to react, you never know what he's actually going to do in a social situation."

"Fabulous." Bryn followed him to his car. "According to my grandmother, it's just us. They weren't invited, and neither was my mother."

"Really?" Jaxon looked perplexed. "That's strange."

"Maybe your mom just wants to see you," Bryn said.

"I guess we'll find out." Jaxon drove them to Westgate Estate in his fancy black sports car.

His mother waited for them inside the foyer with Asher on her hip and a huge grin on her face. "I'm so happy to see you two. Come with me."

Either Asher made her supremely happy or she'd been drinking wine before they arrived.

"Where are we going?" Jaxon asked.

"You'll have to wait and see," Lillith said. "It's a surprise."

Jaxon didn't love surprises. His mother had to know that, but it's not like she could say that to Lillith, so they followed her down the hall, up a flight of stairs, and past several closed doors before reaching a small dining room with an oval mahogany table set for four, plus a bassinet in the corner.

"This is cozy," Bryn said.

"I thought so, too." Lillith sat. "I've missed interacting with people and Ferrin is rarely home, so I thought it might be nice for us to catch up."

This seemed a lot more low pressure than she'd expected, especially if Ferrin wouldn't be joining them.

"How's Asher doing?" Bryn asked.

"He's wonderful," Lillith said. "Would you like to hold him?"

"Sure." Bryn took the baby, holding him in the crook of her arm like she'd seen Lillith and her grandmother do. He was sleeping at the moment, making soft snuffling noises that melted her heart. "He's adorable."

"I know." Lilith sighed. "Especially when he's sleeping."

Ferrin entered the room. He stiffened when he saw Bryn. Was it her presence or the fact that she was holding Asher? Did he think she'd rub off on him in some weird way? If she was marrying one of his sons, holding the other one shouldn't be a big deal. And that was an odd thought.

"Bryn, what an interesting surprise." Ferrin said the word interesting like he meant unwelcome. "I wasn't aware you'd be joining us this evening."

"I did say I wanted to have dinner with our family," Lillith said.

"It would seem we define that term differently," Ferrin responded.

"This is going to be loads of fun," Bryn told Jaxon, not bothering to keep her voice low. If he could be obnoxious, so could she...in a respectful grown-up way, of course.

"Ferrin doesn't like surprises," Lillith said. "That's all."

Bryn was pretty sure that wasn't the root of the problem but knew when to keep her mouth shut.

"Any news on the Quintessence-siphoning dragons?" Jaxon asked his father.

Nice topic change.

"No. We've followed down the vague leads given to us, but the imbeciles didn't know who they were reporting to."

Asher started to fuss, so Bryn handed him back to Lillith before Ferrin could accuse her of doing something to the baby.

"I still wonder if the whole thing isn't some sort of distraction," Jaxon said. "But I'm not sure from what."

"Or a way to throw suspicion on the new students," Bryn added.

"It's not the students from Sanctuary that are the issue," Ferrin said. "It's the adults."

And there was no way that wasn't a slam against her parents. Bryn sat down, put both of her elbows firmly on the table, and leaned forward, smiling at Ferrin. "Is this how it's going to be? You're going to spend the evening slighting my parents? Because I'd like to point out that you're the one that agreed to the marriage contract."

Ferrin turned away from her and walked to a sideboard that held a crystal decanter full of amber-colored alcohol. He poured himself a glass, took a sip, and then said, "Believe it or not, the world does not revolve around you. I wasn't referring to your parents, because as far as I'm concerned, the Sinclairs are your guardians. Anyone else that you may unfortunately share DNA with is not worthy of my recognition."

Chapter Twenty-Four

Bryn turned to Jaxon. "From now on when your father speaks I'm going to hear that teacher from Charlie Brown who goes, 'Whah Whah Whah Whah Whah Whah.' So you can handle the rest of this conversation."

Jaxon looked like he wasn't sure if he should laugh or be outraged. He sighed and said, "Okay then. Let's rewind the conversation to your concerns about the adults in Sanctuary. What's going on?"

Ferrin glared at Bryn and then turned to his son. "We believe there are some dragons living in the old mines below the town. The residents who have registered and are settled into the new housing have passed all of our tests, but we think there are some hold-outs."

"I still think it seems like too much of a coincidence that they targeted students connected to the Directorate," Jaxon said.

"It takes training to be able to siphon Quintessence from another dragon," Ferrin said. "So even if this isn't the Silver Cult brought back to life, some group is draining students and sending them out to do the same to others."

Bryn regretted removing herself from the conversation. She tried to mentally prompt Jaxon into asking his father what happened to the two men they'd questioned. Were they locked up in the cells below the library? Apparently, she and her future husband weren't telepathically connected because he started talking to his father about something else. Bryn leaned over to Lillith.

"What happened to the Silver dragon-pires they arrested?"

Lillith frowned. "It might be better not to ask such questions. They attacked the Speaker's son, so once the Directorate collected all the information they needed there wouldn't be any reason to keep them around anymore."

"Oh." So maybe she'd turned the one guy into a giant ice cube, but she hadn't wished him dead. Then again, he did feed on other dragons' life force and he had dumped her unconscious body in a field by the stadium. A maid with a W sewn onto her uniform pushed a trolley full of food into the small room. She glanced around and then said, "Are you ready for dinner, or should I come back?"

"You can serve the food now." Lillith stood and took Asher over to the bassinet in the corner. After placing him inside, she pushed a button and the basket slowly swung back and forth. Why didn't they make beds like that for adults?

Bryn was already seated on the long side of the oval. Jaxon sat across from her. Ferrin sat at what must be the head of the table, and Lillith sat on the other end. The maid delivered plates of something brown and squishy. She made it a rule not to eat anything she couldn't identify, even though it smelled good. Her three companions dug in. Jaxon caught her staring at her plate.

"It's basically steak with truffles," Jaxon said.

"Steak with chocolate?" Chocolate was awesome on most things, but on beef?

"Not the candy," Jaxon said. "The mushroom."

"Oh, that makes much more sense." She took a bite. It was good.

"People debate whether it's a mushroom or a fungus," Lillith said. "Arguments can be made for both sides."

"It's a good thing I took a bite before you mentioned fungus," Bryn said. "Because that is not an appetizing description."

"So, I hear that your grandmother has started planning an estate for you," Lillith said.

"Where did you hear that from?" Bryn stared pointedly at Jaxon. "I thought it was supposed to be a secret."

"Your grandmother shared the information with me," Lillith said. "She comes over to spend time with Asher and we discuss all sorts of topics."

"Good to know that I don't have to keep it a secret anymore," Bryn said. "I was worried you might be upset." Or try to stop it. And there was no way she was living under the same roof as Ferrin. This dinner was difficult enough.

"I understand that you two will want your own home. And your grandmother has wonderful taste, so I'm sure whatever she comes up with will be spectacular."

"The next time you speak to her, please let her know that I want the W's on the front gates to match the ones here at Westgate Estate," Jaxon said. "It's a tradition I'd like to continue."

Ferrin seemed to brighten at that news. "Good to know you've inherited my pride in our family name."

"Did I mention that I'm considering keeping my maiden name after we're married?" Bryn said.

Jaxon's mouth fell open.

Frost shot from Ferrin's nostrils.

Bryn grinned. "Sorry, I couldn't resist."

Lillith pretended to be coughing into her napkin, but Bryn was pretty sure she was laughing.

Once they finished their main course, Bryn hoped for some sort of dessert, but they ended the meal with coffee. What was up with that?

Ferrin excused himself once his cup was empty. Once he was gone, Bryn said, "No dessert?"

"Ferrin isn't a fan of sweets. Unlike your grandfather, we don't end most meals with dessert."

"That's just wrong," Bryn said.

Lillith grinned. "Go open the box next to the crystal decanter on the sideboard."

Bryn walked over and opened the intricately carved wooden box. Inside she found individually wrapped pieces of chocolate. "That's much better." She grabbed six pieces and carried them back to the table, giving two each to Jaxon and Lillith.

"I prefer this type of truffle myself," Lillith said.

"Me, too." Bryn finished off one truffle in a few bites. While unwrapping the next one, she said, "Jaxon mentioned that you were concerned about me spending time with my mother over the holidays, so I wanted to let you know that I'll be visiting them at their cabin tomorrow. And it might be better not to try and involve my mother in any Blue events."

Lillith frowned. "You're probably right. I spoke to Marie after I talked to Jaxon and she didn't think it was a good idea. I guess it will take time for them to come to some sort of understanding."

What could she say to that? "I think my parents will be part of the community at Sanctuary and I'm thrilled to have them back—and alive—and I plan on spending time with them, but I doubt my grandparents will ever invite them to any events at Sinclair Estate. Co-existing peacefully in separate locations might be the best we can hope for."

"Maybe after the holidays we could set up a small dinner for just the women in our families. Honestly, I've always been curious about your mother and I'd love to meet her." She glanced at Jaxon. "Do not share that information with your father."

"I'm going to pretend I never heard that odd bit of knowledge. In fact, I'm going to my room for something. Bryn you can stay here and visit with my mother." And then he fled.

Lillith laughed. "Poor Jaxon. He's so proud of his father, but he also understands that it's best if certain things are kept private because Ferrin isn't easy to live with."

"No?" Bryn feigned disbelief.

"Hard to believe, I know," Lillith said. "But honestly, I've had a good life. Part of the reason I'm curious about your mother is because my life is her nightmare. It's hard for me to wrap my head around."

Bryn was pretty sure she could explain but didn't think that would be polite.

"You and Jaxon seem to be getting along better," Lillith said with a knowing grin.

Was Lillith looking for some sort of confession? That wasn't going to happen. "I think the news about the house really threw him, but other than that we've been figuring out how to spend time together without annoying each other too much."

Chapter Twenty-Five

Bryn wasn't sure what to expect at Sanctuary. The words "old mining town" conjured a vision of dirt roads and rundown buildings. In reality, it looked more like a camp, with cabins, in an overgrown forest.

Clint and Ivy rode with Bryn to the front gate where her parents stood waiting.

"Thanks for coming with me," she said. "I'll introduce you when you come back from Dragon's Bluff."

"Have fun," Ivy said.

Bryn climbed out of the SUV and approached the guards standing at the admission checkpoint.

"Who are you visiting?" the guard asked.

"My parents, Ian and Sara McKenna."

The guard made her sign in and gave her a lanyard to wear which had a numbered pass card. "This is so we can keep track of who comes and goes. Don't lose it."

"I understand."

The guard waved Bryn through the gate and she ran to hug her parents.

"There's my girl," her dad said.

He looked more like himself, standing tall without assistance. She pointed at his leg, noticing the different brace. "That's new, and you don't have your cane anymore."

"No." Her dad took a few steps to show how the brace worked. "Your friend Garret is a genius."

"He is pretty smart," Bryn agreed.

"Come on." Her mom hooked her elbow through Bryn's. "I can't wait to give you the tour."

They walked down a dirt road which branched off in three different directions. "Straight ahead is the Community Center, but our cabin is this way." They walked down the right-hand road, passing several cabins, which appeared rustic but well restored. They reminded her of Valmont's cabin. The wood was bleached with age and vegetation grew up some of the walls making it look like the wooden structures were part of the landscape.

"Did you have to chop back the plants to find the cabins?" Bryn asked.

"Sometimes," her dad said. "But we left some of the greenery because it helps insulate the building, and in some cases, it seems to be holding the logs together."

When they reached her parents' cabin Bryn understood what he meant. The vines grew up and around the house, looping around some of the logs which gave the whole structure an otherworldly appearance.

"It looks like something out of a fairy tale," Bryn said.

Her mom laughed. "That wasn't the case when we first came here. It was more like something out of a horror movie." She led Bryn up the walk. "Come inside. That's where you can really see what we've done."

Bryn entered the house. The front door opened onto the living room with a couch and rocking chair. One step up from the front room was a kitchen with an apartment- sized stove and a refrigerator. Shelves above the farmhouse sink held dishes and utensils. Off to the side stood a pantry which looked like it had been partially sunken into the wall. Intricate carvings of leaves and vines decorated the doors in an almost geometric pattern.

"That's cool." Bryn pointed at the cabinet.

"Yeah." Her dad rubbed his chin. "That was one of those make-the-best-of-it moments. I wanted to put in a storage closet, but that was beyond my woodworking skills." "He almost brought the whole wall down." Her mom laughed. "But some neighbors helped us reinforce the area and then they built the cabinet to fit inside the niche that was left."

"I like to think of it as a happy accident," her dad said.

That's one thing she loved about her parents. Their outlook on life was so positive. "Who did the artwork on the doors?"

"A very talented Green-Black hybrid carved the design into the doors. It's funny, we've met hybrids who have such interesting skills." Her mom pointed down the hall. "The dresser doors are even more amazing."

Bryn followed her parents down the short hallway to a room which held a bed and a custom-built dresser that extended the length of one wall. The drawers were decorated with carvings of flowers and small woodland animals. Bryn looked closer. "Is that a skunk on the bottom?"

"Yes," her dad said. "I think a Black dragon would have known that a skunk isn't something you particularly want in your art, but when I asked why he included the skunk he said that due to his Green side, he felt the need to accurately represent all of the animals that live in the forest."

"Interesting. I guess you'll have to be more specific in your requests for art from now on." Bryn stepped back into the hallway. There was one more door on the other side of the hall. "I'm hoping you have a restroom and not an outhouse," she said.

"It's functional, but a little cramped." Her dad opened the last door. "See for yourself."

Bryn scooted past him and was relieved to see a pedestal sink, curtained-off shower, and toilet. The blue-and-white striped curtain and towels gave the room a happy vibe.

"It's cute," Bryn said.

"Let's go back to the living room," her dad said.

Once they were seated on the couch, her mom said, "Some people are having trouble adjusting to the tight space. But it's not much different than our apartment."

It was smaller than Bryn's dorm room, which made her feel guilty. Then again, so was the apartment she'd grown up in and she'd never felt crowded when she'd lived there. It was all a matter of perspective. "It's really cute and homey," Bryn said. "How is there so much light?"

"Look up." Her dad pointed at the ceiling.

Bryn checked out the ceiling. Two rectangular skylights allowed sunshine to flow into the room.

"Since we had to patch the roof anyway, it wasn't too difficult to add the skylights."

Her mom laughed.

"Fine," her dad said. "They leaked like a sieve the first time it rained, but we figured out a better way to seal them and now they're fine."

"A lot of this stuff has been trial and error," her mom said. "But everyone has pitched in for the greater good, and we've all learned as we went along."

"I have to confess, I was a little worried about what it might be like out here," Bryn said, "but this is really cool."

"I know my parents probably think we're living in a slum," her mom said. "But this works for us."

She didn't want to talk about the strained relationship with her grandparents. "How many cabins are there?"

"We've restored about fifteen and built another ten," her dad said. "I have to credit whoever is keeping us supplied with materials because there hasn't been a shortage. We have enough lumber to build a dozen more. It's just a matter of time and manpower."

"What do you do all day out here?" Bryn asked.

"I'm teaching yoga classes at the community center," her mom said. "And your dad has helped with the building." Bryn leaned back against the couch cushion and sighed. "You have no idea how worried I was about this visit. I was afraid you were putting on a brave face about the whole situation, but this is really nice."

"Our only complaint would be the lack of information about what is going on at the Institute. We've heard rumors about the increase in security, but we don't know why," her mom said. "Can you fill us in?"

How much should she tell them? She didn't want to worry them, but she didn't want to lie, either. "Honestly, we aren't sure what's going on. Some college students have been caught trying to siphon Quintessence from other students like some old cult used to do."

"Why?" her dad asked.

"Apparently, there are some dragons who think extra Quintessence will help them become all-powerful. They apprehended two dragons who were involved in the attacks and they're holding them for questioning."

"I don't understand what they hope to gain," her mom said.

"Power, I guess. Clint coined the phrase dragon-pire."

"That's funny, but not really appropriate," her dad said.

"What about out here? Have you run into anything strange?"

"Not really," her mom said. "Why?"

"Ferrin suspects there are dragons living in the mines, avoiding detection."

Her dad laughed. "As far as I can tell, the old mine is just a hole in the ground. I wouldn't even call it a cavern. If anyone is coming and going through there they'd need to be excellent climbers. There isn't even room to shift and explore."

"And how would you know that?" Bryn asked.

"It can get a little boring out here, so some of the people tried to go exploring. They didn't get very far. Said the tunnels made them claustrophobic."

After being trapped under the library, Bryn had no desire to investigate anything underground ever again.

"There are rumors about other entrances to the mines," her mom said. "You'd think there'd have to be, for airflow and safety standards, if nothing else."

"I wouldn't ask too many questions about that," Bryn said. "Since Ferrin is the one looking into it. I kind of pissed him off when I joked that I might want to keep my maiden name after the marriage."

"You said that to him?" her mom asked.

Bryn nodded and laughed. "I couldn't help myself."

"That's my girl," her dad said, once he stopped laughing.

"It was pretty funny, but seriously, I think the Directorate is watching everyone in Sanctuary—just waiting for someone to mess up."

"It feels that way," her dad said. "It's been a long time since we walked on eggshells like this and I'm not happy to be doing it again. In the human world, we kept to ourselves and people left us alone. Now it feels like we constantly have to be aware of where we are and what we're saying."

"I know," Bryn said. "It can be exhausting but it's not like there's another alternative."

When her mom and dad didn't jump in to agree, an uneasy feeling washed over Bryn. "Please tell me you aren't planning on running away again."

"No," her mom said. "I mean we discussed it, but I have the feeling we might die in a car crash if we tried."

Bryn frowned. "That does seem to be a common issue around here."

"We would never go anywhere without telling you," her dad said.

"Good." Bryn's stomach growled. "I believe you said something about feeding me."

For the rest of her visit, Bryn and her parents kept to pleasant topics. A knock on the cabin door made her father frown. "Who could that be?"

"It's probably my friends Clint and Ivy. They said they'd come back and meet up with me since we aren't supposed to go anywhere alone."

Her mom opened the door and Bryn sighed in relief. Clint stood there with his Mohawk and lightning tattoos on his arms. Ivy had her wild hair and tattoos. Both looked a little less sure of themselves than they normally did.

"Mom, Dad, these are my friends." Bryn performed a round of introductions.

"It's nice to meet you," Ivy said. "We've heard a lot about you."

"I hear you could teach me how to build better card houses," Clint said.

Bryn's dad laughed. "I haven't thought about that since we've been here."

Clint pulled a deck of cards from the Dragon's Bluff shopping bag he was carrying. They were new, still in the cellophane wrapping. "Then here's a housewarming present for you."

Her dad smiled. "Thank you."

"Not to cut your visit short, but we should go," Ivy said. "The driver said he needs to return to campus."

Bryn hugged her parents. "We should pick a day to put up a Christmas tree."

"Let's set up a date to go shopping for Christmas ornaments," her mom said. "Because the only thing we have access to here is a tree."

"I'd love that." Bryn's throat grew tight. "I know it's stupid, but I don't want to leave you guys. I'm afraid you might disappear again."

"We're not going anywhere, but why don't we walk you to the gate," her dad said.

Bryn took a breath and blew it out. "No. You should probably stay here. I don't want to tear up at the gate."

Her mom shook her head. "I recognize those Blue genes, and it's frightening."

"Tell me about it." Bryn gave them another quick hug and then left.

Once they were in the SUV, Ivy started talking rapid fire. "Dragon-pires have been reported in Dragon's Bluff. A student was approached behind one of the stores. He was buying a Christmas gift so he was by himself. He managed to get away, but he said the attacker was a Green female. He didn't see her face because she wore a mask."

She hated letting them believe the Silvers were Green, but she'd promised Jaxon she wouldn't share. There had to be a way around this situation. "I'm really beginning to hate these dragon-pires," Bryn said. "Why can't they be happy as they are?"

"I don't know," Ivy said. "Not to mention the fact that this is total crap because it's almost Christmas."

"They don't seem to be in the holiday spirit," Clint said.

Once they were back on campus Bryn invited Clint and Ivy up to her room. When they were seated on the couch, she paced back and forth.

"What's going on?" Ivy asked.

Bryn stopped pacing and turned to them. "Here's the deal. I know something I can't share because I promised I wouldn't tell anyone, but I don't want to keep it from you guys."

"Interesting." Clint leaned forward. "You can't tell us, but what if we guessed?"

That gave her some wiggle room. "I can live with that. Here's your clue. If the dragon-pires were hybrids, what kind do you think they'd be?"

"They have to be part Green, right?" Ivy said.

"That's a good guess," Bryn responded.

"Green-Red, Green-Black, Green-Orange?" Clint said.

"Green-Blue," Ivy said.

Bryn nodded.

"Oh my God," Ivy said. "The brains of a Green with the drive and desire to rule of a Blue? That makes so much sense in a twisted sort of way."

Bryn collapsed in the chair. "It was making me crazy not telling you guys."

"What about Garret?" Clint said. "He should know about this."

"You can't tell him," Bryn said. "And you can't ask him to guess. I promised Jaxon I wouldn't tell."

"I'm glad you're hanging onto your rebel roots," Clint said.

Once her friends left, she called Jaxon, partly out of guilt. "Did you hear about dragon-pires in Dragon's Bluff?"

"I did, which means you won't be going back there anytime soon.

"Excuse me?"

He sighed. "Let me rephrase that. We shouldn't go to Dragon's Bluff until they find whoever is attacking students."

"I still don't like it but saying it that way doesn't make me want to shoot a fireball at your head."

"Right." Jaxon snorted. "I'll remember that. Good night, Bryn."

"Good night."

Bryn hung up the phone. How would this news affect Dragon's Bluff? The no-loitering issue had already changed how people behaved in town. Now that there were evil Silver dragon-pires running around, what would that do?

Chapter Twenty-Six

Sunday morning, Bryn woke up with a sense of excitement. She ran to look out her terrace window, and there was snow. Glorious, fat, fluffy snowflakes swirled through the air. And she needed to get right out there because nothing was more exciting than soaring through icy air.

Rationally, she knew the first snow excited Blue dragons beyond a normal level. She didn't even care about breakfast or coffee right now. She just wanted to play outside. Dressing in jeans and a sweater, she grabbed her phone and dialed Jaxon's room.

It rang and rang. Where was he? She shouldn't go out alone. Not that a ton of other dragons wouldn't be out and about, but she was trying to do the right thing.

Knock. Knock. Knock.

Bryn hung up the phone, ran to her front door, and yanked it open. Jaxon stood there with a huge grin on his face. He grabbed her hand and pulled her out into the hallway. "Thank goodness you're awake."

Anticipation ramped up inside of her. "We're going outside, right?"

"Of course we are." They dashed down the stairs along with most of the other students. Everyone was talking and laughing and acting completely out of character for Blues. It was wonderful.

Once they made it outside, Jaxon released Bryn's hand. They both shifted into dragon form. Bryn focused to make sure all her scales were Blue. Since Jaxon didn't say anything she figured she'd succeeded. He shot up into the air, and she followed him. Blue dragons filled the sky... no one was racing or trying to nudge each other out of the way...everyone just flew in figure eights or slow spirals or soared in the sheer joy of flight.

The snowflakes slid against her scales, invigorating her senses. She wanted to fly higher, go farther, dive faster. Bryn stayed near Jaxon and he seemed to be keeping an eye on her, too, which was kind of nice. After a while, dragons from other Clans joined them. Clint and Ivy approached Bryn.

"We thought we'd find you out here," Clint said.

"The only thing that could keep you from your coffee would be the first snow," Ivy said.

"Isn't it wonderful?" Bryn, inhaled the cold, metallic air.

"It's pretty cool," Ivy said.

"I'm glad it happened on a weekend instead of a school day like last year," Bryn said. Last year she'd flown with Valmont before going to class. Was Valmont out playing in the snow with Megan? Maybe. That thought didn't bother her as much as it would have a month ago.

Jaxon flew over to where they were treading air. "I'm hoping you're just being social rather that telling Bryn she has to go somewhere to investigate crazy Silver dragon- pires."

"No dragon-pire information to report," Clint said.

"And I have no desire to investigate anything," Bryn's stomach growled. "Although I might want to take a break for breakfast before I fly some more."

Jaxon looked disappointed. "Fly with me for awhile longer and then we can go have breakfast with your friends."

He'd never asked her to spend time with him just to have fun. "Okay."

"Come find us when you're done," Ivy said. She and Clint took off, flying in another direction.

"Let's go." Jaxon shot off straight up in the air.

She laughed and followed along until he slowed, hung in the air for a moment and then effortlessly did a backward dive which turned into a spiral toward the ground. She imitated his maneuver but knew she didn't look quite as graceful...okay probably not half as graceful as he did but still, it was fun.

Jaxon leveled out as he came toward the ground then shot off into the air again. She was torn between following him and wanting to watch him. Seeing him so at ease and happy was a rare thing. Maybe after he'd had awhile to get past what had happened with Rhianna he could be like this all the time? How much nicer would her life be if he actually liked her and wanted to spend time with her? She shook herself. Rather than focus on the future, she decided to concentrate on having fun in the moment.

After several more spiraling dives, Jaxon flew up next to her and said, "Ready, set, go." And then he shot off.

"Hey." Bryn laughed. "That's cheating." She flapped her wings, pushing down with force in an attempt to gain on him. She caught up with his tail.

He glanced back and flicked his tail at her. She briefly considered biting him, as a joke, but that might be weird, so she focused on powering her wings up and down, arcing up above him, and then diving right past his snout and taking the lead.

He roared, and frost hit her flank. She twisted around midair and blasted him with snow.

Diving under her, he looped back around and came to fly by her side. "One of these days," he said, "I'll outfly you."

She laughed. "Not likely." Her wings were tired. "I'm ready for food." She looped back and forth until she settled on the ground near the dining hall. He followed after her, shifted into human form, and she did the same. "That was fun," she said.

"It was." He smiled at her like they had shared something special and her heart tripped a beat.

"Ready for breakfast?" she asked because she didn't know what else to say. This was uncharted territory.

"Sure."

Clint and Ivy landed nearby and shifted. Jaxon spotted them and frowned. It was like someone flipped a switch on his mood and the happiness drained away from his face. "Why don't you go eat with your friends and I'll go eat with mine?"

"We could all eat together," Bryn said. "It's not like our friends haven't met."

"It's a Clan tradition," Jaxon said. "We eat together after the first snow. You wouldn't understand."

What the hell? "Excuse me?"

"I said—"

Bryn did her best to keep her voice down. "I heard what you said. I just don't know why you said it."

"I'm just telling you the truth."

"No. You're just being a dick. We were having fun. Why are you deliberately trying to—" she almost said hurt me, but she didn't want to give him that much emotional power, so she went with, "Why are you trying to piss me off?"

He wore that blank expression she'd seen for most of the summer. "You're being ridiculous."

"No. You were enjoying my company. Even if it was due to the first snow, and now you're acting all aloof and obnoxious and annoyingly Blue."

"I am Blue," he said. "I'm not the one who is acting."

Flames sparked in her gut. He wanted to point out her mixed heritage? Fine. She'd help him remember. She took a deep breath and shot a ten-inch fireball at his stupid head.

He blasted sleet to keep the fireball from reaching him. "Don't do that again."

"Continue acting like a jerk and you're going to be dodging fireballs for the rest of your life," she snarled and then stalked toward the dining hall.

Clint and Ivy caught up with her.

"What happened?" Ivy asked.

"I have no freaking clue," Bryn said. "Can we get carryout and go to your room, because if he says one more word to me, I'm going to lose it and really try to hurt him."

"Sure," Ivy said.

They went through the line in the dining hall, loading up a few carryout containers. People stared and whispered.

Bryn held it together until they reached Ivy's room and then she sat down and put her head in her hands. "I don't get it. We were having fun together. You saw him. He asked me to stay and spend time with him. Flying was great. When we landed he was good and then something set him off and totally changed his personality." She recapped their conversation.

"I'm not crazy, right?" she asked.

"No. It sounds like he was being a jerk on purpose to make you mad," Ivy said.

"And that comment about him not having to pretend to be Blue," Clint said. "That's like textbook passive-aggressive behavior. Even if he didn't realize it, he was trying to push you away."

"Why?" Bryn opened her container of food and dug into her French toast sticks. "Since we're stuck together, why not have fun? A better question is, why turn into a total jackass after we had a good time?"

"Do you think it had something to do with Rhianna?" Ivy asked. "Maybe he felt like he was being disloyal to her memory or something?"

"I don't know," Bryn said. "And if that was the case then why not talk to me? Turning into a total asshat doesn't help anything."

"It's almost like he's sabotaging your relationship so you won't become close," Clint said.

Bryn took a giant drink of coffee and thought about that statement. "He came to my room. He asked me to fly. He asked me to stay longer. We had fun. And then he freaked out and did something to make me mad so our relationship would continue to be a non-relationship?"

"That about sums it up," Clint said.

"Okay. Say that's true," Bryn said. "Why not just admit to that fact? He could tell me he doesn't feel right having fun because of Rhianna. I'd get that. If he continues down this route, there's going to be a funeral rather than a wedding, because I am not putting up with that level of bullshit."

"And you shouldn't have to," Ivy said.

"Here's my next question. Is he sitting somewhere telling his friends about what he did, or am I totally off his radar like an out of sight, out of mind thing?"

"I have no answer to that question," Clint said. "But I am willing to run reconnaissance as a spy. I could go back to the dining hall...pretend we need more coffee."

"No. He made his choice to be a jerk. He can live with it." Bryn sighed. "I hate that I let myself have fun with him... that I let myself believe things might be working out."

"Things could still work out," Ivy said. "He has to have some sense of self preservation, if nothing else. Pissing you off is dangerous. He'll have to make amends of some sort... right?"

"I don't know." Bryn sipped her coffee. "And I can't change him. The only thing I can change is what I expect from him." Bryn blinked. "I swear it's like I'm channeling my grandmother." And then she had another disturbing thought. "Oh my God. I'm Lillith."

"What are you talking about?" Ivy asked.

"Ferrin wanted my mother. After she disappeared, Lillith stepped in to take her place. She said it took her awhile to realize that Ferrin could never be emotionally invested in her because she wasn't the one he'd really wanted. Jaxon wanted Rhianna. I'm stepping in to take Rhianna's place...Jaxon will never care about me like he cared about Rhianna. So now I'm Lillith."

"Wow," Ivy said. "History has a strange way of repeating itself."

"I know," Bryn said. "I'm marrying the son of the man my mom rejected and even though I'll be his wife he'll never be close to me because he'll always wish I was Rhianna." She reached up to rub her temples. "All of this leads me back to the conclusion that my life sucks."

"Jaxon may be a dick, but he isn't as bad as Ferrin," Clint said. "So there is a chance he'll wise up. Who knows... maybe the key to living with Jaxon, or any Blue, is having low expectations. That way when he does something considerate it will be a nice surprise."

"Maybe," Ivy said, "you should go hang around in Sanctuary and see if you can meet a nice hybrid guy."

"I fantasize about finding someone else, but then I imagine what that would do to my grandmother."

"Can you sick your grandmother on Jaxon?" Clint asked.

"No." And that's when Bryn had a funny idea. "Should I call Lillith and see if she has any advice?"

"While that would be highly entertaining," Clint said, "I'm not sure you want to run to his mother."

"And given their stupid level of Clan loyalty, she'd probably be on his side," Ivy said.

"So what do I do?" Bryn threw her arms up in disgust. "I literally have no idea what my next move should be."

"Well, I guess you wait and see what he does," Ivy said.

"My dad mentioned that he forgot how annoying it was to walk on eggshells all the time. I refuse to do that. If Jaxon wants to be pissy, that's his problem. I'm not going to tiptoe around for the rest of my life."

"What we need to do is figure out something you can do that will bug the crap out of him," Clint said.

Not a bad idea.

Ivy snapped her fingers. "I've got it. Your hair. Change your hair back to red and blond stripes with the black streaks."

Would it be worth the backlash from her grandfather? Then again, he wouldn't have to know. And then it came to her. "I have a better idea. He's all about pointing out that I'm not a real Blue, right?"

Ivy nodded.

Bryn stood and went into Ivy's bathroom. She closed her eyes and imagined her hair various shades of blue with some purple thrown in for good measure. When she opened her eyes, she smiled. She played around a little bit with the color, getting the shades just right before going back out to show her friends. "What do you think?"

"It's awesome," Ivy said.

Clint grinned. "It's not like he can claim you're not blue now."

After they finished their breakfast, Bryn and her friends went back outside into the snow to show off her new look. They flew around, ignoring the gawkers. Jaxon stayed away, which suited Bryn just fine. She still couldn't believe how mean he'd been...and maybe how stupid she'd been to believe something good might ever happen between them. She wouldn't make that mistake again.

When they were tired from flying, and Bryn felt emotionally exhausted, she went back to her room. Clint and Ivy offered to hang out with her, but she didn't want to take up all their Sunday togetherness time.

Once she was back in her room, she wasn't sure what to do. She could call her mom, but her parents' only advice would be to run away. Who else could she gripe to that would understand and maybe have helpful advice? No one. She could call her grandmother, but she was pretty sure any advice given would be of the let him go his way and you go your way variety. And that didn't work for her at the moment either. Giving up on finding an answer, she grabbed her book. She'd had enough reality for one day. Time to get lost in a story that would end in a happily ever after.

Chapter Twenty-Seven

Monday morning Bryn stared at her blue hair in the mirror. She liked it. Should she keep it? She switched back to her dark blond with a cherry red stripe. That was more her. She met Clint and Ivy on her terrace and flew down to the dining hall with them. If Jaxon spent time knocking on her door that was too bad. She was halfway through her French toast when the asshat in question stalked into the dining hall.

"Let the games begin," Ivy muttered.

Jaxon didn't stop at the buffet, he headed straight for her table.

"You should have let me know that I wasn't walking you to breakfast," he said.

"You shouldn't expect me to be considerate of your time or feelings when you've acted like a jackass," Bryn shot back.

His eyes narrowed, but he didn't respond. Instead he went to the buffet line.

"That was entertaining," Clint said.

On the walk to Elemental Science with Clint and Ivy, Bryn kept a watch out for Jaxon. Since their interaction at breakfast, he hadn't even glanced in her direction. He wanted to give her the cold shoulder? Fine by her. The less interaction they had, the better.

Unfortunately, the seating chart in Mr. Stanton's class had her sitting next to him. Thankfully, they were working on their own, writing essays, rather than interacting in a group project. When class ended, Jaxon stood and looked at her expectantly.

"What?" she said.

"I'm walking you to your next class," he said like she should have realized that fact. "Per our normal routine."

"That doesn't work for me," Bryn said. "Clint and Ivy can walk me to class." She looked at her friends for confirmation.

"Sure we can do that," Clint said. "Let's go."

"That won't be necessary," Jaxon said. "It's my job to escort you to class."

"Nope. You've been relieved of duty due to your piss poor attitude." She walked past him. Clint and Ivy followed. They were halfway down the hall when Jaxon caught up with her. He didn't say anything. He just walked near her with a blank expression on his face. For some reason that pissed her off more.

"Go away," she said.

"This is one of those moments when what you want is irrelevant," Jaxon informed her with a little too much attitude.

"You know there's something I've been wanting to try." She reached up and touched his hair. Focusing her Quintessence, she imagined his hair neon pink.

He jerked away from her, but not before he had a bright pink stripe in his hair.

Clint and Ivy laughed.

Bryn grinned. "That worked better than I thought."

"What did you do?" Jaxon reached up and touched his hair.

Students around them laughed.

"Are they laughing at me?" Jaxon spoke through clenched teeth.

"I'm sure they're laughing with you." Bryn headed into class with a warm, fuzzy, satisfied feeling in her chest.

Jaxon stormed in behind her. "Fix it."

"Bite me," Bryn shot back.

"Bryn, that's not the appropriate use of your medical skill," Medic Williams said from her desk. "Jaxon, come here." She ran her hand over Jaxon's hair and it returned to its normal blond color. "Now go to class."

After Jaxon left the room, Medic Williams raised an eyebrow at Bryn. "Care to explain?"

"He was being a condescending asshat."

Janelle and some other students laughed.

Medic Williams shook her head. "As tempting as it may be to mess around with other people in that manner, it undermines our profession."

Bryn was not sorry.

"Okay, class. You're going to read through some case studies with a partner. Take notes about any questions you have, and we'll work out the answers together."

After the folders were passed out, Janelle scooted closer to Bryn. "Was that as fun as it looked?"

"Yes. I regret nothing." Bryn opened her file. "What are we reading?"

Janelle opened their folder. "A Medic healed a newborn baby."

That reminded her of something. "Are dragon pregnancies fragile? I've heard of way too many women losing babies."

"I think they are fragile up to a certain point." Janelle leaned in and spoke in a quiet tone. "It also depends on how much inbreeding has happened within the Clan. Blues tend to miscarry more often because they tend to only marry within certain families."

"Really?"

Janelle nodded. "There are more Reds than any other Clan. Black and Green dragons are the next largest Clans. Blues are the smallest, outside of the Orange Clan, of course."

Interesting. "I never heard anyone say that before."

"You know us Greens. We like to measure things and track data. The Reds have more children per family. Black and Green dragons tend to stop at two kids. Blues may have more than one child but they space them out so they are practically a generation apart."

"Like Jaxon and Asher."

"Exactly," Janelle said. "Which is also why most Blue siblings aren't close. They don't grow up together. One is an adult before the other one starts elementary school."

"That's so weird."

"It keeps the balance of power for the older sibling as the heir, while allowing for the safety net of having another child to inherit, if something happens to the first one."

...

In Basic Movement, Bryn kept an eye out for Jaxon. She had no idea what type of repercussions she was in for.

"That thing with his hair was brilliant," Clint said as they walked on the treadmills.

"I enjoyed it."

"Too bad Medic Williams changed it back so quickly," said Ivy.

After they finished warming up, Bryn felt antsy. "I'm going to beat the crap out of a Slam Man." She jogged across the room to the Slam Man section where Keegan, one of the few dragons who'd been nice to her when she first came to school, and some other Reds were punching and kicking the man-shaped punching bags.

Keegan smiled at her. "Let me guess. You want to hit a certain someone, so you're going to punch the Slam Man instead."

"You might be right," Bryn said.

"Yeah, I heard he was a jerk. Did you really turn his hair pink?"

"Maybe."

Keegan gestured toward the Slam Man he'd been wailing on. "He's all yours."

Bryn took a few practice punches until she fell into a rhythm of jabs and uppercuts like her father had taught her. After a few minutes, she developed a mantra to go along with it. Jaxon was a jerk. Punch. Punch. Kick. He'd deserved what she'd done. Punch. Punch. Kick. Waiting for payback was going to suck. Punch. Punch. Kick. She stopped for a breather and to wipe the sweat out of her eyes.

If she really did go through with the marriage contract from hell, she'd make sure there was a Slam Man available in their estate. That way when she wanted to punch Jaxon, she'd go take it out on the Slam Man instead. Maybe she should have several Slam Mans. One per floor or one per wing.

Clint and Ivy walked Bryn to the rest of her classes. Jaxon hovered nearby with a you're dead to me look on his face. By dinner that night, Bryn was working on her I don't give a crap attitude but finding it hard to achieve.

"I'm trying to be Zen," Bryn said. "And not worry about what he might be plotting as revenge, but every time I see him my irritation goes up another notch."

"Maybe you should have it out with him," Ivy said.

"If I thought it would do any good, I would." Bryn slammed her fork down. "I know he'll counter any question or complaint I have with some holier than thou Blue Clan logic that will irritate the living hell out of me. And then I won't just color his hair, I'll set it on fire. Any advice?"

"Ignore him and hope he goes away?" Clint said.

"I've tried that," Bryn said. "Didn't work."

"Then either you talk to him or you don't," Clint said.

"And remember we're always available to help you dispose of a body," Ivy said.

After dinner, Bryn started on her homework. She'd just finished her last assignment when her phone rang.

There was a 50 percent chance it was either her grandmother or Jaxon. Steeling herself she answered the phone.

"We need to talk," Jaxon said.

Fire surged in Bryn's gut. "I suggest you rephrase that as a question rather than a command."

"Fine. Can we talk?"

She desperately wanted to say no, but the joy from shutting him down wouldn't last long, and they did need to straighten a few things out. "I'm done with my homework if you want to come over now."

"I'll be there in fifteen minutes."

Bryn loaded up her book bag for the next day and waited for Jaxon to knock on the door. How mad and hateful was he going to be? She took a few deep, cleansing breaths. No matter what he said, she wouldn't show any emotion. If she was going to be in a relationship with a Blue, she'd have to start acting like one. For no other reason than self preservation. Maybe she'd start making voodoo dolls to take her frustration out on.

Knock. Knock. Knock.

Okay. I can do this. She crossed the room and opened the door. Jaxon stood there, holding a book and a container with two cups of milk and half a dozen cookies. He came in and set the container on the coffee table before taking a seat in one of the winged-back chairs.

She sat across the coffee table from him on the couch. "What's with the cookies?"

"A prop to make people believe that everything is fine." His tone was cold and calculated.

"So when you murder me for turning your hair pink it won't look premeditated?"

"Something like that."

"I'm not apologizing," Bryn said. "So if that's what you're here for you might as well leave."

He gave her the silent treatment.

Fine. If he wasn't going to talk, she would. "We had fun flying together during the first snow, and then you said something to make me mad on purpose, in front of the entire campus. Why?"

"I resented you for being who you are."

"That clears everything up." She reached for a cookie.

"I resented you because you weren't Rhianna."

How in the hell was she supposed to respond to that? Rather than trying, she grabbed one of the cups of milk, removed the carryout lid, broke the cookie in half, and dunked it in the milk before taking a bite. She finished two cookies while she waited for Jaxon to say something else. He ate a cookie as if he was waiting for her to say something. Finally, she caved.

"I'll never be Rhianna. I'm not trying to replace her, but we are stuck together, so I don't understand why we can't make the best of it."

"After I had fun with you it felt like I'd been disloyal to her," Jaxon said.

"Okay. I have several responses to that. All or most of them will tick you off. So listen before you yell at me. First off, you should probably see a grief counselor to help you deal with losing someone you loved. Second, according to the contract we signed, your loyalty is supposed to be to me now. Rhianna is gone and she's not coming back. Third, there is only so much crap I am willing to put up with and there are only so many times you can be a jerk before I write you off as a lost cause. Not to mention, I am training to become a Medic. I could probably poison you and make it look like an accident—so you really need to stop pissing me off."

"I'll do my best, but you can't pull a prank on me in public. Ever. Again."

There were so many smart-ass remarks she could make, but she refrained. "I can agree to that."

"Good. I'll acknowledge that you're on Team Westgate. We can work toward being friends." And then he stood and exited her dorm room, leaving the milk and cookies on the table.

Bryn slid down on the couch. She should feel better, but she didn't. Team Westgate sucked.

Chapter Twenty-Eight

Bryn called Ivy and summarized the latest turn in her bizarre life.

"So now you're Team Westgate and he won't be an asshat?" Ivy said. "I'm pretty sure that's not enough to make a long-term relationship work, but maybe it's a start."

"Part of me is relieved, and part of me wants to go chase down a Blue female and pray she's a match for Jaxon so I can push him off onto someone else." Bryn shoved the last piece of cookie in her mouth.

"No one knows what the future will bring," Ivy said. "Clint chased me for years and I swore we'd never end up together but look at us now. You and Jaxon could end up having a real relationship after you're married."

Did she even want that? "It's not so much that I want something real with him," Bryn said. "I just want something real with someone. Does that make me an awful person?"

"No. It makes you normal," Ivy said. "Try looking at it this way, even if Jaxon had never been involved with Rhianna, this whole situation between you two would still be awkward. You'd have to become friends first before entertaining the possibility of anything more. And that's kind of the point you're at now."

"I guess so," Bryn said. "So maybe I should just concentrate on the friendship because that's the first step toward not wanting to kill him on a regular basis. Right?"

"Exactly," Ivy said. "With everything that's been going on, I'm not sure you're paying attention, but school is out for Christmas break soon. You'll be at your grandparents' house again, doing Blue things. You should probably come to some sort of understanding before then."

What Ivy said made sense, but it wasn't necessarily easy to put into practice.

...

Jaxon walked Bryn to breakfast and to all her classes on Tuesday and Wednesday. They were civil to each other but it wasn't comfortable. By Thursday evening, Bryn was tired of walking on eggshells. When he walked her back to her dorm room after dinner, she said, "Can you come in for a minute?"

He gestured that she should open the door and then followed her inside and went to sit at the library table.

She sat across from him. Now what? It's not like she'd rehearsed what she wanted to say. "I'm really tired of things being awkward between us."

He snorted. "When has it not been awkward?"

"Point taken," she said. "But it would be nice if we could dial the awkward down just a bit." There had to be something they could do. She spotted a pack of cards Clint had left behind when they were doing homework. "Have you ever built a card house?"

"No."

"Okay. Consider this a team building exercise." She grabbed the deck of cards and set two cards up to start the base layer.

Jaxon looked at her like she was crazy. "Are we building the same house or are we each building our own?"

"Whatever you want," Bryn said.

He grabbed two cards and copied what she'd done. Once he understood the process, he added more walls and a roof. Bryn put the final card on her roof, and the entire thing collapsed. One of her cards slid over and tapped the back wall of Jaxon's card house, causing his creation to fall apart.

"Sorry," Bryn said, and then she laughed.

"Yes, I can tell you're overcome with remorse."

"Let's build one together this time," she suggested.

"On one condition." Jaxon stood and went over to her bookshelf to retrieve a small wooden chest. "We use this to stabilize the base."

"That's cheating."

"I prefer to think of it as an improvement in design." Jaxon leaned the cards around the box. "The upper floors will still be tricky."

They completed the first floor without incident. They managed to create walls for the second floor. "So far so good," Bryn said.

He added cards for the roof one at a time. Bryn sat back and watched. Maybe the key to keeping him happy was letting him be in charge of things she didn't care about. And wow, that sounded like something her grandmother would say.

When he added the last card for the roof and it didn't collapse, he smiled at her.

"You look so proud," she said.

"I am. The question is, do we start on a third floor or stop now while we're in a good place?"

"I say, stop now," Bryn said. "We can always try for more floors later." After Jaxon left, Bryn wondered if the card house was representative of their relationship. They seemed to be headed back into the friend zone. Once they made it there, she'd be happy to stay at that level. There was no reason to go for anything more.

...

Whether it was due to the approaching holidays or the fact that there hadn't been any recent attacks, the mood on campus seemed festive. Even Jaxon appeared more relaxed than normal.

"Do you think the dragon-pires have moved on to different hunting grounds?" Clint asked over pancakes Saturday morning in the Dining Hall.

"Maybe." Bryn took another bite of her butter and syrup drenched carbohydrate bliss. No matter how crazy her life became she could still find comfort in food. "It might be easier for dragon-pires to stake out some of the subdivisions for now, since all the students will be heading home for Christmas break soon."

"Great," Ivy said. "Now I can be paranoid about dragon-pires attacking at home, too."

"I'll never leave your side there, either." Clint said. "So, you won't have anything to worry about."

"My parents might have something to say about that," Ivy said.

"That is the one downside to going home," Clint said. "Being apart."

"I thought your families spent Christmas together," Bryn said.

"We do," Ivy said. "But there are also Girls' Days Out and entire days of baking cookies that are no-guys-allowed." That reminded Bryn of something. "I wonder if my mom and I could bake cookies at their cabin? Last year, I missed that." She sighed. "Having my parents back this Christmas is the best present ever."

"Speaking of presents," Ivy said. "Have you figured out what you're buying Jaxon?"

Ugh. "No. I mean what do you buy someone who has a freaking forest in their house?"

"A platinum-plated bug zapper?" Clint said.

Bryn laughed. "Funny, but I don't think he'd appreciate it."

"What would you buy him if he weren't obscenely wealthy?" Ivy asked.

"Good question." If she took away the money, what did Jaxon enjoy? "It's not like he has any hobbies that I'm aware of, but I do know that he likes books, cars, and cookies."

"Find out his favorite author and buy him a boxed set of books," Ivy said.

"He is a Westgate," Bryn said. "Maybe a first edition of a book, signed by the author would work."

"That would be cool," Clint said. "Where do you shop for something like that?"

"I have no idea, but I bet my grandmother would know," Bryn said.

After hanging out with her friends, Bryn went back to her room and made a couple of calls. The first one was to her mom. She arranged to meet them the next afternoon for a cookie baking extravaganza. The second call was to her grandmother who pointed her in the right direction to purchase rare books. Now, Bryn just had to figure out what kind of books Jaxon preferred. She hadn't paid attention to what he'd been reading. Maybe Miss Enid the librarian could help her out. She called the library.

"I'm not supposed to share patrons reading lists," Miss Enid said. "But since it's for a good cause, I can tell you that he reads a lot of thrillers."

That didn't narrow the field much. "Thanks." Bryn hung up the phone.

There was one more person who could clue her in. She called Westgate Estate and asked the operator for Lillith.

"Hello, Bryn. Is everything all right?"

"Yes, I was hoping you could help me come up with a Christmas present for Jaxon."

Lillith laughed. "Westgates are notoriously difficult to buy for, but I should be able to help. What have you come up with so far?"

"I was thinking about a signed, first edition novel of one of his favorite books, but I'm not sure what that would be."

"Oh...that is an interesting idea. I know he enjoyed those books about a wizard and a hobbit and something about a ring. We read those over and over again when he was younger. I think he even took a set of them to school."

"Are you talking about the Tolkien books like The Lord of the Rings?"

"That's right," Lillith said.

"As a Westgate, do you think he'd like a nice leather bound copy of the set or maybe a signed copy, if I can find one? Even if it doesn't inspire jealousy and awe in his friends? Is that really important?"

"His father has taken care of the jealousy and awe gift," Lillith said. "So you don't have to worry about that."

"Really? What is it?"

"Sorry." Lillith laughed. "You'll have to wait and see. I've been sworn to secrecy."

"Fine. Well, I guess I'm off to shop for rare books," Bryn said.

"Have fun and I'll see you at the Christmas Ball." Armed with this new and amusing bit of information, Bryn called the rare book dealer her grandmother had suggested in Dragon's Bluff. She didn't want to come right out and say, what is the most expensive version of this book that you have, so she improvised, "I'm interested in rare Tolkien books. What do you have available?"

An hour later, Bryn had used a substantial amount of the money her grandparents had put into her account when they'd accepted her as their granddaughter to buy a first edition, signed, hardback set of The Lord of the Rings. The dealer assured her that he'd take care of the transaction and have the books wrapped and shipped to Sinclair Estate. Hopefully, Jaxon would appreciate the gift. If not, Bryn knew what she'd be reading over Christmas break.

What would Jaxon buy for her? Would he even attempt to find something she'd like, or would he buy the most expensive and exclusive item he could find for the strange game Blues played? With her luck, she'd end up with a book bag bedazzled with diamonds in the form of a giant W or something ridiculous like that. Truthfully, the only thing she wanted for Christmas was to spend time with her family. She'd love to have her parents and grandparents in the same room, but she was beginning to realize that might never happen. For now, it was enough that she'd be baking cookies with her mom and dad tomorrow, which left one question. Who would be riding to Sanctuary with her? She hadn't thought to ask Clint and Ivy if they wanted to go to Dragon's Bluff so who did that leave? Only one person was that interested in her personal welfare. She grabbed the phone and dialed Jaxon's number.

"Hello?" Jaxon sounded irritated. Great.

"Sorry to bug you, but I'm visiting my parents tomorrow and I know the SUVs are Directorate sanctioned, but I wasn't sure if I should ride out there alone."

"What time were you planning on going?" he asked.

"Noon."

He was quiet for a moment. Maybe she should have called Clint and Ivy.

"I can drive you there at eleven thirty and pick you up at two," Jaxon said. "I'm meeting my father in Dragon's Bluff for lunch."

"Thank you. That will work."

Bryn called her parents to update them on the change of plans.

"So Jaxon is driving you out here." Her dad sounded like he was plotting something. "You know, I've never met him."

This wasn't a road she was ready to go down. "You have plenty of time to meet him. If you want you can frown at him from the front gate when he drops me off, but I'm not arranging a meet and greet. Tomorrow is supposed to be fun, not stressful."

"It would be fun for me." Her dad laughed. "For him... not so much."

"Another time," Bryn said. "See you tomorrow."

...

Jaxon wasn't super chatty as he drove her toward Sanctuary, but at least the silence between them was comfortable.

"Thanks for taking me," she said.

"Not a problem," he responded. "I'm glad you didn't ask me to meet your parents."

Bryn laughed. "My dad suggested I bring you along. I told him this wasn't the right time."

"Good answer," Jaxon said. "It's strange. My father raised me to think badly of your mother, and before you gripe at me, I've overcome that. It's funny that he never mentioned your father."

"I will never pretend to understand how your father thinks," Bryn said.

When they pulled up to the gate, Bryn grinned. Her dad stood there, holding an ax casually against his shoulder like he'd just gone out to chop wood. There was a small stack of wood in a wire basket at his feet, but Bryn bet the entire thing was staged.

"Want to come say hello?" she asked.

Jaxon put the car into park. "I can't let the crazy man with an ax think he's intimidated me, so sure, I'd love to meet him."

Bryn laughed. "Okay. Try not to act too Blue. Let's go."

Jaxon snorted. She climbed out of the car and walked toward the guard at the admission checkpoint. Jaxon did the same.

"Who are you visiting?" the guard asked.

"My parents, Ian and Sara McKenna." She pointed at Jaxon. "He won't be staying. He's just saying hello."

The guard made them both sign in, gave them lanyards which had numbered pass cards, and then he allowed them to go through the gate.

"Hi, Dad." Bryn grinned. "Jaxon wanted to meet you before he heads to Dragon's Bluff for lunch."

Her dad set the ax down and held out his hand. "It's nice to meet you."

"It's interesting to meet you," Jaxon said. "The ax was a nice touch."

"Thanks," her dad said. "I thought it would help get the message across."

"What message is that?" Jaxon asked without blinking.

"Despite the strange history between our families, I expect you to treat my daughter with respect."

Jaxon nodded. "In spite of the strange history our families share, I do respect Bryn. So you've nothing to worry about."

"Good."

"I'll be back at two," Jaxon said to Bryn.

"See you then." After Jaxon had signed out and driven away, Bryn pointed at the ax. "I can't believe you did that."

He grinned. "Come on. Your mom is chomping at the bit to make cookies."

As they walked to their cabin, Bryn noticed that he wasn't wearing his leg brace but he was moving well. There was only a slight jerkiness to his walk.

"Your leg seems better," she said.

"Your friend Garret stopped by the other night. The new brace he made for me fits under my jeans. It's amazing."

After a round of hugs and a quick summary of her dad's meeting with Jaxon, they started working on the cookies.

Bryn's mom rolled out the dough for sugar cookies on the kitchen table. "I mixed this batch up last night so we could bake them today."

"There's about half a batch of chocolate chip cookie dough left in the fridge, too," her dad said.

"Half a batch?" Bryn asked.

"I ate the other half." Her dad grinned. "For quality control testing, of course."

"Of course." Bryn laughed. "Where are the cookie cutters?"

"On top of the refrigerator," said her mom.

Bryn grabbed the brand-new package of cookie cutters and ripped open the bag. "Let's see...we have a tree, a star, an angel, and a candy cane."

"And I will be making my amazing snowmen." Her dad reached for some of the dough still in the bowl and started rolling large, medium, and small-sized balls.

Bryn took a shuddering breath as a wave of emotion swamped her. She turned away and wiped at the tears in her eyes.

"What's wrong, honey?" her mom asked.

And Bryn burst into tears. "Sorry, it's just last year I never thought I'd see Dad's crooked snowmen or make cookies with you ever again."

Her mom dusted her hands off on her apron as she came to give Bryn a hug. "I'm so sorry."

"It was my fault," Bryn said. "I'm the reason someone tried to blow up the apartment with you inside."

"That's not true." Her dad came to join them in a family hug. "They came after us because we're dragons who defied the Directorate."

"The reason doesn't really matter," her mom said. "What matters is that we're here together and we have cookies to bake."

"You're right," Bryn said. "Back to the cookies."

They spent the rest of the afternoon baking and eating cookies, and it was wonderful, but it wasn't the same as it had been before all this dragon business happened. Then again, maybe it was because she was older, more aware of the craziness going on in the world, and everything seemed less safe.

When it was time to leave, her mom volunteered to escort her to the gate.

"Sure you don't want to come along...maybe bring a machete or something," Bryn said to her dad.

"No," he said. "I think he got the message loud and clear."

She hugged her dad and then headed out the front door with her mom.

Jaxon pulled up to the gate within seconds of Bryn's arrival. She hugged her mom, signed out, and returned the lanyard. Jaxon opened her car door for her, giving a nod of recognition to her mother before climbing in and driving them back toward school.

"So what did you think of my dad?" Bryn asked.

"He made his point in an amusing manner," Jaxon said. "What did he think of me?"

Her dad had said Jaxon didn't seem as obnoxious as his father, but she probably shouldn't share that quote word for word. "He appreciates your attitude toward me and likes that you come across as more approachable than your father."

"According to my father, Westgates aren't supposed to be approachable," Jaxon said. "My mother had a different theory on the subject, so I landed somewhere in between."

Thank goodness for Lillith.

"Speaking of your mother, how are she and Asher doing?"

"We didn't discuss them," Jaxon said.

And now she was back to thinking Blues were weird. "Anything else going on that I should know about? Any Dragon-pire reports or family drama?"

"I think we are at the no news is good news stage," Jaxon said.

"That works for me. I'm hoping my chaos magnet days are over. I'd love an uneventful holiday season."

"The Christmas Ball should be safer this year. Your grandfather has hired extra guards and installed more surveillance cameras around the estate."

"That's comforting," Bryn said. But I don't think I'll ever be able to relax and believe an event is safe."

"I feel compelled to point out that the common denominator among all the recent chaos has been you."

"And you get to spend the rest of your life with me," Bryn shot back. "You lucky duck."

"I can barely contain my joy."

They drove back to the Institute for Excellence trading comments and laughing. It was nice. On the way to her room, he said, "Do you still have the present I asked you to keep for me?"

Way to put a damper on the day. "I do." Where was he going with this?

"Can I have it back?" he asked.

"Of course." She unlocked her door, letting him into the living room and then went to retrieve the bracelet from underneath her sweaters. Should she admit she'd looked at it? No.

Jaxon accepted the box from her and held it in his palm like he was testing its weight. "I finally figured out what I should do with it." He slid it into his coat pocket and then said, "I almost forgot." He pulled a small white cardboard box from his pocket and handed it to her.

"What's this?" She opened the box and looked inside to find brownies dotted with green Christmas tree-shaped sprinkles.

"I stopped in a bakery to order something for my mother, and I saw those."

That was oddly thoughtful of him.

"I know normal girls wouldn't want to eat brownies after baking cookies all day, but I figured that didn't apply to you."

"It's not like I can argue that statement, so thank you."

"Good night, Bryn."

"Good night." She locked the door behind him before taking a bite of brownie. It was chocolatey fudgey heaven. A small voice in her head whispered that he must actually care about her. The smarter part of her brain said to shut up and enjoy the brownie. No reason to read anything even remotely romantic into the nice gesture.

Bryn stopped mid chew. Wait. What? Did she just think of romance and Jaxon in the same sentence? Sure, he was funny, and smart, and handsome when he wasn't being an asshat, but that didn't mean there would ever be any real feelings between them. Right?

She should shoot for friendship. Friendship might be attainable. If she went looking for anything more than that, she'd be disappointed. The brownie was a gesture of friendship. That was all. Just friends.

Chapter Twenty-Nine

The night before Christmas break, Bryn couldn't sleep. She was looking forward to time off from school and spending time with her family. But staying at Sinclair Estate sometimes felt claustrophobic, which was odd for such a giant building. Maybe claustrophobic wasn't the right term, more like she was cut off from the world her friends lived in. After tossing and turning in her bed, she grabbed her blanket and a pillow and headed for the couch. Maybe a change in rooms would help shut her brain off. Once she had herself situated on the couch she mentally ran through her list of Christmas gifts. She'd found a fancy pen for her grandfather and a beautiful cashmere scarf for her grandmother. The gifts probably weren't up to par, but they were from the heart, so they would have to do.

For her parents, she'd purchased a new set of dishes and silverware, since they seemed to be using odds and ends they'd scavenged. Her grandmother had confirmed that Jaxon's present had shown up at Sinclair Estate so that was taken care of.

Maybe counting presents wasn't like counting sheep because she was still wide awake. Fine. She'd just lie there and close her eyes and eventually she'd have to fall asleep.

When her alarm went off the next morning she struggled to get untangled from the covers which she'd somehow wound tight around herself while she'd been sleeping. She stumbled into her bedroom to shut off the alarm. Then she headed across the hall to turn off the other alarm. The door didn't open. Could it be locked? The only reason it would be locked would be if someone was in there. Who in the hell was in the spare bedroom?

The doorknob was yanked out of her hand. Rhianna stood on the other side of the door looking groggy. "Sorry. I forgot we locked it."

Bryn could only stare. Rhianna was here. Alive? "We?"

"I hate that damn alarm." Jaxon's voice drifted into the hall. "I'm going back to bed. We don't have to be anywhere for two hours."

Bryn saw Jaxon climb back into bed. Rhianna said, "Sounds good to me." And then she shut the door.

What the hell was going on? This had to be a dream. It couldn't be real. Her phone rang, and she went to answer it. "Bryn, how could you let this happen?" her grandmother demanded.

"Let what happen?" Why was her grandmother yelling at her?

"We had Rhianna removed and then you just let her back into Jaxon's life? What's wrong with you?"

"This isn't real," Bryn said.

"Well if that's how you feel then you're no longer our granddaughter. We're cutting you off. Go live with your parents."

Bryn stared at the phone. How could her grandparents blame her for Rhianna not being dead? She shook her head. This made no sense.

"You did the right thing," her mom said.

Bryn blinked and looked at her surroundings. She was standing in her parents' cabin.

"We're proud of you, sweetie," her dad said. "But as you can see, there's no room for you here."

The inside of the cabin was tiny but surely they could let her sleep on the couch. "I don't need a bedroom. I'll sleep out here." She pointed at the couch.

"No," her mom said. "You misunderstood. We don't want you here. You turned your back on us. Left us for dead. Celebrated Christmas without us."

The room went fuzzy and Bryn found herself alone in a rundown cabin. "It hasn't been restored yet, but it has potential," Jaxon said. "You'll be fine. It's not like you ever wanted me in the first place." And then he disappeared, and she was alone in a rotting cabin in the middle of the woods. This wasn't real. Her parents wouldn't abandon her. Her grandparents wouldn't kick her out. Rhianna wasn't coming back to life. This was a stress dream. A stupid nightmare. She closed her eyes and tried to feel the softness of the pillow under her. There. She could feel that. Now she should feel the weight of the blanket. There. There it was. And she was going to wake up now. She opened her eyes and saw the dorm room ceiling.

Thank you, God. She shucked off the covers and went to the spare bedroom door. She reached for the handle and then hesitated. And that was dumb. She turned the handle and the door opened with ease. She flipped on the light switch and looked at the empty room.

The alarm went off, making her jump. How could it be morning already? Whatever. She walked over and smacked the top of the alarm to turn it off and then did the same thing in her room. She felt like crap. It's not like she could try going back to sleep after those disturbing dreams, so she headed for the shower.

She planned to meet up with Clint and Ivy before they all went home. After she was dressed and packed, she headed down to meet her friends outside of her dorm so they could walk to breakfast together.

Over a cup of coffee and an omelet she told them about her crazy nightmare.

"Wow," Clint said. "The only thing missing from that dream was dragon-pires."

"I guess I should be thankful for that."

"On to happier topics," Ivy said. "We should pick a date to meet and have lunch over break."

"I declare that lunch will occur at the Snack Shack on the twenty-eighth at eleven," Clint said.

"Why then?" Bryn asked.

"No reason," Clint said. "I just like making random decrees."

Ivy laughed.

After breakfast they all walked to where Bryn was meeting her grandmother. Two hugs later, Bryn climbed into the backseat of the SUV where her grandmother sat waiting for her.

"I have a surprise for you," her grandmother said. "We're making a special stop before we go home."

"Cool." Hopefully it wouldn't have anything to do with a Westgate. "Can you give me a hint?"

"No." Her grandmother sat back in the seat with her hands crossed in her lap. "I don't want to ruin the surprise."

Okay then. "How are the decorations coming along for the Christmas Ball?"

"Oh, they're lovely," her grandmother said. "I decided to go with the gold and silver trees with the reverse color ornaments and the stars on top are a mix of the two colors."

"That sounds pretty."

The SUV didn't head toward Dragon's Bluff. "We're not going shopping," Bryn said. "Are we going out to my secret estate?"

"It's not so secret anymore. I shared the plans with Lillith and your grandfather. They were surprisingly agreeable," her grandmother said. "And yes, that is where we're going. We're going to pick out a color palette."

When they pulled up to the estate, Bryn was once again amazed that she would live in such a massive and amazing place. The sand-colored stone looked even better in the daylight. The wide front porch with the columns gave it an open, airy feel. Inside the massive front door, the spiral design of the foyer floor looked even better in the sunlight. The veins of silver that ran through the floor and the walls sparkled in the light cast from the giant chandelier.

"The chandelier is beautiful." Made of crystals and silver, it was more modern than anything she'd seen in her grandparents' house.

"I'm glad you like it. If something like this had been available when I'd decorated our home, I would have chosen it."

"Can't you redecorate?" It's not like they lacked funds. "If I changed one fixture it would cause a ripple effect and I'd have to change dozens of other lights and fixtures. It's far more fun to start from scratch." Her grandmother walked up the stairs to the landing. "Follow me."

The hallways were light and airy in a way that Sinclair Estate was not. There were clean lines and random bits of sparkle but unlike Westgate Estate everything was in good taste.

The dining room had a back wall of atrium windows which made the room glow. The giant mahogany table which took up the center of the room was gorgeous. It could seat a dozen people with no one having to worry about bumping elbows, but Bryn hoped for something a bit cozier for her everyday meals. Although, if she ever had a dinner with Jaxon's parents and her mom and dad a little distance between the guests would be a good thing.

Her grandmother sat at the table and opened a large leather portfolio which contained several sketches of the very room they sat in. Each was done up in a different color scheme with samples of paint and wallpaper.

"You totally missed your calling as an interior designer," Bryn said.

Her grandmother nodded in appreciation. "Is there a color scheme you'd eliminate on first glance?"

"I'm hoping there is no wrong answer to that question." She didn't want to offend her grandmother.

"There is not," her grandmother said. "Since we built your home with lighter colored stone, your options for the interior can either continue with a neutral palette." She pointed at the drawing done up in tans, browns, and creams. "Or you can go with any number of colors."

Of her choices, there was only one that she didn't like. "The black and gray one isn't my favorite."

"Then we can eliminate that one." Her grandmother placed the sketch back in the portfolio.

One palette jumped out at Bryn. "I like the fall color scheme with the amber, yellow, evergreen, and red."

"Are you sure you're not just picking that because it's familiar?" her grandmother asked.

Bryn laughed. "Well, I was until you asked me that question."

"I tend to prefer those colors myself. We could use the darker colors as accents while keeping the walls mostly neutral warm tones."

"I trust you."

"Thank you." Her grandmother beamed. "Now I want to show you the adjoining room."

What kind of room adjoined a dining room? She was about to find out. Her grandmother pointed at a door which Bryn had assumed was a closet.

"After you."

Curious, Bryn walked over and opened the door. Inside she found a normal sized version of the room she'd just been in. It had the same atrium windows, but the table was meant for no more than four people.

"I love it."

"I know you prefer less formal meals on a day-to-day basis."

Everything her grandmother did was so thoughtful. "Thank you for all of this. It's amazing."

"You're welcome. It's nice to be appreciated."

After exploring a few more rooms which were unfurnished, they returned to Sinclair Estate. Her grandmother showed her the trees she'd designed for the Christmas Ball. They were gorgeous, of course.

"What's on the menu for dessert this year?" Last year her grandmother had surprised her with the Christmas cookies she'd missed baking with her parents. Now that she had her parents back what would her grandmother want to serve?

"We never serve the same thing two years in a row, so I can order Christmas cookies for you, but we won't have them as dessert at the ball."

"That works for me."

"For the ball, I was thinking about cake, but I wasn't sure how you'd feel about that."

Hmmm, she hadn't eaten that particular dessert since someone had poisoned her using carrot cake. "As long as it's not carrot cake, it might be okay."

"I was thinking chocolate cake with mint frosting."

"Sounds good."

The days before the Christmas Ball flew by in a flurry of activity. Her grandmother involved her in most of the choices for the event which was fun but stressful.

She was in the middle of taste-testing two different types of hot cocoa when Abigail the maid came in and told her that she had a phone call from Jaxon.

"Thanks." Bryn walked over to the phone and waited for Rindy to put the call through.

"Hello, Bryn?"

"Hey, Jaxon. What's up?" They hadn't spoken in four days which was a new record.

"I was wondering if you'd like to show me around the estate your grandmother is building."

That wasn't what she'd expected him to ask. "Sure, but where is this coming from?"

"It's not my idea," Jaxon said. "It's my mother's. She'd like to be invited, too."

Bryn laughed. "Hold on. Let me ask my grandmother." She explained the situation to her grandmother.

"I wondered how long Lillith would be able to stay away. See if they can meet us there this afternoon."

...

Bryn wasn't sure what reaction she expected from Jaxon, but the silent treatment he gave her during the tour didn't seem right. She grabbed his elbow and let Lillith and her grandmother move farther ahead of them before speaking.

"How am I supposed to interpret your silence?" she asked.

"I'm seventy percent impressed, and thirty percent annoyed," he said. "The estate is amazing, but if I'm going to live here I'd like to have some input."

"Oh." That she could deal with. "I have no issue with that. My grandmother won't, either." She looked up expecting to find her grandmother and Lillith. "Where'd they go?"

"I'm sure they're down the hall."

They continued walking and came to the stairs which led up to the second floor. "I bet they went up." Bryn dashed up the stairs but didn't see them. "That's weird."

"Let's just look around this floor," Jaxon said.

"Okay, but I don't think the rooms are finished up here." They wandered through a huge bedroom suite which overlooked the back garden. Bryn spotted her grandmother and Lillith on the veranda in the back yard. She opened the terrace door and walked out. "Hello down there."

Her grandmother looked up and waved. Bryn waved back and then went back into the bedroom, shutting the door. "That's one problem solved. Now that they know where we are, we can do a little more exploring. They finished a rooftop observation deck recently. I haven't been up there yet."

"That sounds promising."

They took the stairs to the third floor and looked around for a way to reach the roof. They'd walked up and down the main hall twice, opening doors that led to more rooms, but there was never a set of stairs to the roof.

"Are you sure there's a rooftop deck?" Jaxon asked.

"I swear my grandmother mentioned it at breakfast yesterday." Bryn opened a door to an office they'd investigated before, but this time she noticed that the window opened onto a set of stairs in the same way that the windows at school opened onto terraces. "I think I found it."

They opened the window and ascended the stairs which wrapped around the outside of a turret and led to a large flat area on the roof surrounded by a low wall. There was a fireplace and more surprisingly, a pool.

"Do we have a pool on our roof?" Jaxon asked.

"It looks like we do."

"That's kind of amazing," Jaxon said.

"My grandmother is awesome," Bryn said.

"Thank you," her grandmother said from behind her.

Bryn turned to see her grandmother and Lillith walking toward them. "I wondered if you'd find your way up here."

"You didn't tell me about the pool," Bryn said.

"I thought it would be more fun to let you discover it." Her grandmother tilted her head and looked at Jaxon like she was waiting for him to say something.

"It's spectacular." Jaxon glanced sideways at Bryn. "Even with the lack of W's."

Everyone laughed.

"I promise you'll have your W's on the front gates once they are installed," her grandmother said.

"We won't show Ferrin until that's done," Lillith said. "Now Marie and I are going to have tea in the small dining room while you two continue to look around. No rush. I feel terrible for saying this, but this is my first afternoon away from Asher and I'm enjoying myself."

"Every mother needs some time to herself," her grandmother said. The two women headed back down the stairs.

Jaxon walked toward the wall on the far side of the pool. Bryn followed after him. She wanted to say something like, See, it's not so bad being stuck with me. Look at the amazing house you get in return. But there was no way to say it without sounding a little bit desperate. So she went with, "Things seem to be falling into place at an alarming rate."

He nodded. "It's like your grandmother is trying to help us acclimate to our circumstances."

"It will certainly be easier to be happy here than in a house we didn't like." It was somehow ironic that her mom was happy in a tiny house with her father, but Bryn needed an extravagant mansion to be happy with Jaxon, or maybe that was what Jaxon needed to be happy with her.

"The view is amazing," Jaxon said.

Bryn tuned back into her surroundings and looked at the forest that stretched out around them. The trees were bare, but there were enough evergreens mixed in to keep it pretty.

"This could be okay." Jaxon turned to look at her. "Don't you think?"

Did he mean them personally or the house? Her answer was yes to both, but she wasn't sure what he meant, so she said, "I do."

He smiled and turned his gaze back to the view. His expression changed. "What's that?"

"Where?" Bryn looked where he pointed. "By that tree. Is someone sitting there?"

It was hard to tell from this distance. "Maybe someone is taking a coffee break?"

"That's an optimistic guess," he said.

Chapter Thirty

"Let's go see." Bryn shifted into dragon form.

"No," Jaxon said. "My mother and your grandmother are here. In case there is an issue, they need to be warned."

"We can still fly down and go in the back door," Bryn said. "It will be faster than taking the stairs."

"Okay."

She waited for him to shift and then they dove off the roof, aiming for the veranda. Bryn came to a stop, treaded air for a minute, and then dropped to a crouch. Jaxon landed gracefully next to her. They both shifted back to human form.

"Your landings have improved," he said.

"Thank you." She opened the back door and they made their way to the small dining room where they reported their concerns.

Her grandmother pulled out a cell phone. "Let's alert the guards." She spoke to someone on the phone and then pointed at the two open chairs at the table. "Have some tea while we wait."

"I thought maybe we'd go see for ourselves." Bryn edged toward the door.

"You thought wrong," her grandmother said.

Jaxon gave her a pointed look, but he didn't rat her out, which was good.

"While we're waiting, did you want to contribute to the color scheme for the house?" Bryn's grandmother pointed to the autumn leaf color palette she'd left on the sideboard.

"Some navy would be nice," he said.

Her grandmother's cell rang. Her eyes narrowed as she nodded along to whatever she was hearing. "I see. Yes. Yes, that would be best." She hung up and sighed. "One of the guards will escort us to our SUVs and back to the house."

"What's wrong?" Bryn asked.

"The man you saw was one of the crew who has been working on this estate. He's alive but unresponsive. They've sent for a Medic."

That didn't sound good. "Silver dragon-pires?" Bryn asked.

"We won't know until after they've examined him," her grandmother said, "but that would be my guess."

"There's no reason to wait for anyone to escort us to our cars," Jaxon said. "I think we should leave so the guards can search the estate without us in their way."

"You think someone could be hiding in the house?" Bryn asked.

"It's logical. There are portions of the building that aren't complete, so it would be easy to find a way inside. Speaking of which, since we flew down and came in the veranda door, the window to the rooftop stairs is probably still wide open."

"We closed it," Lillith said, "but we didn't lock it."

"I'll take care of it," Jaxon said.

"Not by yourself," Bryn said. "No one goes anywhere alone."

"I can take care of myself." Jaxon stood and activated his elemental swords so that twin blades of ice shot from his hands.

"Yes, but we're a team and there might be more than one of them." She activated her bracelet so the sword of fire and ice shot from her right hand.

Her grandmother stood. "I'm pulling rank. Neither of you are going anywhere. I'll alert the guards that the roof access is unlocked. They can take care of it. And to keep either of you from doing anything which requires weapons, we'll leave now." She pulled out her phone and explained the new developments to someone. Then she pointed at Jaxon and Bryn. "Put your swords away."

"I'll wait until we get to the car," Bryn said. "Just in case someone sneaks up on us."

"She's not wrong," Jaxon said. "Mother, let's go."

All four of them exited the dining room and made their way to the front door. Bryn went first, and Jaxon stayed by his mother's side. They reached their rides without incident. Bryn released her sword. "You'll call if you learn anything from your father?"

Jaxon nodded. "And you'll do the same if your grandfather discovers anything?"

"Yes." They climbed into the SUV and the driver took them home.

"Before spotting that poor man," her grandmother said. "How were things going between you and Jaxon?"

"Pre-dragon-pire issues, we were doing good. I think the estate made him happy. It's reassuring to know that no matter how strange things are we'll have a wonderful place to live."

Her grandmother nodded and there were tears in her eyes. "I wish Sara could have understood that."

"We're back to that catch-22 situation. If she had married Ferrin, I wouldn't be here."

"I know." Her grandmother reached for Bryn's hand and gave it a quick squeeze. "You are the best possible outcome from the biggest heartbreak of my life. Sometimes it's hard to reconcile the two."

...

Back at Sinclair Estate, Bryn went to her room and called Ivy.

"Hello, Bryn. What's up?" Ivy said.

"How'd you know it was me?"

"Unlike your grandparents' estate and the Institute, my house has this wonderful modern technology called Caller ID."

Bryn laughed. "I miss that." And then she told Ivy about her eventful day.

"You have a pool on your roof?" Ivy said.

"It's pretty cool. I'll make sure you and Clint have your own guest suite. But beyond that, what do you think Jaxon meant?"

"I think the house made him happy and he can see having a future there with you."

"As a friend?" Bryn said.

"Or more," Ivy said. "As long as dragon-pires don't take over your house as their evil lair, I think you guys will be okay."

"No dragon-pires allowed in the pool," Clint called out in the background.

Bryn smiled. "Tell him he can paint that on a sign and I'll hang it next to the pool."

"All joking aside," Ivy said. "That's pretty ballsy that dragon-pires were roaming the estate.

"I know. And I'm sure my grandfather is working overtime trying to catch these jerks before the Christmas Ball. Last year was bad enough. If dragon-pires crash his party he's going to be furious."

After dinner that night, Bryn sat in the dining room with her grandparents, wondering how to bring up the topic of visiting her parents to decorate their tree.

"What's on your mind, Bryn?" her grandfather asked.

"I guess I need to work on my poker face." Maybe she should wait and bring this up when her grandfather wasn't around. It's not like he didn't know she went to visit them. "I planned to visit my parents and help them decorate their tree. When I was in school I had friends drive out there with me so I wouldn't be alone. Is it okay if one of your drivers takes me out there, or do I need someone else to go with me?"

"I'd prefer it if you didn't leave the estate until we're sure that the dragon-pires are no longer in the vicinity. The man you spotted earlier still hasn't regained consciousness. The Medics aren't sure if he will."

"That's awful." Bryn had assumed he'd have the same experience she did. Not fun, but she'd made a full recovery. "Unlike the past victims, myself included, these dragon- pires don't care about leaving their victims alive?"

"At the moment we don't know the answer to that question, but I'd assume you're right. I have a dozen men searching the building site and the grounds all around Sinclair Estate. Once we've determined it's safe to travel, we'll send an extra guard with you when you wish to visit your parents, but that may not happen for awhile."

"I understand. What I don't understand is why anyone wants to suck the life force from another dragon."

"I'm sure Jaxon told you the conspirators we captured were Green-Blue hybrids. When you combine genius with an unfulfilled desire to rule, the result is an unhealthy obsession for power."

"True. I hate that everyone thinks the dragon-pires are Green. Garret is not happy about that."

"Once we've apprehended the guilty parties, the truth will come out," her grandfather said.

"On to a happier topic, have you seen the reports on Garret's prosthetic wings and braces? He's done some amazing things."

"He is a brilliant young man. I'd be willing to fund anything he wants to pursue in the future. A lot of Greens just theorize, but he creates functional prototypes. That's impressive."

This was a far cry from the man who used to think that injured dragons should stay out of sight because they reflected poorly on the Clan. She was proud of him. Saying that would earn her no end of grief, though, so she kept her thoughts to herself. Although she did chalk it up as a personal accomplishment. He never would have considered funding Garret's prosthetics if she hadn't asked.

Before she went to bed that night she called Jaxon.

"I guess you didn't hear anything about the investigation," she said.

"No," Jaxon said, "but I have a question. If we hadn't gone up on the roof and seen that man would he have died?"

"I don't know. Why?"

"It's one thing to steal someone's life force, knowing they'll recover with medical help. It's another thing to drain someone and leave them to die. Both are crazy, but one is more disturbing than the other."

"When I was attacked, I don't think they meant for me to die. They could've dumped me somewhere no one would find me, but they didn't. Maybe the guy today was the same way. They knew it was a construction site and that someone would find him."

"I think you might be overly optimistic," Jaxon said.

After hanging up with Jaxon, Bryn called her parents and explained what was going on. They agreed that she should stay put. "Don't worry about the tree," her mom said. "We'll just string some popcorn to put on it this year."

"The dragon-pires are messing up my holiday plans," Bryn said, attempting to make a joke.

"At least we were able to bake cookies," her mom said. "And after the holidays we'll go shopping for ornaments on sale so we'll be set for next year."

"Sounds good." She hung up after talking to her dad for a few minutes and making him promise that neither of them would go anywhere by themselves. It did strike her as ironic that her mom still planned to bargain shop for ornaments when Bryn hadn't blinked at the price for Jaxon's gift. Funny how quickly she'd grown used to having cash in her bank account. Not that she planned on becoming an Olympic level shopper, but knowing there was money if she needed it gave her great peace of mind. Maybe she could siphon some of it off into an account for her parents, because she hated to think of them having to pinch every penny.

...

By the time the Christmas Ball rolled around Bryn was keyed up with anticipation. Sure there would still be Blues who wouldn't like her, but she wouldn't be by herself this year...she'd be with Jaxon. She wouldn't have to sit on the sidelines and watch everyone else mix and mingle and dance. Last year that had totally sucked.

Neither Ferrin nor her grandfather had found out any new information about the dragon-pires, which meant she'd been housebound. For tonight she wanted to forget about Quintessence-sucking Green-Blue hybrid villains and focus on having fun. Or, at least, the Blue version of fun.

She checked herself out in the mirror. The black toga- style dress flattered her curves and made her feel attractive. That was important, since she'd be surrounded by golden skinned blonds all night. She'd fixed her hair in a half up, half down style with a French twist in the back secured by a diamond hairpin. She hadn't known what it was when her grandmother had showed it to her. It was the size of a pencil and the diamond was where the eraser would be. There was a matching cap the same size on the bottom of the pencil which sported its own diamond.

All she'd had to do was twist her hair and thread the pin through. After capping the end, it stayed in place. With her new hairdo, dress, and subtle makeup, she felt like she could hold her own against Jaxon. She might be as pretty as he was tonight. That was a first.

She met up with her grandmother in the foyer where they'd soon be greeting guests. Her grandmother wore a dress which looked like it was made from blue ice crystals.

"Very pretty," Bryn said.

"Thank you." Her grandmother smiled. "You look wonderful. Jaxon isn't going to know what hit him."

Bryn rolled her eyes. "Right." But secretly she hoped Jaxon would give her a genuine compliment.

"Our guests should be arriving soon," her grandmother said.

Bryn peered into the ballroom where silver and gold trees lined the walls. The tables were draped with navy linens which featured alternating silver and gold napkin rings. An orchestra warmed up on the stage in the corner. "It's even more beautiful than last year."

"Thank you. We've changed the schedule a bit this year. We won't be relocating to the small ballroom to hand out gifts. We'll have the gifts delivered to our tables."

Since the small ballroom had been the scene of the attack last year that made sense. "I think that's a wonderful idea."

Her grandfather came toward them with a huge smile on his face. He kept walking until he reached his wife and took her hands in his. "You look amazing."

Her grandmother's cheeks turned pink. "Thank you, Ephram. You look rather dashing yourself."

What was that about?

He released his wife's hands and looked at Bryn. "You look lovely. Remember to keep Jaxon on his toes tonight."

"I will." Not that she knew what he meant, but he was in such a good mood she didn't want to do anything to change that.

"I believe our guests are here." He stood on her other side and they greeted everyone as they came in. It was a strange Blue tradition where you thanked people for coming as they entered the room in a slow orderly line. When Jaxon appeared, looking runway-worthy in a classic black tuxedo, he just stared at her like he was confused, rather than responding with the expected, "Thank you for inviting us."

"What?" He rarely missed a step in the social dance. "Your hair," was all he said before he moved on to shake hands with her grandfather.

Her grandmother gave her a sly grin before greeting the next person. Huh? Had she just rendered Jaxon speechless? That was quite the feat.

When they were done greeting everyone, Bryn headed to their table up front, hoping to find a glass of water. Sitting down sounded good, too. Her heels were gorgeous, but they weren't the most comfortable shoes she'd ever worn.

She sat next to where her grandmother would be seated and wasn't surprised when Lillith joined her with Asher. However, his outfit did surprise her.

"Is that poor baby wearing a tuxedo?" Bryn asked.

Lillith ran her finger along the tiny jacket lapel. "It's a onesie tailored to look like a tuxedo. I think they did an amazing job."

"Very convincing." She was glad to know Asher was comfortable. The fact that he was making little baby snuffling sounds as he slept assured her his outfit must be baby friendly.

Bryn sipped her water and glanced around the room at the color coded crowd. She wouldn't let it bother her. Over the summer, she'd grown used to it, but since she'd been at school she'd become accustomed to fitting in, rather than standing out. Not that it mattered. This was her grandparents' house and she had more right than any of these people to be here. And she'd just keep telling herself that until she believed it.

"Where's Jaxon?" Lillith asked.

"Probably talking to his friends," Bryn said.

"He should have come for you before he wandered off," Lillith said.

Oh. She hadn't realized that. "Should I be insulted?" Bryn asked in a joking manner.

"Of course not," Lillith said. "As long as he comes to greet you soon, it's acceptable."

Huh. Bryn leaned in. "I trust you, so please don't make fun of me. I've never worn my hair like this and my dress is slit a little higher than I'm comfortable with. Can I carry this off?"

"Oh." Lillith looked like she understood and it made her sad. "Bryn, your hair is amazing, and the dress fits perfectly. Don't doubt yourself. And if I may offer some advice...don't look for your self worth in a man's compliments. Westgates aren't good at compliments. It took me awhile to figure that out with Ferrin. I don't want you stressing over the same thing."

Bryn was once again struck by her life's odd similarity to Lillith's. "Thank you. That's probably some of the best advice I've received about dealing with a Westgate."

"I did work to make sure Jaxon is more considerate than his father."

"And I appreciate that."

Bryn's grandmother came to the table and sat down.

Her smile slipped a bit. "Is everything all right?"

"Yes," Bryn said. "We were just bonding over having to deal with Westgates."

"All men have their issues," her grandmother said. "You should go find Jaxon and mingle."

"If I could spot him, I would," Bryn said.

"Isn't that him by the orchestra?" her grandmother said. Bryn peered across the room. "Probably, but I'm not chasing after him tonight. If he wants to spend time with me he knows where I am."

"I see your point," her grandmother conceded.

"If he doesn't come over soon I'm going to put him on diaper duty tomorrow," Lillith said.

Bryn laughed. "Thank you for having my back."

"We women have to stick together," Lillith said.

"Speak of the devil," Bryn's grandmother said.

Bryn glanced in the direction her grandmother had indicated. Jaxon came toward her with his friend Quentin. When they reached the table, he barely looked at her, but he said, "Bryn, do you want to mingle with us?"

"Sure." What the heck was his problem? Thank goodness Lillith had reassured her about her hair and dress because Jaxon was putting off a strange vibe.

She followed him and Quentin to a group of students she'd met at school but never interacted with much. The boys congregated together, talking about cars. The girls talked jewelry. Bryn plastered a smile on her face. Why in the hell had she thought tonight might be fun?

"Bryn," one of the girls said. "Where did you find your hair pin?"

"My grandmother gave it to me. I think it belonged to her great aunt."

"Is it a Vanleigh?" the girl asked.

Now that she thought about it, there had been a V carved into the side of the pin just like the bracelet her grandfather had given her last Christmas, which meant it was a one of kind special order piece. "I believe it is."

"It's amazing," another girl said.

"Thank you."

The orchestra started to play a song at full volume which was the signal that they should return to their tables so her grandfather could thank them all for coming, which technically he'd done at the door and she'd probably never understand these Blue social norms, but at least this year she knew what to expect. That was a huge relief.

She joined Lillith and her grandmother. Lillith stood and moved over a seat.

"I did shower today," Bryn said.

Lillith chuckled. "Jaxon will want to sit next to you."

The irritating male in question joined them and sat next to her, but he sipped his water and stared off into space rather than looking at her.

She leaned in and said, "Fair warning, I'm close enough to kick you under the table if you don't stop acting like you'd rather be anywhere but near me, and I'm wearing really pointy shoes."

He looked at her like she was insane. "What are you talking about?"

"Thank you everyone for coming this evening," her grandfather's voice boomed through the room. "In these changing times, it's good to come together as a Clan to reinforce our bonds. I hope each and every one of you has a wonderful time this evening."

Bryn clapped along with everyone else, while she tried to reason with her inner five-year-old who really wanted to kick Jaxon in the shins. Part of her had thought she might impress him tonight. That he might see her as an attractive female, rather than someone he was burdened with. Apparently, that was not the case and she'd just have to suck it up and get over it. It was Christmas. And she was going to have a good time...possibly at his expense.

"Aren't the trees beautiful this year," she said to him.

He nodded.

"Young man, my granddaughter asked you a question and I know your mother raised you to do better than nod at your dinner date and then ignore her."

"I did, actually," Lillith said.

Jaxon froze for a moment and then he broke out the fake Blue smile Bryn had seen all summer. "The trees are beautiful. The juxtaposition of the gold against the silver is stunning."

"I agree," Lillith said. "The trees are stunning. Anything else you'd like to comment on?" She glanced at Bryn.

Jaxon sat back in his chair and crossed his arms over his chest. "Not until there is another male at this table."

"Asher is male," Bryn pointed out.

Jaxon nodded. "You're right, but since he's nonverbal he's not much help."

"Since when do you need help making conversation?" Bryn asked.

"Since all the women at this table seem to be hostile." He stood. "If you'll excuse me, I need to use the restroom."

"I think you're lying," Bryn said in a sing-song voice. Jaxon stood and, in as dignified manner as possible, fled.

"If this wasn't so funny I'd be furious," Bryn said.

"What is going on between you two?" her grandmother asked.

"Remember when you said he wouldn't know what hit him? Well he knows and apparently he is not the least bit impressed."

"I don't understand," her grandmother said.

"Me, either. When we went to mingle he didn't say a word to me. The girls complimented me on my hairpin and asked if it was a Vanleigh."

"It is," her grandmother confirmed.

"Good to know." She sighed. "You know what? As Lillith pointed out, I don't need a male's approval to feel good about myself, but I would like to know what the hell his problem is."

"He'll have to dance the first dance with you after dinner," Lillith said. "That isn't optional, so you can talk to him then."

Chapter Thirty-One

Jaxon came back to the table when dinner was served. Bryn focused on her food and on making conversation with her grandmother, Lillith, and her grandfather who, surprisingly enough, had joined them.

The interaction between her grandparents almost seemed flirtatious, which Bryn found amusing. Maybe, after his Directorate sanctioned straying over the years, her grandfather had realized what a treasure his wife was. The whole marriage is a business partnership that produces children idea bothered Bryn. It would be nice to think of them having a real marriage after all this time.

Jaxon smiled and nodded and gave succinct answers to any questions she lobbed at him. After awhile she gave up.

When the chocolate mint cake was served, Jaxon frowned. "You're going to eat cake?"

That was the first real thing he'd said to her, so she answered honestly. "My grandmother and I discussed it. I can't be afraid to eat cake for the rest of my life. Even though I plan to carry out a lifelong ban on carrot cake, other cake is acceptable. And this particular chocolate mint cake is awesome." She took a bite and sighed in satisfaction.

"I'm not a fan of chocolate and mint, so you can have mine." Jaxon pushed his cake toward her.

"Thank you." Was he over whatever his problem had been earlier?

"If you'll excuse me, I need to speak to Quentin." And he was off like a shot.

"At least that was something," Lillith said.

"Two whole sentences worth of conversation," Bryn said. "I'm such a lucky girl. But he did give me his cake."

As the dessert dishes were cleared away, the orchestra played the opening bars for Blue Christmas.

"That's our cue," her grandfather said. He stood and held out his hand to her grandmother. "May I have this dance?"

"Of course." Her grandmother took his hand and allowed him to lead her to the dance floor.

Bryn watched them dance, moving together in perfect synchronicity. "I think something has changed between them, in a good way."

"I believe you're right, which gives me hope that Ferrin might warm up one day."

"Maybe," Bryn said because she didn't want to burst Lillith's bubble.

As the song drew to a close, Bryn kept a lookout for Jaxon. He wouldn't openly defy convention, would he? Because that would really tick her off. Ferrin came to greet Lillith. He took Asher and held him in one arm while he led Lillith to the dance floor. He managed to dance while holding Lillith and the baby, which was impressive. Maybe Lillith would get her happily ever after one day.

Bryn glanced around. Almost everyone else was out on the dance floor. Less than a dozen people remained seated at their tables. Most of them were older than her grandparents. And most of them were looking at her. What was that about? One of the elderly ladies nodded toward the dance floor like she was suggesting Bryn go out there. She'd love to go out there, but not by herself.

Where was Jaxon? He needed to show up ASAP because people were going to notice that they weren't dancing, and she didn't want to deal with any grief from her grandparents. She waited and...nothing.

Wow. This whole sucky situation felt all too familiar. The only good thing about being contracted to marry Jaxon was that she wasn't supposed to be left out like this again. They were supposed to be a team. Maybe he was just late returning from the restroom. Bryn scanned the area and that's when she spotted him. He was already on the dance floor, dancing with someone else.

What did that mean? Wasn't he "legally bound" to dance the first stupid dance with her? That's the way Lillith had made it sound. Maybe Bryn had misunderstood.

Jaxon turned so that he faced her direction, his gaze glided over her like she was invisible. To him, maybe she was. And that ticked her off even more. Fire stirred in her gut. She focused on snow and pushed the flames down. What was going on with him? They'd been on friendly terms when they left school less than a week ago. Had he decided to publicly humiliate her in revenge for turning his hair pink?

Now what? She could sit here and have everyone gawk at her, or she could leave. She stood and exited the room as calmly as possible. She headed for the restroom, which was empty, thank goodness. She stood at the sink with the water running in case anyone came in, so she could pretend she'd just turned the faucet on and was about to wash her hands rather than the truth that she was hiding out because the one person she was supposed to be able to depend on to ask her to dance had abandoned her. And it's not like she'd done anything wrong. This strange new behavior was all him.

She checked her reflection in the mirror. Her hair and makeup still looked good. Her dress was beautiful. Whatever this was about, it wasn't her. At least that is what she'd tell herself to get through the rest of this crazy train wreck of an evening.

She slapped the water faucet off, squared her shoulders, and exited the restroom. Before she reached the ballroom, her grandmother intercepted her. "What are you doing out here? I thought you'd be dancing."

"I'd be happy to dance," Bryn said, "but no one asked me."

"You can't expect to dance with anyone but Jaxon."

"Funny story," Bryn said with a catch in her voice. "He never came back. He never asked me to dance. He danced the first dance with someone else."

Her grandmother just stared at her.

"And no, I'm not joking." She needed her grandmother to have a solution to this situation. "So any idea on how I should handle this?"

Frost shot from her grandmother's nostrils. Bryn had never seen her grandmother lose control of her element so she was pretty sure Jaxon was a dead man. And right now, she was okay with that.

"Come with me," her grandmother said. "Act like everything is fine."

"Let the fun begin," Bryn muttered as she followed her grandmother back into the ballroom and sat at their table. Someone brought them more cake. Bryn ate cake, smiled, and waited for Jaxon to come back so she could stab him with her fork.

Lillith came back with a smile on her face. She took one look at Bryn and sat down. "What's wrong?"

"Find your son and bring him to this table," her grandmother said in a tone that should have made Lillith fear for Jaxon's life.

"Of course." Lillith came back a few moments later, with Jaxon, who looked irritated.

"Sit," Bryn's grandmother said in a tone that should have cued Jaxon in to the fact that something was wrong.

"What's going on?" he asked.

"Do you wish to dissolve your marriage contract?" Bryn's grandmother asked in a tone that could have cut to the bone.

"What?" Jaxon paled.

"I can't think of another reason why you would publicly snub Bryn by dancing with someone else during the first dance at the Christmas Ball," her grandmother said.

The weight of the situation seemed to register on Jaxon's face. "I wasn't thinking. I didn't mean to—"

"To humiliate me?" Bryn said. "Because even I, with my mixed background and lack of social skills, know that you were supposed to dance with me to present a united front and show everyone that we're together."

Jaxon looked stunned. "I'm sorry. When Rinata asked me to dance I didn't consider what other people might think."

"Oh," Lillith said. "I didn't realize she was here." She looked at Bryn. "Rinata is Rhianna's older sister."

Son of a bitch.

"I now have an inkling of why you might have made such an egregious social blunder, but, be that as it may, your behavior is unacceptable. You will make this up to Bryn. You will think of some way to make it clear to everyone here at this party that you made a grave error in judgement and it is no way a reflection on my granddaughter. Do you understand?"

"Yes ma'am." He took a deep breath. "Bryn, do you want to dance?"

"Honestly, I'd rather stab you with this fork"—Bryn picked up the utensil by her now empty cake plate—"but I will dance with you to prove a point."

Jaxon stood and offered her his hand. She took it and let him lead her to the dance floor. Once they were there, she stared at his shoulder rather than make eye contact with him or with anyone else while they danced.

She waited for him to say something. They danced through two songs before he said, "I am truly sorry."

"I'd like to believe that."

"Look at me," he said.

She sighed and then met his gaze. Sincerity shone from his bright blue eyes. "I didn't dance with Rinata to slight you."

"Even if that's true, at worst, you maliciously abandoned me, and at best you completely forgot about me. Neither of those reasons make me feel any better."

"What can I do?" he asked, pulling her a little closer.

"I don't have a clue," she said. "You better figure something out, because I won't have the entire Blue Clan smirking behind my back all night."

"I didn't think you cared about what other people thought," he said.

"I don't." Although it was becoming alarmingly clear to her that she did care about what he thought and why the hell did being in his arms feel so comfortable? She had to make him understand. "How would you feel if you'd come to ask me to dance like you were supposed to do and discovered I was already dancing with someone else?"

"I'd be furious," he said, "but in this case there were extenuating circumstances."

"I know, but no else in this ballroom is aware of that fact." The song ended. "Honestly, until you make this right, I'm done with you." And she walked off the dance floor, leaving him to look like the idiot for once.

When she reached her table, both her grandparents sat there. She wasn't sure which one was angrier. Before they could ask any questions, she said, "I told him to fix it."

"How does he intend to do that?" her grandfather asked.

"Not my problem," Bryn said. "I'm through playing nice until he does." She was afraid they'd tell her to go suck up to him. That was not going to happen.

"I respect your resolve," her grandfather said, "but you'll still uphold the contract."

"Of course I will," Bryn said. "If for no other reason than to annoy Jaxon and Ferrin."

Her grandmother smiled. "I'm proud of you."

"Thank you. I guess now we wait and see what Jaxon can accomplish before it's time to exchange gifts. When is that?"

"Twenty minutes," her grandfather said. "But I can adjust the time frame."

"Let's see what he does," said Bryn.

"He seems to be up to something," her grandmother said.

Bryn turned to see Jaxon with his mother and Rinata. They were talking to a table of young couples. A few of them glanced over at Bryn. She gave them her best I am not fantasizing about incinerating my future husband with a fireball smile and hoped it was convincing.

Jaxon, Rinata, and Lillith approached each table and made small talk with the Blues sitting there. Occasionally, one of the occupants would join them in speaking to other people which caused a ripple effect.

Would whatever he was doing work? For her grandparents' sake, she hoped so. Finally, Rinata and Jaxon approached their table, while Lillith went back to sit with Ferrin.

"May I join you for a moment?" Rinata asked.

"You may," Bryn's grandmother said.

Rinata sat and Jaxon followed suit.

"We've spoken to every table, explaining that I asked Jaxon to dance so we could talk about my sister and he was too polite to refuse." Rinata turned to Bryn. "I meant no disrespect."

"Thank you for explaining the situation to the other guests," Bryn said.

The volume of the orchestra surged. "If you'll excuse us, Rinata," Bryn's grandfather said. "I believe the gift exchange is about to begin."

"Of course." Rinata stood and headed back to her table. The doors to the ballroom opened and the waitstaff rolled in carts of presents which they passed out among the guests. Per tradition, her grandmother handed her grandfather his gift first. It wasn't big enough to be a box of stinky cigars like last year.

He ripped off the paper and opened the plain cardboard box, revealing a brass telescope with gears and knobs which appeared to be an antique. He seemed genuinely pleased. "Thank you, Marie."

"You're welcome."

He handed her a gift, which was too big to be a jewelry box. She opened it and laughed. Inside was a hat with netting and flowers that looked like a modern work of art. "I love it."

The sound of other families opening their gifts drifted through the air. Her grandmother passed Bryn a key ring. "The estate was a bit difficult to wrap, so I thought this would be easier."

"Thank you," Bryn said.

Was she supposed to exchange gifts with Jaxon now? After the idiot move he'd made, she didn't want to. "Why don't you go spend time with your family? We can exchange gifts later."

"I'm not sure that would be appropriate," Jaxon said. "Mrs. Sinclair, what do you suggest?"

"Bryn, why don't you exchange gifts now and then he can leave."

Crap. "Okay." Bryn shoved his gift across the table. "Here you go."

He pulled a black velvet jeweler's box from his pocket and passed it to her. "Ladies first."

He'd bought her jewelry? She'd worked hard to find a gift that was personal, something he might truly like. If he bought her a generic, look how expensive this piece of jewelry is type of gift, she was going to be pissed. She popped the lid and stared inside at the bracelet. A bracelet she thought she'd never see again. The snowflake bracelet her mother had given her which had been stolen and supposedly pawned to fund the rebel attacks.

Bryn ran her fingers over the interconnecting snowflakes the size of quarters and the diamond in the center of each one that was the size of a dime. "Where did you find it?"

"My father discovered it among some of the items recovered from the rebels, minus the diamonds, of course. I had those replaced because I thought you'd want it back." He sounded like he wasn't sure if he'd done the right thing.

"Thank you." She took the bracelet out of the box and tried to put it on.

"Let me help you." Jaxon fastened the clasp for her. Bryn held her arm up and smiled at the snowflakes sparkling on her wrist. "I love it." And she did. In a strange way, it felt like she had a piece of her family back. Maybe he wasn't a complete jerk after all. She gestured toward the box from the bookstore. "Your turn."

He carefully removed the paper without ripping it. When he saw the leather-bound copies of Lord of the Rings he appeared confused. He picked up the first book and carefully opened the brown leather cover, smiling at the inscription on the first page. "How did you know?"

"I called your mom because I wasn't sure what you'd like."

"Thank you," he said.

"You're welcome."

"Jaxon, I know your father has something he wants to give you," her grandfather said. "Why don't you go see what it is? You can come back for cocoa afterward."

Jaxon left the table and headed to his family. Bryn relaxed in her chair. "That went better than I expected. Now I have gifts for both of you." She handed her grandparents their gifts.

Her grandfather opened his pen and grinned. "Very nice. I can always use new pens." Her grandmother ran her fingers over the cashmere scarf. "It's lovely. And I can wear it with my new hat."

A cart came around with cocoa. Bryn grabbed one cup with marshmallows for herself and one without for Jaxon, which she put next to his books. For the moment, the world seemed to be back on track. All around her, happy families exchanged gifts and chattered. So far no one was attacking the estate like they'd done last year. Life was good.

Jaxon returned a few minutes later, with a huge grin on his face. "What has you so happy?" she asked him.

He pulled a set of car keys from his pocket. "A Lexus hybrid SUV, for those days when I need an SUV rather than my car."

Yes. Because everyone needed two vehicles. She resisted the urge to roll her eyes. He sat and drank his cocoa. Bryn did her best to relax, but it felt like she was waiting for the other shoe to drop. What was supposed to happen after the gift exchange? The ball had been interrupted at this point last year, so she had no idea. "Not that I'm complaining about the calm, but what's next on the agenda?"

"After cocoa, everyone is free to mingle or relax. Guests with young children will head home," her grandmother said. "The evening will wind down, and we'll say goodbye to people as they leave."

Bryn sipped her cocoa. "That sounds nice and uneventful."

"Which would be a change from your usual life," Jaxon said.

She knew he was teasing but felt the need to give him some grief. "I'd like to point out that you, too, tend to be in the middle of the chaos."

"I prefer to think of myself as chaos adjacent," he said. "Mostly due to my interactions with you."

The orchestra started playing at a louder volume again. Several couples went back to the dance floor. The ones that did were looking at each other with what appeared to be love. Maybe they were just thrilled with their Christmas gifts, though it would be nice to think that some of them were happy in their relationships.

Jaxon sipped his cocoa and looked at his book. He should ask her to dance but he seemed to have no intention of doing that. She cleared her throat, to gain his attention. "I'm glad you're enjoying your books, but you should probably ask me to dance."

"Okay." He closed the book and slid it back into the box. "Bryn, would you like to dance?"

"I would. Thank you."

They joined the other couples on the dance floor and started to waltz.

"Did you want to dance," Jaxon asked, "or did you just want people to see us dancing?"

"Both." And that was the truth. "I'd like to think that dancing with me isn't terrible."

"And now you're fishing for compliments."

"If you'd actually given me a compliment, or commented on my appearance at all this evening," she said, "I wouldn't have to go fishing. And isn't that part of your job description anyway?"

"My job description?" Once again he appeared confused.

"Just so you know, there's a little voice in my head, set on repeat, saying, 'Don't kick him in the shins.'"

He stopped dancing. Luckily, the few couples on the dance floor were able to move around them. "We need to talk," he said.

"We can't talk here?" she said.

"No."

"Fine. Follow me." She led him out of the ballroom and up the stairs to the small living room next to the dining room where she usually ate with her grandparents. There were bookshelves and several wing-backed chairs and a chaise lounge. "Does this work for you?"

"Yes." He sat in one of the black leather wing-backed chairs. She sat on the gray chaise lounge that faced him.

"Okay," she said. "We're here. Talk."

"You've been acting strange this evening," he said.

Chapter Thirty-Two

"Me?" She laughed. "I'm the one who's been acting strange?"

"You've threatened to kick me multiple times."

"You're right, I did, and with good cause. You haven't said a single nice thing to me this evening except when you asked me about the cake. I realize you're used to looking good all the time, but I put extra effort into my appearance this evening. It would be nice if you recognized that fact."

He sat forward in his chair. "Seriously?"

It took skill to put so much contempt into such a short answer. Fire sparked in her gut. She closed her eyes and thought of snow. "Do you care to expand on that answer?"

"You're being ridiculous." He stood like he planned to leave.

Bryn ticked items off on her fingers. "You spent the first part of the evening avoiding me. You left me sitting by myself for the first dance and didn't realize it was a problem until my grandmother pointed it out. You did work to make everyone believe that you didn't mean to insult me or try to break our marriage contract because apparently, appearances matter more than my actual feelings, and now you're acting like I'm the one with the problem. What in the hell is going on?"

"Why did you buy me those books?" Jaxon asked.

Okay. He didn't answer her question but at least he was talking to her. "I wanted to find something you'd like. I didn't want to do the impersonal expensive gift. I wanted it to mean something."

Jaxon reached into his jacket and pulled out another jeweler's box. He came to sit next to her on the chaise. "I brought two gifts." He popped open the lid on a sapphire and diamond bracelet that twinkled in the lights.

"Behold the impersonal expensive gift. The one I didn't give you because I wanted to give you something that had meaning, too."

Okay. Where was he going with this? And then she understood. "You were hedging your bets in case I didn't buy you something personal?"

He nodded. "And I traded in the bracelet I'd ordered for Rhianna to partially pay for these. Not because I needed the money, but I needed to do it to move on...to move forward in my relationship with you."

"Okay." How should she respond? "You get credit for that but why did you spend the first part of the evening ignoring me?"

He closed the jeweler's box and shoved it back in his pocket. "I didn't know how to deal with you."

He sat close enough that she could look into his eyes and see he was being truthful. Too bad what he was saying didn't make sense. "What are you talking about? You deal with me every day at school."

"I do." He reached over and touched one of the loose pieces of hair that wasn't bound up by the hairpin. His fingers brushed across her neck, giving her goosebumps. His gaze locked onto hers. "But I've never seen you like this."

Bryn froze. How was she supposed to respond to that comment? What did he mean? How was he seeing her? And why was he sitting so close? Okay, if it was any other guy she'd think he was about to kiss her...but this was Jaxon. He didn't want to kiss her...did he? And even if he did, did she want to kiss him, especially after his weird behavior this evening?

"If I'd never been involved with someone else," he said. "I don't think I'd be so confused."

She'd like to think she wouldn't spend the rest of her life with Jaxon haunted by the Ghost-of-a-Girlfriend past. Not that she expected him to forget, but it would be nice if he could move on. If they could both move on. Trading in the bracelet was a step in the right direction.

"The possibility of us as a real couple isn't something I ever imagined," he said. "Until I saw you tonight. It's strange how your hair could make such a difference."

And what could she say to that? She was still the same person. "It's just a new hairstyle."

"No. It's not. It's me seeing you in a different light. After touring the estate the other day things just feel different, don't you think?"

"Different good or different bad?"

"I'm not sure."

Her heart rate bumped up a notch. Was he asking what she wanted? What did she want? She wanted someone who wanted her, not someone who was stuck with her and making the best of it.

"This feels like a pivotal moment," he said.

"It does."

"So what do we do?" he asked.

How in the hell was she supposed to answer that loaded question? "Pivot?"

"Okay, then. I guess we'll head in a new direction." He closed the distance between them and Bryn tensed as he pressed his mouth against hers. What if the kiss was terrible? And what in the hell was she thinking kissing a Westgate?

But it wasn't terrible. And maybe she just needed to stop thinking and give this a chance. His lips were soft and warm and his hand on her cheek felt natural. She tilted her head to the right for a better angle and kissed him back. And even though he was a Blue and normally cold and standoffish, there was heat.

All her concerns about how this could possibly work between them disappeared as he pulled her close. His arms around her felt right, and he tasted like hot cocoa, so she let go and lost herself in the moment.

When he ended the kiss, she opened her eyes and found him smiling at her. She realized she was smiling back.

"Hey, there," she said.

"So, we're pivoting now?" he said.

"I'm not opposed to the idea."

"Good," and then he leaned in again. Just as his lips brushed across hers, the living room door opened.

"There you are," her grandmother said.

Bryn froze. Jaxon slowly sat back. They both looked at her grandmother who was acting like she hadn't just walked in and interrupted a kiss. Although she was smiling like this had been her plan all along.

"Sorry to interrupt, but you can't just disappear from the Ball. People will talk. Come along."

Bryn's grandmother turned and left the room.

"That wasn't awkward at all," Bryn said, attempting to make a joke.

Jaxon stood. "People are probably expecting only one of us to come back alive. Let's go dance to show them everything is okay."

Bryn stood and followed him back to the ballroom and out to the dance floor. Was everything okay? She wasn't sure. It was more like everything was awkward and strange with a side of my life may not totally suck after all.

When Jaxon pulled her close on the dance floor this time, it felt like she was somehow more connected to him. "Why does it feel like everyone is staring at us?" Bryn asked.

"Because they are," Jaxon said.

"Not helping." She met his gaze.

He smiled at her and it was a smile she hadn't seen before. It was a bit mischievous and somewhat snarky, with a dash of we have a special secret.

"You'll adjust. Westgates tend to attract attention."

And now he was thinking of her as a Westgate, which technically she would become, but holy crap, this was weird. "Why do I feel like they all know about the pivoting?"

"I'm sure your grandmother will be discreet," Jaxon said.

"You're probably right." Or she'd tell everyone, in order to counteract the strange incident earlier this evening, but no way was she mentioning that to Jaxon.

They danced to three more songs before the orchestra announced that it was the last song. The opening notes of "Auld Lang Syne" floated through the room.

"I've never understood the lyrics to this song," Bryn said.

"I think it's about remembering the past, and honoring it, while looking forward to what the New Year will bring," said Jaxon. "Which is oddly perfect for this moment."

Bryn didn't comment. She just held her breath and hoped that this optimistic trend would continue.

At the end of the song, Jaxon released Bryn but he kept one hand on her lower back as he walked her back to the table where her grandparents sat.

"We're going to say goodbye to the guests now," her grandmother said, "and that includes you."

"I already knew that." Where did that leave Jaxon? "I'll help my parents gather their things and see you on the way out," Jaxon said.

Bryn followed her grandparents to the main doors, where they thanked everyone for coming. Jaxon's family was last to leave. Even though she knew there was no chance that he'd kiss her goodbye in front of other people, she was a little disappointed when he didn't.

...

Christmas morning, Bryn woke with a sense of relief. She'd survived the Christmas Ball. Even though Jaxon had been inconsiderate with the whole first dance thing, he hadn't been malicious. And the incident showed he wasn't perfect, which was oddly reassuring. And then there was the whole kiss thing. The singular kiss which hadn't been repeated, but the dancing had been nice. And the smile he'd given her when he'd said good night had been genuine. Butterflies had looped around in her stomach.

She'd been afraid her grandmother would grill her once the Westgates had left, but thankfully, neither of her grandparents asked any questions. Bryn had retreated to her room where she'd fallen asleep as soon as her head hit the pillow.

She showered and dressed in jeans and a cashmere sweater. It was vacation after all. She should be able to wear jeans. She put on boots instead of tennis shoes in an attempt to somewhat appease her grandmother. When she reached the small dining room it was empty. That was strange. Maybe they were in the atrium. She went up the stairs and headed toward her grandmother's favorite area of the house. Sure enough, the rich scent of coffee mingled with the smell of green growing things.

"Good morning," her grandmother said from the table where she sat drinking coffee by herself. Uh-oh. There was a platter of fruit, bagels, and Christmas cookies, but the table was set for two. Did her grandparents want to eat alone? Was she interrupting?

"Where's your other half?" Bryn asked.

"We had breakfast together about an hour ago."

Okay. Then this spot was for her. She sat and grabbed a bagel, slathering it with cream cheese.

"I thought you'd go straight for the Christmas cookies," her grandmother said.

"I was trying to act mature, but if you insist." Bryn grabbed a star-shaped cookie covered with green icing and took a bite before pouring herself a cup of coffee.

"So," her grandmother said, "how do you think the ball went last night?"

Did she really want to discuss the kiss with her grandmother? "No one attacked, so I'd say it went well." She finished off her cookie and picked up her bagel.

"That was a relief," her grandmother said. "And how about what I interrupted when I came looking for you?"

Bryn's cheeks warmed. Then again, who else could she talk to about this? "That was a surprise, but a nice one." She told her about Jaxon's comment about seeing her in a new light and how it had confused him.

"Good. Although I'm still displeased about the first dance. Did he explain that?"

"Sort of. I'd be lying if I said it didn't bother me, but I'd like to think it was just a mistake."

"On his part, perhaps, but I'm not sure about Rinata's innocence," her grandmother said. "She would have heard that his marriage contract had been approved."

"Maybe it was her way of standing up for her sister," Bryn said. "I've been worried Rhianna would always come between Jaxon and I, but I think he's made peace with the situation."

"I don't see any reason why you can't have a good relationship with him."

Since they were sharing, Bryn said, "Speaking of relationships, is it my imagination or do you seem to be getting along better with your significant other?"

Her grandmother smiled. "It's not your imagination. We've decided to spend more time together socially. After the attacks I think we both realized how much we could have lost. Whatever the reason, I plan to enjoy it while it lasts." That made it sound like she didn't expect it to continue. "I see that look on your face. Heed my advice. Enjoy the time you have when Jaxon is being agreeable. His personality will change with the political climate. Don't allow that to blindside you."

Talk about conflicting advice. "So I should be pessimistically optimistic?"

"Yes."

Bryn sighed. "Just when I think I understand how things might work, they change."

"You've just summarized life in general," her grandmother said. "We should talk about dinner tonight."

"Why does it sound like you're about to say something unexpected and possibly disturbing?"

"Because you're perceptive." Her grandmother grinned. "A few ground rules. No jeans allowed, and you should wear that hairpin again."

"Why?" She was pretty sure she knew the answer to that question.

"I believe Lillith is trying to make up for Jaxon's social blunder last night, so she's invited us to Westgate Estate for Christmas dinner."

"Oh." She'd thought her grandmother was about to say that Jaxon and his family would be coming here. Going there added a whole other layer of anxiety.

"Care to elaborate?" her grandmother said.

"I'm not sure whether I should be excited or slightly terrified," Bryn said. "Jaxon's mood can change in a split second. Not to mention the fact that I'll have to spend the evening with Ferrin."

"You'll become accustomed to Ferrin. Soon you won't even notice when he's in the room."

Bryn laughed. "Right. He might have agreed to the marriage contract but that doesn't mean he likes being around me any more than I like being around him. I always feel like I'm waiting for him to insult me."

"It's just his way," her grandmother said. "Be grateful that Lillith tempered his influence on Jaxon."

"I'm grateful for that every time I'm around Ferrin," Bryn said.

"Do you want me to help you pick out a dress for this evening?"

"Yes, because I don't want Ferrin to have any excuse to insult me."

...

Bryn checked her reflection in the mirror. "Are you sure this dress isn't too much?"

The black dress her grandmother had suggested Bryn wear was a little revealing. The V-neck plunged deeper than anything she'd ever worn. "I mean I want Jaxon to like me, but I hadn't planned on flashing my cleavage at him or anyone else...ever."

Her grandmother smiled. "That is a perfectly respectable neckline, but if it makes you feel awkward, we'll go with something else."

"Thank you." She could do awkward all on her own without a revealing dress.

Her grandmother went to Bryn's closet, which seemed to be magically stocked with new clothes on a regular basis.

Maybe her grandmother belonged to a Fashion Finds of the Month Club where clothes were shipped to the house.

She returned with a navy off-the-shoulder dress that had three quarter sleeves. Bryn changed into the new dress. "Much better. I don't mind showing my shoulders."

"I have the perfect necklace to go with that neckline."

Bryn followed her grandmother down the hall to a room that had a keypad rather than a doorknob. Her grandmother entered a long series of numbers and the door swung open. Even though she'd been inside the special room which was basically a jewelry vault, she was still amazed by the display cases full of jewelry made with every precious stone imaginable. Everything in the vault had been passed down through generations of Sinclairs and would put most jewelry stores to shame.

"Since Jaxon gave you the snowflake bracelet, I think you should wear this." Her grandmother approached a case of diamond necklaces and retrieved one which had a diamond snowflake as the centerpiece.

"It's beautiful." She accepted the necklace and held it in place while her grandmother fastened the clasp. It was stunning. "I swear it still feels like I'm playing the part of a princess in a fairy tale and someone is going to announce I'm an imposter."

"That's ridiculous." Her grandmother's tone was a tad defensive. "You are my granddaughter and you're exactly where you belong."

"Thank you." Bryn hugged her grandmother. "If Ferrin is mean can I stab him with my hairpin?"

"No."

Chapter Thirty-Three

Her grandfather seemed overly cheerful on the ride to Westgate Estate. "What has you in such a good mood?" Bryn asked as the SUV bounced up and down on the forest roads.

"There are several answers to that question. It's Christmas. Plus I always enjoy going to Westgate Estate because Ferrin goes above and beyond to try and impress his guests. After Jaxon's social blunder last night, I'm sure he'll pull out all the stops."

A sense of uneasiness trickled down Bryn's spine. It's not like Ferrin would punish Jaxon for his mistake. Would he? That would make the evening loads of fun.

"No one is going to bring up the first dance issue tonight, right?"

"Not in so many words," her grandmother said. "But I'd be surprised if Ferrin didn't refer to it in some manner, since it reflected poorly on the Westgates in general."

Great.

The foyer of Westgate Estate still had the obnoxious gold W inlaid in the center of the floor. Thank goodness Jaxon didn't expect her to carry on that tradition. She leaned over to her grandmother and whispered, "Has anyone ever pointed out to Ferrin that if you're standing on the other side of the room it looks like an M?"

Her grandmother grinned, but said, "Don't even think about mentioning that this evening."

"Fine," Bryn said. "I'll just file it away as ammunition to use at a later date."

"Welcome and Merry Christmas," Lillith said as she met them in the foyer with Asher on her hip.

"Merry Christmas to you, too," Bryn's grandmother said. "Thank you for inviting us."

"You're most welcome." Lillith grinned. "I'm fairly out numbered now, so it's nice to have some other women in the house."

They followed Lillith into the arbor-areum which had been transformed into a Christmas wonderland. Every single tree was covered in fairy lights. Some were white, some were blue. Some were a combination of both.

Bryn stared in awe. As obscene as it was to have a forest in the house, she had to give credit where credit was due. "This is magical."

"Thank you." Ferrin's voice came from behind them, startling Bryn and causing her to turn around.

Ferrin had just thanked her? That had to be a sign of the apocalypse. Then again, she'd just complimented something he was proud of. The world had turned into a strange place.

"It is amazing," Bryn's grandmother added.

"This isn't even the best part," Lillith said. "Follow me." She'd taken a few steps when Jaxon appeared from behind a nearby tree. He was smiling, but he appeared tense, like he wasn't happy to be here. "Sorry, I'm late. I was seeing to a few finishing touches."

"Is everything in place?" Ferrin asked. Jaxon nodded and fell into step beside Bryn.

She needed to break the tension. "Do you have Santa's workshop hidden in here?"

"Something like that."

She slowed her steps, allowing her grandparents and his parents to move ahead of them. Jaxon stayed by her side. "Everything all right?" she asked.

He glanced at her. "That will depend on how this evening goes."

She stopped walking. "What does that mean?"

Jaxon placed his hand on her arm. "We need to keep moving. If everything is perfect this evening, my father will be much easier to live with."

Crap. She didn't like the way that sounded. "He'd never do anything to physically hurt you or your mother, would he?"

"What?" Jaxon appeared shocked. "Of course not. He might take away the keys to my car, but he'd never lay a hand on either of us."

And now she felt like she needed to apologize. "Sorry. From my perspective he's a little scary." She wanted to add unbalanced, but that wouldn't help the conversation.

"He is fierce. As he should be. And might I remind you, your father is the one who greeted me with an ax." He grinned at her, and it was a real smile.

The tension she'd felt earlier receded. "You have a point. Now what's the big reveal?"

"You'll have to wait and see."

They continued down the path and caught up with the rest of their family members at a table set for dinner next to a giant evergreen decorated with navy and silver glass balls that sparkled in the lights. A life-size sleigh was parked by the tree. And wait a minute. "Are those reindeer?"

"Yes," Jaxon said. "Rudolph was booked but we managed to bring in Dasher and Dancer."

The majestic animals had velvety brown fur and big amber eyes, not to mention impressive antlers.

"Can I pet them?"

"See that basket of carrots?" Jaxon pointed at the silver metal basket sitting under the Christmas tree.

If she wasn't wearing heels, she would have run to the basket. Instead she walked over, grabbed two carrots, and headed for the reindeer. They raised their heads and sniffed the air as she came closer.

"Hello, there." She held a carrot out to the closest reindeer, which he accepted without hesitation. While he chewed, she ran her hands along his neck and side. His fur was thick and soft. The other reindeer stamped his front right foot and looked at her expectantly. "Sorry." She moved around and gave him a carrot, petting him in the same manner. "They're beautiful."

Bryn's grandmother approached. "They are lovely."

"You have an enchanted forest with reindeer," Bryn said. "Do you have Santa Claus stashed nearby?"

"No, he's a little busy this time of year," Jaxon said.

"Too bad," Bryn said.

"If you'll wash your hands and come to the table, dinner is about to start," Lillith announced.

Okay, she had just run her fingers through the deer's fur, but where was she supposed to wash her hands. She glanced around.

"This way." Jaxon led her to the back of the giant evergreen to what looked like a water fountain. There was a crystal soap dispenser which she made use of and then she rinsed her hands.

"Was this here before the reindeer?" she asked.

"No. My mother had it installed this morning."

"Wow." Bryn couldn't think of anything else to say. She was about to have Christmas dinner, complete with reindeer, at Westgate Estate. She fought the urge to giggle. A year ago she would have been 80 percent positive Ferrin would poison her food. Now she was about 80 percent positive he wouldn't.

Keeping her thoughts to herself, she followed Jaxon back to the table and ended up sitting between him and Lillith. That worked. Her grandparents sat across from her while Ferrin sat at the head of the table. Asher lay in a bassinet by Lillith. He seemed to be captivated by a snowman mobile spinning in lazy circles.

"Thank you for coming this evening," Ferrin said. "I'd be lying if I said I'd ever imagined this situation, but Jaxon and Bryn do seem to be a good match." He raised his wine glass. "To new beginnings and a happy holiday."

Bryn raised her water goblet while the adults raised their wine glasses. Jaxon copied her move. After the toast, Ferrin pressed a button on a small remote and a maid appeared from behind a tree pushing a cart down the slate path. In no time at all, dinner was served.

Lillith kept the small talk flowing while they ate. The food was amazing, and everything ran smoothly, which was strange. After a dessert of Christmas cookies, Ferrin said, "Let's move on to the next part of the evening."

"What's next?" Bryn asked Jaxon.

"I'm not ruining the surprise," he said. "Come on."

They walked deeper into the forest and ended up at what looked like a frozen pond. There were benches with ice-skates lined up on them.

Bryn pointed at the glass like surface. "Did you use your breath weapon to create an indoor skating rink?"

"No," Jaxon said. "We, or rather some Green dragons and an Orange dragon, used technology to create it, while making sure it wouldn't hurt the trees."

"It's pretty cool," Bryn said.

Jaxon shot her a look. "Was that pun intentional?"

"Maybe."

"Do you know how to skate?" Jaxon asked.

Before this whole shape-shifting dragon business, she'd skated as a human. Or rather she'd tried to skate and spent most of her time falling down. "Not really, but I'm sure I can learn." She looked down at her dress. "I'm not sure this is appropriate ice-skating attire."

Jaxon pointed at a small tent-like structure off to the side. "My mother stocked the dressing room with clothes for you and your grandmother."

At the moment, her grandmother emerged wearing a cream and navy cable-knit sweater and navy pants. "Wow. Your mom thought of everything."

Ten minutes later, Bryn realized she might've been wrong about the whole skating thing, as her feet went out from under her, yet again, and she landed on the cold wet ice with a thump. Thank goodness for the wardrobe change or she would've flashed Jaxon and everyone else half a dozen times by now. Speaking of Jaxon, he stood there, the picture of grace and ease on the ice, doing his best not to laugh and failing miserably.

"Instead of smirking at me, help me up." She held out a hand.

He glided over on his skates, like he was floating on air, and grabbed her hand. She fought the impulse to yank on his arm so he'd fall down, too, and instead allowed him to pull her to her feet.

Once she was standing she pointed at her skates. "Maybe the blades are defective."

Jaxon pointed at his parents and her grandparents who were skating effortlessly on the far side of the ice rink. "They don't seem to be having a problem."

"Instead of mocking me, why don't you teach me how to skate?"

"That won't be nearly as much fun," Jaxon said. "I think you're pushing too hard. The idea is to glide, kind of like you fly, but use finesse, rather than strength."

"That's not my strong suit," Bryn muttered. Jaxon held out his hand. "You can do this."

She took his hand which, oddly enough, felt natural, and pushed off, using half the force she'd used before. Huh. That did seem to work better.

"Push and glide," Jaxon said.

"Right." She didn't glide quite like he did, but with him holding on to her, she managed much better and they actually made it around the entire pond.

"In honor of you making a complete circle without falling down, I think we should stop and have a drink."

"Works for me." Stopping while she was ahead seemed like a good plan.

He helped her off the ice to the bench where Bryn had left the boots Lillith had supplied with her outfit. After changing back into normal footwear, she felt much more relaxed. Shoes were not meant to have metal blades on the bottom of them.

In the middle of the bench was a carafe of hot cocoa, a small container of marshmallows, and two cups. Jaxon poured and then pushed the bowl of marshmallows toward her. "Help yourself."

"Thank you." She added three big marshmallows to her cup. For the moment, all was right in her world, which was strange because she was with Jaxon at Westgate Estate. Rather than think too much about it, she blew on her cocoa and then took a sip. It was velvety chocolate goodness.

Jaxon shook his head at her, but he was smiling while he did it. "I've never known anyone who liked food so much."

"I think my grandfather is the same way, but he doesn't let it show in public," Bryn said.

"That is the Blue way of life," Jaxon said. "Give nothing away in public."

"Why?" Bryn asked. "Why is it so important to act perfect?"

"It just is. Blues are responsible for keeping the world in order, which means we must appear to have everything under control all of the time."

"But that's unrealistic."

"Not to be rude, but until you came along, everyone believed the Directorate was in total control."

"Don't blame me," she said. "I just pulled back the curtain. I didn't cause the problem."

"Right, but before you showed up, even I believed they were all powerful and could do no wrong. They were very good at presenting that image. Now everyone knows they aren't perfect, but the Directorate is still responsible for keeping everyone safe."

"I know that. I'm impressed with how quickly the Directorate has assimilated. They aren't preaching Clan purity anymore and they're far more accepting of hybrids and throwbacks than I ever thought they'd be."

Jaxon glanced out at the pond like he was checking to see how close the rest of the group was. "My father isn't having the easiest time adjusting. Your grandfather, due in no small part to you, is leading the charge."

A sense of pride filled Bryn's chest. "I'm glad to hear that. Now if I could only get him to speak to my mother."

"Don't hold your breath. Loyalty is hugely important in our world."

Bryn rolled her eyes. "Really, I had no idea." It's not like she was a complete outsider anymore.

"I know you're aware of that, but I'm not sure you know how deep it runs."

"What I keep coming back to is the fact that I wouldn't be here if my mom hadn't run off." She pointed at Jaxon. "If you make some comment about how you'd be better off if I wasn't here, I will accidentally spill my hot cocoa on you."

"Even if I said it, I wouldn't really mean it." Jaxon grabbed her free hand that wasn't holding the mug.

Warmth bloomed in her chest and it had nothing to do with the hot cocoa. If they were alone, now would be the perfect time for Jaxon to kiss her.

He stood. "Let's go for a walk."

"Okay." She set her mug on the bench and let him pull her to her feet. Should she tell her grandparents where they were going? That would kind of ruin the moment she and Jaxon might be having, so she shelved the idea.

Hand in hand, they walked down one of the slate paths back into the trees with the fairy lights. "This place is amazing."

"This has always been my favorite part of the house. I used to spend a lot of time out here."

"Doing what?"

They walked down a path and into a stand of trees. Several single swings and a double swing where two people could sit, like a porch swing, were suspended from the trees. There was also a staircase that spiraled around a tree and led up to a walkway suspended between the trees, high up in the branches.

"Can we go up?" Bryn asked.

"Sure."

The spiral steps were easy to climb, but the walkway was higher up in the trees than it appeared from below.

"What do you think?" Jaxon asked.

"I think it's the perfect place to hide from the world." Wait a minute. "You made fun of me last year when I said I wanted a treehouse."

"This isn't a treehouse, it's a far superior tree bridge."

"Right," Bryn mocked. "That makes sense."

Jaxon tugged her back toward the platform of the first tree. "There's more." Around the back side of the tree there was a bench. "If you don't feel like walking, you can sit."

"As one does when one is tired from adventures on their tree bridge." She sat and relaxed back against the trunk of the tree, very aware of Jaxon's proximity and the heat coming off his body.

"Exactly," he said.

She laughed. From inside the tree the fairy lights seemed even more magical. "You know this is basically a tree house without walls."

"No. That doesn't work for me," he said.

Bryn rolled her eyes but didn't comment.

"I saw that," Jaxon said.

"You were meant to." Joking around with him felt comfortable. "This is nice."

"The tree?" he asked.

"No." She pointed back and forth between them. "This. Us. No pretenses or small talk...just us."

"Speaking of us." He leaned in, slowly, like he was giving her a chance to move away. She met him halfway and pressed her mouth against his. Time seemed to slow down as his hand touched her cheek and then cradled the back of her head. Heat thrummed between them, burning bright as the kiss grew, which was strange yet somehow right.

Chapter Thirty-Four

Bryn waited for Ivy and Clint at the Snack Shack, per Clint's decree, at eleven o'clock on the twenty-eighth. Actually, it was twenty til eleven, but she'd been so excited to see her friends she was early. The two guards who had driven her here were stationed in the lot across the street, keeping an eye on everything just in case evil Silver dragon-pires decided to make an appearance.

She'd worked her way through half a bucket of caramel corn by the time her friends arrived. Ivy came over and hugged her before sitting down. Clint grabbed a handful of caramel corn and shoved it in his mouth as he took his seat.

"Hungry?" Bryn asked.

"I told him he couldn't badger you with questions about Jaxon, so I think he's stuffing his face as a preventative measure," Ivy said.

"You can ask as many questions as you want," Bryn said. "Not that I have any answers."

"What do you mean?" Ivy asked. "I thought things were falling into place. You're on good terms with your parents, your grandparents, and Jaxon. From what you said, even Ferrin is playing nice."

"I know, but there's this voice in my head that won't let me relax and enjoy and my life. It keeps waiting for the next tragedy to hit."

"I think everyone has that voice now," Clint said. "I'm grateful we made it through Christmas without any major catastrophes."

Ivy arched her eyebrows at Clint. "Well, there was that one incident."

"No." He smacked his hands over his ears. "No, there was not."

Ivy laughed.

Clint dropped his hands. "You wouldn't think it was so funny if it was your parents we'd walked in on."

"Walked in on?" It took Bryn a moment to understand. "Oh my God. Seriously?"

"Clint was going to spend the evening at my house, but he forgot the tin of peanut butter fudge he was supposed to bring over, so we both went back to his house to pick it up and let's just say, his parents were making merry under the mistletoe in the kitchen."

Bryn cringed. "In the kitchen?"

Ivy laughed. "Thank goodness they didn't realize we were in the house. We snuck back out, abandoning the fudge. There were more than enough Christmas cookies at my house to make up the difference."

"Now that you've shared with Bryn," Clint said, "we will never speak of this again. I have to spend time in that kitchen with my parents every day over break. Rehashing the nightmare is harshing my ability to live in denial."

"Okay," Ivy said. "I won't mention it again."

"I don't have any stories that are nearly as entertaining," Bryn said.

"Nothing strange happened at Christmas dinner with Ferrin?" Clint said. "I find that hard to believe."

"It was weird because it's like he switched modes to some sort of host who was trying to impress us. I have to admit, the setting was magical. On a side note, I did learn that I sucked at ice skating." She told them about the frozen pond Ferrin had added for Christmas.

"It's like Ferrin lives in some alternate reality where he can create whatever he wants," Clint said. "Maybe that's why he doesn't like it when he can't control situations."

"Interesting logic," Bryn said. "And you're probably not wrong."

After lunch, they decided to go for a walk down Main Street.

"Are you sure we're allowed to window shop?" Ivy asked. "We could get in trouble for loitering."

"My grandmother and the Women's League have been butting heads with the Directorate over this whole situation. So far, the guards have agreed to stay alert and watch for anyone who might be a threat without badgering people who appear to be shopping."

"It'll be hard." Clint rolled his shoulders back and puffed out his chest. "But I'll try not to appear threatening."

"Uh-oh," Ivy said. "Is it my imagination, or is that guard following us?" She nodded her head at the guard across the street.

Bryn checked to make sure before she said anything. "That's Derek. He's with me. My grandmother sent him with orders to stay nearby. Before that might have annoyed me, but now I'm okay with it."

"Plus he's kind of cute," Ivy said.

"I hadn't noticed," Bryn said, practicing her polite Blue social skills because Derek was cute and God forbid anyone overheard her say that and pass the information back to Jaxon.

"Nice diplomacy act. Anyway, are we actually shopping for anything, or are we browsing?" Ivy asked.

"I wanted to pick up some Christmas ornaments for my parents," Bryn said.

"They should be on sale now," Ivy said.

"Funny how everything is on sale after you've spent all your money," Clint said. "If we were smart we'd wait to buy gifts after Christmas and exchange them on New Year's Eve."

Bryn nodded along, despite the pang of guilt at having a ready supply of money, due to her grandparents. She'd never had money growing up. Having a bottomless purse now was fun, but it also made her uncomfortable.

"Let's go by the art store," Ivy said. "They had ornaments from local artisans which were really cool. Maybe they have some left."

When they reached the art store, Bryn found hand blown glass ornaments that were amazing. "I love this one." She held up a globe made from swirling blue and green glass.

Ivy picked up a tear drop with white-and-red streaks. "I think I need this one."

"Oh, that is pretty. Is there another one like it?" Bryn asked.

"They're all unique," Ivy said. "But here's another red one your mom would probably love."

Bryn accepted the swirling red globe Ivy held out to her. "How many should I buy?"

"That depends," Clint said. "How big is your mom's tree?"

"They dug up a three-foot tree that they're going to transplant to their front yard after Christmas," Bryn said. "So I have no idea what size they'll have next year."

"Whatever you pick can be a starter ornament set," Ivy said. "They can always add more each year. That's what my parents did."

Westgates didn't do starter anything. Maybe Bryn should pick out some ornaments for the tree she'd have one day.

Clint picked up a red and blue globe with swirls of purple where the colors blended. "I think your parents need this one. It's kind of symbolic."

"I like that." By the time she was done, Bryn had a dozen ornaments wrapped in tissue paper and sealed in protective cardboard sleeves inside another larger box.

After paying for the ornaments, Bryn said, "I wonder if I could ride out to see my parents and deliver these ornaments now?"

"We could go with you," Ivy said, "if that would help."

Bryn reached for the handle to the door when it was flung open and Derek the guard rushed inside. "Everyone get back," he warned as he turned to face the door.

Bryn stumbled backwards dropping the box of ornaments. She reached for her wrist and activated her elemental sword. Her heart hammered in her chest while she waited to see what was coming.

The door banged open and a man with dark skin and eyes the color of steel entered the store. He seemed unconcerned with the large Red guard who stood blocking his path. His eyes were on Bryn. "There you are. That is an impressive weapon, young lady. I hoped you'd have it with you."

"It's of no use to you and I know how to use it," Bryn warned. "So get the hell out of here."

"How rude. I thought your grandparents would've raised you better."

"They didn't raise me," Bryn said.

"That's right. Your parents mentioned that."

"You know my parents?" That didn't seem right.

"I am acquainted with them. Right now, they are my guests."

"Don't come any closer," Derek said. "You're not welcome here."

"I'm merely here to extend an invitation. Bryn, you're invited to join us in Sanctuary for a belated Christmas dinner. Your parents and I will be waiting for you."

Bryn gripped the sword tighter and pushed down the fire blazing in her gut. "What have you done with my parents?"

"Nothing permanent, yet."

"Who are you and what do you want with Bryn?" Clint asked as he produced balls of lightning in both of his hands.

"My name is Adden. And I'm a Silver dragon." He seemed to be waiting for them to be afraid or impressed.

"That explains the funky eyes," Clint said.

"What do you want with me?" Bryn asked. She wanted to save her parents, but she also wanted to know what she was walking into.

"It's simple. I'm using your parents to get to you. I'll use you to get something I want—starting with that bracelet."

He wanted her bracelet which was meant for a Red Blue hybrid? It would kill him and right now she didn't feel so bad about that.

"Let my parents go, and let us go, and I'll give you the bracelet," Bryn said.

"You'd just hand it over?" Adden said. "I find that hard to believe."

"My parents are more important than a bracelet. Where are they?"

Adden pulled a phone from his pocket and hit a button. "There's been an interesting development. Put her mom on the phone." He pushed the speaker button.

"Bryn, are you there?" Her mom sounded stressed.

"I'm at the art store with some asshat named Adden.Where are you?"

"We're in our house with some uninvited guests, but we're fine," her mom said.

"Your daughter lacks manners," Adden said.

"Hurt her and you'll be lacking your balls," Bryn's mom growled through the phone.

Adden blinked. "I see where she gets it from. Stay on the line until your daughter gives me her bracelet."

Bryn removed the bracelet but held onto it. "I give you this, your people leave my parents' house, and you let everyone go."

"Agreed."

"Is there a back door?" Derek asked the girl behind the counter.

She nodded.

"Go," Derek stood between her and Adden. "All of you go. Bryn, give me the bracelet."

She didn't trust Adden to keep his word. "I have a better idea. We'll all back up, and I'll leave the bracelet here." She deactivated the safety and set the bracelet on a display of colored pencils. "We back out of the store and you come get this."

"That is acceptable." He chuckled. "Leave the McKenna's home," he spoke into his phone.

Bryn backed away from the bracelet. Derek stayed between her and Adden. Clint and Ivy and the cashier headed for the exit.

"They're gone, Bryn," her mom said. "Are you okay?"

"Yes. I'll call you soon," Bryn hollered so her mother could hear her as she dashed toward the exit.

Adden confidently strode across the store and picked up the bracelet. He bent the ends out so it would wrap part way around his wrist. Bryn hovered in the doorway, waiting to see what the disembodied voice would do to him when he failed the Trial-by-Fire. With the bracelet in place, Adden stiffened and closed his eyes. This was it. He would fail because he wasn't a Red-Blue hybrid.

"Yes," Adden growled. "I knew I was right." A sword of fire and ice shot from his hand. He smiled at Bryn. "Surprise."

What the hell? "How is that possible?"

"I'm a master of all five elements," he bragged. "Therefore, all the artifacts will work for me." He came toward them, swinging the sword, cutting through book displays and bins of paint brushes.

"Time to go," Clint said.

"Move," Derek ordered. He shoved Bryn out the door while he grabbed his cell phone, barking orders at whoever was on the other end.

She didn't know where they were, but she followed Clint and Ivy. They made it out onto Main Street where everything seemed perfectly normal. Her grandmother's SUV sped toward them and screeched to a halt inches from Clint.

"Get in," Derek ordered.

Clint yanked the door open and shoved Ivy inside, climbing in after her. Bryn went in next. Derek followed. Despite the fact that no one seemed to be chasing them, the driver sped away like a bat out of hell while Derek continued to talk to people on his phone.

When they reached Sinclair Estate, Ferrin greeted her at the door with, "Why in the hell did you give him your bracelet?"

"I didn't think he could use it. Only Red-Blue hybrids should be able to use that bracelet."

Her grandfather put a hand on Ferrin's shoulder and pulled him back. "We had no way of knowing he'd be able to use the sword."

"Plus, they had people in my parents' house," Bryn reminded him.

"We sent guards out there to make sure they were okay," her grandfather said. "They're fine. I've left someone to watch over them."

Ivy held out her wrist. The black pearl bracelet shone in the light. "It's a good thing he didn't know about my bracelet."

"And if he ever finds out, you'll know not to hand it over without a fight," Ferrin snapped.

"Bite me," Bryn said.

"You've caused yet another mess—" Ferrin started.

"Keep yelling at me and I'll name your grandchildren after my parents," Bryn shot back.

Ferrin blinked, looking dumbfounded.

"Hey, look at that," Bryn said. "I have a new way to annoy Ferrin."

Clint and Ivy both turned away, trying not to laugh. Her grandfather sighed and rubbed his eyes. "Bryn, I need you and your friends to give a factual account of everything that happened. Come with me."

Ferrin stalked ahead.

Clint caught up to Bryn. "That was freaking brilliant."

"Thanks. It just sort of came to me."

"Next time," Ivy said, "tell him you'll get his grandkids tattoos like Aunt Ivy and Uncle Clint."

Bryn laughed. When they entered the dining room she did her best to put on a serious face.

"Derek, come with us," her grandfather said. "Bryn, we'll be back for you in a few minutes."

They walked across the hall to the small living room where she'd first kissed Jaxon. Her grandmother came into the room, followed by Abigail who had a cart of snacks and drinks.

"Bryn, I thought we discussed this," her grandmother said in a joking tone before coming over to give her a hug.

"Sorry, my status as a chaos-magnet continues."

"Help yourselves to whatever you like," her grandmother said to Clint and Ivy. "After you've given your statement I can have a driver take you home."

"My car is in Dragon's Bluff," Clint said.

"Then we'll take you back there," her grandmother said. When Derek came back into the room, the veins on his neck were bulging. Her grandfather or Ferrin must have ripped him a new one.

Before walking across the hall Bryn grabbed a soda and took it to him. "Thank you for protecting me today."

"I did what I thought best at the time." He accepted the drink. "Thank you."

Bryn went across the hall and told them about everything that had happened in the art store. "I don't know where Adden came from, but Derek made sure he couldn't physically reach me. I swear I thought the bracelet would poison him or kill him."

"And you were okay with that?" Ferrin asked.

"He had my parents. I would have been happy to see him drop dead."

"Now he knows he can use any artifact," her grandfather said. "We need to round them up to keep them out of his hands."

"Ivy has her bracelet and Jaxon has his cuff links. What else could he be looking for?"

"Don't," Ferrin stated like he was king of the world.

Her grandfather ignored the decree. "We had several more knight volunteers who retrieved artifacts for us. There are weapons for Orange and Green dragons as well as Red. We were considering taking hybrid volunteers to find more weapons like yours."

"What did you do with the knights?" Bryn asked.

"They were released once the artifacts were found."

"So you think Adden and his Silver friends will be looking for anyone with an artifact? What does he plan to do with them?"

"Is there any point in asking you not to share?" Ferrin asked.

"No," her grandfather said. "From what we've read, combining certain artifacts will create some sort of super weapon."

"That does what?" Bryn asked.

"We have no idea. Miss Enid has been scouring the history books for us, but she's yet to find anything conclusive."

Something about this didn't make sense. "Why would they need weapons if they're immune to all of our breath weapons?"

Her grandfather squinted at her. "Why would you think they're immune?"

"I was curious about the Silver dragons, so I read some articles in the library."

"The Silvers may develop control over all of our breath weapons once they've fed off enough dragons from each Clan, but they're not impervious to them. They may have claimed immunity to make themselves seem more impressive, but that's not the case."

"Good to know." It made them seem little less threatening.

"You can share what we've told you today with your friends and Jaxon, but no one else."

"Why even bother to keep it a secret?" Ferrin asked.

"What has your panties in a bunch today?" Bryn asked.

Ferrin rounded on her. "I am the Speaker for the Directorate. You will treat me with respect." Frost shot from his mouth. Her grandfather was giving her a look like she'd crossed the line. Maybe she had.

"You're right. That was rude. I apologize."

"Send Clint in," her grandfather said.

Bryn went back out and whispered to her friends. "I set Ferrin off. Tread lightly." In a louder voice, she said, "Clint, you're up."

Bryn went to the phone and called her parents. After trading assurances that all was well and confirming that someone was watching their house, she sat and ate some more Christmas cookies.

After giving their statements, Clint and Ivy had a guard drive them back to their car in Dragon's Bluff.

Once they were gone, Bryn sat on the chaise lounge and reran the day's events in her head. A wave of self-doubt hit her. Had she been stupid to give Adden the bracelet?

"May I sit with you?" Derek asked.

"Of course." She scooted over to the edge so he'd have plenty of room.

"I wanted to apologize for what happened today," he said. "I never should have let Adden enter the store."

What could she say to that? "You protected me. You have nothing to apologize for."

"I saw him coming down the street, blasting ice in different directions. I didn't know what he was doing, but I knew he was trouble. I should have blocked the entrance until backup arrived," he said. "But all I could think about was making sure you were okay and I couldn't do that from outside the store."

"You can second-guess yourself all you want, but it won't do any good." Not that she wasn't guilty of the exact same thing. "I'm just grateful you kept him from reaching me, so don't beat yourself up over the rest of it."

"Thank you." He cleared his throat. "I just wanted to say my piece before your grandfather reassigns me."

That wasn't right. "You think he'd reassign you because of today?"

"I believe he will. As is his right."

"That sucks," Bryn said.

He smiled. "It would be best if you didn't mention this conversation to anyone. We aren't supposed to interact on a personal level with the people we protect."

"That sucks, too," Bryn said.

He laughed, and his green eyes sparkled, and his smile was genuine. Ivy was right. He was cute, and it would be easy for a girl to fall for someone like him.

Male voices could be heard coming down the hall. Derek jumped to his feet and stood off to the side in guard mode a split second before Jaxon entered the room.

"What in the hell did you do?" he asked.

She glared at him. "Do you want to try that again?"

"You know what I mean." He pulled her to her feet and hugged her. "Are you all right?"

"Yes." She relaxed against his chest for a moment. Being wrapped in his arms was comforting. It was funny that his heart was beating fast. He must have been worried. She looked up at him. "Seriously. I'm okay."

"Good. Now. Answer my first question."

Bryn stepped back and sat on the chaise. He joined her, still holding her hand, which was nice. She repeated her tale of weirdness, ending with, "And if anyone had told me there was a chance Silvers could use a hybrid weapon I never would have given it to him."

"I would have used the same logic," Jaxon said. "No one can fault you for that."

"Your father disagrees," Bryn said.

"I'm not surprised," Jaxon said. "Now what?"

"I don't know. My parents are safe. I'm not sure where the other artifacts are being kept, but I'd love to look and see if there was anything else I could use."

"Do you think you could use a weapon meant for a Blue?" He held out his free hand, showing the cuff link.

"I'm not sure I'd want to try. If I was wrong, the results might be fatal." And then she had a funny thought. "Could Garrett or one of the Greens make another bracelet for me?"

"Good question. I'm not sure who made the artifacts in the first place."

"Me, either," Bryn said. "They're old. Miss Enid said she'd only heard of elemental weapons in myths and legends. And if they could be created now, I doubt the Silvers would be trying to steal ours."

Bryn's grandfather entered the room. "We're going over footage of Dragon's Bluff. Come and look at the video with us. See if you recognize anyone from school."

They gathered around the dining room table to watch the screen. "Adden was parked across the street from the Snack Shack. He seemed to know where you were and then he followed you, acting like he was window shopping."

"If only there had been some law in effect that would have kept Adden from loitering in his car and on the streets," Ferrin said, taking sarcasm to a new level.

"Who knew your plans for today?" her grandfather asked, like he hadn't heard Ferrin.

"We talked about it in the dining hall at school—before Christmas," Bryn said. "Anyone could have overheard."

Bryn watched the video play out. It cut from one angle to another. Adden looked perfectly normal when he walked down the street. He nodded at people and said hello, but he didn't stop to speak to anyone. One of the people he walked past was Janelle.

Bryn pointed at the screen. "That's a girl from my Medic classes. She didn't interact with him but she's the only person I recognize."

"Since she had no contact with him, I doubt she was involved," her grandfather said. "We'll find out why she was in Dragon's Bluff and what she did, just to make sure."

"This is where it becomes disturbing." Her grandfather pointed at the screen. Adden raised his hand and blasted ice, and the screen went blank. The video switched to another camera feed and the same thing happened.

"Derek had been watching the art store from across the street. He saw Adden's strange behavior and realized it could be a threat, so he ran to join you."

"Adden knew where the cameras were," Jaxon said.

"The cameras are there for everyone's safety," her grandfather said, "so we try to make them blend with the architecture but we don't hide them."

"To sum up, there are crazy Silvers trying to get ahold of dragon artifacts which are meant to be individual weapons, but when combined they might make something worse," Bryn said.

"Yes."

"I'm sure they know about my cuff link swords," Jaxon said, "but I doubt they realize Ivy's bracelet is also an artifact. Where are the other items?"

"They're being studied to see if they can be reproduced," Ferrin said.

"Any luck in that area?" Bryn asked. It was probably too much to hope that she could get another bracelet.

"They have had a modicum of success focusing a dragon's element into a dagger, but it doesn't hold its form for long."

"Are they working on campus?" Bryn asked.

"Yes," her grandfather nodded.

"Do you think the Silvers were looking for artifacts," Jaxon asked, "or your experiments on artifacts, on the Friday you cancelled classes?"

"You think they wanted us to quarantine students so they'd have time to search the campus?" Ferrin asked.

"It makes sense," Jaxon said. "They had to know that multiple students feeling ill would cause a quarantine and the Medics would investigate."

"There was an attempted break in at the Vaults of the Library that day," her grandfather said. "They made it down the stairs to the main chamber but were unable to open the doors, since they didn't have a knight."

"How'd they get the key to go down there?" Bryn asked.

"A dragon-pire fed on Miss Enid, knocked her out, and then used the key."

Poor Miss Enid. She'd be very unhappy about being duped. Not to mention losing the key.

"There are a few more orders of business. Derek will be your shadow until you return to school," her grandfather said. "We'll station him on campus to keep an eye on you but you won't notice him," her grandfather said. "Now, you and Jaxon can spend some time together before he leaves."

...

Feeling like she wanted some semi fresh air, Bryn suggested they go up to the atrium. She and Jaxon walked among the flowers and stopped at a bench nestled into the plants. "This isn't nearly as nice as your tree bridge," she said. "But it will have to do."

"It would be nicer without your shadow," Jaxon said. Derek stood off to the side, about a hundred feet away, staring down the hall like he was ready to lay down his life if anyone tried to join them.

"He's doing his job," Bryn said.

"When I'm with you he isn't necessary," Jaxon said. "His presence is insulting."

She wanted to laugh but that would be wrong. "My grandparents are going to be hyper protective for awhile. It's no comment on your abilities."

"From now on, he won't be the only shadow you have," Jaxon said. "This will probably make you mad, but no more solo trips to Dragon's Bluff. Clint and Ivy will have to adjust to my presence sooner or later, so we might as well start now."

"Fine. We'll figure out some manly bonding thing you and Clint can do while Ivy and I shop for girly stuff."

"Or, we could just have everything you need delivered to your dorm room so you don't have to leave campus." He nodded like that was a fabulous idea.

"Watch it. You'll make me feel claustrophobic if you tell me I can't go anywhere."

"I'm hoping common sense will prevail," he said. "Although I get the feeling the odds may not be in my favor."

She elbowed him in the ribs, lightly so he'd know she was joking yet slightly annoyed. "Ha-ha."

"What were you shopping for today?"

"Christmas ornaments for my parents. And I found some hand-blown glass ornaments that were beautiful—but I left them in the store. I should call and see if they can deliver them."

Jaxon gave her a strange look. "Christmas is over. Why would you buy them ornaments now?"

Jaxon had never been without money so this was going to be an interesting conversation. "They go on sale after Christmas. My mom mentioned needing ornaments, so I thought I'd give some to her as a gift."

"They didn't have a chance to buy them, or they couldn't afford them?"

"Both, probably. I think they're trading services out at Sanctuary, but it's not like before where they both had jobs."

"I never thought of that." Jaxon furrowed his brow. "I've never thought about not having money to take care of things I wanted or needed."

"There are a lot of dragons that work and watch their budget so they can afford what they need. It's bizarre to me that I have access to my grandparents' unlimited bank account. And it's a lot of fun, but it does make me feel guilty."

"Maybe you should talk to your grandfather about jobs for people in Sanctuary. I'm sure he could have some Greens look into it and set something up."

"Good idea."

"I don't suppose this incident today will be the end of our problems with the Silvers," Jaxon said.

"No. They've discovered that there are fun new toys they can play with, so I'm pretty sure they'll try to steal them."

"Since we know they'll come after my cuff links, maybe we should use them to set a trap," Jaxon said. "That way I won't be waiting for them to jump out at me. We could get them to come to us on our terms."

"You want to be the bait for a crazy cult leader?"

"When you put it that way it doesn't sound as good," he said.

Bryn sighed. "Promise me you won't run off and do something dangerous...without me."

"A normal female would have ended that sentence two words earlier."

"I'm serious. We really are a team now, right?" He nodded.

"Then whatever danger there is, we face it together."

"I will do my best not to have any life-threatening adventures without you."

"Thank you."

...

The next morning Derek stood guard in the hallway outside of Bryn's door. That was new.

He nodded at her. "Good morning."

"Good morning." She wasn't sure what to say next. "So I was heading down to breakfast unless my grandparents have me confined to my room."

"Nothing like that," he said. "I'm supposed to keep track of you. Just think of me as your shadow."

"Okay." She set off down the hall and he fell into step behind her. Should she try and make small talk? Maybe after her coffee kicked in she'd have a better idea of how to handle this new situation.

Her grandmother sat in the dining room, reading the newspaper and drinking tea. She smiled as Bryn came in. "You had a surprise delivery from Dragon's Bluff this morning."

"I did?"

"The lady from the art store said you forgot your ornaments." Her grandmother pointed at the box, which Bryn had left behind after escaping Adden.

She walked over to inspect the box. It was a little dented on one side. Had all the ornaments survived? She opened the outer box and checked the contents. The individual boxes were cushioned between layers of tissue paper, so they seemed to be intact.

"Out of curiosity, why did you buy ornaments?" her grandmother asked.

Bryn headed back to the table and poured herself a cup of coffee and grabbed a muffin from the basket on the table. "I bought them for my parents. They have a tree but didn't have time to shop for ornaments."

"Oh." Her grandmother appeared thoughtful but didn't comment any further.

"So what are the plans for today?" Bryn asked. After Adden's appearance and the discovery that he could use her bracelet, she wasn't sure how much freedom she'd have.

"I planned to meet with the Women's League in Dragon's Bluff, but if you want to visit your parents and deliver your ornaments I could have the driver drop you and Derek off at Sanctuary and come back for you after lunch." She was surprised her grandmother would make such a generous offer. "That sounds wonderful. I'll call my parents and make sure it works for them. One phone call later, Bryn had her plans for the day in place.

When they reached Sanctuary, both of her parents waited for them on the other side of the gate. Her father's ax was absent. "Do you want to come in for a moment to say hello?" Bryn asked.

Her grandmother looked away. "Perhaps another day. I wouldn't want to be late for my meeting."

Bryn interpreted that response as "Absolutely not," but hoped she was wrong.

"All right. We'll see you in a few hours." Derek had already exited the vehicle, carrying the box of ornaments. He came around to open Bryn's door. After checking in at the front gate and receiving their passes, Bryn wasn't sure how to introduce Derek so she improvised.

"Mom, Dad, this is my assigned shadow, Derek. Derek, meet Ian and Sara McKenna, my parents."

They exchanged rounds of the obligatory nice to meet you's and then headed toward her parents' cabin.

"What's in the box?" her mom asked.

Bryn grabbed the box from Derek. "It's a surprise."

The wind picked up as they walked straight down the road before branching off to the right-hand street. Bits of sleet randomly hit Bryn in the face. "Please tell me it's not going to sleet today."

"I heard we might have some snow," her mom said.

"Snow is fun, sleet is obnoxious," her dad said as he opened the front door for them. Bryn followed her mom inside and then heard her dad say, "You're not going to stand out here. Come inside."

Derek didn't argue with her dad, but after surveying the small living room and kitchen area, he said, "I'll keep watch by the door." He moved to stand by the front door with his back to them. Could he even see anything out of the small window set into the door? Better than staring at a wall, but still, it made Bryn uncomfortable.

"Let me take that for you." Bryn's dad plucked the box from her hands and passed it to her mom.

"Thank you." Her mom settled on the couch and opened the package. "Boxes inside a box." She opened one of the smaller boxes and pulled out the globe made from swirling blue and green glass. "Oh, honey. I love it."

"They're handblown. I found them in the art store in Dragon's Bluff."

"Makes me wish we'd kept the tree inside a little bit longer," her dad said.

Her mom unwrapped a purple teardrop ornament and held it up to the light. "They don't have to be just for Christmas. We could hang them from the skylights, like a chandelier."

"I'll get the ladder," her dad said.

Warmth blossomed in Bryn's chest. She'd missed these positive, warm, family moments. She loved her grandmother, but the difference in joy between the two women was astounding.

Her dad brought the ladder back in and handed Bryn a spool of wire. "This should work."

Bryn helped her mom unwrap all the ornaments and attach varying lengths of wire to the ends where the hooks would normally go.

"I'll hold the ladder," said her dad.

Bryn grabbed an ornament, intent on climbing the ladder. "Let me help you," Derek said.

"Afraid I'll fall off the ladder and you'll have to explain the situation to my grandparents?" Bryn asked.

Derek grinned, and his eyes lit up. "Yes, plus staring out the door is boring."

Bryn handed the ornaments to Derek while her dad held the ladder and her mom approved of their placement. When they were finished, the ornaments hung in a descending swirl design.

"I love it," Bryn's mom said. "I'll make us some hot tea." Derek moved back toward the door.

"Have a seat," her dad said. "And I won't take no for an answer."

"The Sinclairs would not approve," Derek said.

"They won't hear about it," her dad said.

"Okay, then," Derek sat on the couch next to Bryn. Her mom sat on the far side, and her dad brought a kitchen chair into the living room.

"How are things going in Sanctuary?" Bryn asked.

"We're turning one of the cabins into a yoga studio," her mom said. "The interior walls had fallen down and no one wanted to go through the work to replace them, so I asked to use the space."

"You're making sure it's safe, right?" Bryn said. "I'd hate to lose you in some sort of cabin collapse."

"We're reinforcing the walls and making sure it's sound," her dad said.

"My uncle works construction," Derek said. "If you need any extra manpower he could probably find some volunteers."

"Thank you," her dad said. "We might take you up on that."

For the next hour, Bryn relaxed and enjoyed her parents' and Derek's company. It was funny how easily he fit in with her family, in a way Jaxon never would. When his cell vibrated, Derek checked the screen and sighed. "They're waiting for us at the front gate. Thank you, Mr. and Mrs. McKenna, for making me feel welcome. I'll wait outside while Bryn says her goodbyes."

"It was nice meeting you," her mom said.

"Good to know you're looking out for Bryn," her dad said.

Derek nodded and headed out the front door.

"If you wanted to trade that blond kid in for this guy," her dad said, "I wouldn't mind."

Bryn sighed. "In another life, maybe." She hugged her dad and her mom. "I'm glad you liked the ornaments."

Stinging sleet hit Bryn in the face when she walked out the door. "This sucks," Bryn said.

They hurried down the road to the main gate where her grandmother's SUV waited. They signed out and hustled into the car. As soon as the car door opened, Bryn was hit with the smell of Fonzoli's pizza. She inhaled deeply as she took her seat. "Is that what I think it is?"

"Four pepperoni calzones. Two for your grandfather and two for you."

"Yum." Her stomach growled. "I don't suppose I could eat one on the drive back."

"No," her grandmother said. "Tell me about your visit."

Bryn told her grandmother about the ornaments, leaving out any mention of Derek.

Her grandmother shifted the takeout bag around on the seat next to her. "Do your parents need anything?"

"Not that I can think of. Mom is opening a yoga studio. She might need some yoga equipment, but she didn't mention it."

"I can't imagine living in one of those ancient cabins," her grandmother said. "But she's happy, isn't she?"

"Not that you want to hear this, but the only thing she's ever really needed to make her happy was my dad."

"I'm beginning to understand that." She smoothed her hand down the front of her coat. "The next time you speak to her mother, tell her the Women's League will fund whatever she needs for the Yoga Center."

"Thank you. I'm sure she'll be happy to hear that." Bryn sat still even though she felt like bouncing in her seat. Had she finally convinced her grandmother to make some sort of peace with the situation? That would be a major victory.

...

The next afternoon, Bryn found herself staring at a sea of furniture in a set of connected rooms on the third floor of her grandmother's wing. Beds, dressers, armoires, and nightstands were packed tightly together, next to sets of dining room tables and buffets. Couches and wing-backed chairs lined the far wall. Bryn turned in a circle, taking in the dozens of beds and tables that could've stocked a furniture store.

"Where did all of this come from?"

Her grandmother walked over and ran her fingers along the edge of an antique dining chair. "These have been passed down through our family. While you're free to purchase new furniture, I hope you'll find some furniture for your guest bedrooms and sitting rooms."

Her grandmother held a stack of blue Post-its out to Bryn. "Wander around. When you see something you like, put a Post-it on it. Derek can move the furniture around if you want to see how different pieces work together."

"One of my many skills," Derek said in a voice only Bryn could hear.

She smiled but didn't comment. "Where will you be while I'm browsing for furniture?"

Her grandmother smiled. "Ephram and I are going out to lunch."

"Have fun."

After her grandmother exited the room. Bryn turned to Derek. "Any suggestions on where I should start?"

"Not with the blue and green paisley couch in the corner," Derek said.

"Agreed." She walked over to a gray suede couch with a matching wing-backed chair. "This is nice." She tagged it with a Post-it. "Do you think anyone would notice if we shipped a few pieces to my parents' cabin?"

"I don't think any of this would fit in their cabin," Derek said. "Can I ask you a question?"

"Sure." Bryn walked over to an end table with a white and gray marble top.

"You grew up like a Red...middle class...same couch for most of your life...right?"

"Yes."

"How do you go from that to this?" he asked.

He wasn't being judgmental. He just seemed curious. She put a Post-it on the table. "When I thought my parents had died, my grandparents took me in. They didn't have to do that. So even though their way of life seems extravagant and sometimes strange, I've adjusted."

"Better than going from rich to middle class, I guess."

"Not according to my mother," Bryn said.

"It's pretty impressive that she gave up all this for your dad."

"True love trumps everything."

"I guess." Derek pointed at a bedroom set across the way. "Is it me, or does the headboard of that bed look like a duck?"

Bryn walked toward the piece of furniture in question. "I think it's supposed to be a swan. Better than a duck bed, but it's still strange."

"No Post-it?" Derek asked.

"Nope." She smiled at him. He was so easy to talk to when they were alone. "You know all about my strange life. I don't know anything about you. Tell me your story."

His smile faltered. "It's not a happy story. My girlfriend, Ana, was fatally injured during the attack on campus."

Well hell. "I'm so sorry."

He shrugged. "You couldn't have known."

Bryn sat on the swan bed. "I'd ask how you're coping, but that is probably a stupid question."

Derek sat beside her. "Ana and I had been friends since we were little kids. It's like my life is off-balance now. Like I'm not sure of my place in the world."

"Oh." What else could she say?

Derek sighed. "I probably shouldn't have shared."

"No. It's okay. You can tell me things. I won't tell anyone else."

"I know you won't." He turned and met her gaze. There was an emotion in his eyes she couldn't quite interpret. Was he sad or nervous? All of a sudden, the situation seemed too intimate. Not that she didn't trust him, but she probably shouldn't be sitting on a bed having deep conversations with a handsome guy who wasn't her future husband.

She stood. "If I don't use up half this stack of Post-its my grandmother will probably be insulted."

"Are you sure you want to pass up this fabulous duck bed?" Derek asked patting the mattress.

"I'll try to live without it."

"That's a shame."

Chapter Thirty-Five

The rest of Christmas break passed by in a flash. She and Jaxon spent some time together but for the most part it was Bryn and the two Derek's. Not that there really were two Derek's, but there was the Derek who talked to her and joked with her like a friend and maybe even flirted with her a tiny bit, and the Derek who was all business. If Jaxon ever found out about the first Derek he would not be pleased.

They decided to continue the tradition of a Welcome Back to School party which they'd started last year. Unfortunately, that meant Bryn and Jaxon were stuck playing hosts again. She was surprised at how touchy-feely he was being when they were in public. As they greeted students, he kept his arm around her shoulders or around her waist. Not that she minded, but she wondered if he had an ulterior motive.

When the last group of students filtered, in, she said, "I declare that it's snack time."

"Unfortunately, I believe it's time to mingle and make useless small talk."

"Nope. My stomach says food first, then useless social chatter." She batted her eyelashes at him. "And you know how unreasonable I can be when I'm hungry."

"Point taken," he said. "Let's visit the buffet."

He stuck close to her as they filled their plates with cheese, crackers, and fruit. When she turned to head over to the table where Clint and Ivy sat, he turned in the opposite direction where his friends were seated.

"Meet back up for useless social chatter in fifteen minutes?" she said.

He paused. "Maybe I should come with you."

"I appreciate the thought, but I'll be less than a hundred feet away," she said. "And my shadow is around here somewhere." She figured it was best if she didn't give Derek's identity away, in case someone was listening.

"I'm painfully aware of that fact," he said. "I'll come find you in fifteen."

Bryn joined her friends and noticed Ivy wasn't wearing her bracelet. "Did you forget your jewelry tonight?" she asked.

"No, the clasp on the bracelet Clint gave me broke, so it's at the jewelers being fixed," Ivy said, like that was the truth rather than the story they'd come up with to throw any Silvers off her trail.

"That's a bummer."

"It wasn't the most expensive bracelet in the world," Clint said. "It's not like I have access to Bryn's grandma's jewelry vault."

"No one has jewelry like my grandmother," Bryn said.

"We should sneak in there one day and play dress up." Ivy suggested.

"So, half of our senior year is over, and we have half to go," Clint said, changing the topic.

"It's funny. Finishing your senior year in the human world means you'll either get a job or go to a different school for college. It's weird to me that I'll be here for college, too."

"Our way makes more sense," Clint said. "You can take pre-college courses that lead right into your major, like your Medic classes."

"True." Bryn looked around. "That reminds me, I haven't seen Janelle yet."

"Maybe she decided not to attend, because honestly, if this wasn't your thing, I'd be in my room eating pizza in my PJ's," Ivy said.

"I understand." Bryn checked the time. "Jaxon will be over here any minute to sweep me away for exciting small talk."

"You're such a lucky girl," Ivy said.

Bryn checked the table where she expected Jaxon to be. He wasn't there. A strange uneasy feeling tiptoed down her spine, giving her goose bumps. "You don't think history could be repeating itself, do you?"

"Let's go see." Clint stood.

Bryn made a beeline for Quentin. "Excuse me, not to be rude, but how long has Jaxon been gone this time?"

Quentin narrowed his eyes. "Let's take a walk and see if he needs our assistance."

The four of them headed for the restrooms. Clint and Quentin went in and came right back out. "No blood, but no Jaxon either."

Derek came stalking down the hall. "Bryn what's wrong?"

"We've lost Jaxon," she said. "This is where he was ambushed before."

"I saw him head out the dining hall doors a few minutes ago."

"He better not be using himself as bait," Bryn said.

"What do you mean?" Derek asked.

"He has something the Silvers want," Bryn said.

Derek pulled out his cell phone and made a call. "We should stay here. Other guards have been alerted."

Yeah, that didn't work for her. "Do you plan to physically restrain me?" Bryn asked. "Because that's the only way I'm not going to look for him."

"If it were my choice, yes," Derek said. "But it's my job to follow you. So let's go."

"Did he say he was going anywhere?" Bryn asked Quentin.

"No. He just excused himself," Quentin said. "I thought he was going to meet you. Maybe I should return to our table in case he comes back. He could just be running an errand."

"True. If he shows up go to a guard and have them call me," Derek said.

Quentin returned to his table while Bryn, Clint, Ivy, and Derek casually walked toward the front door. Bryn's heart rate ratcheted up a notch as worse-case scenarios played out in her brain.

When they made it down the steps of the dining hall Bryn wasn't sure where to go. "No sign of him. Did any other guards see him?"

Derek shook his head. "No one reported seeing him after he exited the building."

"Let's check the Blue dorm and the library." Bryn shifted. "Derek and I will fly up to my terrace. Clint, Ivy why don't you check the library?"

"Got it," Clint said. He and Ivy shifted and took off.

Bryn launched herself into the sky and powered past the treetops. She landed on her terrace in a stumble step because she didn't have time to gauge a graceful landing. Her terrace window was wide open. That was wrong.

Derek landed beside her.

"I didn't leave that window up."

Derek stepped in front of her and entered the hallway. She followed, a ball of fire ready in one hand and ice in the other.

Her bedroom door was open, and her room was trashed. Someone had searched through all her things, tossing clothes and shoes all over the floor. The door to the spare bedroom was open. The mattress was pushed off the bed and the drawers pulled from the dresser.

"What were they looking for?" Derek asked.

"I don't know." In the living room, they found the same thing. "Whatever it was I didn't have it." She headed out her door to the hallway and ran to Jaxon's room. She knocked and of course he didn't answer.

"Step aside," Derek said. He rammed the door with his shoulder twice, and it splintered down the middle. One more hit and there was a hole big enough for Bryn to climb through. Jaxon's apartment had suffered the same fate. After a quick check to make sure he wasn't in any of the rooms, Bryn turned in a circle and threw her arms up in the air. "Now what?"

Jaxon's phone rang. "That can't be good." She picked up the receiver.

Derek came and put his ear next to the phone so he could hear, too.

"Hello, Bryn. This is Adden."

"Do you have Jaxon?"

"I do. Your friends Clint and Ivy popped by, too. You should come join us at the library."

Derek stepped away and dialed his phone. Hopefully, he was calling for reinforcements.

"I'm hosting a party right now," Bryn said. "Maybe I could stop by another time."

Adden laughed. "Come now. There's something you should see."

"I've never been fond of surprises. Why don't you tell me what it is?"

"If you're not here in five minutes, I'll drain the life from your friends."

Bryn slammed the phone down. "We need to move."

"Other guards have been alerted. They're converging on the library. We're staying here."

"If a psychotic asshat didn't plan on draining the life from my friends, that might work for me." Bryn headed for the terrace window.

"We're supposed to stay here," Derek objected.

"No. You're supposed to follow me." Bryn threw open the window, climbed out, and shifted. He could follow her or not, but he couldn't keep her from going to her friends. She dove off the terrace, aiming for the library. Derek joined her. They landed on the front steps, shifted back, and entered the building.

Miss Enid stood at her desk. "It seems we've been here before," she said. "Adden is waiting for you in the vaults."

"Why? I can't open them any more."

"We've kept them open by stationing guards inside," Miss Enid said.

"Bad idea," Bryn growled as she hurried past Miss Enid into the room with the trap door in the floor. She descended the narrow staircase, knowing Derek would follow.

At the landing she saw the doors to the main room were open. Adden stood there with Jaxon, Ivy, and Clint. He was holding her elemental sword. And that annoyed the crap out of her.

"I want my sword back," she said.

"Then you shouldn't have given it to me." He gloated. "Oh, that's right, you expected me to die. Sorry to disappoint you."

Jerk. She turned to Jaxon. "What happened to meeting for small talk?"

"Sorry." Jaxon shrugged. "I stepped out for some air, and Adden suggested I join him in the vaults. He's such a sparkling conversationalist, I couldn't refuse."

Right. She doubted Adden snuck up on Jaxon. This had to be some sort of plan. A plan he'd neglected to tell her about.

"So many jokes," Adden said. "So little control over your fate."

"What do you want?" Derek asked.

"Finally, someone who gets straight to the point," Adden said. "I want the other artifacts. They're down here somewhere and you're going to help me find them."

"What do you want with us?" Bryn asked.

"I required Jaxon's cuff links." Adden held up his arm to show he had the cuff links in place on his sleeve ends. "Plus you're my insurance policy and my bargaining chips. There's only one way out of these vaults. I'm not going to strand myself without a get out of jail free card." Adden pointed at Clint and Ivy. "These two are worthless to me, so if either of you tries anything I'll drain them in front of you."

"That's just rude," Clint muttered.

"Let's go," Adden said.

"Go where?" Bryn asked. "We can't open the doors without a knight."

"You can't open them, but the guards stationed inside can." He pointed at Derek. "Call them and explain the situation."

Derek looked to Bryn. "What do you want me to do?"

It's not like they had much of a choice. "Make the call." After a few terse comments on the phone, a door opened.

Bryn expected to see the library table and stacks of books like she'd seen months ago. Instead, the room appeared sterile. There were file cabinets and desks crammed into the space, along with microscopes and lab equipment.

"That's new," Ivy said.

"What do you mean?" Adden asked.

"Before it was artifact-ey," Clint said. "Now it's all science-ey."

The guard inside the room smirked at them. "Something I can help you with?"

"Where are the artifacts?" Adden asked.

"They've been removed for study," the guard said.

"You're lying. This is the most secure area. Where are you keeping them?"

"There are other doors," the guard said. "Perhaps you should try one of them."

Bryn sidled over to Jaxon. "He's being awful agreeable."

Jaxon's face gave nothing away. "It's his job to keep us alive. And to some extent, Clint and Ivy."

"I heard that," Clint said.

"Just stating a fact," Jaxon said. "Adden, why don't you let Clint and Ivy go, the guards aren't as invested in their wellbeing."

"But Bryn is," Adden said. "So stop trying to out maneuver me."

"Can we just get on with this?" Bryn asked. Maybe they could shove Adden into a room and trap him there.

"Do you want to try another room?" Derek asked.

"If you would be so kind," Adden said.

A door which was slightly ajar appeared on the back wall.

"What's in there?" Adden asked Bryn.

"Last time I was here it was a storage room for scrolls and books."

"You can open the door," Adden said. "Just in case the guard inside decides he wants to try something."

Bryn stepped forward and opened the door. This room was all scienc-ey, too. There were microscopes and tables and a row of computers.

"Someone has been redecorating," Bryn said.

Adden pushed past her. He looked all around the room. "Where are the artifacts?"

The guard inside said, "They pay me to sit here and open the door. I've never seen any artifacts unless they're tiny slices on those slides." He pointed at the boxes of slides near the microscopes.

"You think you're so smart," Adden said. "Where's the next door?"

Jaxon placed a hand on Bryn's arm and shook his head. Suspicion confirmed. He was in on this.

The guard pointed to the right-hand wall. "Back out past the main room."

"Show me," Adden said.

Derek led them back past the first guard into the main room and down a hall to a normal door.

"This isn't what I asked for," Adden said.

"They store artifacts here. It's the only way to access them." Derek pulled out a set of keys and opened the door to a hallway.

Jaxon held Bryn's arm so she wouldn't enter behind Derek. "Follow my lead," he said.

For now, she nodded. Later she'd yell at him.

The hallway had several visible doors. Adden walked to the first door and pulled it open. Inside were display cases with antique swords and daggers.

"That's more like it." Adden entered the room. "Come along."

They shuffled in behind him. The cases resembled the ones that had poison dart defense systems. If a dragon tried to open a case containing artifacts which weren't for his Clan, the cases would shoot arrows with enough poison to kill him in seconds.

Adden walked over and opened the case. Bryn held her breath and hoped to hear the zing of poison darts. Nothing happened. Damn it.

"Look at this." Adden held up a ring featuring a giant sapphire. "Probably meant for a Blue." He slid it on his finger and waited. Nothing happened.

"Just a pretty bauble?" Bryn said.

Adden frowned. He rifled through the case but didn't find anymore jewelry. He stalked over to the other case. "There must be something here." He pulled out daggers and swords, carelessly tossing them on the floor. "Aha." He held up a ruby ring. "Reds don't wear jewels like this. Only Blues. This must be something." He put it on his left hand and closed his eyes.

Jaxon yanked Bryn backward out of the room. Clint and Ivy also lunged backward.

"Yes," Adden said and a dagger of fire shot from his hand. He opened his eyes just as Derek slammed and locked the door.

"That won't hold for long," said Bryn.

"This way." Jaxon tugged Bryn down the hall. Clint and Ivy followed. Derek dashed ahead and unlocked a door. "Inside. Quick."

The sound of screeching metal was like nails on a chalkboard. Adden was breaking loose.

Derek locked the door with a deadbolt from the inside. They ran down a hall which led to some stairs. Up they went into a room without a door. Derek spoke on his phone and a door appeared on the back wall and swung open. They rushed through to a room with a dozen guards.

No way this was happening by coincidence. "You used yourself as bait and didn't tell me," Bryn said.

"I'll explain later," Jaxon said. They followed Derek to a real door which he opened with a key. Three of the guards came with them. They were in a stone hallway that tilted up at a mild angle. It reminded Bryn of when they'd walked under the library...forever. She spotted a playing card with the number two on it. "Shit. We're a long way from the exit."

"Not really," Derek said. "But we should probably jog."

"Nothing like running from a psychopath to make the Welcome Back to School party really special," Clint said.

Chapter Thirty-Six

They jogged down a hallway, went up a set of stairs that seemed much newer than the surrounding stonework, jogged down another hall, and up more stairs until they reached a normal door that opened into a normal storage room full of books.

"Not to be ungrateful," Bryn said. "But where are we?"

"Through that door is a hallway that leads to the landing and back up through the trap door into the library. Go and make sure Miss Enid locks the door," Derek said.

"Adden has a key. What good will that do?" Clint asked.

"The lock is on the outside of the door," Bryn said. "He can't unlock it from this side, right?"

"That's right," Derek said. "We're leading him into a trap."

"But you'll be trapped down here with him." That didn't seem like a smart idea.

"Your grandfather installed an emergency exit. If worse comes to worse, I can exit that way. Hopefully it won't come to that. Now go."

She did not like this.

The sound of a battle drifted to them from beneath their feet.

"He's coming." Jaxon tugged on her arm, so she went. They made their way to the landing, while the sound of fighting seemed to come from all around them.

"With all these damn tunnels you can't tell where anything is coming from," Clint said as they dashed up the stairs and through the trap door. Miss Enid stood there. For some reason Janelle was there, too.

"I'm sorry," Miss Enid said.

"Janelle? What are you doing here?"

"Allow me to show you," Janelle placed her hand on Miss Enid's forearm and at first it seemed like nothing was happening. Then Miss Enid's eyes closed and she swayed.

No freaking way. "You're a dragon-pire?"

"Do you have any idea how hard it was to act like I didn't know what I was doing in that stupid Medic class?" Janelle said.

Miss Enid moaned and dropped to her knees. "Stop it," Bryn said. "You've taken enough."

"Enough? You think so? There's never enough power. There's always more to be had."

Miss Enid slumped to the side and if Janelle didn't quit soon, she'd die. Bryn produced fireballs in both of her hands. "Let her go."

"So sentimental," Janelle said. "It's a weakness." She pushed Miss Enid's unconscious body through the trap door and down the stairs. Then she locked the door with the librarian's key. "Don't worry. She'll recover just like you did."

"Why are you doing this?" Bryn asked.

"My IQ is off the charts. Garret is a flyspeck compared to me. But everyone has all these rules which I'm expected to follow."

"What about Adden?" Jaxon said.

"Now he's trapped," Janelle said. "He thinks I work for him, which is hilarious." Janelle's eyes changed from brown to steel gray and her hair went from dark to silver.

"They make hair dye for that," Clint said.

Janelle flicked her hand at Clint and a blast of wind sent him flying off his feet and through the door out into the library.

"Anyone else have a comment?" Janelle asked.

"No," Bryn said. Maybe she could talk her way out of this. "You're more powerful than any of us. Adden has what you want. Why do you need us?"

"Well," Janelle said. "I don't need her."

She flicked her hand at Ivy and sent her flying backward into the wall. There was a crunching sound, Ivy cried out in pain, and then she dropped to the floor, clutching her shoulder.

Fire roared in Bryn's gut. Smoke crawled up the back of her throat. "You crazy bitch." She blasted flames at her former friend. Janelle blocked the attack with a tornado made of sleet. It extinguished Bryn's flames.

Shit. How was she supposed to compete with that? "Play nice," Janelle said. "And you'll all walk, or at least limp, out of here."

"Let Bryn and Ivy go," Jaxon said. "You only need one of us to guarantee safe passage.

"Sorry," Janelle said. "One of you is for me and the other is for Adden. He should be along any moment now."

"I thought we were friends." Bryn growled.

"Fine," Janelle said. "Since you were nice to me, Ivy can leave."

Maybe Janelle wasn't completely unreasonable. "Thank you." Bryn turned to Ivy, who looked conflicted. "Go."

Ivy nodded. Clutching her shoulder, she ran out the door.

The floor shook, and a wave of power came up through their feet.

"Adden is using sonic waves." Janelle chuckled. "Such a show-off."

Best to reason with Janelle before Adden made his appearance. "My grandparents will give you whatever you want, if you let us go now," Bryn said.

"Are you afraid to face Adden?" Janelle said. "Don't worry about him."

"Janelle," Adden's voice came through the trap door. "Are you there?"

"I'm here, my love," Janelle said. "Did you need something?"

"Let. Me. Out."

"So crabby," Janelle muttered. "On one condition. You have to share your toys."

Bryn moved the slightest bit toward the doorway which led out into the library. Jaxon followed suit.

"I have a lovely sapphire ring for you," Adden said.

"It's not an artifact," Bryn whispered. "He's trying to trick you. You want the ruby ring." If she could turn them against each other maybe they could make a break for it.

"I prefer rubies," Janelle said. "If I open the door, I want the ruby ring."

"Fine," Adden said. "Just let me out of here."

Janelle put the key in the lock. Adden pushed from below and it popped open.

"You had me worried for a minute," he said, "leaving a librarian in my way. That's quite rude." He climbed out and then slammed the trap door. "Still, you're my favorite conspirator." He held out his hands. "Pick a ring."

He wore a ring on almost every finger.

"Oh, they're so sparkly," Janelle said. "Which ones are artifacts?"

"Most of them produce daggers," he said. "Take two if you want."

She pulled the ruby ring off his left hand and a black pearl ring off his right.

He gasped like someone had stabbed him. The knuckles of both of his now ringless fingers were bleeding like someone had cut him with a scalpel.

"What's wrong?" Janelle asked.

He stared at her as foam bubbled from his mouth. His eyes rolled back into his head and he started to twitch.

"Oh, one of the rings was poisoned? I didn't see that coming." She turned to Bryn. "Did you know about this?"

"No." Bryn cringed as Adden dropped to the floor, where he gagged and coughed up bile and blood. "But some of the glass cases had poisonous darts. They had the same effect."

"Well, we should leave," Janelle said. "I know your cuff links and Bryn's bracelet are safe to take. Too bad about the rings." She grabbed Bryn's bracelet and then started to remove the cuff links from Adden's sleeves. "This is what happens when you get greedy," she told Adden.

Wow. Janelle was crazy.

"Now I only need one of you," Janelle flicked her hand at Bryn. A gust of wind slammed into Bryn's chest, enveloped her, and moved her forward.

"No." Jaxon blasted frozen flames at Janelle, but she shot sonic waves at him with her free hand, shattering his ice.

Janelle latched onto Bryn's arm. "Now I'm going to show you how to really use your Quintessence."

Bryn felt a strange pulling sensation on her arm. Janelle was going to feed off her? She had to stop this. Dizziness hit her. She could hear Jaxon yelling. Blocking everything out, she grabbed Janelle's hand like she meant to break her grasp, instead, she focused her Quintessence into Janelle's veins, reaching into her blood and imagined the blood thickening, moving sluggishly, clotting and no longer flowing.

"What are you doing?" Janelle tried to push Bryn away, but she held on tight.

"I'm ending this." She reached further into Janelle's veins, turning her blood into clotted sludge, slowing and then stopping the beat of her heart.

"Bryn." Jaxon's tone sounded like it came from far away. "Bryn, you have to hurry. There's a bomb."

She released Janelle's arm and Jaxon shoved her toward the door. "Run."

She stumble-stepped and then ran. Just as she made it out the door someone tackled her. She growled but went rolling over and over before she could stop. She sucked in a breath to blast her attacker and then realized who it was that had her pinned to the ground. "Derek. What the—"

K-boom!

The floor shook and books toppled off shelves. Bryn shoved Derek aside, and half crawled, half ran toward the sound of the explosion. Smoke filled the air, obscuring her vision. No. No. No. This could not be happening.

Clint stumbled toward her, carrying Ivy. Thank God.

"Jaxon?" Bryn tried to push through the Red guards in her way. Everyone was shouting at once. Where was Jaxon? He had to be okay. He had to be.

"Jaxon?" This had all been part of a plan. His plan. He must have known what he was doing. Right?

"Move." She shoved at a guard.

He turned and blocked her path. "Believe me, you don't want to see this."

"No?" Flames ignited in her gut. Sparks shot from her nostrils. "Let me through," she growled.

Someone grabbed her from behind. "Wait. Let the Medics through first," Derek said.

Jaxon might be hurt. She could help him. And she was done letting other people call the shots. She shifted into her dragon form, breaking Derek's grip on her arm. Then she plowed through the guards knocking them aside. "Move," she roared to the people ahead of her.

Guards backed out of her way. She could see the Medics gathered around someone on a stretcher, but she couldn't see who it was. When she was within a few feet she shifted back to human form, digging her nails into her palms as she moved close enough to see. The scent of burned flesh filled the air. Bryn clutched at her stomach, afraid she was going to vomit...afraid of what she was going to see. She held her breath and stared at the form on the stretcher. It was Jaxon. His hair was burned down to the scalp and his forehead was blackened and blistered. His eyes were wide open, milky-colored, and staring up at nothing.

"No!" Flames roared in Bryn's gut. She stumbled away from the image of Jaxon, battling the flames in her gut. This could not be happening. They'd just figured everything out. He couldn't be gone. He just couldn't be. She focused on cold and blasted sleet down an aisle of books, roaring out her pain and frustration. She clutched at the edge of the bookshelf and blasted out her grief until her throat was raw and there was nothing left inside of her.

...

"I'm so sorry about how this all turned out," Derek said to Bryn as he sat next to her in the medical clinic.

Bryn nodded because what could she say? Jaxon should have told me. I should have been part of the plan. I'm furious at everyone who knew and didn't clue me in.

"I know this isn't the best time, but I wanted to ask you something. Did you ever think that history might repeat itself?" Derek's cheeks colored. "Like with your mother and your father?" Intensity shone from his bright green eyes. "Because when I'm around you it feels like maybe I've found my place in the world again."

It took her a moment to understand. And then she got it. Her mom had married a Red. How much easier would her life be if she loved someone like Derek? She reached over and covered his hand with hers. "I'm sorry. Maybe if circumstances had been different."

He nodded. "I understand, but you can't blame a guy for trying." Leaning in he kissed her on the cheek. "It would be for the best if I asked your grandfather to reassign me. Take care, Bryn." Derek stood and exited the room.

Clint and Ivy came over to join her. She'd focus on her friends for now.

"How are you?" Bryn asked.

"Much better," Ivy said. "Thank you for talking Janelle into letting me go. Sorry I wasn't more help."

"If someone had told me about the freaking plan, I could've been more help." Tears filled Bryn's eyes. "I'm so mad at Jaxon. He should've told me so I would've known what was going to happen." If she'd known she was on a timetable with a bomb going to blow, she would have killed Janelle faster. And that was a disturbing thought. She'd used her medical skills to kill someone. She hadn't admitted that to anyone yet. And maybe she never would. Who would want to be treated by a Medic who'd taken someone's life?

"I guess no one counted on Janelle being there. They thought Adden would walk out of the library trading Jaxon for his escape before the rings detonated. And if he tried to take any of the rings off he'd be poisoned."

Medic Williams came toward Bryn, chugging a container of chocolate milk. "When you're ready, we need to talk about what happened with Janelle."

"Not now." Bryn was barely holding it together.

"I understand, but this conversation isn't over," Medic Williams said. "You can see Jaxon now. Fair warning we still have a lot of work to do."

Bryn swallowed over the lump in her throat. "Thank you." She walked down the hall to the private room and put her hand on the doorknob. How bad would this be? She pushed the door open and walked in. Jaxon lay on the bed. They'd healed the blisters, but his exposed skin was still red. They hadn't bothered to regrow his hair. His eyes...his eyes were open. They were back to their normal bright blue and they were looking at her.

"What in the hell were you thinking?" she shouted at him.

He smiled and then grimaced. "That's my line."

"That's not funny. We're supposed to be partners."

Flames ignited in her gut. Smoke drifted from her lips. "We're supposed to be a team."

"I was trying to protect you."

"That's not how this works." She growled and sparks shot from her mouth.

"It's my job to protect you," he insisted.

"No. Wrong. It's our job to protect each other. And I can't do that if you're running around making half-assed plans without me."

"So you'd rather I make full-assed plans with you?"

"Not funny." She took a deep breath and focused on cold. She walked over to the bed and reached for his hand but stopped when she saw how red it was.

"I probably look like you did after the explosion at your grandparents' estate."

She gently laid her hand on his shoulder which was medium pink rather than bright red. "Please. They just had to regrow my eyebrows. You're practically bald."

"Yes, but I'm a Westgate, so I'm sure I look fabulous."

She rolled her eyes. "Of course you do."

"Listen. I really am sorry I didn't tell you. I was hoping to keep you out of the battle. Then Clint and Ivy showed up. Once Adden had them I knew you wouldn't be far behind.

If it makes you feel any better, this wasn't my idea. My father and your grandfather approached me and told me about the poisonous rings they'd planted, knowing Adden would try and take them. It was my job to lead him to the library. They thought the poison or the explosive in the rings would do the rest."

"Once you're fully recovered, I'm kicking your ass," Bryn said. "When I saw you on that stretcher I thought you were dead. I grieved you. I destroyed an entire aisle of books with ice because I was trying not to burn the damn building down."

"Hey, I've seen you look pretty bad, too," Jaxon said.

"Yes, but you didn't love me back then so it doesn't count." And holy shit, had she just told Jaxon she loved him?

He stared at her bug eyed. "Did you just—"

"Nope. Rewind. That never happened."

"Yes, it did," he said.

Okay. He was right. It did. And now was the time he needed to chime in and say that he cared about her, too, but he was just staring at her. Great. This was freaking fabulous. She stood and stalked out the door.

"Bryn, get back here."

"Nope." She'd had enough drama for one day.

"I'll call your grandmother," Jaxon shouted.

"Seriously?" Bryn turned around and stormed back into the room. "You'll call my grandmother and tell her what?"

"I'd tell her you're stubborn and you have a terrible temper, and it's almost like we were made for each other. Which is probably why I love you, too."

"Really?"

"I'm not saying it again." Jaxon gestured. "Get over here."

She walked over and stared down at him. "You're a mess," she said.

"Right back at you. Mentally, rather than physically, of course."

She arched her eyebrows. "Another trait we share in common."

"Probably." He grinned. "Stay with me for awhile?"

"Sure." She sat in the chair next to him. "I'm going to tell you a story. Once upon a time there was a cute princess and a handsome prince. When they first met, the prince hated the princess because his father was still mad at the princess's mother. Once they became acquainted, they went on many adventures together and became friends. Then the prince did something really stupid and scared the crap out of the princess, forcing her to see that she loved him, but that was okay because he loved her, too, and he swore never to do anything stupid ever again. The end."

"Never again?" he said. "That might be a hard deal to keep."

"But you'll try, right?"

"I'll try," he said. "And now I'm going to tell you a story. Once upon a time, a prince thought he understood how the world worked. He believed everything his father told him. Then this strange princess with multicolored hair barged into his life and threw everything off course. She showed him there was more to life than shiny objects and fast cars. Not that those things aren't awesome—because they are—but she showed him that sometimes, all you need is someone who will sit with you, read books, and share their cookies and milk. Although she wasn't very good at sharing cookies, but that's a story for another time. The End."

Epilogue

The sounds of the orchestral version of "The Wedding March" drifted down the hall. Bryn clutched her flowers. Was she ready for this? No. Not really. But it was time, and she couldn't disappoint everyone who'd come to Sinclair Estate today.

Bryn prayed she wouldn't somehow trip on the silk runner as she entered the ballroom. Her grandmother would never forgive her if that happened. Why was she so nervous about this? It wasn't a big deal. She and Jaxon had practiced the evening before. Speaking of Jaxon, he stood waiting for her at the end of the aisle, looking amazing in his black tuxedo.

Taking slow, measured steps, she made her way toward him and then stood to his right, clutching her flowers and smiling like an idiot. There was no reason to be nervous.

The orchestra played the first notes of "Here Comes the Bride" and Miss Enid appeared in the doorway. Her dark skin looked lovely against her cream-colored wedding gown. Mr. Stanton looked rather handsome, if a bit pale in his black tuxedo next to Jaxon.

Bryn had been thrilled when the Directorate had declared that Mr. Stanton and Miss Enid could finally marry. The two had been faithful to each other for all these years, carrying on their relationship in secret. Now they could finally be together out in the open. Once news of this spread, maybe other couples would step forward and have the legal recognition of their relationship they'd always wanted.

Once the ceremony was over, and they'd congratulated the happy couple, Jaxon grabbed Bryn's hand and pulled her out onto one of the terraces.

"What you did here today, helping them marry after all this time was a good thing."

"Thank you."

"I guess we can add that to the list of things you've changed since you barged into my life."

"Barged?" Bryn said. "You used that word once before, and I don't think it's a nice description."

"Well you didn't glide in like a graceful swan," Jaxon told her.

She couldn't argue that point so she changed the subject. "I'm just happy Miss Enid, or rather, Mrs. Stanton, made a full recovery." The door down into the vaults had kept the librarian from feeling the effects of the blast but it had taken her a few days to recover from Janelle sucking out three quarters of her Quintessence. "Do they have any more leads on the crazy cult?"

"They found Janelle's journal in her room," Jaxon said. "Being part Green meant she made detailed notes about the dragon-pires, including the higher-up Silvers who restarted the movement and the feeders who fed on multiple students to make everyone mysteriously ill. She and Adden took out the higher-ups and sucked the feeders dry because they wanted all the power for themselves..."

"So they made everyone sick to shut down the campus so she and Adden could search for artifacts?"

Jaxon nodded. "I'll miss my cuff links, but it might be for the best that they were destroyed. Janelle believed the artifacts could be combined to create some sort of super weapon. No more cuff links equals no more super-weapon."

"She was insane," Bryn said. "And I had no clue."

"She was brilliant and insane, so she outsmarted everyone."

"Power hungry unstable super geniuses are a scary discovery."

"Speaking of scary discoveries," Jaxon said. "We graduate from high school in less than a month and I have it on good authority that your grandmother has already scheduled half a dozen events for us to attend over the summer."

She didn't find that news as disturbing as he did. "As long as there's food, I don't think I'll mind."

"Why is that?" he asked.

She moved closer and reached up to play with the hair at the nape of his neck. "Maybe because I finally agree that we're a good match."

He wrapped his arms around her waist and pulled her close. Leaning forward so their lips almost touched he stared deep into her eyes. Her heart rate sped up. Why wasn't he kissing her?

"I have a question for you."

"Now?"

"Yes." He brushed his lips across hers in a feather soft kiss and then leaned away, keeping his arms around her waist. "We ended up in this relationship by default. To avoid any confusion, I thought maybe we should rewind the situation."

Where was he going with this? She wasn't sure. He wasn't pushing her away, but he was making her nervous. Flames flickered in her gut. "Go on."

"I was wondering if you'd like to go on a date. Not because we signed a contract, and not because your grandmother and my mother pushed us together, but because I like you for who you are...a temperamental hybrid with strange hair."

She laughed. "You were doing so good up until that last part."

"You didn't answer the question." He seemed a bit nervous.

Should she torture him? It was tempting, but this seemed like another pivotal moment. He'd taken a chance by asking her out so she went with her gut. "Even though you have a temper to match my own and annoyingly perfect hair, yes, I'd like to go on a date with you."

"Good." He kissed her and something about it felt different. Like the last piece of the puzzle had fallen into place. Maybe because now they'd chosen to be together rather than being together because of a contract. There were sure to be many challenges in the future, but they would face them together as true partners.

Acknowledgments

I'd like to thank Erin Molta for editing my dragons into shape. Thank you to all the readers who left reviews and made the continuation of this series possible.

About the Author

Chris Cannon is the award-winning author of the Going Down In Flames series and the Boyfriend Chronicles. She lives in Southern Illinois with her husband and several furry beasts.

She believes coffee is the Elixir of Life. Most evenings after work, you can find her caffeinating and writing fire-breathing paranormal adventures, romantic comedies, or paranormal cozy mysteries. You can find her online at www. chriscannonauthor.com.

www.ingramcontent.com/pod-product-compliance
Lightning Source LLC
Chambersburg PA
CBHW030936260626
47169CB00002B/500